SHOW-ME SERIES

SLEUTH WORKS 1955
ESCAPADE 1952
NOH *FOOLING THIS TEACHER 1949*
SHIVAREE 1946

SLEUTH
WORKS

Margery A. Neely

authorHOUSE®

AuthorHouse™
1663 Liberty Drive
Bloomington, IN 47403
www.authorhouse.com
Phone: 1 (800) 839-8640

This is a work of fiction. All of the characters, names, incidents,
organizations, and dialogue in this novel are either the products
of the author's imagination or are used fictitiously.

Published by AuthorHouse 05/29/2018

ISBN: 978-1-5462-4371-7 (sc)
ISBN: 978-1-5462-4370-0 (e)

Library of Congress Control Number: 2018906323

Print information available on the last page.

This book is printed on acid-free paper.

In 1899, Congressman Willard Duncan Vandiver in Philadelphia said, " . . . frothy eloquence neither convinces me nor satisfies me. I'm from Missouri. You have got to show me." *2010 World Book Multimedia Encyclopedia:* Version 14.0.0 (r) World Book, Inc. (www.mackiev.com)

TO MY SISTER, DORIS NEELY NEIL,
FAMILY SCRIBE EXTRAORDINAIRE
AND MY LATE BROTHER ARTHUR
DEE NEELY, A WITTY ONE

CONTENTS

PART ONE
TRACE

CHAPTER ONE

The doorbell from the door downstairs clattered in the office causing Ken to jump up, pace hurriedly over, and press open the connection to the call bell. "Sleuth Works," he announced. Ken was once more pleased that he had rescued an old communication connection between an upstairs bedroom and the apartment's downstairs kitchen, inserted the contraption from the foyer to the entrance by the doorbell. The family could screen callers without walking down to the door.

"I'm an attorney wishing to interview you for an investigation," came the garbled syllables.

"I'll be down, sir."

Ken hastily went through the living room doors, sliding them shut behind, him, through the office to the foyer, sliding those doors shut behind him, opened the door to the downstairs, and walked down sedately, knowing his steps could be heard on the solid oak stairs.

"Come in, come in," he greeted the short, older fellow, gesturing him up the stairs. The stranger took off his hat from a bushy head of hair as he climbed and said, "I repeat: I'm looking to engage an investigator. Am I in the right place?" He looked askance at the small room.

"Kendrick Massey here, one of the Sleuths," said the WORKS partner. "May I take your coat?"

The visitor shook his head, unbuttoned and took off his coat, then placed it on the coat tree.

"And who might you be, sir?" Ken asked. He sat down at the little desk in the foyer, gesturing for the fellow to be seated.

"I'm not 'might be,' I'm actually Walter Raleigh, and would not be anyone else," the fellow answered with a slight smile. "I have a law practice across the street in Country Club Plaza. An acquaintance, a police officer retired from your Air Base south of here, Phil Tyler, said you're in the business of tracing people, data, and/or things, Ricky."

"Please call me Ken, Walter, as *I* actually am."

"Sorry. And your profession? Was I correct? You follow clues?"

The two men's slight frowns showed that they each knew that they were off to an uncomfortable start.

"Yes, sir. I finished my Air Police hitch, under Tyler part of the time, got hitched, and charged headlong into being a sleuth." Ken rose, shook hands formally across the desk, and handed over a business card.

SLEUTH WORKS
Telephone 2345 P. O. Box 123
Kansas City, Missouri
Kendrick Massey, Investigator
Belinda Jones Massey, Librarian and Accountant
Holly Osborne Jones, Owner and Manager

"The company is named **Sleuth Works** because we trace whatever is lost." Ken thought that it was hard to tell how to deal with this guy who seemingly examined everything.

Little sense of humor usually went along with that oh-so-serious personality. "What type of an inquiry would you would like us to undertake?" Ken kept his voice even and respectful. He wasn't going to describe the allocation of who ruled each aspect of their housing/business domain––with, of course, input from others––but ultimately each did rule, made the final decisions in the area of expertise. He had the interviews; Belinda led the nursery and account ledgers; and, Holly ruled the household help and the firm . . . and owned more than half of SW.

"These three people compose the outfit that undertakes investigations––the 'we' you mentioned?" Walter asked. "I see you here in your office; I note that there are two ladies mentioned on the business card; but, there's no mention of a secretary or other staff, unless they would be ensconced on a corner shelf. I see no one except you."

Ken patted himself on the back: Roger, wilco . . . this guy was into detail work. "My wife, Belinda, is a former librarian and is my partner 'til death do us part. My mother-in-law, Holly Jones, is an experienced administrator as well as the senior partner. Their workspaces are on both sides of a desk in the main office. We all know how to type and spell." *Dang, don't get sarcastic.* "Why do you ask?"

"Oh. It's a lot different than my office, and I'm the only owner, but I have a secretary." Raleigh studied both the small, sparsely furnished room and Ken's face. Because Ken's hair receded from his brow, people often mistook him for being older than a mere three decades. Walt's facial hair and scalp, in contrast, sprouted every which way and did nothing to conceal his middle age.

The only decorations in this anteroom were two

watercolors, both of the same apple tree, one from the winter and one from the spring. They certainly had not been painted by Georgia O'Keefe but were more in the two-dimensional naïve style of Grandma Moses.

The visitor sighed. He sighed again. "I indicated that I need an investigation carried out. Would you please give me some idea of your procedures? I suppose that means that the others have to hear this as soon as you can round them up. Or get it as second hand gossip."

"No, sir. We have our main office next door and live in an adjoining apartment, and we can go into the office to involve them. We don't like to advertise that we live where we work, in case things get dicey. If your request seems to mesh with our talents, we will go in there. So, tell me a bit about it."

"I need the ownership traced of a donated set of items to the local art museum."

Ken rose and hit a bell on his desk that was heard as a faint, single tingle. "That, I am sure we can do. I'll ask my partners to join us in the main office next door."

Walt Raleigh nodded and seemed to relax a bit. "I noticed that you advertised only a phone number and a post office box number both in the yellow pages and on this card. I can certainly understand that. My wife is not only a teacher, but is also a sometime diplomat. The State Department calls upon her to help host dignitaries from the Far East. We too have learned to be circumspect about our private lives.

"Actually, my wife was asked by an acquaintance to trace that information, and that is why I am here," Mr. Raleigh revealed. "You can introduce me with that." He followed Ken's lead, stood, straightened his shirt cuffs, and touched the knot on his dark blue silk tie.

A door that fit smoothly into the wall slid open to reveal a little boy clinging to the denim slacks of a tall lady. "Yes?" she glanced at both men as she spoke and stepped back with her hand waving them into a high-ceilinged space. The stranger looked over at the tall blonde who bested his height by a couple of inches while her husband was a good five inches taller than he.

Ken Massey signaled his wife with a wink, nodded at the visitor said, "Belinda", as an introduction. She picked up the boy, left the room through sliding doors across the room, and returned with a steno pad. She had shut both sets of the sliding doors quickly. Walt did not get a glimpse into the private apartment space.

To the left side of the office stood a large, oak desk in front of an alcove with an oriel window. A captain's chair fit behind the desk. The window glass was very old and showed imperfections when a person looked outside, viewing the building across the street or the (usually) blue sky with a resultant crinkled perspective.

An elegantly dressed older woman was already seated at a round table on the right, and Belinda sat down in the alcove behind the desk.

Ken said, gesturing the others, "Mr. Walter Raleigh is an attorney and has another of those delicate type of matters to discuss with us, ladies. He's checking our bona fides regarding confidential matters."

He pointed at a cushioned chair next to a round table, indicating where the client was to sit opposite Mrs. Jones.

Belinda's first words were a warning. "Now, as to

security in our approach to cases. If you tried to get into our files, you'd never figure out our filing system. My husband was an Air Policeman for eight years and learned a great deal about security. My mother ran the principal's office in a big high school, and she occasionally dealt with teenage scoundrels. I was a librarian and prevented purloining of books, and have an accounting degree."

Next to the oriel desk area, several framed certificates hung beside the window, above a row of low file cabinets, all padlocked. The circular table against the wall had six grey cushioned desk chairs around it. The large room had dark wainscoting below embossed wallpaper that was decorated with delicate green vines.

Raleigh turned his look toward Belinda and asked, "You combine your work space and living room?"

She answered, "Not really: this is our main office, with the foyer serving as the entry point. Our home base is past that wall. For credentials, our diplomas and Kendrick's Air Force awards and discharge are posted over there; files are in those wall cabinets; supplies are in the desk. Typical office as you may have observed but certainly not a living room as usually defined."

"Intriguing description, Mrs. Massey," the visitor said smoothing the air with his hands as though he thought she had been irritated by his question.

"Please call me Belinda."

"Do you really think this is a secure area? From your children when you or your mother are not keeping watch because you're busy with work?"

Belinda responded smoothly to the query, "The nanny keeps our children out of the office; they're usually upstairs.

I hardly ever have my boy with me when I'm near here. Today was unusual when I heard talking in the foyer while I was reading to him in the living room next door."

Mrs. Jones sat regally beside the table, studying him.

Belinda Massey pulled out a shelf with a wooden leg that unfolded immediately from a slot on the side of the desk and placed her steno pad and pencil on it.

Ken sat in a swivel chair and said, "The walls to this office are soundproofed. Try yelling for help if you don't believe me. Furthermore, we all know how to use pistols, shotguns, and bows and arrows. The area is secure, sir."

Raleigh looked back at the door to the foyer. He could discern the sliding door's outline because he knew where he had entered, but there was no knob. He glanced at the wall opposite the foyer and again discerned the outline to a sliding door, that one evidently leading to the living room, and, again, no knob.

"This is rather like an extremely large priest's hole."

"Cromwell's time?" Mrs. Jones asked.

"Yes." Raleigh looked surprised. "In fact, it's a European connection that brought me here. But from four hundred years later." He slapped the table gently.

"And, how may we help?" She was still appraising him.

"No," the lawyer said, "I can't tell you yet. I need to have some references. About your results from snooping. That it's above board and legal. I limit my practice to Civil Law and stay away from Criminal Law. That is, I will deal with issues that could deprive you of your property and/or time but cannot take your life. And therefore I must know specifically what types of investigations at which you are experienced."

Belinda stirred, her mother nodded in understanding, and Ken simply raised an eyebrow.

Mrs. Jones said quietly, "I object to the word 'snooping,' sir. We don't know how you found us, but we investigate; we don't listen at doors or focus binoculars on trysts."

"For some reason, your taking umbrage makes me feel better. The onset of this inquiry may sound complicated, but it's only a chain of friends. My wife, Meg, has a friend who needs ownership of some items chased down for an art museum."

"Sounds clear so far. Suit of armor? Ancient painting?"

"I'll fill you in after you supply references that I can check. My wife, Meg, knows your former sergeant, Ken, one Phil Tyler, and I have met him. I checked with him and with an attorney I know who lives near your last Base."

"But you're saying you already know about our reputations from checking with your wife's friend and a lawyer back there in Granstadt." Holly Jones made the observation in her quiet manner. "Yet, you want more references about cases we have taken on?"

"Of course. But those earlier were checking about Ken's character and due diligence. I need some idea of how you proceed and how successful you are. And your fee schedule."

Holly Jones replied evenly, "We'll give you the names of, say, four cases for whom we've traced ancestors or items, sir. Those are the ones most relevant to the task you're describing. They have, of course, given us grateful permission to use their names. And, as you said, you've already checked with other names regarding Ken's integrity . . . which will rub off on us, naturally."

Raleigh laughed after absorbing her remark. Ken had

to appreciate his mother-in-law's sneaky injection of the compliment. He was glad she had not sounded insulted by the man's superior tone of voice.

She added, "Let me describe our procedure. I take down the information provided by a client, work with Ken and Belinda on how differently names may be spelled over the years or in the census because differences do occur for the same person. We have several ways to check documents. We have not yet been involved when a legal issue was at stake, if that's what you're asking: we stay away from crimes. We did trace a stolen family item to a pawnshop. That was our first case but had nothing to do with a crime because it was an internal family matter, and, moreover, it led to another task for the same family."

Mr. Raleigh nodded and responded with an order. "Those will suffice but kindly prepare that list for me so that I may check with the people who experimented with hiring you. You merely sketched your methods, and you haven't mentioned your fees. I believe that this will be a minor investigation that I cannot devote time to but does involve a legal conclusion."

Ken responded to the challenge. "Sir, I'll add some detail. We trace people such as relatives who want to find heirs, phone or address changes, names in marriage or divorce. We find data that are related to ancestors: birth, death, sickness, licenses, real estate, insurance, cars, boats, hunting, farms, dairies, diaries. Things that have been stolen/pawned/lost, mistakenly discarded, heirlooms, cars, books, statues. For tracing people, we have the Bureau of Vital Statistics in Jeff City, Jackson County courthouses here and in Independence, graveyards, telephone books,

Census Bureau by Bannister Road––you'd be surprised, sir, perhaps, that twice the person was found in the very town of the seeker; once, she was merely around the corner."

Belinda chuckled before she explained. "AND we don't do crime scenes, any more than you do, although, as I mentioned, Ken has the expertise from his career as an Air Policeman. We turn his expertise into using his keen eye, low-key interviewing skills, and knowledge of the way people respond to situations. My mother dealt with high school rascals for 23 years. She ran the principal's high school office."

"I heard. When may my secretary pick up that list of references?"

"We'll be happy to bring it over tomorrow," Holly Jones said. "Just whereabouts is your office, Mr. Raleigh?"

"Walk all the way across the Plaza to the west end to the brick and stone building, Mrs. Jones. The directory is inside beside the doorman's chair. The second floor has my office."

As Ken rose to escort him out, Raleigh nodded at Belinda and Holly and rose as though weary. Ken had the foyer door open when the attorney said, "We have to pay a lot for our address, and here you have one quite nearby, and, yet, I bet you don't pay a third as much rent as I do."

Ken simply grinned at him, opened the outer door, and said, "Goodbye for now, sir."

Raleigh glanced at the ceramic letters mounted on the outside wall by the door. The door plate had been Mrs. Jones' design"

Sleuth Works
People, Data, and Things

We Finders, You Keepers
2345

"I'll have my secretary schedule you to see me. She'll call you," he said.

"Yes, sir."

After he watched the man put on his overcoat and hat and then close the door behind himself quietly, Ken turned, walked back to the inner room, and swiveled his chair toward Belinda and Mother Holly.

"Was he trying to rile us, dear? I heard his remark about rent."

Ken merely chuckled. "We'll let him stew over that one." In fact, Mother Holly Jones had bought this building after her husband died. They didn't pay a dime in rent—the other tenants paid rent to *them*.

"Serves him right," Mrs. Jones added. "I do believe he thinks I'm the nanny, too!"

Belinda said, "Wouldn't he be surprised to find out that we have two servants, and that Mom's job is to supervise them as well as the building's tenants and our office?"

Seating herself at the desk, Belinda then pulled the cover off the Remington and began typing on a piece of their letterhead stationary. Her steno pad had four names and addresses on it.

"Yes, I think he was establishing the pecking order. The time will come when he will find out, but not from us. It'll be a bigger revelation if we don't bother to brag. He doesn't know yet that we're so serene and superlatively satisfied with our lives that we're hard to shake. We're cloak and dagger, not choke and stagger."

"Oh, you state that so beautifully that you should be on the Chautauqua Circuit. Except it went defunct some decades ago. People get their education elsewhere today. Like from television. Oh, and colleges." Belinda finished typing and whipped the sheet out of the roller.

She looked fondly at her husband, pen raised like a dagger, and grinned. "Both of you men looked as strong as if you'd stepped out of the Charles Atlas ad from the back of a comic book. But, your bespoke suit looked more expensive than his did, you handsome Massey massive man with the muscles to match."

"He did appreciate the doorplate, I saw, because he actually grinned at the last line."

"That's what I intended people to do. We aren't in the business of seeking a tragic solution to a problem." Mother Holly chortled and waved an imaginary flag in her hand.

Belinda looked at her mother. "Would you care to dictate a cover letter, mother, to accompany us when we reveal our inner workings?"

CHAPTER TWO

Holly, Belinda, and Kendrick stomped their galoshes on the mat inside the entryway in Walter Raleigh's office building. The snowflakes were hard to shake off, having already started to melt on their heads and shoulders.

Holly acted as though her head had her knit cap frozen in place. Pulling off both mittens and stuffing them in the front of her coat, she then yanked the hat off by the pom-pom on its top. A few pieces of yarn flew to the side. "Blast it. I knew I should have knitted it myself, instead of buying it at the arts and crafts sale."

They all looked up the stairs at a lady slapping her feet hard on each step as she descended. "That woman," she fumed, coming down the stairs quickly toward them. "That woman." She thrust a hand under her blond bangs and slapped her right ear.

"I beg your pardon," Belinda said, stopping as the doorman straightened up, saluted, and stared up at the lady. "Were you speaking to us?"

"Oh, no. Sorry. I just dealt with, or I was dealt with, by my husband's secretary, Marnie King. She's so very efficient, so very precise, so very exasperating, so very unlikeable."

"I've met one or two people like that." Belinda started up the stairs ahead of the other two sleuths passing the lady who was going down.

"Are you Belinda Massey? I'm Mrs. Raleigh." A hand was touching Belinda's coat to stop her ascent.

"Yes, I'm Mrs. Belinda Jones Massey. My mother, Mrs. Holly Osborne Jones, and my husband, Mr. Kendrick Massey." She nodded at each of them.

"Please, please, don't you go off on me, too. I mean I'm Meg Lowe Raleigh. Donna Aldrich Tyler down by the Granstadt Air Base is a very good friend of mine as well as yours. She said your business company could help my friend, Merrilee Anderson. I had called around asking for names of people who'd know what to do. Donna was the only one who helped."

Holly offered her hand. "How do you do. Donna is a friend of mine, too, a friend whom I miss a lot. She and Belinda worked at the library together and were teammates on the firing range. I'm following your train of thought, although someone else might not. The secretary goaded you a bit, I guess. Yes, we are on our way up to see your husband about your friend's problem. But I can easily challenge the secretarial harridan to a duel if necessary to get in the door."

"Watch out for that hag. She's always coldly boiling CO_2, sweetly poisonous to me. Car engine lethality. Black widow spider. If those contradictions are possible in one humanlike body. I really wanna watch your contesting her, but Walt wouldn't like it. Pure serendipitous, synchronous, and solicitudinous to meet you-all on the stairs. I had come over this morning hoping to meet you face to face and look what transpired: we did meet."

Belinda laughed. "Thanks for the warm welcome. We'll be careful, but discreet in facing her, and thus you probably won't hear about how I snub her skillfully. Nice meeting you, too."

Meg said, "I'd like to visit with your family. Maybe you could call me at home some night, Belinda? We're in the phone book. And we could go to the Y on some weekend--if you've time? I heard that you and some other girls participated in archery and rifle practice on my parents' farm. I've always liked hunting in the forest around home, but the target set-up happened some years after I left my folks' place."

"Yes, several of us formed a cadre in Granstadt three years ago and made good use of the Lowe farm. We called it a National Guard Auxiliary Auxiliary: having the right to bear arms as a well-regulated female militia. I'll call you before this Saturday. I'm not busy then."

"Hot ziggedy! I'm free, too. At the YWCA we can exercise and swim. Too bad that there is no firing range there. The gyms and pools have re-opened after being closed during the polio epidemic last year. Praise be to Jonas Salk for his vaccine."

Ken, climbing the stairs behind his two colleagues and pushing their shoulders to urge them forward, looked back at Meg and commented that his family had lined up immediately to receive the first polio vaccinations. He bid Meg farewell as she walked toward the entrance door. He didn't want to be too late for their appointment because so doing would not make a good impression regarding their efficiency.

On the second floor, a brass sign was outside each office. Belinda shook her coat off of one arm while holding a folder up in the air with the other hand, then switching. The coat fell to the floor. She retrieved the coat and turned it inside out, preventing it from making their folder of documents damp. Then she handed the folder over to Ken. He knocked on the office door bearing the sign "Walter Raleigh, Esq., Attorney at Law" and opened it, gesturing at his two colleagues to enter.

Holly entered first. A secretary, short, with hair tightly pulled back from her head and enormous glasses on a tiny nose, jumped up from her chair as if under attack.

"What do you want?"

"We have an appointment to see Mr. Raleigh. I'm Mrs. Jones here with my partners."

"You're too late. Your appointment was for ten o'clock sharp."

"Sorry. The sidewalks are slippery, and we had to walk slowly. We're only a few minutes late because we were visiting with Mrs. Raleigh downstairs."

"Just give me the folder, and I'll see that he gets it."

Ken tilted his head, a tiny frown on his face. Mrs. Jones demanded in an assured voice, "Please ask if he'll see us. He may wish to ask some questions that only we can answer." Holly spoke directly at the little rigid figure. "See, miss, you wouldn't have the slightest idea how to provide subtle shadings pertinent to our professional submissions."

The secretary straightened and replied, "I certainly could do that. You can wait over there if you must." She pointed at a horsehide sofa. "Be careful, though, ungainly people tend to slide off that onto the floor." She knocked gently on the door to the office.

"I'll stand, thank you, although I certainly wouldn't slide off." Belinda squared off and mildly challenged the guardian dragon by also looking straight at her without seeming to be angry or insulted. The lady's body remained stiff. She stared back but then did knock again.

The room was warm, almost too warm. The walls were painted a delicate blue color that set off the white backgrounds of floral pictures on each wall. The pictures were matte photographs, Belinda decided, as opposed to paintings, framed in unpainted wood.

Ken kept the folder securely in one hand and unbuttoned his own double-breasted, heavy, dark blue wool coat. Holly's hat was still tucked inside the front folds of her coat, until it fell to the floor. He stooped, picked it up, and handed it to her. He sized up the elegant surroundings, glancing at the beautifully carved desk where the secretary was now seating herself, and noticed a nameplate that read "MISS M. KING."

Walt Raleigh finally opened his office door and beckoned them in. "Hold my calls, Marnie. These people are on my schedule."

"Yes, Mr. Raleigh."

He took the trio's coats and put them on a coat tree near the door. "Please be seated." He waited as they arranged themselves on chairs in front of his desk. "I'm glad you came over. Now, go through the cases you've brought and describe what the clients wanted as well as how you found solutions to their problems. I hope you did not intend to describe cases from people I cannot contact to verify your conclusions. That would waste my time."

Holly assured him of their discretion. "The people we're citing see no reason to stay silent. There are no embarrassing linkages in the findings. We would not reveal confidential matters."

"I'll check with these clients of yours later this week. You indicated before you had some clients who preferred to remain anonymous."

"It's just a matter of promising confidentiality unless a crime were involved. We are clear in our contracts that we would turn matters over to the legal system if iffy things were involved."

"But, can you be sure that nothing illegal is involved?"

Mother Holly was a great organizer when setting out tasks dependent on each partner's strengths. Thus, Ken admired the appropriate and executive demeanor on Mother Holly as she replied, "I assure you, my dear sir."

"And is discretion observed by your partners?"

"Yes, sir. By all of us." Belinda did not elaborate further, even when he gestured for one of them to continue. She produced a steno pad and a pencil, prepared to jot notes of the interchange.

"Oh, I get your reluctance to say anything further–– that might tell me something you cannot reveal! Very well, tell me about this first reference." He looked down at the outline Belinda handed across the desk.

Holly took charge of the interview. "Case Number One. A daughter had disappeared. She left a note saying she was going to the east coast. When the family wanted to look for her some three years later, we found her here in Kansas City, working at a library. She has turned out to be a useful colleague, as a matter of fact, helps with our research, and, of course, is reunited with her family south of here. You'll have to call long distance to talk with the father."

"I see. Not very relevant to my needs. All right, the second case is also from here in KC. I judged that from looking at the address and phone number of the reference."

Holly spoke again. "The father was trying to find a cemetery where his childhood recollection said a great-uncle was buried. He was correct, but it was a graveyard on a farm outside of the city. Records had been kept in a family Bible and another place. He didn't know how to decipher the information. We did, plus we found the farm with the sunken granite grave marker."

"That's interesting and somewhat more related to what I'm possibly retaining you to investigate." His words were spoken briskly.

Ken would give Belinda credit for cracking that one, used as she was to digging in library archives in earlier days. She had refused to give up on shifting through dusty files, faint writing in church ledgers, and surly clerks. That grumpy guy finally smiled at her and eventually led them to a forgotten corner in the basement of the little brick church for a look at a deceased rector's funeral notes.

Holly continued the reporting. "And the third case is related to the first, as you may notice from the address, sir. The family had lost an ancient icon of a saint, first stolen from their house by an escaped prisoner and then stolen by the daughter. We made the rounds of antique stores, pawnshops, and churches. We found it in a shop in a little town north of here, all covered with dust."

Ken waited, sitting back and watching Raleigh's face, listening for any subtle hints in voice or demeanor that would suggest that the man was not as disinterested as his brusque statements suggested. Ken recollected the turmoil back in Granstadt that had accompanied the stolen icon, the disenchanted daughter.

But Raleigh seemed to relax a little as he said, "That seems as though you are only reporting three references, instead of four."

"I mentioned four cases, not four references. We are able to provide more names, but don't wish to hassle any more people than necessary."

The secretary had opened the door after giving a brief tap and asked, "Do you want anything, Mr. Raleigh?" She eyed each face turned toward her.

"No. We're about finished. Thank you. Please shut the door." He waited until she complied.

"She seems concerned about something," Belinda noted, raising an eyebrow.

"My wife doesn't like the way that Marnie hovers over me, but I think it's cute. My Meg was teaching in Japan for two years while Marnie's father employed me in his law office before I struck out on my own. You three have already told me your former occupations. I'm telling you this so that you know in turn something of my background. Mr. King's law office has built a lot of prestige because he has been the defense attorney in several famous cases." He brushed a hand over his scalp, but the hair remained sticking up.

"I see," said Belinda politely, leaning forward in genuine interest at the historical review of the Raleigh couple's careers.

"You might want to look up Clifford King's name in the newspapers of the past quarter century to see how I've been trained under him. I realize I should be as much under your scrutiny as your office is under mine. I'm sure you're all aware of the types of criminal activity that have been noted in this city since the twenties. Mr. King and I simply believed in 'innocent until proven guilty'. We did deal with criminal matters but I no longer do so. Those gangster days are pretty much gone now anyway. Well, so, to your last case, Mrs. Jones."

"Yes, sir. So on with it. The fourth case was that of finding a divorce filing from 1908. We checked with the local courthouses. Everything in them is filed in basements and rooms and dumped in file folders or in various other containers. That took quite a while because we had to have permission and be accompanied by a clerk the whole time. We had little to go on, but the divorce paper was found filed in East Courthouse. Better than fine. Check with the people, and they'll tell you more if they wish to."

He picked up a fountain pen and made a few notes. "That case fits even better with mine. Very well. I'll call these references tomorrow, as I said, because I'm due downtown in a few minutes and will be gone the rest of the day. I'll schedule another appointment with you if things work out. My problem involves a rather old, long family line so it'll take hours of your time if I engage you. Just be warned. Is your fee schedule in this folder?"

"Yes, last sheet. Mileage at 3 cents a mile, time at $1.20 an hour for each person used, calculated in 15 minute segments."

"That is precise. It's satisfactory––if I choose your business."

He rose, helped Holly on with her coat, shook Ken's hand, turned to help Belinda and escorted the sleuths to the outer door––where they were watched every step of the way by his Marnie hen. Ken wondered if she feared they were going to steal a paperclip. Maybe she just didn't like people. Particularly female people.

Belinda pulled her hat down over her ears and stuck her hands in her red mittens as she walked down the stairs. Ken's brown felt hat still had drops of water on the brim from melted snowflakes. The snow had left wet spots on all their winter coats added to the fact that they still had to walk more than three blocks back home, collecting more wet spots and colder appendages.

Ken objected that it was too cold outside for Holly to leave off her tacky tam. She grudgingly admitted that he was right, although she commented that his own ears weren't covered. His rebuttal included a comment about the wide brim of his felt fedora preventing snowflakes from dropping in his eyeballs.

There was no place to stop off for a minute to warm up except at the antique store, but the proprietor was suspicious of people who simply browsed.

The local restaurant of note demanded dress-up, meaning hat, gloves, heels, and hose for the ladies and did not include mittens, tams, and galoshes. Ken thought about how they were going to arrive at the restaurant in snow-free shoes when they kept their reservation there Friday night. Limousine? Sleigh? A sleigh would be elegant, romantic, looking up through snowflakes at the Christmas lights on the rims of the roofs on the Country Club Plaza.

Good thing the coffee pot at home was always ready to burble when the gas ring underneath was lighted.

Ken opened the doors that they had to pass through at the entrance and up the stairs. Inside their foyer, they unbuckled galoshes. Belinda handed the left one and then the right to him. He placed them carefully on a rug inside the foyer door. He hurried inside in his own wet boots to answer the phone.

He returned a few minutes later, looked his cohorts solemnly in the eye, and said, with a poker face, "That was Mr. Raleigh calling, and we are now on his time clock. Hi-dee-ho! He'll be here shortly after one o'clock to outline the problem we're to solve. He'll make it brief because he has other appointments. He likes it that we're near his office."

He watched their faces light up, Belinda's in particular, with that way the eyes seem to become more round and more blue, beaming on him. "We didn't have to tell him much. I think he was already ready to hire us."

"I agree, plus even more so after we explained the cases to him," Holly said in a delighted tone.

"He did say that he had called the references after we left. That meant one long distance and two local calls, given that two cases involved the same family. He obviously did not dwell on that odd way of citing four cases, thank goodness. I'm glad the people were home when he called."

Mother Holly nodded in agreement. "I need a cup of coffee. And a question occurred to me as we tramped through the snow. How are we going to be able to enter that restaurant Friday if we've tramped through snow in galoshes? That would be *gauche*."

Ken had that problem figured out. "Oh, we'll take a cab. The restaurant not only has the walk cleared but also places a rug over to the curb. It doesn't like wet shoes on its expensive carpet, as you must have guessed."

"Good. Tell Cook we're home, and I also need a cup

of coffee immediately." Belinda had removed her black cardigan sweater and leather shoes and was rubbing her feet.

Holly slipped into the living room and continued toward the kitchen.

Ken tossed some fuzzy slippers at Belinda from the doorway into the apartment.

"Thank you, Oh, Venerable Investigator," she said and tossed him a salute in return.

"You're welcome, Lady Librarian. Need to keep your tootsies warm."

"Did you clip yours? I'm tired of having to mend your socks."

"Yes. And, I washed my hands and ears. Nothing but pure clean thoughts under my hair, either. Want me to show you where to plant a purely clean smooch?"

Belinda came in, slid the office door shut behind her, sat down on the couch by him, and kissed his cheek. "Oh, my, and you shaved your face clean this morning. You are all ready for a smooch. You still smell like shaving foam––I see a speck on your neck, here I'll get it off––and after-shave. Yes, my clean, pure, and righteous husband. I think we're in business with the Raleighs. And, he's certainly starting us off quickly. Must be some urgency to it. I hope it's more interesting to investigate than what we've had assigned to us before."

CHAPTER THREE

Walter Raleigh, Esq., placed photographs on the desk in the small front foyer of **Sleuth Works**. "There're three newspaper articles in that bunch, with stories reporting what I'm about to expand upon. Two are from 1946 and one from last September. Shouldn't I talk to all three of you?"

"Yes, sir," replied Ken Massey. "Let's go into the main office. Belinda is typing up our notes. Holly Jones does the assignments after we all decide on a plan. Please let me have your coat, and you go take a seat at the round table. First, though, you remove your wet boots, then we'll move into the warmer room away from the draft up those stairs from the front door." He picked up the newspapers photos and waited to slide open the door.

Walt Raleigh put his coat on the coat tree himself and sat down to remove his wet overshoes. Finished with that chore, he rose and followed Ken went into the office. Ken spoke easily about the inner office, to establish a deeper acquaintance with his client, as one would to one's intimate friends. "We have that thick old plate glass on the oriel window to keep the chill down in this inner room plus it faces south. We seldom draw the drapes over it. We do feel that there's more chill in the air because of the increased moisture here at the confluence of the Missouri and Kaw rivers than where we met each other and worked down by the Big Blue River."

"I heard that you were stationed at the Air Base south of here?"

"Correct, sir. But, I grew up over by the Mark Twain forest in a kind of backwoods home. Graduated from Pulaski County High School in 1949. After being drafted and moved around various airfields, I had to keep adjusting to more traffic and taller buildings, stoplights that I had never seen before, and having to use street addresses and maps. At home, we'd just give directions such as 'go past the church two lanes and up to the silo and turn left to the house.' I met Belinda at my last Base, and we married almost three years ago."

Raleigh smiled. "I separated from the military in 1944, went straight through undergraduate college and law school. Took the bar in '50 and married Meg Lowe."

Within the office, the other two Sleuth colleagues ignored the men's chatter. Belinda continued typing while Holly was absorbed in some paperwork at the circular table.

"Should we read these papers before you begin with additional information, sir?"

"Yes, of course." Walt settled down into chair cushions and folded his small hands. "I marked each pertinent article with a star over the headline. I managed to find copies that had the date and exact placement of the articles on each page. Those two things indicate the importance of the article——at least to the editor. Articles above the fold are more important. The relevant information begins with two news articles from 1946 and continues with one from this year."

"The maid will bring in some coffee in about fifteen minutes," Belinda told them as she finished typing and extracted a sheet of letterhead from the roller.

Ken and Holly quickly reviewed the articles' photographs, and, finished, looked at Raleigh. Holly with one eyebrow raised, said, "Shoot. I'm interested in this article about *Arrest Made in Cemetery Death.*"

Belinda came over and picked up the photograph copies. She quickly perused them and then collected her steno pad for making notes while the others discussed the case.

Raleigh explained while looking up to the left. "Well, the articles describe a death in a cemetery, the appraisal of antique jewels and subsequent placement at the art gallery, and the recent death of the jewels' possible heiress, Natalie Kilmer. She and her husband died in a car wreck that looks to me suspiciously different from an accident. After all, they were motoring on the highway on a fair weather day in September. No ice. No rain."

"I noticed that the newspaper articles did not allude to questionable findings on the wreck, sir." Ken sat across from Raleigh and next to Holly. His elbows rested on the thick wood armrests.

"The editors were careful about alleging anything weird about the wreck. Richard Kilmer was not an upstanding citizen and has 'friends.' No one wants to be a target."

Holly reacted quickly. "Are we being caught up in something dangerous here? How are we to stay clear, actually to know what is dangerous? After all, we're just setting up shop. We're not conversant with Kansas City history or dynamics, Walt, because I and the family have been here only a year and a half."

"I anticipate no problems whatsoever. Sorry if I alarmed you unnecessarily. Only seek information from people who are mentioned in the articles. Check with me first about ones whose names you may hear rumors about."

"Duly noted," Holly Jones agreed.

Walter Raleigh continued, "Now, the problem is that the jewelry was duly loaned to the museum in line, first, by Natalie Kilmer's mother, although she had died in that cemetery before actually signing the loan papers. That is mentioned in the one article. She hit her head against a tombstone when she fell. The tombstone was that of her father and mother. Her mother was a twin and the twins came to St. Louis to be married to brothers now living in Kansas City. All emigrated here during the turmoil in Austria. Natalie approved her mother's art museum loan later. Currently, the issue is that the title to the gems needs to be cleared."

"Thus, we need to trace back to the emigrants' arrival to determine if other relatives sailed in, too, given the article's mentioning antiquity," Belinda said.

"Yes, you may be correct. Apparently, the jewelry was brought to the United States by twin girls during the mid 1800s turmoil in Europe and handed down through one lady's descendants through the years," Raleigh stated. "No one is clear if it was simply a one-sided, not twin-sided heritage."

"Shouldn't be hard to trace records."

"Oh, yes, but it is. There are no heirs, no children, who are descendants of the Kilmers. However, a local woman says her mother is a direct descendant of the twin girls, is a descendant parallel in line to that of Natalie's mother. We have no clue as to any other heirs. Finding any of those is your assignment."

Belinda said, "I do not understand why your 'local woman' isn't named in the newspaper articles."

"She's my wife's friend, name of Merrilee Anderson. She was asked by the museum to acknowledge no claim to the jewels when she decided to inquire about them. She knows little about her third cousin, Natalie. Different social groups."

"But why did Mary asked about the jewelry if she had never been involved with Natalie?" Belinda persisted.

"Because *Merrilee,*" he spelled the name, "is a direct descendant of the second twin."

"And that means simply finding old wills, sir? Remember, we are not much interested in criminal investigations if you meant us to work on the accident angle."

"No matter. The police, with the help of my old colleague, Clifford King, are supposed to be handling that aspect of the issue. I'll admit that nothing seems to be moving very quickly toward a conclusion about the Kilmer deaths. You need only find any wills and also birth and death certificates of relatives. Those documents will be scattered around the state but will enable you to trace any other descendants."

Holly said thoughtfully, "Yes, sir. We do that sort of tracing. Our firm has already found that events such as epidemics, hard times, and wars disrupted many forms of correspondence among family members. People grew apart, moved away. Didn't meet, couldn't afford a stamp or to call long distance if they could even afford a phone."

"That is a valuable insight. Too, relatives do lose track of each other when they're busy with their own families. Here are Merrilee Anderson's address and phone. She is the wife of Slim Anderson, a local newscaster. We see them socially. Their phone number is unlisted because people tended to call all hours of the night and bother them. People keep gossiping to me and Meg about the late Kilmers, some shady tales, seems like, but those I give over to Clifford King, my former boss. He likes to keep up on rumors. Merrilee knows a little about mutual ancestors linked with her cousin Natalie Kilmer. She can put you in touch with any others who can probably fill in more."

Belinda asked, "I see. Well, may I go ahead and call Merrilee, Mr. Raleigh?"

"Yes, but remember the number is not in the phone book. Don't lose that number. The actual name is Horatio Anderson, anyway. Slim's a nickname."

Raleigh looked on with astonishment as the far sliding doors parted, admitting a teacart pushed by petite, and young, brown-haired maid. The heavy wooden cart held a china coffee pot, china teapot and metal strainer, cups, saucers, sugar and cream, tiny spoons, and a platter of several types of cookies. The cart she placed by the big desk on Ken's side and put delicate linen napkins trimmed in lace by each person before she left the room.

Ken slid back his chair and glanced around at the sturdy furniture pieces that had been brought over from the ancestral farmhouse. Mother-in-law Holly had joked that the low seat cushions, covered with heavy grey material edged with grosgrain, were replaced religiously every quarter century––unless a child had an "accident." That particular event required a complete cosmetic makeover, she added.

Belinda said, "Thanks, Harriet" as the maid left the room. Ken and Holly changed places and also called 'thanks.'

Holly poured tea or coffee as requested as they pondered their moves. Ken didn't want to have an accident, such as a car wreck, himself. Ken wondered aloud if the Kilmers were mixed up with the people from the historically criminal side of town? He looked at Walter Raleigh who seemed to have alluded to such an interpretation.

Ken asked softly again, "Suspicious wreck?" Raleigh nodded slightly but also shrugged. Obviously, reluctant to answer.

Belinda seemed not to notice the interchange between the men because she remarked, "It's great that you've found one line of descendants. Do you know anything of these Volks mentioned in the cemetery story?"

Holly added another question. "Or anything more from the article about the Schmidt woman, Natalie's mother, being killed next to the Volks' monuments back then? You haven't explained the article about the death in the cemetery."

Raleigh smacked his head. "Oh. That. Richard Kilmer was first charged with murder, then later a boy was. Finally, it became obvious that it was decidedly an accidental death: the woman was surprised by the boy popping up; she slipped; and falling hit her head. The boy was also blamed with the death but freed down in Raumville.

"So. That cemetery is obviously where you must start. I know only what is quoted––the discovery that the jewelry was valuable and had been loaned to the art gallery. It is the gallery's board that wants the hoard of jewels traced and ownership cleared. Is this ten-dollar retainer enough? It will cover eight hours of time and some mileage." He stood, looked at his watch, and, opening his billfold, extracted the money he passed over to Holly.

"Yes. The session yesterday and our delivery of references to your office are *gratis*. And, you correctly guessed that the actual charges started the minute you walked in the door today." Holly handed the payment to Belinda.

"I have to get back to the office because an accountant and I are helping with a major merger and acquisition of auto parts manufacturers," Raleigh revealed proudly. "I wouldn't have even paid attention to this request if the art museum hadn't been concerned or if Merrilee hadn't recommended my office to them. It's really a minor case. Just time-consuming."

Raleigh rose, shook hands, and all said their goodbyes. Ken Massey followed him down the stairs from the foyer, and shut and locked the door to the lobby after he left.

Belinda said, "That case doesn't sound very difficult. We're good at the task of searching for records."

Ken heard her as he returned upstairs and remarked, "I saw you cooking up a plan, Mother Holly. Whom do I interview first?"

"Of course, those in the obituary," she said, then sipping her tea and putting down the cup into the china saucer. She wiped her mouth and looked over at him.

"First here, though, do you want any more tea or coffee, girls?" Ken asked his wife and mother-in-law. He gestured to the cart, but they both shook their heads. "Well, it may be a minor case, but it will expand our reputation hereabouts. Okay, then, Mother Holly, time for Belinda to start a new ledger, and you to set up our drawer of files. Tell me what the labels will be. I think we learned a little more that is significant from our discussion with Raleigh than what we found in these articles. The goal is to clear the title to the jewelry for the art museum. That should be a snap." He sat down in his comfortable chair and sipped his coffee.

"A car wreck wiped out the titular owner who had loaned the stuff to the museum," Belinda said, putting down one picture of a newspaper article.

"Yes, after her late mother initially loaned the gems to the museum years ago. The earliest articles are about the jewels and the cemetery death." Ken took another sip.

She shot him a look of merriment. "Oh. Huh. A cemetery death. Very puzzling, I'm sure, for that to occur."

"Keep reading, funny girl. Raleigh hinted, however, that the recent car wreck was suspicious. That isn't good. I noticed that the newspaper did not say anything about another car running into them, that is, involved in any way in their wreck. And, he also said the Kilmer fellow was on the wrong side––of the law, that is, not the road. I trust that he is correct that those particular Kilmer items need not concern us."

They memorized dates and times by muttering aloud. The yellowing page of the September newspaper was fragile; therefore they handled it carefully. The two photos and the one recent article were kept flat on the desk and not held in their hands.

Mother Holly said, "I suggest that we order these names chronologically. I have another weird password for the padlock combination to the file cabinet. Are you ready?"

The couple nodded, grinning at her and then each other.

"The news articles say that the ancient tomb stones were dedicated to two couples--the men both named 'Volks' and their wives' maiden names, 'Jufellear'. Those are German names. The password clue is 'beer' because of the Teutonic names. The code to the file cabinet padlock will be by the yellow pages index under 'Alcohol.' Look for the phone number of the first listing under that. The folders inside the cabinet will be ordered chronologically when we have the data."

The couple knew to flip the lock backwards a couple of times, land on the first two digits from the phone number, go forward past the next single digit from the phone number, and return to land on it; and, go backwards and land on the next two digits. Weird, but workable, Kendrick Massey thought, looking fondly at his mother-in-law.

"And that assemblin' a folders is our job, sho nuff," Kendrick said.

"Those cemetery monuments would identify the elder Volks man, whose folder will be followed by that of his Jufellear wife, assuming the girls are younger than the men. We will be starting, therefore, in the mid 1800s, assembling family trees for descendants. You look puzzled."

"Are the dates for the husbands' and wives' births and deaths listed under their names on the granite slabs?"

"Most assuredly. Those do not show up in the news articles. Someone is going to have to go over to that cemetery . . . someone like Belinda."

"Okay, mom."

Ken smiled, stood, removed his jacket from his broad shoulders, and sat down again.

Mother Holly beamed at him and said, "I hope you

noticed I came up with the system for a secret password quickly, like a drunk might do with an excuse when stopped by a cop. Different from the other filing systems I've concocted. Think you could remember it?"

She eyed the youngsters. Belinda shook her head at her mother's frivolous tone; Ken grinned again.

"You know we can," he said.

"I thought so. And we needed a chuckle. Next, we have unknowns: children's names descending from the two Volks' couples. We'll have to fill in that gap. Then recently, we have the dead Kilmer lady and any other relatives of Merrilee. As the last living ones, I mean."

Belinda remarked, "So far, I don't see any living relatives being mentioned except Merrilee, so I don't understand why you assume her mother or others are alive when Natalie's died years ago? I'm going to call Meg tonight and see if she knows anything more."

Holly said, "Ah, the linkages across the world never fail to intrigue me. Let's find the birth or death certificates of the oldest people. If they were immigrants, the marriage certificates from churches or registries may be the first and only legal sources, except for the ten-year census. After 1900, it listed all family names, not just the males' names or only the heads of household names, as the census did in prior decades. We know the cemetery where the Volks are buried, and that helps. Next, birth certificates of children and then wills that may have been filed. If needed, we'll dig up census reports, although many are written in very faint ink."

"All right. Government Offices will be closing several days for Christmas and New Year's at the end of the month so I'll get hopping," Belinda said. "I'll take the two Jackson County courthouses to start with."

Ken outlined his own work. "Maybe some neighbors know more. What I am going to do is interview people. I'll start with the pallbearers and the church that held the Kilmers' funeral. I don't want you gals getting anywhere near the outfit that Kilmer worked for; that is, talking with people that may have been at the funeral. That car accident that might not have been an accident!"

"Don't be so suspicious. Mr. Raleigh said nothing's being mentioned in that regard. I don't like the possibility of violence, Ken, for you, either. We're not police; we're not attorneys." Belinda shook her head.

"Walter Raleigh already told us he'd handle any legal stuff that arises. We just investigate and provide him with our best summarization. When we have something to report."

"I'll type the letter on each label for the files, Mom. Do we have enough folders?'

"Yes. The bookstore had them on sale last month, and I bought two boxes. We'll put them in drawer 'B.' 'B' for 'Bier.'" Holly laughed. "I hope you didn't try to memorize the letter 'A' for 'alcohol because it's not there in the yellow pages. I just looked and discovered that I had to go to 'B' for 'Bars and Taverns.'"

The youngsters nodded. Neither had tried to find the padlock number yet. Mother Holly loved to tease, and Ken adored her teasing even when it was a bit strained in reaching for an actual witticism.

CHAPTER FOUR

The next hour was spent arranging schedules, putting tabs on folders, searching for addresses in the phone book for the relevant government buildings, and making notes.

The bell on the desk tingled through its outlet. "Supper," a voice wavered. Ken hit the bell and said, "Coming right in." Once a week they dined early so that the children could have their usual bedtimes but also moments with their parents.

The children were already in high chairs and had bibs around their necks. The maid, who was also the cook named Harriet, ladled chicken soup into five bowls and left the dining room. A young nanny, Lillian, fed oatmeal to the children on either side of her. She and Harriet also had places at the table. Some animal crackers were already on the floor from the pile on the boy's chair, a boy who was about to grow out of his high chair.

"We need to get a booster seat for J. B.," Holly said, pointing her spoon at the child. "Next agenda. When shall we put up the Christmas tree?"

"I think after some people are asleep the evening of December 24th," said Ken. "Stockings can go on the lower limbs, or might be better on the fireplace mantel. I'll buy a fir out on the highway that day."

"Good. We need some more crackers, Harriet," Belinda

called to the cook in the kitchen who was dismantling a roasted chicken. They heard her pull open a drawer.

The cook could be seen next in the butler's pantry, a six-foot long hall between the dining room and kitchen. On one wall were serving shelves, with drawers beneath, and cabinets to the ceiling. On the other side were more drawers and cabinets all the way up. The wood was polished mahogany.

The dark passageway had an elegant overhead chandelier with its lights reflecting on china plates and etched glassware inside the plate glass doors in the middle cabinets. Harriet finished filling a basket with crackers, brought it in, then took the soup tureen from the table, and returned to the kitchen.

After that, Harriet brought in the platter of chicken and immediately followed it with the bowl of asparagus and basket of cornbread. She sat down and began on her bowl of tepid soup. The others moved their bowls toward the table's center from off of their plates and passed around the main course.

"Are we having the asparagus that you canned?" Ken asked Mother Holly.

"Yes, of course." She stood before she moved over and lifted J. B. up, carrying him back to her place and plunking him onto her lap. "Have some greenies?" she wheedled, moving the boy's hand away from her plate. Her spoon held a tiny bit of asparagus.

The toddler took a bite and bit the spoon.

"Want more?"

"Wyeth, Nana." She gave him two more little bites while the nanny, having rapidly finished eating, took the younger girl out of the room, Alberta first having been presented to her family members to receive kisses and a tickle.

"J.B., what sound does your airplane make?" asked Belinda.

He gave a growl and swooped his hands in the air.

"See, Daddy, he's going to be in the Air Force, too. He's looking sleepy. I'll take him up to Lillian." Nana Holly Jones cuddled him in her arms. And hummed the Air Force song softly as she walked out of the room toward the stairs to the children's nursery.

The couple talked little while finishing supper. Going back into the office, Ken made a list of pallbearers' names mentioned in the Kilmer obituary. His approach would be asking for an appointment to trace Natalie's relatives. Maybe the church had addresses for everyone mentioned, because two of the names were not in the telephone book.

Also in the office, Belinda called Meg and arranged to meet her at the YWCA at 10 Saturday morning. Merrilee could be invited, too, Meg offered. The Andersons were not listed under "Slim" Anderson, a nickname, Meg revealed with a giggle, because his given name was Horatio. But Belinda remembered that Walter Raleigh had told them the same thing plus that the phone number was unlisted and had given it to them earlier that afternoon. Meg chatted on about mutual acquaintances that they might have. Unfortunately, Belinda had to keep saying, "no, not acquainted" with only two yeses. She finally was able to say goodbye.

Belinda next called Merrilee for information about her relatives' names, addresses, and phone numbers. She jotted the list in the back of the address book, not by the alphabet pages. In turn, Belinda gave Merrilee the **Sleuth Works** information.

Belinda cradled the phone and asked Ken, "Did you know that Meg knew Donna and Phil Tyler from when she was teaching in Japan? I know Phil was your Air Force superior, but there was no reason that Phil would mention Meg's name to you. Donna and Meg played tennis together when serving in Japan. All irrelevant but gives us more background connections to her and hubby Walt."

"No, I never heard of Meg until we ran into her this week at Raleigh's office."

Holly had returned to the room to note the time already engaged by each of them, any long distance calls that would show up on next month's phone bill, and the cost of supplies (for income tax purposes). She handed the list to her son-in-law. "Did Mr. Raleigh understand that he's paying $1.20 a hour for each of us?"

"Should have. We're all employees of our firm. He himself has a secretary and worked downtown for another lawyer for some years. I told him about each role we play." Ken looked over the statement before handing it to Belinda, and she entered items in two columns.

"Well, we've already used up half his retainer."

"Good show." Ken saluted Mother Holly.

Belinda snapped shut the ledger, looked over at Holly, and asked, "Now, what more do you want me to do, Mother?"

"I'll line up things to do after you finish at the courthouses. Maybe you could go to the Volks' gravesites next. Have to use the car."

Belinda asked, "Mom, about the holidays you mentioned

at supper, where are we putting everyone the Friday night before Christmas? Shall Ken and I give our room to Uncle Chuck and Aunt Deedee?"

"Oh, no. We're not moving out of our places for one night. Or for any amount of time. We have plenty of room. I'll put your brother Barney and my three nephews out on the winterized porch. There're the four couches out there, and it's long enough that they can practice catching a baseball; it's about forty feet long––as you may have noticed last summer chasing J. B. from one end to the other playing peek-a-boo. Chuck and Deedee can use the spare bedroom on the second floor at the other end of the hall from the servants' rooms. It has the guest bathroom attached behind the full bath in the hallway. Remember how it duplicates the layout of your suite, except the bath facilities are reversed? I've had Harriet cleaning the rooms all week, turning the mattress, and fluffing the pillows."

"Good thing I had already moved our luggage to the storeroom off the porch," Belinda commented. "I don't remember anyone except Uncle Chuck very well. We haven't seen them much. I remember how we had to work every day, dawn to dusk, on our farm, Mom. I liked living in town better and still prefer it. I'm so glad you sent me to high school in Granstadt: I met a lot of friendly people and won my prize Kendrick!! I could always get enough fresh air and exercise to suit myself without tossing bales of hay."

Holly replied, "You're welcome, daughter. On reflection, I've never known Deedee to any degree of intimacy, either. She's standoffish and seems to consider me a rival, I think. She doesn't like it that Chuck and I show our mutual love by trading insults—all in good fun, of course. We've done that since we started to talk. I'm two years older than he. He joined the Army in the Great War, and we grew apart because I had married and moved to my husband's farm closer to Kansas City. When we sold that we moved to Granstadt after you did, and I worked at your high school year round. Times were that Chuck and I didn't see each other or correspond for years," Holly sounded remorseful. "I'm glad they're able to afford the trip now. We need to drive them around on the freeway system that's springing up here, easing traffic. Pretty good city planning going on here. Nice parks and museums and other entertainment."

"Where did he meet Deedee, do you know?"

"Some neighborhood bash, or church social, most likely, Belinda. Everyone in a twenty mile radius tried to go to those for entertainment that cost next to nothing, as you well know."

Belinda nodded. "And, as I said, I liked living in town after I left home. Although I had to go down the hall to the bathroom at the boarding house, everything else was enticing. The work and school games and church and holiday celebrations meant we were totally surrounded with a lot of people all the time. I had forgotten how our farm families became used to solitude. Although luckily, our farm was close to my elementary and junior high schools so I never had to miss class because of the weather."

"Yes, we were family-focused. On the farm, husbands, wives, and children become deeply concerned with each other's lives, because we had to cooperate to make the work pay off. Influenced each other a great deal. It usually worked, unless one member was terribly beastly, but that didn't happen often--to my knowledge, anyway, Belinda," she said, picking up the evening paper to signal an end to the conversation.

"I believe that I mentioned that I, in addition, when living in town could go down the hall to the bathroom, instead of outside to a privy."

"All right, Belinda Jones Massey, that's enough editorial opinion for the day. And also enough forever."

Belinda left on the trolley car for the downtown courthouse before Ken came back into the office with his coffee refill. The people he had tried to reach were out of town or, at least, had not answered the phone. He re-read the newspaper accounts. Perhaps the archives at the newspaper would give more background for Mother Holly to sift through for clues to relatives of the Kilmers. He was still a bit worried about the lack of certainty that threats would not reflect on their work. The newspaper's allusions to the suspicious circumstances--with the words "investigation is continuing" about the wreck--must have something to do with the infamous old gangs that Raleigh mentioned.

Ken informed Mother Holly, "I'm going out through the kitchen down to the garage. The front door is locked but Belinda has her keys. Maybe you should also take time to finish some Christmas shopping and mail your packages if you find nothing easily in the newspaper archives," he said, struggling into a long black wool coat, and placing a felt hat on his head.

She replied, "I have no packages to mail to anyone. My relatives will be here. Ignore that car wreck, you hear?"

"Okay. See you, Mother Holly. What a great name during this season. Great lady all the seasons." He gave her cheek a kiss. "I hear you. I'm going to follow your prudent suggestion as long as I get some results. Realistically, the Kilmer car wreck is a minor issue. Raleigh said he'd handle that. I'm off to see the church to find out about pallbearers mentioned in the obit. Close friends should know any relatives. I'm going to see the minister then I'll do pallbearers. None were mentioned in the obits for Natalie, just those for Richard. I'll come back and call around. Maybe I could even visit one before noon, and one in the afternoon. I'd grab a bite somewhere and finish those calls early this afternoon so that I can pick out a Christmas tree at a farm outside town which means I should be home in time for supper, if you'll tell cook for me, if you follow my digressions. I must run because I'm pressing my timing too closely with these digressions. To the church first."

"Take care. Take notes. Take down minutes spent to the quarter hour and mileage." Mother Holly looked up from the desk and rested the gold fountain pen on her lip. He saw that she next added another name with a question mark and put the pad inside a locked drawer, the key on a chain around her neck. Although he was familiar with "mileage" reimbursement from his Air Force days, he made no comment on her order to track time.

She sighed but then snorted. "Ignore the wreck, Kendrick! Some fellows can be much too dangerous, my dear retired AP. I'm reluctant to share these rascals' names I've read about over time in the newspapers. Unless absolutely nothing else helps us trace relatives, I'll see if there's any mention of social doings with the Kilmers in the society pages. It's Natalie Kilmer's friends and relatives that are relevant, not her beloved's. Merrilee Anderson gave

Belinda that short list of kinfolk. I agree that I don't see how knowing who Mr. Kilmer's relatives or friends would help trace Natalie's kin, anyway. Or even that knowing the cause of the accident would help, the wreck that killed them."

CHAPTER FIVE

Kendrick Massey had decided to visit the church to see if a guest register had been lodged there, or find out which kin had taken it. Both Kilmers had been eulogized at the same service and were buried in a new graveyard on the edge of town.

Icy flakes were falling on the DeSoto's windshield but the wipers worked fine. He sneezed twice, running over the centerline during the second one before he brought the steering wheel back in line. Have to stay away from the children if he comes down with a cold or the flu, dang it. The kids had been active and cross the night before. He escaped in case they were still out of sorts today and hollering because, truly, he was, himself, feeling out-of-sorts and might holler back. No, but might scowl and scare the pants offa 'em.

The Methodist minister, Pastor O. Owen Palmer greeted him from behind his desk, half-standing up from his chair with his hand outstretched. He started right in chatting. "Come in, sir. Glad to be of any help I can be. We ministers are transferred every few years, I was transferred here three years ago from Raumville, and I'm glad I was up here by fine hospitals when an old war wound caught up with me. We have really fine hospitals in the area. Papa OOPs is what my grandchildren call me when I start to ramble. That's a nickname from my initials." He pointed at his nameplate on the walnut desk. "Early in life, I was called 'Otto' but when the war started with the Nazis after I finished college, I opted for my middle name 'Owen' and have kept it ever since. Even my wife is exasperated sometimes and says 'O. Owen' in a weary tone. Enough about me. You're here about some parishioners according to my clerk."

Walnut frames held paintings of fighter planes on the walls, alternating with those of those of Biblical scenes, a strange contrast. All of the walnut wood in the frames and furniture had a deep, polished appearance, dark grain showing through. The walls were an off-white color that permitted the paintings, as well as a metal cross on the wall behind the desk, to catch one's eye.

Pastor Palmer sat down abruptly with a wince. He had a little wiry hair around a bald spot. Ken bent to follow him down because his hand still held in the handshake. The pastor let go, making a brief apology. "Sorry. I hurt sometimes."

"Yes, sir. Well, as I told your receptionist on the phone, I've been engaged to trace any relatives of Natalie Kilmer. The funeral service was here last September." Ken handed over a business card. He needs to move this visit along. In fact, the phone had been busy the first three times he tried to call the church. Phone lines always busy with parishioners needing solace. Someone would probably drop in in the next minute, and he'd be ejected.

Pastor Palmer replied, "The couple were not regular attendees. I bet I had met them only twice before they were killed in the wreck. No family members came forward to introduce themselves to me either here or at the graveyard service. However, the pallbearers for Mrs. Kilmer were all members of our church––volunteers they were. But only six of Mr. Kilmer's pallbearers were from our congregation. The other two were friends or kin to him."

"I saw his listed in the newspapers. No names were mentioned for her attendants. Do you still have the guest book?"

"Probably. I'll ask Charlotte to check." He knocked on the desk with a gavel, and a lady appeared. She was dressed all in black and had a morose expression. "Yes, Mr. Palmer?"

"Would you see if we still have the guest registry for the Kilmer funeral for him to check? It was back in September."

"I remember. I know where I put it. I'll be right back."

"I see no problem with your reading the names and statements they may have written in sympathy, but I am reluctant to let you take it," Mr. Palmer said.

"No difficulty there, sir. I'll just make a note of names if I might have a place to work."

Charlotte returned with a small padded book the size of a girl's diary and handed it to the minister. He leafed through it while saying, "Show Mr. Massey to a desk in the classroom, please. He's going to take notes but will leave the book with you when he's finished."

"Thank you, Reverend Palmer." Ken stood.

"You-all come to church sometime. I assume you're married, young man."

"Yes, sir. Thank you, sir. Oh—I noticed you have pictures of planes. I was in the Air Force, a few years back. Were you in the Army Air Corps?"

Rev. Owens raised his voice, pride revealed in his tone. "Yes, indeed. The Great War. We're mainly in cartoons, now, but we followed up on the Wright brother's inventions. I doubt they realized how useful those would be in war. Even in peacetime Amelia Earhart became a famous aviator, but she disappeared in 1937. She's from near here: Atchison, Ks."

"I heard. Thereafter, we used bigger and better planes even more in the Second World War."

"Yes, sadly. Say, I'd bet that you have children," Palmer raised his voice at Ken's back.

"Yes, sir."

"We have Sunday School during the nine a. m. church service."

"Yes, I'll tell my wife." Ken turned back, leaned over the desk and shook hands before he followed the clerk from the room to settle in a Sunday School room.

The clerk pulled the door shut and gestured toward the Sunday School room with its little chairs and desks.

Charlotte flipped quickly through the pages and said, "Most of these people do not belong to our church. I'll put a star next to those who do." She leaned over the table and marked them with a pencil she had had nested behind her right ear. "That's the few names. The crowd wasn't very big. I'll be happy to provide those phone numbers that I have of our members. These two couples, names of Shannon and Lincoln, aren't members. I think the men were pallbearers for Mr. Kilmer."

"I've tried to find them in the phone book, but they weren't listed. Those others attending might help me trace Natalie Kilmer's relatives. I would like addresses, too, if you have a church directory."

"It's only published for members. You could ask for those by telephone."

"Yes, all right. I prefer to make an appointment to talk with them in person if they're acquainted with Natalie." Maybe, just maybe, one would know of some of her relatives.

Ken wrote down in a notebook all the names and any comments that were besides them. He counted about twenty names that were not starred; most apparently being married couples because a single surname was provided with a male or female name. That meant a total of eight couples and four single persons. His phone would be busy this afternoon, he grouched a bit. He grumbled under his breath that these church people were the worst possible witnesses, wanting to gossip about everything in the subjects' lives. *Oh, well, had to be done.*

Charlotte returned with the telephone list and addresses, reached over and added a second star by three women's names. She said the women came together to every event and were not likely to provide anything more than a single one of them could. Actually, calling the list of church members was last on his list. Non-members of the church who had attended were more likely to be friends of the Kilmer couple.

Ken took the list home and had a snack with the kids and the nanny and Mother Holly. His mind was organizing the tasks before him. He phoned and, as luck would have it, made appointments with the two pallbearers who were not members of the church who had attended Richard Kilmer--a Mr. Shannon and a Mr. Lincoln.

After backing the DeSoto out of the garage into the back alley again, locking the wide wood doors, and returning to the front seat, Ken drove down Main and turned on 63rd to be able then to turn south on Ward Parkway. The address he was looking for turned out to be a huge stone house on the east side, atop a long sloping lawn. Turning at the next cross street and coming back north, he pulled into a wide stone and concrete driveway. Shallow steps led past boxwood shrubs up to a granite porch with etched stone pillars. Everything except the lawn had been cleared of snow and ice. He parked, climbed out, looked around, and then walked up onto the porch, pulled a lever next to the elaborate screen door and waited for the Shannons to answer. And waited. He stamped his cold feet.

Finally, he glanced at his watch and pulled the lever one last time––he could hear it jangle––and followed that by twice knocking hard.

Turning around he saw a late model Chrysler pulled into the driveway behind his car, diminishing his to puppy size in front of a Great Dane. A chauffeur, garbed in a maroon uniform, climbed out of the driver's seat, donned his matching cap, and opened a rear door for a lady in an ermine coat and fur hat. She's a replica of the Teddy bear. An animated one. The tall, burly dark chauffeur walked around the car to open the door for a gentleman wearing a black cashmere overcoat with a fur collar.

The chauffeur came stomping up the stairs ahead of the couple that moved slowly. He stared haughtily and directly into Ken's eyes. "Sir! You are blocking our way into the driveway garage and family entrance."

Ken blinked. "Sorry." He watched the elderly couple mounting the steps with smiles on their faces.

The white-haired and mustached gentleman said, "Unlock the door, Chaz. We've an appointment with Mr. Massey and are a tiddly bit late. I'm Mr. Shannon, Mr. Massey, and this is my wife, Mrs. Shannon."

51

The chauffeur, Chaz, obliged, grudgingly, giving Ken one last disdainful look as he turned around holding open the screen door. Ken handed the chauffeur the keys to his own car and bowed his head graciously, giving him permission him to move it, and entered after the couple.

From somewhere, a uniformed butler made an appearance at the front entrance hall. The guy had ignored the door chimes! Maybe he was uninformed regarding the meaning of the sound of a doorbell.

A virtual ceremony took place with the butler helping remove coats and taking the proffered scarves, gloves, and hats. An additional person, in the uniform of a housekeeper materialized, ushering the couple and Ken into a parlor, with her arm steadying the mistress. They were being seated by a fire before the butler entered and laid another log in the fireplace. It was like being in one of the first motion pictures released in color. Every move was dramatic; every color startling, contrasting with other hues in one's sight; all movements appearing stylized.

The room paid homage to gorgeous, varicolored damask cloth. Even a coffee table was padded and covered with deep green and blue embroidered damask, with one little rose in a corner. The old couple wore richly colored clothes that blended in well with the setting. Ken's dark, intelligent eyes kept taking in the surroundings while not staring, merely glancing as if impressed, though he most definitely was.

The little rose on the damask covering reminded Ken of the poignant lone flower in Pablo Picasso's *Guernica*. The painting had been completed in the late 30s during the Spanish Civil War. It depicted the destruction of the town and its people. The flower on top of a hand on a severed arm indicated that a little hope still could be found in the sad conflict.

"Some hot tea, Mamie, and scones, please," said the mistress to the housekeeper. Mrs. Shannon had her grey hair pulled back, a pearl on a hairpin stuck through a chignon at the nape of her neck. Her dress was of elegant grey embossed material with a dusky rose-colored collar and side panels. An ivory cameo brooch was pinned in the area below her Adam's apple. Her eyebrows were painted as dark arches.

Mr. Shannon had on a dark grey tweed suit with leather patches on the elbows. He wore an ascot tie of a wavy black and white design. His horn-rimmed glasses seemed to be more for show than for vision problems, because he soon laid them aside.

A ritual tea service in the offing, not even delayed until four o'clock, was preceded by pleasantries exchanged about the weather, the season, favorite childhood Christmas present, and number of children––and in the Shannon's case, doted upon a late grandson.

A maid entered with an English-style teacart more delicately framed than Harriet's sturdy contraption. The anonymous maid poured the tea, the mistress having hands that trembled too much to do so, and it not being a task for men. She handed cups on saucers to each person, served the scones, and left the room.

Mr. Shannon took a sip, had a bite, and placed the cup on a side table.

"Yes, now, what did you want to ask us about the poor Kilmers? He simply must have been speeding down that little highway, as he was wont to do, don't you think so? The accident was merely due to inattentive driving by a reckless chap, don't you think?" asked the lord of the manor, accompanying his description with a swoop of his hand to indicate the car flying away from the highway and crashing.

"I didn't know him. Just as we've been discussing about our kinfolk," Mr. Kendrick Massey began directing the interview easily, "I am interested only in relatives. Do you know any of Natalie Kilmer's? We know she had no children. Her mother was Jacqueline Schmidt, a descendant of a Volks' couple."

The couple looked thoughtfully at him and glanced at each other. Shannon replied, "I don't think we do. I gave a eulogy and was a pallbearer for Richard only because I had known him since he first started out with my company. He worked for me for thirty-five years as a, hmmm, a security man. I barely knew Natalie. I didn't flip through the guest book at the church or funeral home to notice names of any other people. Not many people there. The caskets weren't open because the bodies from the car crash were terribly mangled. Sorry, my dear, don't mean to put you off your tea."

"Would you know who kept any of their legal documents or address books with her phone numbers of friends?" Ken asked.

"Usually the family. Except you said there is no family that you know of nor that I know of. It might still be at their house although I heard everything had been carefully cleaned out. It'd be a cleaning service that worked their place over. And took it. If such a list existed. Good luck finding it in that case." Shannon laughed, for no reason that Ken could fathom.

"More tea?" asked Mrs. Shannon. "No more for you? Well, my dear sir, my friends and I believe Natalie may have been the only child of her daddy, Herr Schmidt, but, frankly, her mother Jacqueline Volks Schmidt was a bit of a scamp when we were young. And," she poked her husband's shin with the toe of her tiny shoe, "she and her mother disappeared for a few months in 1906-7. Told us that they were off to the continent *for the season*."

Her husband tilted his head toward her, a knowing look on his face. He laughed again.

The lady laughed, too, and wiggled her thin eyebrows. "We always knew what that meant back then: round heels."

Kendrick Massey waited, maintaining his composure but not sure how to pursue the matter and not quite sure what she meant. Finally he said, "You think she maybe had one out of wedlock? Excuse my being so blunt, ma'am."

She took a careful sip, holding the cup in both trembling hands, and carefully replaced the china on the delicate saucer. "All of us debutantes thought so, even when she returned in time, months before the spring ball, and came out with us. Look at the society pages from spring, 1908. She's certainly put on weight from her brief vacation. In Paris for the season, she insisted it was. Simply must have been the season for partaking of very fat *escargot* if she were not *enceinte*." Mrs. Shannon actually chortled.

"That is interesting, my dear, but the Massey fellow here isn't interested in gossip, no matter how discretely and colorfully you word things."

"Oh, my, perhaps I have been remiss in suggesting that there's another shirt-tale relation out there in the blue. But, the Volks family couldn't have gone to the continent because there were terrible plagues scaring people away at that time. And, she wasn't at parties here." Her chin was stubborn.

Mr. Shannon said sharply, "I don't think he wants us to speculate on what might have been. If there's nothing further, I have had a busy day, Mr. Massey. My chauffeur will keep an eye out for you if you need help around town."

Ken doesn't dispute the fellow about speculating, but this Paris rumor is an unexpected I-beam support to add to the edifice of background facts he is building. On his way to the living room door and hallway, he and Mr. Shannon chatted a little about the Kilmers, vague notes. Mr. Shannon seemed awfully interested in anything Mr. Massey might want to know about the accident, and Ken had to insist, rather forcefully, that the accident was of *no* interest. It was Natalie's relatives that he is interested in. Ken did not think he should mention the jewelry and art museum linkage because the Shannons were focused on Natalie's husband and rumors about illegitimate children.

The men ended their conversation with reference to the marvelous Christmas program at the Episcopal Church this coming Christmas Eve. Ken promised to bring his wife and mother-in-law to the service, made his courteous goodbyes, and found his keys on the desk by the front door, next to the butler (who still seemed to materialize) there to help him into his overcoat. Maybe to also ensure that he left.

The DeSoto had been parked facing down the driveway, perhaps to speed his departure. He turned right and right again to go toward the eastern suburbs of Kansas City. Along the way, he noticed one of those diners that resembled a long trailer and usually had some fantastic tasting pie. Hungry, he pulled into the lot and entered, like a hamburger, into a wrap-around delicious aroma. His lunch was thus clearly suggested without his having to read a menu. The waitress put down a mug of coffee and took his order for the burger, potato chips, and the special for today, gooseberry pie.

As he sat pondering the recent conversation with the Shannons, he decided to jot down notes about the 1908 dates, a young debutante who went to Paris the year before, and more vague descriptors of the accident/wreck. He also had a hint of the involvement of the Kilmer guy as "hmm, a security guy."

Mother Holly would know how to search phone books to see if there was a Catholic orphanage in Kansas City. Or, maybe she'd have to search newspaper archives to check if one existed during the first decade of the century. If a Volks daughter had a child born before she wed a Schmidt, it would have gone into such an establishment for adoption.

Some clerk could help Mother Holly trace newspapers that were in print back then, as well as others during the Kilmers' lifetime. Maybe even find archival information on the ancestral Volks. Belinda should be able to find a last will and/or any testaments today.

The pastry arrived along with a coffee refill as well as his check allowing him an excuse to stuff his little spiral notebook back into his jacket pocket, and enjoy the pie, savor the pie.

Belinda was already delving into sources for ancient death certificates, too. That information would round out what Mother Holly found in the news. Someone had once told him that *proper* people were mentioned in the newspaper only three times: when they were born, married, and died. **Sleuth Works** needed more information than that about the Volks' kin, for sure.

CHAPTER SIX

It was still a bit early for the next appointment with pallbearer Mr. Lincoln. He dawdled over the second cup of strong coffee but laid money on the check to give the waitress a chance to clear the table––except for the mug––and perhaps end her shift. And take the generous ten-cent tip.

Exiting the diner fifteen minutes later, he spied a telephone booth by his car at the curb and called home. "Mother Holly, I'm glad I caught you before you left. I might have a another name to add to the Volks' clan. Remember that the lady killed in the cemetery was Jacqueline Volks, Natalie's mother? This couple I just interviewed insinuated that Jacqueline might have had a baby before her marriage, around 1906-7. In addition to searching names in the newspaper archives, please look for any Catholic orphanages extant during that era."

He listened to the phone. "Yes, first decade of the century. I'm on my way to the suburbs. See you later."

The highway was relatively clean of snow, with the tar pavement and shoulders colored the way that s'mores looked, with the dark brown graham cracker laid smoothly on top of a piece of oozing Hershey's chocolate and white marshmallow on the edges. Traffic was light so he made good time to the next appointment.

The Lincolns' house he located was a junior copy of the

Shannons' stone one. However, this once elegant old house needed scrubbing and point work on the stone, the walk and driveway needed snow removal, and the gardens needed a clean-up because dead limbs and piles of leaves peeked through the snow. Ken carefully walked up the driveway. He feared it was too steep and icy to be safe backing down in his car. He knocked on the warped screen door, and the door opened abruptly. Ken retreated a step backwards on the wood porch, butting against a splintered wood railing. That wood needed replacing, too.

"You're the nosy parker looking into Kilmer's wreck?" a burly, flat-faced man said, reaching out, grabbing Ken's arm, and pulling him into a dusty, musty hall. The pockmarked walls indicated some hard objects had been thrown around. Ken immediately vowed that he would not be one of those objects.

"Mr. Lincoln? Yes, I'm Mr. Massey. Not really interested in the wreck. I'm trying to find Natalie Kilmer's relatives."

"That's not what I heard on the phone when you called." A teenage boy with a purple cheek watched from a doorway down the hall.

"Sorry if I didn't make myself clear, sir. Are you Mr. Lincoln?"

The man snorted as he nodded.

"Did you know any of her relatives?"

"Why should I? I didn't know her and don't want to. And where'd you get my name?"

"I saw it mentioned in the obituary column because you were a pallbearer for Mr. Kilmer. The church members seemed to be most of the pallbearers for the Kilmers except two, you and Mr. Shannon, for Richard Kilmer. I looked you two up in the phone book and called for appointments. I didn't mean to make you angry about it. In fact, that puzzles me--I mean that I'm seeing you so put out, but that's not my concern. It's Mrs. Natalie Kilmer I need to know about."

"That does it. I told my wife to take our name out of the phone book, but she don't obey and says she couldn't have her sorority sisters without a number to call, which only wastes money talking talking. You can get out of here now. I ain't knowin' nothin' about any wreck of that Richie Kilmer or his wife. It was good enough riddance, bye bye, to him. And I'd be really really careful if I was you. We'll be watching. It were an accident like the newspaper says. I mind my business. You mind yours--and stay away from mine."

The man jerked open the door and pushed Ken away from the heavy screen door and the foul smell from the interior. "Don't bother to come back. And, stay away from my friends and I. And, I'd take good care of that DeSoto of yours, fella. Don't want an accident, too, like Richie, do you? I could sic my son and friends on you, iffn needed."

"Yes. You. Could. Sir." Ken kept his tone neutral, although he could've taken the guy down in nothing flat if he'd been attacked. Good thing Mother Holly had warned him about rough characters in the area or his AP training might have taken hold . . . and instantly disabled the old guy. And that included if the teenager had tried to assist. His usual interviewing skills, paying quiet attention to the person's tone of voice, even when choosing not to respond to sarcastic threats, did not work with this Neanderthal.

He nodded and walked slowly, carefully down, not

running scared, down the damaged concrete in the driveway, climbed into the car, and waved goodbye.

Ah, well, time to stop by the Christmas tree farm I'd seen on the way here and reserve a tree to be cut down Saturday, the 24th, just 17 days from now. Also, I'll pick up my suits from the cleaners and check on the progress at the jewelers for my girls' brooches. Belinda and her mom are such competent and efficient colleagues that they rival the guys I used to work with in the Air Force. Brooches are the closest things to medals of honor I can award them.

Like the Seabees sing, Ken promised to remember today, the Seventh of December, every year of his life. He stepped from the car, blew wisps of air from his lungs toward the afternoon sun, and inhaled the smell of pine boughs. Small, medium, and large wreaths were for sale. They were made of those pine boughs, red satin bows, and cones. He thought about buying a couple but wasn't sure if Mother Holly would like the idea of hammering a nail or two to latch the decorations to, too.

The tree farm was busy with people hewing branches or cutting down tall evergreens, beautifully proportioned fir and pine trees. Evergreen limbs brushed his hat. Ken carefully stepped from one large flat stone to the next. The dirty piles of snow around the path were flattened here and there by small footprints of children. He strolled around, found a choice tree that he gauged was of the right height and breadth for the living room, and had his name attached to it by the workman.

The jewelry he had ordered at the 10th Street downtown store was ready in beautiful padded boxes. The brooches were made of different materials and nestled inside the boxes. Belinda's had pieces of slim green jade of various colors arranged like reeds that were waving on a pond. Mother Holly's had tiny garnet beads arranged in a rose pattern on a thick piece of nacre.

In addition, at his next stop, the cleaning was ready in six bags, long ones for the two evening dresses and his suit, and short ones for the jackets. He had stopped checking the mileage after Lincoln's place in order to have an accurate and truthful accounting.

Belinda and her mom were already home when Ken came up the stairs from the garage, bonked his head again on the lintel, walked through the kitchen, strode down the length of the butler's pantry and dining room, and finally entered the living room. "You know, people who built this edifice must have been really short. I always hit my head at the top of the stairs."

"Why aren't you a one-trial learner, dear? Once should have taught you. Bow your neck, be humble," Belinda said.

"I guess I deserve a knock on the noggin every time, Belinda." He laughed as he inclined his forehead. "I'll put these away." He walked to the hall doorway with the evening dresses and suit trousers draped over his right arm as he held the hangars high in his left hand. "One more load to come," he said and went back down to the car. He had left the garage door open in order to have enough light to see by. The remaining cleaning he hooked with the hangers in one hand because it was neither heavy nor awkward, shut the car door and the garage door, locked the latter, and returned upstairs, locked the porch door at the head of the stairs, and strolled down the hallways to put the hangers in his closet.

He felt good about his accomplishments so far. He walked carefully across a series of throw rugs on the carpet, entered the foyer, and, as he worked to strip off his overshoes, the telephone rang. "I'll get it," he called to the living room.

Because his leather shoes felt stiff from the cold, he moved carefully back across the room to the phone. A young man's voice asked for an appointment that evening for himself and a friend after their last class was over at seven p.m. Looking through the telephone yellow pages, the friends had lit on the *Sleuth Works* advertisement and wanted to consult the firm.

Ken pulled open a drawer and removed a pencil. He jerked the notepad from his jacket. "Your names?" He wrote something with his left hand. "Where do you want to meet?" He listened for a minute.

"Yes, I can come to the library at the University. I know it's south of the Nelson museum. But, if you have time, why don't you come here and meet my colleagues, too? We're only a few blocks away, and the sidewalks are clear as far as I can tell."

After a pause, he said, "Yes, we're free for the next hour or so." After settling the receiver back into the cradle, he revealed the topic of the call to his partners. "Another case, my dear colleagues! Voice sounded colored. Some college kids want us to trace brothers who were in the Second World War. Now this one calls upon my particular military expertise for a change!"

"Colored college students here in Kansas City?" Belinda asked, surprised.

"Oh, honey, the university admitted its first colored student back in 1947. And, now that the Brown vs. Board of

Education of Topeka case has been decided, public schools are no longer segregated. What is purely wonderful is that the University of Kansas City was first named the *Lincoln and Lee* for Abraham and Robert E. Honoring both sides of the Civil War, see?" Holly almost gushed the information.

"Mom, I'll never catch up with your knowledge of history. But I'm not sure the Brown vs. Board act pertains to private universities."

"Doesn't matter, ours here is a community leader with its several majors. And you're correct about knowing history: you'd probably not be as aware as I am. I've lived through a lot of years of it, for one reason."

Ken said, "Nice to know that college's history. The kids will be over between classes." Finally, he found a chair in the living room to sink into, thankful that his chores were finished. "Have you finished your work already?" he asked.

Both nodded, and Belinda waved at her mother to start the reports.

"I started with the newspapers at the library from 1907, looking at the society pages. I took a Polaroid snapshot of the Volks' debs. They are both pictured there from spring, '08, debutante ball. Jacqueline is Natalie Kilmer's mom, and Marlena is Merrilee Anderson's mom." She handed over a snapshot.

Ken and Belinda both studied the grey and white grainy reproduction of the newspaper photograph and passed it back to her. The photo showed that the debs had proud smiles and rich looking evening gowns, sporting jewels in their hair and on their arms.

Ken said, "Let me interject something here, Bel. I told your mom that the first interview I had today was with a rich, old couple. There I elicited the rumor that one of your debs there may have had a child before marriage––the lady said the girl was a 'real scamp' and disappeared for some months in the year before the 1908 coming-out ball."

"I don't know where we'd be able to trace that." Belinda shook her head, her curls tied into a ribbon on either side of her neck and bouncing around.

"Well, as Ken suggested, I found that there was a Catholic orphanage here before the first of the century that the archivist said didn't close until 1947," Mother Holly said. "Ken's written reports are best supplemented by hearing him describe his meetings. His emphasis on certain words and his mimicry abilities add a great deal of information. Nuances absent from print."

"I've notice that, too, Mother. Hmmm. We could also try Vital Statistics in Jeff City for birth notices. Or a church that's mentioned in the weddings or funerals or obituaries. Babies are usually baptized or christened."

"Let me finish up," said Holly. "I looked for obit notices and found this short one: Henrik Volks in 1903 at age 58. He left a son, grandson, and granddaughter, but no names were given."

"I found him, too," Belinda said, "in the old courthouse for the west part of Jackson County. The record was hard to read because the records back then were hand-written, not in print. I copied it down. I didn't find anything relevant otherwise, but I did eliminate quite a number of records. And, lastly, I found some marriage certificates for men named Volks, but not with given name of Henrik. Tomorrow I'll go to the cemetery where the Jacqueline lady was killed near the Volks couples' tombstones. Maybe Henrik is one of the two buried there. If no other records are kept there, at least the tombstones should have the couples' names, birth and death years. Then, although it's quite a distance away, I can also drive over to the courthouse in Independence that serves the east side of Jackson County."

"Fine job, daughter. Any data that that I found were in newspapers. I'll call around tomorrow to see if I can locate the orphanage records stashed somewhere to check that faint rumor that you heard." Mother Holly saluted Ken and Belinda.

Ken said, "Another sense I caught today is that Richard Kilmer may indeed have been the victim of a gang war. The first gentleman wondered why I wanted to know about him, but I assured him I was interested only in Natalie's relatives, if any existed. I was a little threatened at the second interview but didn't let the fellow know that I am raw-ther skilled at protecting myself against physical attacks, unless it's a beautiful blonde throwing herself at me," he said with a knowing smile on his lips. "One named Belinda. Say, following up on your idea, why don't we take a few days and drive over to Jefferson City, tour the capital building, and look for other records. I figure it'll take us most of the day to drive over. Let's say we're gone for four days, to give ourselves two days there. Little vacation."

Belinda grinned. "That would save me from having to drive all the way over to the courthouse in Independence."

Both women nodded. Ken chose not to add that he figured getting out of Dodge would be prudent right now. He simply knew too little about the undercurrents here but could sense some tugs and eddies.

Belinda said, "I have been working on diagramming the

family for our chronology. Look." She held up a paper with room for the two capitalized Volks names at the top, with Henrik's name penciled in at the top. She now looked at the notes made by her mother. "Evidently, we don't know which girl was married to which fellow?" Belinda asked. "And Henrik may actually be the younger brother, but I wrote the name in pencil so that I could easily correct it. Or I can erase it if he's not one we want."

"Don't know. Didn't say in the obit I found––just the scant information that I told you the obit had." Holly then handed over her notes to be typed. "Okay, Ken. Enough work for today. I have a mystery for you concerning a historically famous man's name. It is a duplicate of a British sport."

"Cricket?" Ken guessed.

"No."

"Mr. Rugby?" Belinda joined in.

"Nope."

"Beer and skittles, I bet!" Ken threw up his hands in victory.

"No, sorry. Never heard of anyone named skittles."

"What was Lord Mountbatten doing when he was murdered? Would it be called sailing, boating, fishing, yachting?" Belinda muttered her question.

"No, no, and no. Not even close."

"Fox hunting?"

"Now you're getting closer." Mother Holly teased Ken with the comment.

He fell silent and then grinned, "Polo! You're talking about Polo, as in 'Marco.'" Ken liked Mother Holly's whimsical puzzles and especially when he solved the riddle.

Himself, he knew, had no inclination toward the invention of enigmatic matters.

"Am I supposed to make a label for Marco Polo?" Belinda asked. "I think he preceded our travelers by maybe a few centuries, Mother."

"No need to get het up. You-all were getting too serious. Life is really a comedy, as well as an on-going puzzle; you both need to realize those perspectives in order to survive bad times. Also, Polo and his dad and uncle brought a lot of jewelry home with them from the Far East. Our jewelry emigrated from east of here across the broad Atlantic. That's the leap of logic I made."

"Come back to the facts and quit digressing, Mom. I'm getting hungry and want to finish up the notes. We can find out in the 1900 census the solution to our puzzle of who's married to whom, somehow finding maybe from whence cometh the jewelry. And, what the reason is that Merrilee can't donate them, and Natalie could. And, I'll get to that census next," said Belinda. "After I finish going over another dozen years of records at the cemetery and courthouse. If my eyes survive the spidery writing."

Ken interjected, "I'll make hotel reservations for Monday night, and we'll spend Tuesday and also Wednesday, if we need another day, on the Jeff City records. That should speed us up better than trying haphazard searches here in Jackson County. On the other hand, we do need to know what we can locate here first to finish off our meandering through the labyrinth of local record storage."

"On another note, I had a letter from Chuck's wife, Deedee, this morning," Mother Holly said. "She is bringing a German feast for Friday night. I'll let Harriet and Lillian off about five o'clock that night for the weekend. Ken, see if you can locate some German beer, please."

Belinda kept talking as she jotted notes. "I'll leave blanks for names and fill in here lower down the more recent names that we know. The blanks also are for the mothers of the Schmidt and Harver females (using their married names) who were born about 1891, married about 1908 or soon after, and who were mommies to Natalie Schmidt Kilmer and Merrilee Harver Anderson. Born about 1926. Got that?" She chuckled a their bemused expressions.

"Make a chart for those names because it's a bunch of potluck stew otherwise. Ken, when you note the hours you have worked, please do not count your lunch hour. Eating lunch may have been part of your duty in the Air Force, but we do not charge clients for the time."

"Yes, all right, Mother Holly, I'll scratch out my time sheet and resubmit it."

She said, "I'm glad that it's almost time for tea with the children. You can look into the tea leaves to prognosticate the outcome of our investigation while I use a break."

Ken rose and said, "I'll be back shortly. I'm going to get my slippers."

When he entered their bedroom, he took his shoes off and removed the slippers from his closet. He then slipped the two brooches into his hunting jacket's pockets. He suddenly remembered that his high school letter jacket had not been on the back seat when he made the final trip downstairs for the rest of the cleaning. He was almost positive that it had been in its plastic sheet along with the other items. Hands on his hips, he stared at the clothes in his closet. He'd have to ask the washerwoman next week if she had left it off at the cleaners the last time that she took things there.

Taking off his suit coat and tie, he put on a smoking jacket, although he didn't smoke, and stopped by the nursery to read to J. B. The boy had a number of toy planes to swish around and swing on strings. Two larger airplane replicas hung from the ceiling. Ken set those swaying with a brush of his hand before his son caught him around the leg.

"Hickory dickory dock, what runs up the clock?" Ken said.

J. B. squealed, said, "Mouse mice."

"And J.B. runs up my leg," Ken said as he picked up the child. "And who ran around the mulberry bush?'

"Weasel went."

"You win," answered his father, picking up the nursery rhyme book, too, and nodding to the nanny reading in a corner. Lillian was middling tall with strong arms and shoulders as though she'd grown up pulling a plow through a stony field. Her age was hard to guess; probably she was in her forties because her hair was an unusual taupe color, brown and grey.

"We'll have a bit of tea to whet your whistle in a few minutes while your nanny goes for her supper." Getting the hint, Lillian picked up Alberta and left the room to change her into a dinner smock and hand her over.

The boy tried to say, "Whet your whistle," but it was a teeny bit garbled, to Ken's delight.

His dad started, "Patty-cake, patty-cake, bakers man," and the boy put up his hands to match his dad's movements. Then the boy voided into his pants. Ken hadn't been revolted by the smell of manure on the farm when he was growing up. He hadn't been nauseated by bloody bodies pulled from a jeep wreck while working as an AP. But this accident in J. B.'s pants caused him to choke back bile. "Lillian," he called frantically. The nanny came flying up the stairs.

"I left Alberta with Harriet. I'll clean up the big boy. Harriet is also setting out your tea things by the dining room table. She already put the high chair there." Lillian took the boy to the bathroom. Ken picked up two toy logs and put them back in the Lincoln Logs box.

CHAPTER SEVEN

For the first time up here in the nursery room, he heard Belinda jingle the bell from the front office. He took the stairs, turned to the left at the landing, dismounted the final five stairs, and entered the dining room, then walked swiftly through the living room sliding doors to the office.

Two young, short, dark-skinned people stood there. "We called you about tracing our brothers, sir. I'm John Johnson; she's Nettie Ruggers."

"Pleased to meet you. I'm Mr. Massey. This is my wife, Mrs. Massey, and mother-in-law, Mrs. Jones. We're the *Sleuths*. Please sit down." Ken smiled and reached out to shake hands with the young man and young lady. They sat in the deep cushioned chairs by the round table.

"I'm Nettie." Ken nodded. He'd already been introduced, but she was obviously nervous. "We're students at the University of Kansas City. One day we were talking and discovered that each of us had an older brother who served in the Second World War. Neither of us has ever heard from them since then. We'd like them traced."

"Yes, Nettie. We can do that. I was in the Air Force for eight years and know where records are kept. Why do you think that you have never heard from them?"

Belinda said, "Why do you think you haven't heard?" at the same time.

The diminutive girl smoothed down her full skirt, wrapped her arms around her knees, leaned forward, and answered, her black eyes drooping, "Well, I was in the second grade, and John was in the fifth grade in 1945 when it was over."

The boy said, "I'm John, as I said. Our folks died while we were each in high school. We went to different schools until we met at the university this year."

Mother Holly said, "The fact that you were so young and that your folks passed over would explain why the brothers probably don't how to find you yourselves!"

Ken smiled at each of them. "I'll have some forms drawn up for you to sign later this week. But, now, my wife will take down anything you can remember about his service, John, spelling of his names and units. Any and everything you can remember. Mrs. Jones will take notes from you, Nettie."

The two young people each spent some thoughtful minutes. They often interrupted each other across the room at first so that things became confused. Mother Holly took over making notes for Nettie in the foyer, and Belinda ushered John over to the desk. Ken walked between the rooms and occasionally inserted a question clarifying a detail now and then that one of them had revealed about their memories from the war years.

The maid brought in tea and cocoa on the cart from the dining room, surprising the young people who each shyly took a cup of cocoa and a cookie. The whole group gathered around the cart in the main office. The students each also accepted a second cookie and, later, a bag of cookies to take with them.

"College kids are always hungry," Mother Holly noted as they went down the steps leading from the foyer after Ken escorted them to the door. He had given them each a card with revised fees that he drew up especially for them. Reduced fees. "We'll have them over for supper when you find the records, Ken."

"I need to have Walter Raleigh devise a release form for me to search military records for them," Ken said. "The students are old enough to give me their information and have it be official. I know what agencies to check, and I'm quite sure I'll have to present legal releases."

"I wouldn't have thought of that. We don't need permission to see the documents we've already been tracing," Mother Holly said.

Belinda said, "I'm glad we don't. What a nuisance that would be. I'll go see if our kids still need their afternoon tea with us. We may have to feed them supper, instead." She found out the kids were already fed. And, thus, the adults ate a small supper. Without the children to entertain them and make a mess to be cleaned up.

On that Wednesday, December 7, the evening newspapers remembered Pearl Harbor from 14 years before just as Ken had thought of it earlier that day, the bombing that wiped out isolationist sentiments in the United States. The bombing that brought us into war across both of the oceans that lined our coasts. The bombing that united Americans.

Ken thought again of *Guernica* and also of a photograph by Margaret Bourke-White, the first female war correspondent. During a nighttime clash of artillery after Hitler broke his pact with Stalin, she photographed a memorable, terrifying picture of shells exploding brightly over the Kremlin. The Nazis certainly attacked as many countries as the Japanese did, although the Japanese invasions started decades earlier.

Ken was thoughtful after he had eaten, read the paper, and hugged Belinda fiercely on the way out to find some German beer. He had looked under *Alcohol* as well as *Bars and Taverns* in the phone book, mainly to check out Holly's padlock combination, but he also looked under *Liquor Stores* for an actual source of German beer. And found one: returned home to sample it, looking around the cantilevered porch as he paced.

Back in the middle of the Great Depression, Jeremiah and Holly Jones and their family had started a fruit farm that they ran successfully for twenty years, staying away from bank loans and possible default. With some help from tenant farmers, everybody had adequate food and shelter throughout the drought years that followed.

Ken wondered if his deceased father-in-law would have known of any Jackson County lore because the farm had been in the outlying area that is now favored by the aggressive real estate developers. Subdivisions seemed to be growing everywhere around the edges of Kansas City. He had been amused by Mother Holly's depiction of her negotiations with a conglomerate.

Just before he passed away, Jeremiah (and Holly, the owner of the farm) had held out against the first offers for the farm. They had already retired to Granstadt where Belinda had gone to high school, living in the boarding house as she mentioned earlier.

A conglomerate wanted to build a lot of houses between Granstadt and Kansas City in a subdivision to be named The Meadows. The Jones couple eventually walked away with a bundle of cash for most of the land. Holly, widowed soon after, quit her job at the Granstadt High School.

Mrs. Holly Osbourne Jones, sole owner of the property, had inherited it. She subsequently called up the local representative of the conglomerate that had bought the farm property, a Mr. Jerry Wrenslow, and offered to swap the remaining farmhouse and leftover acreage for an apartment building in this lovely central Kansas City area. She hadn't realized that he ran the conglomerate's office from this particular building until the negotiations began, and they met in the office/living room to wrangle. She outlasted every maneuver he could propose.

The conglomeration was pleased with the final deal, and the Wrenslows moved out of this apartment several months ago. Moreover, she was also pleased and invited her daughter's family to move in to this area--convenient to stores, hospitals, and libraries. Her next idea was to build an investigative agency. Holly had grown up on Dashiell Hammett books.

Maybe Mother Holly also would know names of the shady people who could have threatened the Kilmers if the same business people had purchased her farm. The next morning, back inside the office, he pushed the bell attached to her rooms. It rang back immediately, meaning she would be there shortly. He stood up and stretched his arms high into the air, the ceiling still four feet above him and covered with a stippled light blue celestial design. The crick in his nape cracked, releasing a jammed muscle-joint-bone; he wasn't sure which one.

Holly strolled in, dressed in a dark plum-colored dress that beautifully set off her graying hair.

"I'd like to know how you and Jeremiah conducted the sales transactions for your farm. I mean I'm interested in names of the people you worked with when selling it, Mother Holly. I'm not talking about the money."

"Would it help with our present investigation?"

He nodded. "Maybe."

"First, you should know that men usually own the farm property, have their names alone on the deed. In this case, my father had left my brother and me each one farm. I never put Jeremiah's name on mine. Therefore, I had to be present at all the meetings with The Meadows Corporation. Rather, I insisted that I be present. I, to tell the truth, was scared of what they might do to my husband if I were not present when we met up here at their dingy office."

"You mean that ladies were not often threatened."

"Yes. But men are, for sure. There had been some bloody pictures in the papers now and again in all the Missouri newspapers. We'd go in; meet with Tom, Dick, and Harry; look at them stoically; and, leave with a final––and we always increased it––demand because they hadn't met our earlier offer." She waved her hand elegantly.

"I didn't know that. That was gutsy. I admire your bravery." Ken saluted her.

"Or foolish effrontery on our part."

"Any names that would have gone up against this Mr. Kilmer?" Ken leaned forward.

"Why on earth should there have been? None of the articles said he was involved in real estate."

"I am trying to making sure that we are not getting into something dank and rank in our tracing the ownership of the jewelry."

"No. I don't think it was the same outfit as Kilmer's local connections seem to have been. Anyway, after some weeks, the head guy from out-of-town came in and said to get the negotiations over with. We sold the fields and kept the house and small acreage."

"Good maneuvering."

"Yes. We were so tickled at our windfall selling that farm by Granstadt that we went to St. Louis for the weekend, took the kids for the last weekend in August the next month. I'm glad we did. Jeremiah had that sudden stroke in January and died quickly. Sooo, then, I met face to face with the men again, and we swapped my house and two remaining acres for this building and its tenants. And, here we are."

Mother Holly fell silent, apparently lost in memory. Took out an embroidered handkerchief from its place in her sleeve and wiped her eyes. They were both silent a minute as she composed her features back into their usual commanding look. Her lithe figure straightened as she brushed at her grey curls and wrinkled her plucked eyebrows.

She opened a drawer of the desk and removed Belinda's steno pad. "The men that the Kilmer man in this investigation associated with are likely to not be nice men, Ken, from what I surmised hearing Walt. I've read the newspapers over the years about nefarious goings-on. I think you'd be better off interviewing a police officer about the events and evidence regarding the Kilmer accident, if needed. I underscore the word '<u>if</u>.' I'll write out the names of our developers, but as I said, I really believe they're from out of town, not associated locally with any syndicates. I'll also put down names of gangsters I've read about. Or heard rumors about. One front page story was called the *"Union Station Massacre"*. It concerned some gang being mowed down."

He sat back and began aligning his tasks with Belinda's and Mother Holly's. Belinda needed the car to drive clear over to the cemetery on one side of town but was skipping the other Jackson County Courthouse this afternoon. Mother Holly would be taking the streetcar to the newspaper office to delve into the archives. He himself would tie up the telephone. First up was that call to Walt for drawing up permission forms.

While Mother Holly had been at the library yesterday, she had checked out a book about the strife in various countries in the mid-1800s. She had told him that she'd concentrate on German speaking countries. But, she advised, Walter Raleigh needed to give them the first estimate of the jewelry's value from the appraisal that had been mentioned in the 1946 article. And, strangely, explain why he had not said more about the possible provenance of the jewelry. Had the daughters of the jewelers brought items that their father had designed to the United States or had they themselves been heiresses from older relatives? The art museum should have given Raleigh those facts.

He might have to trudge over to the attorney's office to collect a copy of the information and talk privately. Having the list of jewelry and estimated values should have occurred to him earlier. And, were the Sleuths actually supposed to determine provenance--or merely ownership?

To ensure peace for his whole family, he'd better remember to tell ole Walt Raleigh about the veiled threats from the pallbearer named Lincoln and from Mr. Shannon. That and the need for a release form for the college kids to have notarized.

Belinda greeted him with a kiss and hung up her coat. She said, "I bet Mother's gone to the library to check old telephone books. I'll grab a peanut butter sandwich and glass of milk before I drive over to the cemetery. The snow is letting up but is supposed to return harder this evening. That is, according to the weatherman. We need to take Harriet to the A and P tonight or tomorrow. She has a long list of staples that need replenishing."

"The streets aren't too bad yet. I'll feel better if you return before dark so that I can do that grocery run tonight. We still aren't too familiar with some parts of Kansas City, and I'm not sure that the area you'll be driving through is safe along that north side."

"I have a map that shows a wonderful system of streets and major highways. I promise I won't drive into the river by mistake." Belinda hugged Ken again.

Ken said, "History note: did you know that Kansas City was first called 'Kawsmouth' because settlers began camping at the mouth of the Kaw River that runs into the Missouri River."

"You must be joking."

"Nope. Look it up. Don't navigate into that one, dear one."

"I won't, dear two. I've wondered why sometimes the

tribe is called Kaw Indians and sometimes Kanza Indians. Do you know why, Ken?"

"Don't know, maybe what other tribes called them. The Assiniboine Sioux in Montana supposedly translate their name as 'one who cooks in a pot' but other tribes translate the name as 'snake in the grass' because of their warriors."

Belinda had not been paying attention and didn't chuckle as he thought she would. She continued her own train of thought. "But then, I answer both to 'American' and to 'Yankee.' So more than one designation is acceptable. Maybe the word is 'assignation.'"

"Sometimes to 'Missourian.' Sometimes to 'show me.' Sometimes yes, sometimes no. Sometimes to 'honey.'" Ken couldn't help grinning. Sometimes Belinda sounded absent-minded. But still adorable **and** intelligent.

Belinda kept an absent-minded tone in her voice as she mused, "Mom's the history buff. She's been reading in the living room about Marco Polo's travels to the East in the 1200s. I'll remember to tell her that Meg Raleigh teaches history; they can explore ancient times together. Meg was teaching in Japan in the Far East, but I doubt that they have polo there, and I don't know if Marco was there, either. Oh, well. You just thought I wasn't paying attention to you. Here's the phone so you can have some success ferreting out information, too, two dear."

"You simply must drive me to work, mustn't you? Push me into slavery." Ken grinned and held up his arms in surrender.

"I read last month in **Time** about a lady who was so mad at her husband that she ran their car straight through the front window of a bar, leaped out, and hit him with a two-by-four. I do swear that I won't do that, my darling."

"And I read that a guy in Canada was fined because he was driving recklessly. He said he ordinarily steered by celestial navigation but mistook a TV tower for the evening star and ran into a ditch. Bet he'd also been in a bar. So, don't be gone so long that you might have to drive by starlight, please."

She held up her hand, "I promise as well as swear." Taking a swallow of milk, she toyed with the car keys as though uncertain about leaving just yet. "Go ahead. Start calling the whole list from the church. Maybe you'll feel less threatened than when you met up with those two pallbearers. Don't pretend," she scolded him, "I saw your distracted manner when you returned last night. I'd like to learn how you handle such calls seeking information from strangers."

"Look 'em sternly in the eye, keep shoulders straight, hold forehead up, exhibit no frown. Perfectly intimidating!" He demonstrated each in a dramatic manner, grinned, and whirled her around before plunking a kiss on her forehead.

CHAPTER EIGHT

Ken selected the starred names with phone numbers on the church list and began calling. He first tried one of the double starred names to eliminate those three women he'd been told about but elicited nothing useful about Natalie Kilmer. The next calls were answered by ladies who knew nary a relative of Natalie Kilmer's, just as he expected.

He then found one elementary school friend who thought some relatives lived in the Ozarks somewhere. When he hung up and mentioned the possibility to Belinda, she said, once again, that they already had information on Merrilee's mother (MMM: Merrilee's Mother Marlena) and siblings down south.

She brought him a glass of milk and a peanut butter sandwich on a tray, making his own lunch a duplicate of hers. He asked for a second sandwich, and she obliged.

"I wonder how many times we're going to be given Merrilee's name and told about her mother's. We've known that stuff since Day Two," she complained.

"Please just call her mother yourself; we should have taken care of that first." He slapped the desk and shook his head. "But get out the map first, then we'll see if we can stop by where her mom lives. Raumville. We could drop down by there on the way back from Jeff City," he said. "Find out old man Harver's name, I mean the given name of the widow's husband. You saw how important, legally, it was to know Slim Anderson's given name, even when the phone number is unlisted.

"Slim's name isn't listed so that they won't be bothered by people with a news flash about missing jewels, Ken," Belinda said and giggled. He grinned back, and she asked the long distance operator for the Harver number.

"Sh. It's ringing. Mrs. Harver? I'm Belinda Jones Massey working on tracing relatives of some people named 'Volks' . . . I'm glad Merrilee already told you, Marlena. First, please tell me if these are the current whereabouts of your children. Merrilee gave me the names earlier." She began reading from the list the names of a daughter and three boys but stopped. "Oh? You were given a jeweled pin by Natalie Kilmer after her mother died in a cemetery?" She paused for some time. "Uh huh." She mouthed, "Marlena Harver's looking for her address book."

"Oh, yes. Yes. Correct. And, your husband's name? Given name. I see. Oh, dear me, yes, I'd love to have the names of your ancestors. I never thought to ask." She gave Ken a triumphant look.

Belinda spoke the names as she wrote them down. "'Christian and Frieda' and 'Henrik and Helga.' Yes, I spelled them correctly. You mean that the men and the twin girls Frieda and Helga Jufellear were born in some country that spoke German because of the girls' last name (meaning Jeweler). Did you say that they were married in St. Louis to the Volks men who were from Kansas City? Got it, okay. I appreciate the information, Mrs. Harver."

Ken handed her a note that read, *Ask for the name*

of a hotel in Raumville, and I'll cancel Wednesday night's reservation in Jeff City.

She had found out Marlena Harver's maiden name, hubby Harver's given name (Sam), and added proof that Merrilee's information that she already had was correct. In addition, Belinda was provided gold strike of ancestral names, a Raumville hotel name, number, address, etc., etc. The 'etc.,' Ken observed, included their own business post office box and phone number that Belinda gave to Marlena in return.

"There now. What a success I have finally had at digging up these data," she crowed. "See how well I learned to elicit information simply from listening to you for a few minutes doing so? Well, hear this, Dearie: she said nothing about any jewelry. Now we have to know why Merrilee's so interested in it. And, I wonder why MMM has never had them. She said she and Natalie's mother used to dress up with jewels and old dresses at her aunt's house."

"I hadn't thought of that ownership possibility. Curious."

Belinda looked at the clock chiming its head off on the wall. "I'll be off now for my further investigations. I'll make a formal chart of the names when I return. I don't want to drive after dark."

"I don't want you to, either. Congrats. I admit you had more luck with one phone call tracing deceased people's names than I did with a lot that numbed my ear. Fine work, Belinda."

She didn't seem to hear him as she took the car keys from the desk before she pulled on her mittens. "I now have the old Volks ones' names and will just have to look at their monuments to get their life spans." Her mind was already turning to the task of searching at the cemetery and courthouse in Independence.

"Belinda." Ken kept patting the desk hard and harder to capture her attention after she'd replaced the receiver.

"Yes."

"If we left Jefferson City early enough, we could stop for lunch at my folks' place."

"I enjoyed your parents at our wedding. Wonderful people. I'd love to see them again, and see Devil's Elbow where you grew up, my little imp." She whirled around in a jog, flapping her mittens over her ears as though she were an elf, her green wool snow pants snuggling her knees as she hopped forward and up.

"Oh, our home is a ways out of town beyond Devil's Elbow, but we can drive by DE slowly. Not that there's much to see. It was named by lumbermen who hated the log jam in the river bend below."

"I was hoping for a more lurid story behind the name. Oh, well. I'll mark up my map when I return, and Mom will calculate the mileage. We don't wanna scam Walt and Meg too badly with the mileage we turn in."

"You do that. Be back soon. Before dark. It starts getting dark in four hours."

"I already told you that I promise to do so. I'm careful."

Silence fell after she left. What was odd was that the next three calls he made to the unstarred list were all answered by ladies, and the information to his inquiry became a ritual answer. "Don't know them. Goodbye."

He guessed that one of the first ladies he called had anticipated the calls he would make in his research and thwarted him by warning other wives of his request for information. Word certainly gets around fast.

He telephoned Walter Raleigh, Esquire, and asked for the information about the appraisal of the jewels. Walt questioned him closely about his need for the data.

Finally, Walt said, "The value actually was pretty general knowledge after Mrs. Schmidt told her circle of friends ten years ago, although the appraisal data were not revealed in print or newscasts, just general hints. I'm free at three this afternoon if you would drop in. I'd like to know how you're progressing."

Mother Holly returned from the library but said nothing, just nodded and went to her room. She returned with two books in her hands and remained in the living room.

Three o'clock was only twenty minutes away. Ken typed some notes about the tasks Mother Holly had assigned to each of his team, placing the notes inside an envelope and that inside his jacket pocket. Snow was coming down thick and wet outside and could penetrate cloth, even a layer or two, and he needed the list to look professional.

"I'm free of the phone, Mother. Walt has some information we need, and I'll run over to his office. Belinda won't be back much before dark, I think." He turned to slide the door shut behind him after his announcement but stopped to hear her answer.

"Good. I was just contemplating calling around to see where the records of baptisms and christenings are held. We have been getting enough dates, or approximate ones, to pin things down a bit. Remember to lock the front door. I hope the snow doesn't create difficulties for Belinda. She's been driving for years but some of these town people do idiotic things in traffic."

Ken arrived in the lawyer's office already prepared to be instructed. His usual demeanor while interviewing was to look interested while a subject was gesticulating, with big eyes, tight mouth; he was seldom shocked if the subject had a wrinkling nose or bilious reaction; nor was he disgusted, or fearful if the person being interviewed flinched or seemed otherwise threatened or was pale. Many times several emotions were working on the subject's face and eyes and body. His Air Force colleagues had depended upon him for his nonjudgmental approach to other people.

After sitting down with his coat off and refusing a cigar, Ken mentioned the jewelry appraisal.

Walter Raleigh said, "Meg wanted me to call a friend of hers in southwest Missouri who had had some things appraised. He'd brought them back from Japan with him, and they turned out to be rare coins. She thought we should retrieve the jewelry from the museum and have it looked at again before we advised the Volks' descendants. However, I'm not willing to do that unless some difficulty arises. The museum should pay for the appraisal itself."

Ken said, "I agree, but I understood all we were hired to do was find ownership. So, why do you say the 'Volks'" descendants?"

"You know that you must find out what person has title to them to clear the title for the museum. That is all. Here is a list of the pieces of jewelry. List dates back to 1946 when they were appraised. What I'm going to tell you next is not for publication. I had hoped you would find the ownership without having to attend to any other details. But here we are." He eyed Ken.

Ken nodded. "We know how to be discrete and or mum."

"In the original donation to the museum, ownership was claimed by the donor lady, Jacqueline Schmidt. The actual history is rather convoluted that, to start with, the jewels were brought over by the younger brother, Henrik Volks, not either of the twins who became the wives. He had apprenticed himself to the twins' father, who was a jeweler. Henrik earned some of the jewels, and he evidently collected historic ones. The twin wife of the elder brother was also given the jewels to wear on appropriate occasions. It's the younger Volk brother's lineage that is at the heart of the matter. I'm not sure whether Merrilee Anderson is unaware or, maybe, concealing that fact. We have to tread lightly. Having the gems go to the museum is the best, non-litigious solution."

Ken sat contemplating the information, his eyes distant, and then reached for the list, scanned it, and put it down. "I'm still absorbing your revelation of the history, Walt. To change the subject a teeny bit, I'm puzzled about some of the descriptions on that list. I've never heard of bloodstone or carnelian. Or moonstone or zircon. Or feathers as jewelry."

"I was also puzzled. I had to look up 'faience' and 'lapis lazuli.' The man who did the appraisal died, and no one else locally situated appraises such old jewelry. Items have to be sent to the Manhattan, New York, museum curators. Or an auction house that engages knowledgeable consultants, mostly from Europe. Or, wait for one to drop into town."

"I'd like this list for our file. I can hardly wait until Belinda and Mother Holly see that the jewelry consists of a girdle, a pectoral––that probably looks like a bib of beads––a collar, a feather cap, and so on. I really want to see how that girdle was worn. Are these things currently on display?"

"No. I'll have a copy made of the list. Marnie, please come in."

"Yes, sir?" The door came open immediately. Ken suspected that she had been listening.

"Please type a copy of this list for Mr. Massey."

"Glad to be of help to both of you," she said, simpering a bit.

As she was walking out the door, Ken said, "I want to tell you that the pallbearers for Mr. Kilmer that I interviewed threatened me overtly for bringing up the funeral."

Her walk slowed perceptibly.

"Oh, I bet that was the automobile dealer where Kilmer worked and had purchased his new convertible for a discount. The dealer may not have wanted bad publicity about his cars. Name was Lincoln, I think, selling Lincoln cars. His business is actually owned by Mr. Shannon." Walt downplayed Ken's remark as he looked askance at Marnie near the door to the outer office.

Ken said quietly, "That's strange. Now I see how that could be. But, no, Walt, the threat to drop it was more concerning the publicity about Richie Kilmer's dying than the wreck itself. And I received suggestions at both Shannon's and Lincoln's interviews. The Kilmers' other pallbearers were members of the church as were the attendees at the church funeral."

Walt put his fingers over his lips and shook his head, shifting his eyes toward the door where Marie had just left.

"I realize that you're not familiar with the background or underground here. Both were probably concerned about the death as well as the wreck, because they could be bad publicity for the dealership." Walt sounded insistent and shook his head and frowned toward the door. "I'll make a note of your comment. Maybe I ought to have the police look up the accident report. I haven't heard that there has been anything in the news about signing off on the accident report. My former colleague, Clifford King, has some contacts in the police. I'll ask him to inquire into the reports on the accident."

"Yes, please do so."

"On a lighter note, could you meet me at my club in the morning? I'd put your name in for membership if you liked it," Walt said.

Ken looked at him in surprise. "Well, yes, I could meet you. But if it's a gentleman's club, my wife and mother-in-law are my partners, remember. It might not be prudent for me to join. We'd be better off with a country club membership where we could all play golf or something like that."

"We'll see about being prudent. Ten o'clock down on Twelfth and Broadway. Kansas City Club on the door. I'll leave your name with the valet. I also can put your name into membership at my country club. I used to bat baseballs, but now I hit golf balls. I was a better batter than I am a hitter." He smiled.

"I would enjoy golf, although you'll out-par me. I appreciate your suggesting that membership, and I'll look forward to seeing you tomorrow."

Walt kept smiling. "The Club is a place you need to

know about, where all the movers and shakers drop by." He started to stand, signaling the end of the meeting.

"I can understand that." Ken sat back in his chair and crossed his legs, not leaving just yet. "Walt, I'd like to ask you to draw up some legal forms for me. Frequently I need to have permission to examine some records. Right now I need legal permission slips for a college boy and girl with their signatures that could be notarized by you or any notary public. I need to access veterans' records for them. They're legal age," Ken added, "And you can deduct the charge for drawing up that form from our fees on the statement I handed you."

"I'll do that this afternoon. Do you want all three members of your firm to sign them or each to do so legally but separately."

"Separately."

"That'll be an easy one. I'll bring the copies tomorrow. You can have more printed."

"Thank you." Ken stood, leaving the office with a wave at the King girl, and walked casually back home, thinking over his duties. He was surprised to see a University of Missouri stuffed tiger in a drugstore window. Just the thing for J. B. As soon as he walked up into the nursery, J. B. held out his arms but didn't seem to know what to do to open a sack. Ken showed him, made the tiger growl, and then bury itself into J. B.'s stomach. After an hour of playing with his son, he returned downstairs to find Belinda curled up on one sofa.

"You're back already? Astonishing. Did you fly over hill over dale or into the wide blue yonder?"

"No, my Air Force friend. The cemetery is on a steep

hill, too icy and snow-covered to climb. I went into the sexton's shack to ask if he had information on the Volks folks. He said that he'd been helping the po-leese solve a murder ten years ago. He'd had several snapshots made of himself next to the two gravestones and sold them to his friends for a quarter. I dug out 50 cents, and here are our first four names!"

She gestured at the coffee table. Mother Holly looked up and smiled at her. "Awesome, fast accurate clues to move us along."

CHRISTIAN VOLKS (1843-1893) by FRIEDA
JUFELLEAR VOLKS (1846-1897)

HENRIK MANN VOLKS(1845-1903) by
HELGA JUFELLEAR VOLKS(1846-1898)

"Ignore the grinning sexton at the edge of the tombstones."

Ken bowed and threw her a kiss. "My sleuth of sleuths."

"The highway was clean, and I moved right along, arriving by 2:30 and turning right around after talking with him."

Ken forgot about the list of the odd jewelry that Walt had given him. It was in his overcoat pocket. He was busy relating the story of J. B. and the tiger, how the boy had it attack him, and he fell to the floor, J. B. cheering.

"Your brother, Barney, is going to go to the University next semester, Belinda; ergo, we'll have a real Mizzou tiger in the family." Mother Holly opened her book. "I wonder what you've found out, Ken?"

"I interviewed a couple by the name of Shannon and

a man by the name of Lincoln. Both of the men were pallbearers for Richie Kilmer."

Mother Holly interrupted his report as she looked up to her left. "The Shannon name seems familiar. Something to do with the negotiations for this apartment building. Well, it'll come to me." She started reading.

Belinda went to the office desk to type up the information on the Volks. Ken picked up the evening newspaper and settled into the sofa cushions, a cup of coffee near at hand.

PART TWO

THREAT

CHAPTER NINE

Walter Raleigh began his talk in a strained voice the next morning with Ken. He had his shoulders pressed back into the chair at the men's Kansas City Club, his downtown rendezvous. "A police sergeant told me––in a nasty tone of voice––that the Kilmers should have been laid to rest and left there. He was responding to pressure from my old partner, Clifford King, to reveal the cause of the accident. Next thing, King called me from his office to ask more about what Marnie told him she overheard you and me talking about." Walt said, "I had been afraid she'd overheard your remark when I was trying to downplay your report. That's when I signaled the warning to you. We should tread more warily."

"I don't understand much about what you're telling me, except I sense that you felt threatened," Kendrick Massey replied before taking a sip of his bourbon and water. Even though he had not been trained as a therapist, he could recognize when a man's ego was bruised. "But I'm not sure whether it's your old colleague, Mr. King, or the sergeant that threatened you."

Walt considered who it was, reaching for his tumbler, swishing it around, while he stared at the ceiling fan rotating slowly as if he found it odd for that to be moving in the middle of winter, with eyes finally dropping back down to

Ken's face. His own face was corrugated like an old sheet of tin, with his whiskers serving as the splotches of rust on his jaws. Five o'clock shadow, it was called, even in the morning.

A faint scent of sealer and varnish accounted for the beautiful light-colored oak boards. The thick smudge of pipe and cigar smoke meant the boards were destined to darken again. Chairs were set askew around the room; their backs had wings concealing men's faces but a spiral of smoke or newspaper page indicated a person's presence. It was similar to being ensconced in a wooden cigar box, the way Ken and his dad had sequestered a baby chick once. Without the smoke.

Seated, the two men were approximately the same height. Ken kept his gaze interested while he patiently waited for an answer. Also, he wasn't used to having alcohol before lunch. Needed to take it slowly. Both the drink and the revelation.

"Early in my association with King's office, I started overhearing bits of conversation that puzzled me at first, and then alarmed me. Young men talked with middle-aged men who talked with elderly men. It was always about 'moving up.'"

Ken took a sip and urged him on. "I guess you do not mean a wooden ladder but another type. Promoted up through the ranks, like in the military."

"Yes. Exactly. Moving up in the organization. When a police officer also could be heard in one of these interchanges, I decided that I'd seen too much of war, too many battles, been shot at enough, for a lifetime. As to the recent threat, it's from *both* of them, King and cop, because somehow this

Kilmer matter has ignited fury. No matter how subtle they try to be, I feel it."

"But why, Walt? We're interested only in Natalie, not her husband. I have said that I felt threatened after I interviewed Mr. Shannon and a guy named Lincoln, who were pallbearers for her husband, to see if they knew anything about Natalie."

"Good grief, man, you shouldn't have broached any topic with those guys. See, remember that I told you I wasn't interested in dealing with Criminal Law? And that was why I left King's office and set up my own practice? Unfortunately, I was naïve enough to take Marnie along with me to 'help set up my office efficiently,' as King told me to," Walt said. "I quickly found out that she routinely reported back to him about the cases I was working on. I became discreet about my conversations and the reports I had her type. Instead, I would have my Meg return with me in the evenings to type up notes, discuss procedures. And those men are some that Mr. King had as major clients. Involving criminal law."

"Isn't what Marnie is doing a violation of confidentiality?"

"I would be interested to hear how you would handle both typing volumes of notes and all the while searching out the relevant laws and documentation and data all by yourself," Walt answered sharply. "You gotta have an assistant who knows her way around. That reminds me, here is your master document permitting data searches." He pulled up a leather briefcase and extracted a few sheets of paper. "I made some extra copies." He set the briefcase at his feet.

"I appreciate having these permits to release information

to me, acting as a third party. And, of course, now I see what you mean about needing assistance that you can trust. All right. Marnie tells her dad, and he tells the clients or the police, and something is amiss. Correct?"

"Correct. Our esteemed Mr. Lincoln of Lincoln Motors is your classic criminal type. That old man trained himself to be suspicious of everyone, and you would have hit his antenna with a lightning strike mentioning Kilmer. He never raised himself above the thuggery class. It didn't help that you earlier also engaged an upper rung in his environment in conversation."

"Well, how was I to know if someone was above him? I don't get it. Why isn't Lincoln arrested if everyone knows he or his dealership did cause the wreck? I was merely trying to interview the pallbearers to see if they knew any of Natalie Kilmer's relatives."

Walt took a puff and asked, "The other pallbearer, Mr. Shannon, whose name was mentioned in the newspaper, is the one up the ladder. King did forcefully mention it to me."

"Yes, I told you all that on the same day I saw that roughhouse Mr. Lincoln and later chose a Christmas tree, as if that pertains to anything, I saw him earlier," Ken almost snapped his reply, feeling criticized. "It was Mr. Shannon's dear, old wife that started us on the wild-orphan chase that Meg and Merrilee picked up on and raced on hoping to find a lady they knew was an orphan."

"Not important. On top of enraging Lincoln, you happened to visit the eminent Shannons. Hmmmm. Shannon owns Mr. Lincoln and his dealership. That particular Shannon, Ken, has been the virtual chieftain of all crime in the city since he had lost his baby teeth. He inherited a syndicate that controlled the booze and babe joints during Prohibition and just kept building it."

"But he and his wife, sweet old Mrs. Shannon, were so, uh, so *upper-class*," Ken exclaimed.

"Money can sometimes buy anything, Ken. And he, *he*, is far more likely to be behind the efforts to keep us from finding out anything whatsoever about Richie or, less likely, about Natalie. Mr. Lincoln was merely one of his barefoot boys who had been with him through the upsetting business with his daughter being left at the altar and therefore always was a reminder of the Kilmer treachery."

"One of his what?"

"Haven't you heard about the underlings who want to fill the boss's shoes—and go barefoot?"

"No, I had not. Who left her? I can't get my mind around it. I need another drink. But, Walt, we are not trying to find out about the wreck of the Kilmers! Why won't anyone listen to me?"

Walt swallowed the remainder of his Scotch and signaled a butler by holding up two fingers. "Who jilted whom is not pertinent, as you would say. Now, Clifford King finally filled me in, reluctantly, after I told him that someone took a shot at me when I was talking with a policeman at my front door last week. I had called my cop friend and your old sarge, Phil Tyler, in from a suburban precinct to complain about someone stealing my Christmas decorations from the hedge. I hauled Phil inside when we heard the shot. He circled around the yard from the back entrance to the front. He saw someone hieing off, however, who maybe did the shooting."

"Oh, hell's bells. You never mentioned this. You know

Phil? How about his wife? Are you telling me that we really are under threat? I'm not sure where you're going with this."

"Yep. The cop started after him, but the kid ran down an alley and disappeared over a fence. I told Phil that I was sure it was the Lincolns' son. Here is a lesser bug biting at me: Shannon orders Lincoln who orders his son, *ad infinitum.* Tyler was sweating and cussing and vowing that the kid would pay. He thought the kid had shot at him. I didn't disavow that. King said I was the origin of the problem, because I had hired you."

Ken pondered the events a few minutes, sipping now and then. "He evidently doesn't think that you made a smart move. Why haven't the city police been more involved? It seems to me that if the Kilmer fellow had some connection to the crimes in KC, from all the information I've read about the dark element and the law, he should have been jailed. Plus I mean now that he died, they should be interested in discovering the truth about what happened to him."

Walt explained, "Here's one possibility. Clifford King revealed that Richie Kilmer had jilted Shannon's daughter and also stolen money from Shannon's firm. He has hated him for years but stayed back, nursing the grudge, until no one would suspect that he had been behind retribution, namely--a car wreck. Most importantly, last summer Shannon's only grandson died leaving no heir to carry on his name. That triggered the revenge against Kilmer, and Natalie, the wife, was an incidental casualty."

The butler deposited two more glasses. Ken noticed that Walt's usually cold mien was thawing, warming up to an occasional smile, animated during their talk, his speech becoming confidential instead of being brusque.

Walt took a long, thoughtful time sipping his drink. "You're correct. One kink in the logic is that sometimes the downfall is just what some other major figure wants. Ken, we've had quite a reduction in crimes and felons the past few years. That doesn't mean the problem is deleted. I've mentioned, too, King's linkages to both sides, law and crime. Now someone has taken aim again, stirred things up, even inadvertently as it may be, I bet things will start to move on determining the cause of the Kilmers' wreck. I mean you stirred things up by visiting both men; you are investigating something for me; and, you are an ex-cop from the esteemed Air Force. These innocent seeming links intertwine in those warped minds. This has been misinterpreted as pertaining to the wreck."

Ken asked, "Should I start going around armed?" He let his Kentucky bourbon sit there, and the leavings mellow some more.

"I am," Walt answered calmly, pulling back a jacket that cleverly fit over a sidearm. "I served in the Second World War in the Pacific, and I survived. I'm not going down in my own town. Nor is my family. That's unforgiveable. I don't want two smirking pallbearers carrying my casket, a gesture of triumph over me, as they did Richie Kilmer's."

"Speaking of him, how did Kilmer get off the charge of murder that appeared in the article on the cemetery death of Natalie's mother, his ma-in-law?"

"It isn't really pertinent to your investigation. But, he wasn't responsible. Some dumb kid had startled the lady up near the tombs, and she tripped, hitting her head. The kid was so scared at his trial that everyone believed his description of events. He spent a few months in jail for trespassing on the cemetery grounds."

Ken looked him in the eye, studying his face. "Well, I'm grateful that you finally warned me about the underground sewer people here that I've stirred up. Maybe I'll be able to rat them out. No, no! Belinda and Mother Holly would object except maybe we have no choice. I'm pleased, very pleased, to know that you know how to protect yourself. But what do you mean about our families? Should we arm our girls?"

"Hadn't thought about it. My Meg does know how to shoot."

"So do Mother Holly and Belinda. I don't think the maids do. Both of those grew up in the city. Should we seek advice from your Mr. King?"

"God, no. I've stayed away from any direct involvement in his doings. Tried to keep my hands and reputation clean. This is a new era. I want to survive in it. Don't want to play ball using Chicago White Sox tactics, end up being Black Sox nor do I want to end up in a brown box in the ground."

Ken commented, "You've been in war zones. I've been in live fire at the training camps but not war. I think we're smart enough to outfox any incoming fire. Let's lay some ideas on the table. For instance, it occurs to me that publicity is not sought willingly by underground enterprises."

"Hah! That sets up an immediate Plan A. Of course, showing up on the front page means your mug is more clearly in the line of fire. Or someone might hurl a caber at you."

"I'm not following. Do you mean 'sabre'?"

Both of Walt's bushy eyebrows rose, and his nostrils

widened like the entrance and exit tunnels to a highway mountain pass. His voice was stern. "Oh, sorry. No. We had been talking about our backgrounds, I made a side connection, and me folks is from Scotland. We Scots take a long heavy pole, called a caber, and see how far we can toss it . . . and stay out of range while the game is going on."

Ken's voice slurred. "Not exactly the rodeos I'm used to. Maybe we can spread the news about fun and games here in town. Ask who is red and white and thus pinko all over? Get the HUAC, House UnAmerican Activities Committee, involved? What do you say? People in the military were abnormally afraid of being tainted like that."

"For Plan A, I suggest we not only involve Slim Anderson, Merrilee's husband, for a chatty interview on KMBC-TV but have Meg do one of her dramatic presentations inviting listeners to guess who's a pinko? As though it's from a show at Swope Park Theater. You should see her in front of a classroom or raising money for the Symphony. She could pretend it's a philanthropist at work with a segment from the new show: *Our Kaycee Gang*, for Adult Audiences Only."

Ken laughed, "I'm getting what you mean. News is truthful news, if it's broadcast. And could frighten the cruds more than the threat of the Feds."

"I mean exactly that, with how the truth is presented."

"And?" Ken was not used to drinking 100 proof alcohol, much less drinking before lunch he kept reminding himself. Walt appeared quite unaffected by the liquor although he was at least one drink ahead.

Walt put down his drink, lowered his eyes to slits and his voice to a sinister tone. "Don't you know the *Our Gang* silent cartoons that became *Little Rascals* as talkies? They were shorts that entertained kids for years? The films could set up a dramatic moment in short order, so to speak. Here's an historical example: Little did Archduke Ferdinand realize as he set off on that drive through Sarajevo that before the hour was out he would be *stone cold dead*."

Ken laughed again. "I know what you mean. Very dramatic yourself. I can imagine what Meg would do with that to entertain a class." He raised his fist, took aim with a finger, and said solemnly, "Bang. You're dead as a dodo."

Walt brushed his lips with a napkin. "Here in Kansas City, we remember the Great War and the men from here. Those American volunteers served against the militarized Prussians who used the Archduke's death as an excuse to wreak havoc. We're rather proud of the Liberty Memorial over by Union Station. It's the only one in the country recognizing the American military from that Great War. The Austrian-Hungary Empire, the Prussians, the French, the English were the first ones in the Great War. And my dad was with our AEF––the grand American Expeditionary Forces––that arrived in time to end the war on the eleventh month on the 11th day at 11 a. m."

"Yes. I know that date quite well. We grew up in school honoring veterans on Armistice Day with parades and the Pledge of Allegiance. I still don't know why they added 'under God' to the Pledge last year."

"Because of Senator Joe McCarthy's sneak attacks on Communists that he imagines behind the sofa in every living room. He has these drunken scenes and articulates them. Caused Truman *et al*. to order loyalty oaths. As if every American isn't grateful for our country."

"I heard he's a drunkard, but Eisenhower has to let the

senator continue his paranoiac campaign. Of course, there *are* people who joined the Communist party in the 30s because it was the 'in' thing to do."

"Similar to the ways people invite the powerful criminals to the exclusive clubs. I'm not talking about *your* being invited here," Walt said and gave a grin.

"But it is a nice Club, and I have enjoyed our talk. I really need to get back home and alert Mother Holly and Belinda," Ken said, pushing back his chair. "And I'll fish out my pistol and load it."

"Good idea. I'll just run our drinks on my tab here. We need to talk more about our news chat. I'll call you after I get Meg's take on it. Yes, I need to discuss it with her, for sure. I have to run by the office first, so take your time coming over to our place. One subparagraph: we cannot prove that Kilmer's car was rendered lethal at Lincoln's motors; we're just guessing. I know, I know. The car was picked up at his lot that morning by the Kilmers. Nevertheless, we have to stay away from both libel and slander. But a picturesque request to reveal a little story of derring-do is acceptable."

"Thanks for the drinks. And, Walt, I have now realized that our company needs someone in the legal profession as backup when we stumble into danger, as we have done here. May I depend upon you?"

Walt shook his head. "Notary forms I can do, not others. Anything involving criminal law would pull me into an arena I have escaped from. I'll think about someone to recommend as your backup. There are new lawyers in town who do not owe anything to the shady side."

He relaxed and smiled broadly, revealing a black lower front tooth. No wonder he'd always seem grim when they talked: he didn't grin. *Ah, vanity, thy name is Walt man.* He stumbled a bit when he stood, and Ken put out a shaky hand to steady him.

"Thank you for both types of assistance, too." Ken tried to speak carefully, without slurring his words.

The men surrendered their claim checks at the cloakroom for their wool overcoats and fedoras. They stepped out onto the chilly doorstep and shook hands. A shot rang out, and they both dived for the pavement. Ken was down ahead of Walt by two seconds and heard a thunk after something flew by his ear.

Someone had shot at them. Probably.

"THAT does it." Walt gave a famous Army curse as he quickly tore open his grey wool overcoat, losing a button in the process, pulled out his weapon, and twisted on the ground. "SABU," he shouted. He aimed the revolver around, quartering off the area, saw nothing, and rose.

"Who is it? Who, why? What was that you shouted?"

"Oh, just ANZAC talk. Aussie Kiwi acronym. Uh. **S**elf-**a**djustable **B**alls **U**p. Meaning we're clearing up this mess pronto, Ken. I will thraw a caber to threap that creep. You've awoke the Ness monster!"

Ken said, "Well, I can throw a bowling bowl—ball--in a split, spare, or strike, even throw it down the alley at a monster, but I don't know exactly what it is you'd be doing."

"It's not funny. You've affronted some dangerous people somehow somehow."

Ken was exasperated. "What are you saying? I'm not understanding, and we seem to be in danger standing here! Whom did I affront that means that I be target practice?"

Walt's wide face was red with anger that gradually faded

as he turned to Ken. "I dinna see who did it. Oh, you mean what I said. First, I used an expression I picked up in the Pacific confrontation with the Japs. Then, I fell into childhood lingo. I mentioned that my mother is a Scot, and I learned some expressions from her, more are suitable for mixed-company than the military exclamations. I just said I'd throw that caber pole, the long, heavy pole tossed in the Scottish game, to flatten the laddie who shot at us."

"I didn't see anyone pointing a weapon when I stood up." Ken brushed at the seat and arm of his coat. The paperboy standing across the street looked at them with a startled expression followed by an amused one. A lady, face pinched with cold and a red nose, gave them dirty looks as she swept by. Sounded like she said, "Drunk skunks."

"Neither did I." Walt surveyed the area with arms akimbo. "Let's go back inside. I'm going to make some calls. Give the assailant time to scurry off." Walt's voice slurred the "r's."

"I always thought your southern accent had some other foreign touch in it. It's that Scot burr I've read about."

"Yes. It shows up when I'm angry, Meg says. Let's go find some lunch and prepare an interview for airing on the news, like with that Slim Anderson. I will call him and call Meg to ask her to add us to the lunch at home. Did you know Slim's first name is Horatio, like Horatio at the Bridge?"

"Good. He can help us defend our bridge and game." Making a joke at a time like this meant he wasn't all that scared.

Both men, however, were talking tersely and rapidly. Ken realized that he was actually feeling a pang of panic, that he couldn't downplay it, and that the adrenalin surge was something rarely felt even back during his earliest training in arms.

They reentered the Club to use the telephone. Walt found Slim at home having breakfast. "He gave the late news last night and just woke up," Walt said to Ken as he waited for Merrilee to turn over the phone to her husband. "Walter Raleigh here, yes. Ken Massey and I would like an appointment with you. We need help from you and from my wife."

Ken watched Walt's impassive face, with a slur to his voice that wasn't really a burr, but a bit too much bourbon. The wrinkles helped conceal any emotion he might be feeling, Ken noted. Ken felt a pain in his knuckle, looked at a slow drip of blood, realizing that a chip from the brick foundation had caught him, and stepped outside again to scout the pavement. He found nothing and went back inside. His pistol would be riding his hip this afternoon.

He had implored Mother Holly to install a safe behind one of the big-framed landscape paintings in the living room. That allowed his "gat" and Belinda's target pistol, both wrapped in oily rags and then in an outside covering of oilcloth, to have a home away from the children. The safe also held up to thirty dollars for emergencies. In contrast, numismatist Holly had stuffed her coin collection temporarily behind a splintery plywood board in the dumbwaiter, because she was afraid the gun oil might leak onto her coins.

"No, first I have to talk with my wife because I want to involve her. We're facing dire straits, to put it mildly."

After a pause, Walt said, "Let me put Ken on for a minute while I take a latrine run."

Ken took the handset. "Hello, I'm Ken Massey of **Sleuth Works**." He listened. "Yes, your wife indirectly involved my outfit in tracing some items for her art museum problem. The effort has pulled me and Walt and our families into a minor war zone. We need your help. Here's Walt again." Ken handed the handset back.

Walt whispered to him, "Didn't want to piss away our intriguing him." On the phone, he said, "I'm back." Stopped to listen. "I understand your puzzlement." Walt held up a hand as though to stop Slim from expostulating although the man couldn't see him through the telephone. "No, not that soon, nor to fight. To send out the news to notify our foe like the Revolution army did to Cornwallis: 'surrender or else.' Oh, sure, I understand why you'll wait to agree to it until after you heard our ideas."

He nodded at Ken. "Yes, Two o'clock this afternoon at the Library. Thank you."

The cloakroom attendant stood with arms folded on the counter, listening to their end of the conversation. Walt frowned at her as he replaced the handset and shoved the phone back toward her. He revealed to Ken, "The Library is a nice bar down on Main. I'm already meeting Tyler there. He's bringing back some photographs that Meg sent for his wife to see of our son.

"Incidentally, the Library is also a well-fortified building. And, your Phil Tyler, recently promoted to police sergeant in his suburban district, might help us."

"Phil was an extra fine sarge at Granstadt before he retired!"

"Nice to know." Walt brushed off the comment sharply. "First, I need to go to the office to finish my calls. I want Meg to be at home and give us lunch. Second, see you at my house in an hour. Or do you need a ride?"

Ken shook his head. The men stepped back outside only to be faced with another explosion. Walt ignored the noise and moseyed toward his car.

Ken dived to the ground again. He wouldn't swear that it had been another bullet because he heard nothing strike nearby. The resulting two shots of adrenalin reacting to the blast cleared the two shots of bourbon from his brain.

A little girl in a blue, dirty snowsuit with skates slung over her shoulder asked, "Are you all right, mister? Do you want me to help you?"

"No, thanks. I must have stumbled." Embarrassed, Ken rose and dusted off his overcoat again, his fedora, and his blond crew cut, in that order. His cheek stung where he'd hit a chunk of ice. He looked around warily, but the only sound he heard apparently came from a car that had backfired, and was now coughing, starting up, and moving off with a faulty muffler. Ken felt his mouth twitch at the corner. "Count down: two 'shots' swallowed, one shot missed, zero shot fired."

He and Walt both sank rapidly into their car seats. Driving easily through the traffic, Mr. Kendrick Massey realized that he was actually feeling exhilarated, not threatened. The adrenalin had subsided. Here he was, back in a semblance of police work that he had done in the Air Force.

CHAPTER TEN

Stopping at home to tell Belinda where he would be for lunch, he showed her the permits. He tried but was unsuccessful in his attempt to call collegian John Johnson. He wanted to see the kids about signing the forms and having them notarized. Belinda said she'd keep trying to contact them and have Ken see them at their university registrar's office that had a notary public.

Ken, therefore, was just a minute behind Walt in parking his car and going up the porch steps to greet Meg. Inside, they both set their winter garments on a bench and moved into a beautiful room decorated in gold and green. A recording of a jazz band was playing "Has Anybody Seen My Gal."

Off-handedly, Walter said, "I'm going to have to do something about Marnie listening into my calls. Maybe I should bring in a new cabinet with a record player and play our jazz records. We like jazz a lot."

"Our family does, too. We like about everything except Country-Western."

"Would you-all like to go with us sometime to the 18th and Vine clubs? We also belong to The Symphony patrons' group. Meg loves everything from Wagner's *Overture* to *Tannhauser* to the Marx Brothers' *Who's Sorry Now*, and I'm following her lead. Been a wide range of excellence so far." Walt waved a decanter at him, but Ken shook his head, liking its feeling of clarity in the brain.

"Oh, I'm sure we would like both jazz clubs and the symphony orchestra. I like Dixieland, but Mother Holly likes be-bop, classical, and swing: that is, she just likes to listen to every type of music. She regrets she never learned to play an instrument," Ken replied, a pleased smile on his face. "We're free in the evenings as a rule. Our nanny, Lillian, watches over the children every evening except Saturday."

During a quick, rather delicious lunch preceded by aperitifs that Meg set before them, they joshed about their ideas for diverting the thugs. She had prepared some tomato bisque soup with cheese sandwiches. Meg kept expressing puzzlement over why the boys were set on throwing down a gauntlet on some people for some reason that she couldn't grasp. She gave up trying to comprehend and played along as they prepared their script for a try-out with that suburban police sergeant, Theophilous Tyler, whom she knew was sarcastic and didn't want to be around. And the boys heartily agreed that it was an amusing interview possibility for TV newscaster Slim Anderson . . . if he agreed when he met them at the Library.

"Walt, I have a hard time dealing with Phil Tyler," Meg complained, wearily anticipating trying the skit out on cynical Tyler. "He was always rude to me when I knew him during my teaching stint during the Occupation in Japan." He arrived as the clock struck twelve on the local church tower. She greeted him as he came into the room with a nod and a wave and a passive face. "How's Donna these days?"

"Fine, as always."

"Did she like the pictures? Did you bring some of your kids?"

"Yes. Here're three of our girl and son."

"Oh, what a cute daughter washing her brother's face," Meg replied.

Phil looked at her blandly and sat down. "I'd like a glass of water before I leave."

Walt drew a glass of water and put it on the table. "I wonder if you'd play-act a TV interview with Meg. I'll give you a time for dime."

"What?"

"I reimburse you if you'll help here now this minute," Walt laughed.

Phil said, "Why?"

"Well, the boy you arrested after he shot a bullet at us has done it again . . ."

Phil interrupted. "That boy escaped, you know."

Walt stopped. "No. I wasn't sure. Maybe that explains why someone shot at me again, and that someone is the kid, Lincoln's kid. It ties in with the reason we're trying to get Slim to do a subtle interview with Meg. Will you query Meg, interim newscaster Tyler?" He raised the whisky bottle toward the two men. Ken nodded; Phil shook his head.

Phil sighed. "Go on."

Meg said first that she would tell some jokes. He rolled his eyes.

Meg looked him in the eye, stilling the eye roll, sat makeshift microphones (i.e., small *cloisonné* vases) in front of herself and him. "'Mr. Anderson. We were at the zoo recently, and a guide asked if we knew what was black and white and red all over. One teenager said, 'A newspaper?' The guide said, 'No, an embarrassed zebra.'"

She waited for a chuckle or smile, or grin, and Tyler obliged her with a sickly smile.

She continued, "But on a more serious note. This is what has happened recently. A scorpion crept into my friend's life. It is trying to bite. It must be stopped," she widened her eyes and held up her hands in apparent horror. He, acting out his part as the newscaster, snarled, "Please explain what you are talking about. Our audience will be interested, I am sure, even if this story is not funny."

"Well," Meg leaned toward him, widening her dark blue eyes, blond hair brushing forward over her ears, "A teenage, insect-like son of a local assassinating man tried to help his father's boss by shooting at a house where a child lived with his parents. That fellow had no reason to act like a brain-dead zombie instead of sticking to selling cars and retiring in an elegant fashion among the elite. I feel blue about the red and white that shows up as pinko strategy." She waved her fingers with a disgusted look on her face.

"I see. I guess you mean someone has been trying to commit a crime because of some imagined slight, Mrs. Raleigh?" he said in a snide voice that seemed to be one he used with her because she gave a reluctant shake of her head. He next feigned puzzlement with lifted eyebrows, exaggerated lifted eyebrows.

"Yes. And my husband and his friends served bravely in the war and survived because they cannot be threatened . . . and they know how to protect themselves and win. They will not be assassinated like our eminent President Lincoln. Or also slain like the other three almighty Presidents. Or businessmen around here. The opposite is more likely to happen: the unmighty will fall. I just wanted to share a little timely local news today. Thank you, Mr. Anderson."

Walt and Ken clapped their hands. Phil Tyler looked resigned and shook his head. "Dumb," he muttered. "You two, her husband and friend, are a bit high and can't carry on with this ridiculous idea. Anderson will never go for it."

"It would be perfect," one man said gurgled into a glass. "That was a fine replication of what we want Slim to do tonight in interviewing Meg. Go over it a couple more times. Then let's go see him at the Library."

And so went at the practice for, possibly, the ten o'clock newscast. Might have been pertinent if the grandfather's behest had been given to his pimply-high-school-dropout of a grandson--but they somehow forgot that they knew the grandson was dead: forgetting results from fumes on brains. Or that the task was instead given to the son of a employee, a son not too bright in the brain region, even without alcohol fumes, which was likely the scenario. If the story were fashioned clearly enough to be interpreted by the enemies of the Lincoln and Shannon families. Then some laughter would be heard in dark bars downtown as the newscast ended, some knowing laughter. If not, oops.

"For us in our little political arena, Meg's news flash should work as well as Richard Nixon's maudlin Checkers speech did to keep him on Ike's ticket in '52," said Walt in a positively ebullient manner. His drink was darker than the water in Phil's glass.

"You know more than we do about how the tensions stretch and flip back and forth around here. Let's hope," Ken said. Ken's drink was also darker. He slurred his words a bit.

"I'm positive that Shannon and his underling Lincoln will heed the message. Even if it means that the Federal authorities use income tax evasion to put someone out of business and into jail, as they did with Boss Pendergast, the law eventually wins out. Hope it doesn't take thirty years. They'll be here quick as a blink to investigate his Commie link.

"Let's ride in my Plymouth to the Library." Walt rose and lurched to one side.

"No, thanks," said Phil. "I have errands to do before I head home before dark."

"Be sure to bill me," said Walt. He moved his hand in a semblance of a duck's bill.

"Tell Donna I said, 'hi'," called Meg.

Phil nodded to Walt, turned to Meg, and, in an innocent voice, asked, "Do you mean 'hai', meaning 'yes', to a question she hadn't asked, or mean 'hello' as I'm saying 'goodbye' now?"

"Oh, Phil. Tell her hello. I'd love to see her and the kids up here sometime when the weather's better."

"Donna told me that you found it inexplicable why I seem put out with you. Well, Meg, your continuing sideshows in my life seem ineluctable!! Bye, now."

Ken added his decision, about moving on. "I'm going to take my own car because I need to get back home to continue my cases."

As they all walked out to the driveway, Ken stopped Phil to offer, "How about coming over for supper. You know Mother Holly and Belinda from when they lived in Granstadt."

"No, I have to be going home. I could drop by in a couple of hours, though, for a cup of coffee."

"Great, I'll be home way before then."

Ken backed out of the driveway after Phil had backed out and waited by the curb to follow Walt and Meg after he backed out. The Library was a couple of miles away. The two cars were parked sloppily at the curb on the narrow street, and the three people walked gingerly across an icy patch of snow.

Inside, the Library was maroon. Glass-covered bookshelves 12 feet high were lined with maroon (leather?) books with gold lettering on the spines. The wall by the entrance had paper maroon patterns, the rug had solid maroon tufts, and the chairs were, groan, cushioned with maroon material . . . but a checkerboard pattern with blocks of cream that made Ken's eyes cross.

Clifford King came storming into the Library room just as they were shedding their coats. "Just what in the blue blazes are you idiots doing? You are children playing with dynamite."

The Raleighs and Ken reared back in alarm at the furious message. The hatcheck fella watched with interest.

Mr. King continued roaring. "Get your message across on television to watch some fireworks, are we, children? Start Federal investigations here? Are we ready for bloody scrapes and fearful nights? Are we ready to set up barricades to protect our families from the explosions? Don't you dare, don't you *dare*, do anything to escalate a few minor incidents? *Do you understand me?*"

Three people looked at him in shock and finally

registered his words; Walt simply nodded, Meg shuddered, and Ken looked astounded.

"Minor? You call being shot at 'minor?'" Ken exploded, and, because he did not know Mr. King, he shoved the man's shoulder.

"You want to see 'major?' You'd not be alive to see it. But you might feel it before you passed." King still roared. He stared at Ken with anger.

"No, no, but really, whoever you are, what business is it of yours?"

Walt said, "Uh, Kendrick, this is Mr. King." He pointed to Ken with a limp wave, then at Meg. "You know my wife, Meg."

"Oh," said Ken, backing away. "How you doing?" said Meg.

"I know who all of them are. They better heed me." Mr. King left the room with long strides, his feet stomping leaving wet maroon tiles behind him in the entryway.

"Whew!" said Meg. "That was certainly a coherent chastisement. Do we cancel this because of his attitude?"

Walt had waited somewhat impatiently for her to finish. "Yes, Yes. We must: too powerful. King's too close to the undercurrents for us not to pay attention. Marnie must have sussed out that we were coming here for lunch and called him. She must have listened again to my phone calls to you guys."

"What are you recommending?" asked Ken, somewhat shaken.

"All right, all right, I tell you. I'll go outside now and waylay Slim. Tell him thanks for coming, but we decided it wouldn't work. Mr. King does know what he is talking about. Cancelling our amusing play with the pinko labels may have seemed necessary but was a pretty stupid idea to start with, now that I put it in the larger picture of diverting that Lincoln guy's kid. Oh, well, we can laugh about it." Walt was studying the far wall. They put back on their coats, and somewhat sheepishly, left the Library, abandoning the plan. Walt and Meg lingered to speak to Slim who would probably be put out by the cancellation and waste of his time. His deep voice would be calm and dispassionate, as always, regardless of his irritation.

Back at home, Ken was told that he was to meet the two university kids at their library administration office at five. He, in turn, told Belinda and Mother Holly that Officer Phil Tyler would drop by for coffee about 1600 hours.

He lay down for an hour's nap while Belinda typed in the information on the releases that he dictated. *Mr. King was a grand antidote for dispelling a head full of tasty spirits.* He had that sober thought, suddenly rose, walked into the typing desk, sat down, and composed cover letters to two veterans' offices for Belinda to type and mail tonight. They should have records on the veterans the kids wanted to find. about

Belinda typed them swiftly and remarked while doing so. "I think the afternoon mail should be here. Why don't you trot down and see?"

Officer Tyler was hit by the lower door being opened by Ken. "Ouch, Kendrick Massey. I was simply studying your **Sleuth Works** sign. I wasn't planning on stealing it!"

"Oh, I'm sorry. I was just coming down for the mail. Let me get it while you start on up to the office. There's a coat rack and a mat for your overshoes in the little foyer. Donna and Holly are expecting you. The percolator is percolating, the cook assured me."

Ken followed Phil up the stairs, looking at the magazines he'd taken from the mailbox. One was for Mother Holly's interest in coin collecting, one was for Belinda with short mysteries, and one was for his interest in news from around the world.

Phil was being greeted warmly when Ken came in behind him. He said, "I can stay about 20 minutes, but I wanted to tell Donna that I'd seen you."

"I'm glad you took the time. It's always been interesting to hear what's happening back there. And, Phil? We have a guest bedroom and a nanny full time, so why don't you and the family come visit us some weekend? You can bring us up to date on what's happening in Granstadt." Mother Holly said. "I remember when I gave you that yearbook from the high school to check on the high school boys who were playing tricks during a stressful time."

Phil replied, "Oh, yes. That mystery that Belinda and Donna helped solve. Oh, Belinda, here is a copy of a puzzle Donna made at the end." He dug a small slip of paper out of his pocket."

THE CASE OF THE MISSING CLUES

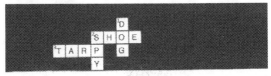

Across
2. What didn't fit? [SHOE]
3. What is wrapped around body? [TARP]

Down
1. What barked in the night? [DOG]
2. Who sneaks around? [SPY]

"That's amusing, even if at that time the case caused a roil of scary speculation in the town. At least it ended."

Belinda copied off a sketch of the puzzle to put in her scrapbook. She returned the paper to Phil.

"Here's Harriet with the coffee. Cream? Sugar? Cookie?" Mother Holly pulled the cart toward her chair, lifting the coffee pot up.

Phil shook his head, took the saucer gingerly and sipped the hot coffee quickly from the small cup. "I like this black. I'll take a rain check on the cookie."

Holly Jones added, "We always have enough food in our pantry to entertain friends with their kids if you make a last minute decision to come."

"I'll pass along the invitation to Donna, and we'll let you know when the weather permits us to come up and take the kids to the Swope Park zoo. Your two and our two should have a great time together," Tyler said, rising, bowing to the two ladies, and shaking hands with Ken.

"Wish you could've stayed for supper and met our kids," said Belinda.

Phil smiled and shook his head. "It's darkening outside already, and I need to be on the road home."

Ken escorted him to the door. Phil lowered his voice. "Stay far away from trouble, hear? You remember all the massacres and gangland stuff from earlier decades. That has not been forgotten. Vestiges are always germinating."

Ken nodded. "I'm back to toting ma six-shooter, Sheriff." He watched Phil don his black jacket over his black policeman's uniform . . . the clothing looked tailored, not issued. Expensive black wool cloth. Phil must have found a black sheep somewhere.

They shook hands. Ken followed Phil downstairs to make sure the lower door was locked tightly.

CHAPTER ELEVEN

The old brick YWCA building, half a block wide and two stories high, had a small parking lot, slots made for old Model T's and not big enough for the DeSoto. Belinda Massey drove around the block and spotted a space close at the curb only a block away. She climbed out in her heavy winter outfit, patted the hood emblem, an image of the head of explorer Hernando DeSoto, and trudged to the YWCA doors. Inside, the halls had tiles on floor and walls, antiseptic, cold white tiles. She sloshed in her wet boots to the reception desk, an oval monstrosity with a huge wall clock behind it. Because the ceilings were so high, the desk and chairs, chairs built with tall legs where the receptionists were seated, seemed rightfully designated for their placement.

The registration fee didn't set her earnings back much nor did the rental of the gym suit: blue shapeless cotton blouse and bloomers. Belinda had brought her own swimming suit and white rubber cap in a small suitcase, along with comb, brush, hand lotion, and deodorant.

In the locker room she found Meg, who introduced Merrilee Anderson as they emerged from behind the white curtains hanging across metal stalls. Soon garbed in the loose outfits and having stowed, and stuffed, their belongings in their rented lockers, they entered the gym.

An older woman served as the gym teacher; she had the dozen ladies line up after each had taken a pair of tenpins from a big container. Well apart from each other, the gym teacher had them swing the wooden tenpins up, down, around, behind, in front, over and over to a John Phillip Sousa record playing song after song, march time.

After replacing the *Cro-Magnon clubs*, as Meg christened them, in the bin, the teacher put half of the ladies on one end of the gym facing the other half. They ran, slapped hands, touched the far wall, turned, and ran the other way, slapping hands once more.

Belinda was aching and sweating. A basketball net situated at one side provided an excuse to continue running around in a circle and tossing the ball upwards for another hour. The three shook perspiration from their foreheads, headed for the showers, put their swimsuits on afterwards and went to the basement pool.

The pool gave off its stringent chlorine order, while the air was hot and damp as though they had wandered outside on a humid, steamy summer day. The uncomfortable dank, stinky air was a great encouragement to the three girls to jump into the pool.

"I'm really out of shape. Last night we went to that lovely restaurant in the Plaza, and we shared a chateaubriand. My stomach ached before we finished, and yet I had a baklava for dessert," Belinda said as she clung to the side. "My dress fit beautifully before we left and was too tight when we returned home."

"I like the chef's offerings there," said Merrilee. "I tend to eat too much as though I would starve to death otherwise. Undeterred I'll be interred."

Meg said, "Amusing choice of words, Merrilee. About that menu, I'll agree: yep, me, too. I enjoy word play. Yours reminded me of something. I've always teased Walt about a solecism in what he wrote me that he'd 'just read a big tomb'. He meant 'tome'." She spelled the two words, climbed out as they chuckled, strode to the diving board, and made a sharply clean dive into the deep end.

"I seem to put on weight quickly ever since I had the babies a year apart," moaned Belinda. She guessed that she was maybe ten years younger than Meg and 15 years younger than Merrilee. She needed to establish rapport without insulting them.

"It's worth moaning about. We can't have kids. Slim was injured in the war, so don't ask anything else about why, okay?" Merrilee replied coldly.

Belinda squinted at her before nodding. *Blew that attempt, blast it.* She looked out at the slight wake that was moving her up and down in the water.

Meg Lowe Raleigh was the cause of the wake. She swam beautifully, her arms barely seen above the water as she moved like a dolphin, turning under at each end of the pool and going fast. Waves followed after her strokes.

Belinda and Merrilee paddled around the shallow end hanging onto plastic tubes and talking. Belinda asked if there were any facts that Merrilee remembered about the Kilmers. What Ken actually wanted her to find out was exactly why Merrilee was interested in jewels that had been loaned by a relative, one not in her family, to the museum.

"Well, Slim and I went to the Kilmers' funeral because, as you know, my mom was a cousin of Natalie Kilmer's mom. Tally and I'd be second cousins, I think. She sent a semi-precious pin to my mother after my husband helped at the cemetery where her mom died in an accident. Where her mom died bonking her head on a tombstone when a boy frightened her. Tally's mom had loaned it to the art museum. The jewelry is probably mine now."

"Figuring it out, I think that to Natalie, you're a third cousin," Belinda said. "My firm is trying to establish the heritage of that art museum jewelry as you requested of Walt."

"Oh, really? I first met Tally years ago at the cemetery when her mom named Jacqueline––Smith? no––Schmidt, was killed by that accident. She ran into a young hobo up there. He was from down around Raumville, my hometown. Slim told me the boy was also 'accidentally' involved in two other deaths and spent a few months in jail. The kid's family wasn't well known down home there. The police chief had a brother who had been one of the dead victims, but, outside of him, none of the deaths occurred to anyone prominent enough to make a flap. All deaths were some kind of accident. Slim thought that's why the kid was let off lightly. No one much cared. But you do?" Merrilee had a quizzical look on her face as she turned to face Belinda and continued an exercise kick, hanging onto the side of the pool.

Belinda paddled away with a thoughtful look on her face and came back. "You were the one who asked that the ownership of the jewels be clarified for the art museum?"

"Yes. My mother is next in line, apparently. She'll need to sign off. Why?"

"Here's something. My husband found out that Mrs.

Schmidt, your Tally's mother, might have had a child before her marriage. First decade, around 1906 or 1907."

"I certainly do not think so. That's shocking. That's a long time ago. How did he hear that?"

"Talking with a woman who knew her when they were young."

"That reminds me. Years ago Slim told me that the hobo kid had parents who were *both* orphans. But then, orphan trains came through here from New York and dropped off kids on farms throughout the Midwest." Merrilee shook her head. "But, what if the hobo kid's parents are orphans? Then one is related to me? Doesn't sound feasible. I don't know. I'm ready to go home." She heft herself up onto the granite and stood.

Meg swam over to a ladder and climbed out of the pool, taking off her swim cap and shaking her hair loose. "What are you two gabbing about?"

Merrilee replied, "You remember that kid accused in Raumville court of imitating people's voices and making harassing phone calls? He was the one accused of being present when some people died, including cousin Jacqueline Schmidt over there at the cemetery? Teddy something."

"I read about it, but that was long ago. I'd moved over to my folks' farm from the college dorm by the time the trial was held. I vaguely remember reading about his responsibility for something like two or three deaths." Meg rubbed her shoulders with a towel.

"No, it turned out that those deaths were all accidents, and he was sent to jail for just a little while, three months or so for something else. Well, Belinda just told me the

Schmidt woman may have had a child before her marriage. And Slim had told me the kid's parents were orphans."

"And that means precisely what?" Meg demanded.

"Maybe nothing, maybe something."

"I'll call your sister, Carole, in Raumville, Merrilee. I had her in history class a long time ago, in 1943, I think. Do you know her number? Just to see if she knows anything about that kid's family, see if she knows if his mom or dad is an orphan." Meg took charge.

Merrilee raised an eyebrow at Meg's suggestion. "That's pretty far-fetched, I know, Meg. The Schmidt woman would have been my mother's first cousin. Isn't that right, Belinda?"

"No, they would have been second cousins if I'm following the connections correctly, and descended from different grandparents," replied Belinda. Belinda worded the obvious statement carefully, not wanting to imply that anything suspicious was suspected, if that's a well-phrased phrase.

"Come to think of it, she was removed permanently and rather abruptly that day by knocking her head against a gravestone . . . Hope I didn't offend you girls by my flip remark. Please do call Carole, Meg. I've told her your husband was investigating the jewels' ownership for us. And now I've met Belinda from the outfit that your husband has investigating ownership." Merrilee showed no alarm—was talking serenely.

"No harm in trying, Merrilee. I'm getting cold. Let's get dressed and grab a bite at my home first. I've had the cook prepare ingredients for *tempura*, which are fantastically delicious fried vegetables, and boil some rice for us.

I couldn't find any *sake*, a Japanese rice wine, but we'll substitute Chablis. I am adamant about matching tasteful wine properly with meal flavors." Meg started off to the showers before the others had climbed from the pool.

After taking showers and donning their garments, the three drove their cars to Meg and Walt's house. Meg cautioned them upon entering that baby Lynn was asleep upstairs and suggested that they talk in the kitchen. She said that the cook wouldn't mind, it being her own naptime, and a phone was positioned near the back door.

Meg set a tin crock on the table over a sterno lamp, heated some oil, and added long slices of vegetables that were coated with dough. The rice was ready, letting her direct Merrilee to fill bowls while Belinda filled wine and water glasses. On the table, bottles of soy sauce and salt and pepper shakers were centered.

Meg grinned. "I didn't bother to put out chopsticks. The utensils we're used to will serve as well."

She quickly dished out slices of carrot, some type of squash, potato, and yams fried in light dough. They chatted about the Y and its reopening after the polio scare was over, the way the gym instructor had biceps like a man, and the awful chlorine smell that lingered in their hair. Meg casually asked Belinda after she sat down, "How did you meet Ken?"

Belinda answered, "We met at a church social. Same church where we were married after Dad died. How about you and Walt?"

"Oh, we met in college, back in the 40s. I went to his softball games. He came to Japan where I was teaching, and we were married in the chapel."

They both looked at Merrilee. She revealed, with a

laugh, "My story is better. We met at a jazz club downtown when I was visiting a friend one year. He was the announcer for the band. They played Dixieland Jazz. They were so good. "Maple Leaf Rag." "Twelfth Street Rag." Scott Joplin's works. We were married in a judge's office, because we eloped. Some friends came so they could tattle to Mom. He was on leave but was serving a long stint in the Army. Afterwards, he worked for a radio station in Raumville." She smiled at some memory.

Belinda ate two pieces of *tempura* and wiped her mouth with a tan linen napkin. "I'm so full. It was wonderful, Meg. I do need to be getting home. Could you check out the story with Merrilee's sister, Carole, now? Before I leave?"

Rising from their seats, they stacked their dishes and walked over to place them on the drain board. Each took a cup of hot coffee, black, and sat back at the table.

Meg telephoned Carole long-distance after both of the others suggested questions. She engaged in the typical pleasantries and family remarks with her former pupil. The other two ladies glanced around at the lovely green appliances, tan counters, ivory painted walls, and carved cabinet doors. One cabinet on the wall beside the kitchen table had glass windows, behind which were large decorated plates in unusual red, green, and blue designs.

Meg finally said, "Hey, Carole, do you know what happened to that Teddy--you, know, the Killer Kid?--or his Clarmont family? Are they still in Raumville somewhere?" She was silent for a number of minutes.

"You don't know specifically?" She opened a kitchen table drawer and took out pencil and a tablet. Finishing with promises to meet sometime in the future, sometime in the New Year, somewhere in Missouri, western Missouri, or southwestern Missouri, Meg at last replaced the black receiver. And, revealed that the Teddy kid's parents could be orphans.

"They moved to the wine country west of St. Louis." Merrilee and Belinda shook their heads. Neither knew anything about that part of Missouri. Meg admitted that she also had never been to that part of the state. "But it's a famous section, settled by Germans. Maybe a hundred miles west of St. Louis. Hermann, Missouri, wines, I think." Merrilee offered her knowledge with a shrug, tapping the pencil gently on the tablet as she thought.

"Carole didn't know where exactly. She did say that one of the boy's sisters married the winery owner's son, and they may be the owners now."

"Can we get phone books anywhere for that part of Missouri?"

"I haven't the slightest idea. Let me call the operator," Meg said. She asked the long distance operator for a person-to-person call to Mr. Ted Clarmont in Hermann, Mo. She hung up and said, "No luck. But I bet those wineries are in the yellow pages somewhere, maybe even in the St. Louis phone book. Walt has Ma Bell phone books from all the major USA cities in his office. I'll look Monday, and let you both know."

Belinda said, "My mother is looking at the telephone books in the library downtown, too."

Goodbyes were said, coats donned with agreement to meet the next Saturday at the gym.

Upon her return to the apartment and recital of the

possibility of an orphan's identity as a Clarmont, both her husband and mother showed skepticism toward Belinda's enthusiastic disclosure.

Belinda argued, "But what if the Clarmont mother is the child of a Volks' girl? Ken, you believed that the lady who told you about that was enjoying the revelation. No one's going to be embarrassed now. Mrs. Jacqueline Schmidt's husband, daughter, and son-in-law are dead and buried. Not a single other relative, except Merrilee and her mother, ever came forward to admit being related to the dead Natalie. The museum wants Walt, through us, to prove that no one is going to bring up some arcane claim in the future. It wants everyone who is identified to cede claims against the property instead of having a hole in the issue. Or it could settle with such a claimant."

Belinda was working pretty convincingly to persuade them, Ken thought. He said, "All right. We might as well check it out. We'll get a hold of the list of vineyards from the phone books from Walt. Make calls when we arrive in Jefferson City. Costs less from there. Just ask if there's an employee named Clarmont, okay?"

Belinda nodded.

"And then I'll call my folks and Merrilee's mom, Marlena Harver, and change our dining plans to Wednesday night and Thursday. We'll use the extra day in Jeff City if nothing takes us up by Hermann's wineries. We'll know by Monday night, I think, if it's worth tracing the adults who were orphaned. And hope that the weather cooperates."

Holly said, "The distance to St. Louis is close to 300 miles. But you would stop about 100 miles west of that to the Hermann area. See, here's Highway 94 up out of Jeff

City to Hermann that is north of the Missouri River. I've just circled it on this map so you know. I'll draw the whole route so that it's easy to follow, even if there's a detour. I can keep the bigger atlas with that map in my lap. Call if you need help, kiddos."

Belinda added, "Yes, Mom, good. I'm convinced we need to check out that Clarmont family. Even if one of the parents is probably not the orphan we need to identify, if there is such a one, they might know something about others from when they were little. Plus you found where the orphanage records are located."

"And," Mother Holly said, "I'll stay here, and you call me to check my atlas on any changes in the route. I'll be here for the servants and children, for Mr. Walt Raleigh, plus I can go search the orphanage records for 1906-1908 and find out if there're any relevant names. Furthermore, I don't think the difference in phone charges to the vineyards would be much different from Jeff City compared with here. We don't have to be that frugal, guys."

"Agreed," said Belinda. "Ken?"

"Sounds like an excellent plan. If nothing pans out about the winery employees, we'll take extra time with my folks."

"That's settled. Mom, your idea sets out efficient plans, as I should have expected. Thanks be to you." Belinda picked up her mom's hand and kissed it.

The dinner bell tingled, and a wavery voice announced "supper."

"I didn't realize it was already seven o'clock," Mother Holly said. "Pork roast and scalloped potatoes are on the menu tonight. New label on the white wine someone recommended at the store the other day." They ambled into the dining room.

"Is it from a Missouri winery?" Belinda asked.

"Yes," Ken said, looked at the label, picking up the bottle and moving around the table pouring it.

"What kind of fish dish sounds like a lawn game?" Mother Holly said as she sat with the Masseys in the dining room.

"Spawn tennis?" Ken offered. "Boccie barracuda?"

"I know, Mom. Croquet. You're talking about salmon croquettes, aren't you?"

"Gong, the winner on the first guess," Mother Holly said, raising her wine glass in a salute.

"You keep making these silly things for us to guess," Belinda complained, but showed a "V" for victory sign with her fingers.

"Well, you need to expand your vocabulary, and, as for being a librarian, you don't read much. You learn more about people, places, and things by reading. That's how you become more knowledgeable as a sleuth seeking solutions."

"I can eat a croquette, play croquet, or be a coquette. How 'bout that for vocabulary?"

Holly laughed.

Harriet brought in the bowls and platters with the main course. The three put their linen napkins into their laps and started passing the food. The aroma from the roast plucked at their tongues' sensory buds, and no one spoke for several minutes.

"But that was pretty fishy as a riddle . . . they aren't spelled the same, like polo and Polo are," Ken complained to break to silence.

"And here's the guy who said 'spawn' tennis. Eat your potatoes and grin at your wife's quick bite at the bait," Mother Holly said. "By the way, Ken, you should look at putting a lock of some kind on that dumbwaiter in the butler's pantry. Young J. B. is starting to scout around upstairs, and he might stumble on the old closet and pantry that I've tried to close off up there. I can see him wanting to ride it up and down and getting stuck and hollering bloody murder."

"I'll do that. Hadn't thought that far ahead about our little tiger's possible antics. After dinner, let's watch a bit of television and go to bed by ten. I told Pastor Palmer that we'd come to his church sometime. Tomorrow would be a good time because the weather is supposed to be bright and sunny," Ken informed his wife and mother-in-law. "And, you can check out the Sunday School classrooms, Belinda."

"Ken, my dear sir, we do need to find some friends our own age. Going to church would help us make some social acquaintances, don't you think?" Belinda said.

"Yes, that would work. We do need to broaden our network of acquaintances. Walt offered to put my name in at a country club. And, too, Walt said he and Meg would like the three of us to go with them to a jazz club downtown some night. Some pretty famous names have appeared here in Kansas City."

"I know about those,' Holly said. "I've been reading up on Count Basie and his group and how they toured the country. The famous bands would be here or in New Orleans, and in New York and in Chicago at various times."

"Walt also mentioned that Meg is involved with the Symphony angels."

"We could do that, too. We have eclectic tastes as vast as they do, I would guess." Belinda was pleased at the suggestions. "Even if I don't read books, I engage in other types of erudition, Mother."

Holly looked up at the ceiling and shook her head in amusement.

CHAPTER TWELVE

Ken Massey, with wife Belinda, entered the office of Missouri's Department of Vital Statistics on Tuesday. They had made good time driving to Jefferson City through a sparkling clean, white snow, sculpted landscape, and all it was missing was a snowman waving a hand at them somewhere along the way. They found the proper office and entered and were surprised to learn that a copy of a document cost fifty cents.

Belinda was amused. She said, "Every place I visited last week, I had to pay a fee of some sort even if I cajoled the attendant into letting me do the looking. I myself found little of anything relevant even when I had paid the fee. But, some of them will remember me, and I'll be back to continue searching."

"Did you get receipts for the fees?"

"Of course. I wasn't a librarian for four years for nothing. We charged late fees, you know."

"I kinda think that's how I met a feisty blonde who wouldn't let me heist a book."

"And I kinda remember a handsome fellow trying to tell me he was too legally apt, too absolutely rapt in my beauty to have done such a thing as keep a book past its due date. Then *we* had a date." She touched his arm and grinned up at him.

"Amazing what book learning can achieve for someone, eh, Belinda?" He returned her grin and looked past her down the counter at the clerk coming toward them.

The clerk reported proudly, "I found birth certificates, tracing from the ledgers to the files, with the surname 'Volks' from the 1872 to 1892 in Kansas City area, as you asked. Three males and three females *in toto*. Would you like copies of all of them? That'll be $3.00."

"Yes, ma'am," Belinda said. She clutched Ken's arm in surprise at their luck.

"I'll have photostats made for you, if you'll fill out these forms. I can mail them if you're in a hurry." She spread six applications on the desk with Ken and Belinda each filling out three, using the names they copied from the files provided. Two daughters were born to Frieda and Christian Volks' son, Jost, whom they had already found out was Marlena's dad, Merrilee's grandpa. Jost's other daughter was Irene, who had not been mentioned by anyone.

No birth certificates appeared for the daughters' children because the information would have been filed under the father's name, even though the mother's maiden name would be on the document.

Two sons, Johann and Josef, had been born to Henrik and Helga Volks. Johann had a daughter they now noted was named Jacqueline. Because they had not asked for any later birth certificates under any other surnames, the Masseys assumed that Natalie (Tally) Schmidt Kilmer was an only child, given the lack of relatives at her funeral, except for her distant cousin, Merrilee.

"Okay. I have to make a chart. We're missing vitals on a son Josef and a daughter Irene. The documents could have shown any descendants' births to Josef, but not to next generation Irene because her kids would be under a husband's name," said Belinda. "Also, I think Merrilee would have known about an aunt, a sister of her mother's. Those two, too, may have died early, may be dead so we'd have to trace that information elsewhere."

"I'd bet Marlena would know what happened to Irene, her sister, even if she passed away at an early age," said Ken. He thought of another tack. If a child had been born outside of wedlock to Jacqueline Volks (Schmidt), it had to have been recorded under the Volks' name, although it takes two to tango. He looked over at the clerk. "Would you please check also to see if a Volk's baby was born around 1906-1908, without a father's name being on the file?"

The clerk looked astonished. "That'll take all day. I'll do that when I'm not busy if you'll leave your address. Oh ho, identifying a missing heir, I bet."

Ken nodded his head and emitted a snort. "Ho ho ho, yesss, a prodigal son," he hissed. He palmed a dollar bill to the clerk, who looked surprised, and then gratified, as she took it.

The clerk laughed with both of them. "While you're touring the city halls and statehouse, I'll find out some information you asked for on these forms."

The clerk returned to a distant area as Belinda looked at Ken and said, "Are we getting somewhere or are we getting somewhere? You realize that an orphan child to Jacqueline could have been born in France?"

"Don't get your hopes up: I'm not. Why, even these may not be the Volks-Jufellear twins' children, but some cousins. No, don't slug me: I'm teasing. These have to be our quarry.

We have found all children's names born to the tombstone couples that Holly and you had dug up in Kansas City."

"Sounds like a wild west story by Gary Cooper, Walter Brennan. Merrilee's the one that gave Walt and Meg that article to start with, I mean about her mother being related to the Kilmer lady from the crash."

"I know. I'm glad you talked with her Saturday. That put us way ahead of where we were with Meg's airy assumption about the orphaned vineyard Clarmonts. Of course, that may be a dead end that I originated. I just don't know whether I believe that Mrs. Shannon's gossipy mien." Ken had a thoughtful look on his face.

"And we'll drink a cup o kindness there, wherever they are, tomorrow afternoon at the vineyards. We've lucked into a swift end to our delving into records here." Belinda backed up and sat down on the long bench by the tiled wall.

Ken rested an elbow on the counter and half-turned his body to talk with her. "Are you tired?"

"A bit. That long phone call at the hotel from Mom while I had to take notes meant I didn't get back to sleep readily. First off, remember that she said that some cars in the alley had been tampered with and that a bullet hole showed up in our storeroom's window on the back. Then I thought about what she said about the orphans. I was thinking about the ramifications. Both a boy, Ted, aged about sixteen, and a girl, Barbara, aged about thirteen, escaped, or ran away, disappeared in 1916 from the orphanage records."

"Did you say a bullet hole appeared? What did you mean?"

"Ah, yes. I was talking about the orphans."

"When did that happen?"

"The bullet hole? Or the orphans running away"

"Yes, Belinda, the bullet hole."

"She sounded as though it happened last night," Belinda looked at him with curiosity in her eyes. "Why?"

"I suppose it was simply part of the pranks in the alley, soaping cars, maybe." Ken nodded to distract her, to reassure her.

Belinda continued her stream of thought. "No last names were attached to most orphans, although Mother hasn't traced any of their births, yet. No further information but she was pleased that what she found fit with our possibilities. The time of their disappearance was after the First World War so Mr. Clarmont wouldn't have been drafted then, and he was too young anyway. But no one knows if they ran away together. The dates were close together but not on the same day that each didn't show up for meals. Mom also cautioned me to remember the orphan trains from New York that let off kids to work, mostly on farms. These two may have been sent off to work in a factory or on a farm somewhere. Sounds like a plot for Horatio Alger, doesn't it? Poor urchins who end up being exemplary citizens. Except for their mischievous son."

Ken nodded and said, "People did start working hard earlier in life in those years. Well, the dates also fit a possible out-of-wedlock birth of a child or two. Maybe one is a Volks as the old woman Shannon I talked to last Wednesday hinted at––broadly hinted at. Meg really leaped on that hint, too."

"I liked that you heard that hint, given that nothing else of significance came out of your phone calls and visits," Belinda said.

Ken was not going to go there yet, that "nothing else of significance." He continued, "What I myself liked was how quickly your mom found the wineries listed in the telephone books over at Walt's office. And found the one where Mr. Clarmont works. If he's the boy, he may remember if he engineered an escape––or two––as a youngster from the orphanage. With Mother Holly quickly making an appointment for us with him tomorrow, she has created fantastic progress ahead for our data checks."

"As has a cooperating weatherman," teased Belinda.

Ken straightened as he saw, in the distance, the clerk coming up some stairs with a stack of files. The clerk had a smile on her face, greenish eyes crinkling as she approached. "I think someone at the immigration office misunderstood surnames when your German friends were emigrating. '*Volks*' translates from German merely as the word '*people.*' It's pronounced '*Folks,*' actually. But sometimes the entry clerk wrote down what he heard, and the emigrant didn't know enough English to correct the form to his real surname. And he was stuck with it."

"You are telling us that '*Volks*' really isn't a name?"

"Nope, but the emigrants simply went along with whatever their official entries spelled out. One tale my folks told was of a man who said, in broken English, 'sam t'ing' when his brother moved off, and he was then first in line. The clerk wrote down 'Sam King' as his name and that he was for evermore!"

"Weird."

The clerk explained further, "'*Jufellear*' means '*jeweler.*' That's just a little language lesson for you from my high school German class to your ears. People from about 800

A.D. were often identified by their occupations or residence. I doubt that ladies were jewelers, but their pa probably was."

"Good to know. Thanks for the information."

She continued, "Be interesting to know what the Volks' name really was back in the Rhineland. Hope it wasn't Goring or Schicklgruber."

They all laughed.

"They seemed to be of minor nobility. We're trying to trace their descendants, though, not the ancestry," Belinda said softly. "Yes, these are the ones we need." She handed the files to Ken.

The clerk said, "I found no fatherless children in the files. Maybe a bastard would be listed in a church file. I understand that tracing can also be difficult from people spelling their names differently at different times. Why don't you two go tour the Capitol building and grab a bite. I still have those three certificates to type up for you."

The Masseys agreed, donned their coats, and left for a peek inside the stately Capitol.

"Well, that's the first time I ever heard that "B" word in a business office. By a lady, too."

"The military inured me to words, lots of words, that you've never heard in a business setting. It may not be the last time, Belinda, so harden your sensibilities."

"Are you being an S. O. B.?" she asked.

He laughed. "Gotcha. Polite way to indicate same word."

He drove while Belinda looked at the houses and buildings along the street.

"Your mom was generous about staying home to supervise the domestics. She is good at supervising all of our activities," Ken remarked.

"On top of being the secretary to the principal of the high school most of the year, she had to help handle the migrant workers when the fruit and pumpkins and squash ripened in the fall. Dad had two tenant farmers who helped year round, and their wives helped in the fields and in the sales in the fall. But there were a myriad of details to handle with money, taxes, supplies, emergencies that fell to mom," Belinda said. "My brother Barney and I were not very interested, I'm afraid, in lending a helping hand."

"The farmland back there is beautiful with all those fruit and nut trees. I hope the developers of The Meadows save a lot of them."

"I'm going to be afraid to look at what has become of my parents' farm outside Granstadt," Belinda confessed. "Trees are usually unthinkingly decimated because homeowners aren't crazy about their droppings. Walnut trees drop such a terribly hard crop to glean. Nasty green pulpy outer skins that turn your hands black and sharp-edged shells inside. Hard shells that have to be cracked with a sledge hammer. Well, that was an exaggeration, but then the wood from the trees turns into lovely furniture or flooring. Bulldozers chew up too many trees, and they take years to replace. Rarely does a housing developer seem to realize that little point. Think how much we humans need shade in the summer and the smell of burning leaves in the fall."

"Uh-huh. Remind me to get a receipt for the cost of those birth certificates for our statement to Walt." Ken was not paying attention to her lament.

CHAPTER THIRTEEN

Statues and fountains representing Missouri history graced the main entrance on the south side of the Capitol. The steps, so many steps, up to the building erected from Carthage marble had been partially cleared of snow and ice. Engraved columns outlined the portico.

Few people were in evidence as they entered and stared at the rotunda's walls and up at the ceiling dome dozens of feet above them. Signs indicated that there was a Soldiers and Sailors Museum to the east and a Missouri Resources Museum to the west. The latter museum had Indian, mineral, and agricultural items on display. They wandered around in opposite directions studying the exhibits. The Indian pottery that had been retrieved as shards, vases, dishes, and pipes intrigued Belinda while Ken studied the projectile points, arrowheads, and axes from ancient times.

Murals depicting human progress started on this level and continued upward to the other floors. Belinda excused herself and found the lavatory on the lowest floor before climbing up two floors to rejoin Ken.

He was looking at the statues of Lewis and Clark along with more murals on the third floor.

Beautiful stained glass windows lighted the Senate chamber. In the west House lounge was the mural by Thomas Hart Benton that stirred up controversy because it had villains and productive workers, real and imaginary folk, all associated with Missouri: the James boys; some muscular men working; thus, a whole wall of lore. They moved closer to study it. Vibrant colors still resonated all these many years after it was painted. "Think one of 'em is Jesse James?" Belinda asked, pointing at the villains.

"Could be. He's rumored also to have lived around my old home. As also is a fellow from the gold rush who supposedly buried some 60,000 dollars of gold somewhere. We kids were always on the lookout for treasure. Do you know how your Jesse James finally met his end, after escaping the law all those years?"

"How?"

"Shot—by a friend."

"I suppose an outlaw's friends aren't always the most loyal sort."

"Indeed. It happened when Jesse James was hanging a picture in his living room."

"You're kidding," said Belinda. "I never heard that."

"Oh, yes. We used to act out train robberies when I was growing up. That is, we did that during the recess period at school. No one lived close enough to my house to play with. Just I and my brother were there. And we were always busy with farm work during the spring-summer-fall," Ken replied.

"Sounds like how I and my brother grew up, too, except we tried to avoid that work," Belinda said, walking around, admiring the wall displays. "This building is as gorgeous as that Methodist church we went to last Sunday. But, I am a bit hungry. Let's grab a bite, as that clerk suggested. Are there any real estate deeds we could find recorded here? I didn't think to check with Walt if those would be of use."

"Not so far as I know. I'm not sure why they'd be relevant, anyhow. These are offices for the legislature. Property deeds are filed in city and county offices, obituaries and wills in newspapers and courthouses, and wills in attorneys' offices, too. All of which for Kansas City, Missouri, are in Jackson County."

Seated back in the DeSoto, Ken showed Belinda a map he'd picked up on the way out of the Capitol. "Look. The Missouri River is over on that side of the Capitol, below a bluff. The gardens around this building are described a luxurious. Some day we'll have to return in good weather."

"We should go back to the hotel. Maybe eat at the cafeteria in there. It has the jukebox selections in a strange book on each table against the wall. I won't have to get up to poke in a nickel for each record. Also, I want a coke and onion rings like in high school."

"Are you sure you don't want to see the State Penitentiary or the National Cemetery first?" Ken looked over at her with a kidding look on his face.

"No, but I wouldn't mind taking a peek at the Lincoln University, the only one that always accepted colored students until this year, Mom told me. The first idea for it grew out of men from a colored infantry unit during the Civil War, one that fought for the north. People contributed money, and it was opened right after the war, I think. It was supposed to mirror the curriculum used at the University of Missouri in Columbia that enrolled white students. Now, all colleges in Missouri are open to all students. We're in a land of opportunity, for sure."

"We try to be, we try," Ken replied. "We keep learning how. Just have to show-me how or why or where or when."

At the hotel, Belinda and Ken both picked through their luggage and set items in the bathroom. Belinda brushed her teeth again. "I probably should wait until after we eat, but my mouth felt like garbage smells," she told Ken.

The hotel's cafeteria had just loaded the counters with fresh vegetables, few in number, and canned vegetables, many in number. Waitresses behind the counters served the meats and potatoes. Ken charged the meal to their room. He figured that would be a surer way to be reimbursed than merely stating what he had paid.

After an afternoon rest, the Masseys returned to the State Office building for their parcel of birth certificates. The same clerk greeted them cordially and had everything ready. Ken asked for an envelope to put them in, and she obligingly gave him one—free.

They discussed their next move, and because they had already seen or disliked the subjects of both movies offered at the local theaters, they returned to the hotel. Choosing to rest and rise early for the trip to Hermann, they watched television until they fell asleep. They settled on watching Arthur Godfrey's show: he played a mean ukulele and now and then introduced a fine, new singer.

"I need to call Walt to tell him on our progress," Ken remarked when a commercial came on.

"Maybe there's a phone in the lobby for long distance."

Ken walked downstairs to the phone booth. He put in a coin, and the operator gave him Long Distance. He requested a person-to-person collect call. Ken was thankful that Belinda would not hear what he was curious about.

"Walt. We've found the birth certificates of six Volks' descendants."

"Why call me collect to tell me that?"

"Sorry. What I really wanted to know was about Richie Kilmer's accident. Did you ask the police to look more closely at the car?"

"Oh. Yes. Heard from them and King again today. The car was way out in the salvage lot of car wrecks and covered with snow. An auto mechanic went over it carefully. It hadn't been examined since it was towed in, can you believe that? And, he found that all the brake fluid was gone. It had dripped from a pinhole, not from being crushed or otherwise damaged. I pushed the police to go into the background of Richie Kilmer. And his employer."

"I'd bet your old boss King won't like that. I consider that wreck's evidence that confirms my conclusion. Now, I'm on the Lincoln guy's list. My mother-in-law says that cars were damaged in the alley behind our building and that a bullet hole showed up in the window of our storeroom on that side. And then that blasted gun shot at us outside the Club."

"The police don't want anything stirred up, Ken. The rather feckless son of Mr. Lincoln maybe caused the bullet hole in your window and the cars being maimed in your alley. Probably at the behest of old man Shannon, his ultimate boss."

"I don't want anything happening to my family, hear me, Walt? I'm not going to put up with any shooting at my house nor in harming cars in the alley behind our building."

"Yes. I know what you mean. I'll see if I can square things. I have to go. Good-bye; safe driving. And, say," he whispered, "Remember that Marnie King listens so be careful in my office." The phone disconnected. Ken sat back with a bad feeling in his stomach.

He walked upstairs and confessed the events to his wife. She had to know. "Bel, I have to tell you about some things that I haven't yet, and emphasize that we are being targets." He ran down, in chronological order, repeating or enlarging on the pertinent threats: Shannons and Lincoln; gunshots at apartment window, Walt's house, and outside Club; possible damage to Kilmer's car.

Belinda argued, "You think that we are targets? That's an awfully swift conclusion—it doesn't make sense. I hadn't heard of a Lincoln guy's list. I hadn't heard of your being shot at. I know about the storage room window."

"You have not been at my side in KC. My being shot at doesn't make sense, I agree, unless it's a dicey kid like that cop, Phil Tyler, chased away from Walt's door." Ken paced back and forth.

"Who did what?"

"You heard me!"

"And why am I just now hearing about these threats?"

"Because, sweetie pie, we're halfway across the state, and bullets don't travel this far. King also told us, me and Walt and Meg, to keep things quiet, soothe our fears, and let us plead ignorance of the tensions there."

Belinda said stoutly, "I can't ignore anything now that we've and you've had an overt attack from a weapon. We have children, Kendrick Massey. And maybe the alley vandals were zeroing in on our car, but we have it in Jeff City with us. Our kids are back there! The renters are back there. We have to get home, and call the police!"

He shushed her as he walked to the bathroom. "Some changes are going to be added onto the security measures that Mother Holly has already instituted. Those people who lived in the upstairs apartments were too old to have to worry about at stray bullet or what to do in case of fire, and your mom told us many times about the safety procedures. She went over the procedures with the renters every six months; she gave them written copies of the procedures. She's pretty well thought of everything, Belinda. Be calm. Disasters just can't happen to prepared people."

Some added defense strategy would have to be legal. He tried to conjure up a tactic but everything he thought of was adapted from the military and not part of the civilian procedures. He couldn't scout, snipe, or sabotage. Briefly he remembered a joke about a truck that dropped a box of carpet tacks in a road. The car following swerved around the mess yet the driver was pulled over by a policeman. The Plymouth driver couldn't believe that he'd been given a ticket for 'tacks evasion.' Okay, maybe he wasn't thinking straight, having been through so many records today, but he wasn't ready for sleep, was too much on edge.

After splashing water on his face and scrubbing it dry, he returned to the living room, he shook Belinda's shoulder where she had already fallen asleep on the couch in front of the TV. "Why don't we go for a walk and work off some of our tension, honey?"

"I'm on. I've been unable to do anything except see over and over odd numbers and names on the backs of my eyelids. The TV shows are all about holiday things. Most of the TV movies I've seen before. In fact, I'd really like to run a little if we could find a clean sidewalk."

"I'll ask the desk clerk."

"Good thinking, Ken. I'm going to put on my plaid wool pants suit that breathes better than this rose cotton corduroy outfit. Besides, I've had it on all day, and it's ready to be cleaned from the slight odor I'm picking up. I must have touched something rotten today."

Ken almost said aloud that he, too, had touched something rotten. But, as yet, he had not decided if he had to emphasize further the dangerous aspects of their inadvertent involvement in a side problem that was potentially lethal. How could he have ever imagined that interviewing those pallbearers would create an unintended sideshow?

While Belinda changed into her suit and boots, he put on a clean undershirt, a dress shirt without the top button fastened, and a sweater of a weird yellow color. His trousers he had worn for two days but felt as though they would still move well if he ran in them; that is, they weren't very wrinkled nor did they sag much. His topcoat he would leave in the car.

Downstairs, the clerk suggested that they drive over by the Capitol where so many people went in and out and around. They could run up and down the stone stairs, if no sidewalk appeared safe, because the steps were cleaned daily and might have sand on them.

The car was cold at first, but they scarcely noticed it, so eagerly were they looking forward to some exercise. Both the sidewalks and the stairs appeared free of ice or snow, allowing for a reasonable amount of physical effort. They followed their separate workout routines, and, nicely winded, each arrived back at the car about forty-five minutes later. Now, they wouldn't much notice how cold the car was because the seats would be soft on their stretched muscles and joints.

"Now, I can sleep. Thanks for thinking of this, Ken Massey. It was a wonderful workout in the heart of Missouri in the middle of the city at the end of the day. To put it succinctly." Belinda patted her husband's back as he opened the door to let her climb in the passenger seat.

CHAPTER FOURTEEN

Mr. Clarmont, dressed in brown tweed suit and blue tie, stood as his secretary opened the door to his office to the visitors. "Come right in, Mr. er, Massey."

Ken indicated his wife, "This is my wife, Belinda Massey."

"Glad to have you. You carry yourself like a soldier." The men shook hands.

"Yes, sir. I was an AP in the Air Force until a few months ago."

"I noticed your ring. Myself, I was in the Army, a sergeant in the *Europeeing* Theater. Seems much closer than ten years ago, but then it took me a while to adjust afterwards to civilian life and its surprises," he said, a wry tone that puzzled Ken briefly. Then, he remembered the tales about the Clarmont's son.

"Thank you for seeing us today." Ken had noticed that the room needed painting, the walls being a dingy white color. Simple tan shades were rolled up on the windows, but the furniture looked new or refinished. He sat in a comfortable wood chair next to Belinda's.

"Are you going to be purchasing wine from us? We're gradually getting the vines growing into fertile stages. I suppose you know the area has been suffering since Prohibition laws stopped any legal alcohol production and so no money was available to bring back the grape vines. We're confident we can bring back the earlier reputation for fine wines. It's slow but gratifying to be a part of it. We like to make early contacts with people from other towns."

"Oh, no. I'm guessing I didn't make myself clear to your secretary. We wanted to talk about something that happened a while back. We have an investigative agency in Kansas City." He handed over a business card.

Mr. Clarmont stood so suddenly that his chair rocketed back against the white plaster wall, knocking some flakes to the floor. "If you're newspaper or scandal mongers, you get out before I toss you out by the seat of your pants. And I mean both of you."

Belinda leaned forward and said softly, "We're merely seeking historical data about your ancestors."

"I don't care. I'm not having anything to do with publicity hounds. I've been hounded enough. I hate newspapers and newscasters and magazine editors and pulp writers and true crime digests. It's sickening how they keep coming on. Only our Raumville paper paid little attention, I guess because the events were hushed up."

"No, sir. Excuse me, sir. I want to hand you a birth certificate and ask you about an orphanage in Kansas City." Belinda stood and placed a photo static copy of Jacqueline Volks' birth on his desk. "Do you know your wife's maiden name? Or where she was born?"

"Why? I have nothing whatsoever to say. I am not interested. I demand that you leave me alone. NOW."

Belinda, leaning forward, waving her hands as if placating him, said, "Sir? An art gallery in Kansas City is trying to trace any claimants on a cache of jewels that were brought from Europe in the mid-1800s. We are trying to see if you or your wife were related to the family."

"Just leave." He got up and walked to the door. "Our name has been tarnished enough. We're important here. It's calm here. We want no publicity about anything."

"Please, Mr. Clarmont. We want to know about your wife at least."

He whirled around and glared at her. "She's dead. Is that enough information? Get out."

Belinda said calmly, "I'm so sorry. We didn't know that. But, it's the birth certificate of a female we wanted you to see if she's perhaps related to the family jewels or you guys."

Ken coughed into his hand after Belinda spoke, stifling a laugh.

"Ma'am, you are so persistent. Barbara died right after we moved here so the effort you're making is worth nothing."

"But you do have children?"

He bulked up his shoulders and strode to his chair. "Six daughters, four grandchildren, and one wayward son, as you've probably found out to hassle me about."

"No. That extensive a family was unknown to us. Please see if the birth certificate could be your wife's relative, if not yours," Belinda said again.

Clarmont put his head in his hands after he pulled the desk chair back into place and plunked down in it. He muttered, "We had only had an outhouse on our farm south of Raumville. Here we moved into a modern two-bedroom house. Barbara was so thrilled with the accommodations. She kept everything sparkly clean. One day she was cleaning the toilet with ammonia and bleach, and the fumes killed her. Like mustard gas in the Great War."

The room became silent. Only a faint whisper of an occasional breeze against the window broke the stillness. The Masseys looked at each other. Ken sent her a questioning look. She placed her fingers against her lips and sat back. The silence settled like a pall.

Clarmont shuddered and rose, this time to walk to the window and lean on the sill, staring out at the rows of twisted brown vines that they had passed on the way here from Jefferson City. After several minutes, he wiped some dust from the sill with his forefinger, turned, and spoke to both of them, looking from face to face. "If you promise no publicity, no gossip about the lady I loved, I'll listen. You seem intelligent enough to understand."

Ken avowed, "I promise, sir. The information goes only from us to an attorney. We ourselves would not survive with our investigation agency if we broke the confidence that people placed in us."

Ted Clarmont wiped some moisture from his face and walked over to pick up the certificate. "Barbara and I were placed in a Catholic orphanage shortly after we were born. We had very little schooling and had to work for various people in different jobs. We grew tired of it. I was a bit older and bigger."

"Did you know your surnames?"

"We were 'awarded' names."

"Didn't know your parents'?"

"No. Not at all. We never asked exactly when we were born or where we came from. I doubt that we would have been told. Let me look at this paper a second." He continued musing as he studied the certificate, "We ran away about

1920, tired of being slaves to uncaring people and figuring we could make it on our own. And, we did right well."

Clarmont sat down with his back and shoulders straight and studied the document more carefully. "All right, this could be a mother Volks to Barbara, because she was old enough to have a child--but I never heard a last name for Barbara or me. Volks is a weird name. I have no idea how you'd ever prove it. But, hear this. I want none of this to leak out. I want nothing to do with confiscated jewels. I heard about the artwork that the Nazis stole while I was fighting for my life in Europe, and I'm never going to do something like that. I'm no thief taking advantage. If I need to sign off, refuting any claim, I will be your guest. My daughters do not need anything that interrupts their lives and gets us back into the public eye. We're happy here."

"Would you have a photograph of Mrs. Clarmont or even several of her through the years? That we could borrow? We'll return them," Belinda Massey promised softly.

"Why ever for? We had no money to waste on film."

"We could compare her facial features with those of a few other women in the family tree."

"This is getting personal," he growled.

"Sir. Believe me. We'll return the photos quickly. And, if she had a drivers license--"

"She couldn't read, write, or drive," he said abruptly. "She was, however, a wonderful lady. Deeply caring. Beautiful. I still think of her at odd times."

"Yes, sir. I was thinking of the color of her eyes, hair, her height, weight," Belinda explained calmly. "For example, was she my height?"

"Oh, no. She came to my shoulder. Dark hair, beautiful

black. Brown eyes that could actually twinkle, long eyelashes, firm jaw that stayed firm even as we grew older. She died in 1946, October 21st. We were friends as well as parents. We laughed and grew up together. I miss her so."

The room fell silent.

"Any photos?" Belinda persisted. Ken approved of her taking the lead in this interview, having noticed that Mr. Clarmont seemed less belligerent to her than in replying to him.

"I'll call my daughter Laura over at the big house. She keeps all that stuff. I don't want to hear from you again. You return any photos to her quickly, or you'll hear from me in an unpleasant manner. Leave your calling cards with Laura, too."

He called to his secretary to get Laura on the phone. The Masseys sat comfortably in their chairs and waited. He sat slumped over.

He answered the phone before the first ring ended and barked, "Laura. Some people are here. I'm not going to say any more because they'll tell you. Find those two scrapbooks, please and have them handy. I'll call later."

Clarmont waved them toward the door.

Ken turned and said, "Sir, did your wife have a will?"

"Great Jumping Jehosophat, leave me a will? She wasn't even forty. So, no, she didn't." He looked at them with as much disgust as Gary Cooper had shown at the end of *High Noon* while dropping his gun into the street.

Ken shut the door softly after they moved into the waiting room. The secretary handed them each a bottle of wine, to their surprise, and pointed north to the road on the outskirts of the parking lot. "Two miles that way to the manor house," she said. "Bye now. Drive carefully."

As soon as Ken sat in the driver's seat and started the engine, Belinda asked, "Why did you want to know about a will? You sounded merciless. You hurt his feelings."

"I'll have to check with Walt, but if his wife was a Volks and didn't leave him her estate, then any children she had are all heirs, not Mr. Clarmont."

"Oh, dear me, what a mess. We didn't get their names."

"I know. We'll maybe have a better reception from the daughter, Laura. I didn't want to press him because of his emotions, his turmoil close to the surface, capable of crippling a creative hard working man, and we had caused the problem."

"What emotions?"

"First, he mentioned battle fatigue after the war ended, and that can creep up many years later and catch a guy by his brain and nightmares. Next, he had the shock of a son being jailed, hurting his reputation, as well as bad karma for other members of the family. That catches a man by his ego and integrity. Followed by his wife dying suddenly injuring his heart. Capped by disgust at our bringing it all to the fore."

"I'm regretting our interview." She became thoughtful as they pulled into a gravel road. Broad acres of whipped cream snow lay flat in the fields with straight ripples of brown twined vines running in narrow rows from edge to edge.

After silently reviewing the events so far, Belinda Massey said, "I was thinking about the Volks daughter—Jacqueline-who-became-Schmidt. Remember that Schmidt woman who drowned or some such a few years ago in my hometown of Granstadt?"

"Of course. We guessed that perhaps the fake fellow, who pretended to be our Air Force pilot Haswell, had pushed her into the river."

"What if Mr. Schmidt, the husband and train engineer, is related to Mrs. Jacqueline Schmidt?"

Kendrick Massey mused, "Wouldn't matter. Schmidts don't matter. Schmidts have nothing to do with the inheritance except some Schmidt fellow married Jacqueline. He's not a female who descended from the Volks. He'd have to have been in Jacqueline's will, and the reason that I doubt that occurred was because she had placed the jewels in the art museum, not in his vault. Same problem as the Clarmont descendants. And, I have a feeling there is no Volks/Jufellear connection to them, and we're simply having a pleasant tour of Missouri."

"Oh. Yes. You're correct. I just had another thought. Schmidt might be a shirttail cousin for Mr. Clarmont, from his generation, who could commiserate with him, both having lost their wives."

"Belinda, make sense. You're way off the track."

Belinda ignored his admonition. "And, I was thinking of that Schmidt icon we recovered from the antique store that had jewels around the frame."

"That was more than likely from the tsar's country: Russia. It was an Orthodox saint, I believe, from the outfit it was wearing."

Belinda sighed. "Well, dear, it had jewels on it. I thought for a minute that maybe my old friend Rosie Schmidt might be an heiress of the jewelry. I miss our friends back home."

"Sorry." Actually he couldn't imagine why Rosie should be the heiress. She was the youngest of the Schmidt girls, and dibbies should go to the oldest in their father's will. "I myself wonder why we have been assuming that the twins were the original owners of the jewels?"

"Because they are twin girls! Men wouldn't wear those gems."

"Humph. Think of all the royal families in Europe and Asia: portraits all have the men sporting lovely jewels." Ken gave her a lofty look with his eyebrows high on his forehead, eyebrows not quite able to reach the receding hairline.

"Anyway, granted that that is so, we've been told to focus on the twin Jufellear girls and their descendants."

"Yep."

Belinda sighed and smiled. "I loved it that our first case was for Rosie's father, not only for the icon recovery. That poor man who seemed heartbroken that his daughter had run off to New York. Then, because I knew her sisters, we found out that she had actually run down the highway to Kansas City and was working her way through college with a little help from her sisters. They could help because each had been given an allowance from their husbands. Rosie was determined to prove that she was smarter than her pampered brother John. And do college herself without help from her father. Now, of course, Mr. Schmidt's helping with money for tuition and books. Her sisters don't have to help anymore. And, she told us where she had pawned the icon of the saint. We paid for it, sent it back, and received a bonus on our bill for marvelously good work."

"We're lucky the icon was still at that old antique pawn shop."

Belinda said, "And then there's a peacock shoehorn that a teenager stole from the local lawyer's office during the same month. It could be part of a strange set of foreign stuff."

"Belinda! Stop your connecting this case with people's property in your hometown. All we're engaged to do is to find the relatives of Mrs. Natalie Kilmer and to determine that the museum gets the title for ownership of the jewelry."

"All right, be stuffy. I want some little mysterious happenings in this investigation. The others we've had so far have been too routine for amusement. Wait! Here. Pull over. I think that stately big stone house must be where we're to meet up with Laura Clarmont whatshername. You know what? I just realized that all seven of those orphans' descendants are also going to have to abstain from lodging claims against the jewels if their mother was a Volks orphan. Should Laura have to tell us names of her sisters or brothers?"

"We'll have to ask her for them. I can't understand why Mr. Clarmont didn't say much word about his son. Didn't you hear somewhere that the boy had been in some kind of trouble?"

"Jail. Don't recall why he ended up there. Maybe Laura'll tell us about it."

CHAPTER FIFTEEN

A maid in a white cap and apron over a dark blue dress––Belinda nudged Ken, whispering, "Can you believe that outfit?"––opened the door, held out a tray, and said, "Your calling cards, sir?" Ken put his and Belinda's business cards on the tray, and they followed her to a living room. The room had wood on the lower half of the walls and stonework carved into flowers and vines above. Two fireplaces were going, and Ken noticed a furnace vent at the bottom of the two walls he was facing. The room smelled of fermentation, ash, soot, and must.

Shortly after the maid left, a lady, dark hair tied back, about age 30, came striding into the room carrying a tray with glasses of tea and ice cubes. She put the tray on the coffee table, sat down, and pointed at the love seat. A command to sit.

The hostess was wearing a jacket and pleated skirt of red and black checks, hose and low-heeled shoes. Ken would bet that she no longer was aware of the odor in the house any more than she noticed the freckles on her long nose. He'd also bet that he would feel static electricity in the dry air the minute he touched something metal. And that she was asking to feel such a spark, wearing wool in the dry air.

"Just what is it you want?" She sounded haughty. "My father didn't say much about why you wanted pictures of my mother. She died years ago right after I moved here. Our scrapbooks are somewhere down in the basement in a trunk. We've been too busy to dig them out."

She handed over glasses of tea with a paper napkin wrapped around each one. Laura continued explaining in jerky sentences. "Mother had little time to become acquainted with the history of this Rhineland area of Missouri. This area was famous for its viticulture until the Prohibition era. My husband's family years ago first had to turn the vineyards into cotton fields because of Prohibition, and my family worked as share croppers raising cotton until lately."

"Ah, that's nice." Ken was surprised to realize that the grapes' fermenting had left an odor from twenty years ago before Prohibition shut down the wine making.

"My father, father-in-law, husband, and brother-in-law Gary Greene have been working hard to refurbish the equipment in the winery. Now we've begun cultivating the grape vines from small plantings my father-in-law kept nurturing through the past quarter century. This house is built over a vaulted wine cellar that I can take you on a tour of. Now, what else do you want to know? My mother, as I've said, had nothing to do with the winery."

"It's not the winery we're seeking to discover information about. We're trying to determine if she is a descendant of a family that came from Germany in the mid 1800s." Ken sat forward and put his glass back on the table. Laura immediately picked it up and placed it on the tray. Ken noted her tan, decided she must work in the vineyards herself.

"Whatever for?"

"Your father said that he would tell you about us.

The maid gave you our cards. See, we're working with an attorney about descendants of a German family. If we have your mother's pictures to compare with those of other old pictures of female members, we may be able to answer that question for you."

"Some ten years ago I took two pictures outside our house here on the Fourth of July when the family was visiting. Our dad's a veteran of the Second World War. Maybe I can dig up the negatives, but I fail to see how that will help. Mother was an orphan. My dad and she escaped to the Ozarks when they were young and started a small farm. He went to war and sent us money. Neither one ever told us anything about where their families were from. I doubt if they knew. It seems presumptuous of you to be inquiring about her. All the way from Kansas City, Dad said. I am talking to you only because Dad called after you left and said you were not making news but promised discretion about the family members."

"Correct. We're not from the news media," Belinda assured her.

"We absolutely forbid anything getting into the news. We've worked hard to maintain our good reputation that my brother sullied once. Our family no longer recognizes him. But, I suppose that's not news to you."

"Please, ma'am, we are not interested in him, I swear. We just want to try to trace your mother's origins."

"None of us know. I told you exactly where the information leads and ends: to my father and mother. Period."

"Do you have any sisters?" Belinda asked.

"Five of them, why?"

Belinda gasped because she had not paid attention to Mr. Clarmont's mention of six daughters.

Ken leaned forward again. He asked politely, "May we have the addresses of your brother and sisters. As well as your husband's name?"

"Whatever for?"

"The reason we're after information is because some ancient jewels were loaned to a museum by a family now passed over. The museum is trying to settle any claims that might be made. Any heirs would be asked to cede claims."

"Seed claims? Why would a museum want to start a crop of something? You're confusing me."

"Not 's-e-e-d,' but 'c-e-d-e.' Give up title to."

"I see." Laura sat back in her chair.

The room became quiet. Ken waited with a kindly look of inquiry on his face. Both sleuths were used to waiting, from former occupations as librarian and Air Policeman, to waiting, to waiting quietly.

"I'll call Dad and ask what he thinks. He didn't sound too happy with your visit earlier. And, hear me clearly; he does not know that I have my brother's address in St. Charles where he sleeps when he's not performing on a tourist ship sailing up and down the Mississippi. Dad disowned him for ruining the family's reputation."

"We promise discretion."

Laura left the room, and they could hear murmuring from a room down the hall, probably a study.

A man walked in the front door. "Well, I'm John Helsinger. Are you friends of Laura's?"

Both Masseys stood, introduced themselves, shook hands, and sat again. "We're here trying to clear some information about ancestors and descendants of Laura's parents," answered Ken.

"Don't think you'll have much luck with ancestors. They were both orphans."

"Exactly."

"Where is she?"

"She wanted to check with her dad before providing addresses of her sisters," Belinda replied.

Laura returned just as that remark was made and said, "He was leery but approved. He's going to call my sisters about this and tell them to refuse anything that would be of note to the newsmen. This is the list." She handed a folded sheet to Ken with a warning look he figured meant to convey silence on his part about the brother. "My sister, Ima Jean, is frail and lives with Pa. She takes care of his house."

"Are all of you children 18 years of age or older?"

"Yes. Of course." Her nose, centered in a flat face, was narrow at the bridge and wide at the nostrils, nostrils that now flared. "I will try to find the negatives and send you copies of the pictures. When I have time."

He gave a slight nod and thanked her. Both made their thanks and left, taking highway 19 south to Highway 66, then drove west toward Devil's Elbow. "We have a coupla-three hours' driving to my folks'. If I become tired, you'll need to drive. The 66 route was originally called the Wire Road and followed the trails of early travelers. I think the ridges giving way to sloping acreage are beautiful in any season--except winter. I never know when a little river is going to make a bridge unsafe to drive across because of the ice that accumulates on top," Ken said.

"Remember back when Donna and Phil Tyler were in

charge of a Santa Fey Schooner in the Christmas parade? It was cute. Too bad the boys had to keep rehitching it to the car. They should have used wire or a chain. Dad found a place in a carriage house to construct part of it because he and Mom were negotiating to sell our farm and barns.

"No, I didn't go to the parade."

"An odd float won that year that featured girls dressed as dolls under a Christmas tree. It was odd it won, I thought, because the dolls didn't move while our Santa Fey group kept up a running pageant, including us elves tossing candy." Belinda spoke quietly as though picturing the parade going by.

Ken grunted because he had nothing to add, having not seen the float; having been on duty when the parade occurred; and, having little knowledge of the local families and children involved. Unless the kids presented a challenge to his duties as an Air Policeman at the Base. If that happened, he became acquainted, very well acquainted, with the families and children.

"Good thing we both clicked on Mom's idea of becoming sleuths. I enjoyed tracing down overdue books," Belinda revealed. "Useful for what I do now for our business keeping books and such."

Belinda opened the list of Laura Clarmont Helsinger's siblings when they were several miles down the highway. "I liked that Pendleton outfit she was wearing. Probably has to wear wool all the time in that cold stone house. Shouldn't we go to St. Charles to see this brother Teddie? The sisters live all over the state, from what I know of the towns."

"No. That's way east of here. The family doesn't want us to contact him, and we'll honor that given our current knowledge. We can write or call, if we need to. We'd need a lot more monetary commitment from Walt before we'd interview anyone that far away in person." Ken flicked away the idea with his left hand.

"I'd like to see where the Missouri River meets the Mississippi River. The Siouxians named the tribe here 'Missouria,' meaning 'big canoe people,' and thus, the Missouri River is 'big canoe river.' Maybe I could surfboard it like that Doris Duke who inherited all that Lucky Strike money."

"I'd like to see you surfing with all that money behind you. Flying down the heavy waves. Lewis and Clark and the fur traders found that was somewhat difficult. Strong current to navigate against but very nice to float down with."

"I could do it if I knew how. You know," she became thoughtful, "I don't remember where the word Mississippi, 'big muddy translation' came from."

"I don't either, except that's what it looks like, silly girl. Muddy." Ken was silent before he began, somewhat apologetically, to explain his boyhood home. "At home, we have a creek that freezes in winter. No surfing there. Where my folks live is in a house much older than your farmhouse was, Belinda. The drive and lawn will be muddy right now from all the moisture, or maybe icy. It's a big, drafty old wood house, fireplaces in every major room. They added indoor toilets only six years ago 'cause Mom is having trouble walking. I remember when electricity came to the farm. We had wires installed in three rooms. Dad put lamps or chandeliers everywhere, and we stuffed the kerosene lanterns in the barn. Maybe they've added a furnace so that dad doesn't have to chop wood anymore.

"Darling, that's exactly what we went through about ten years ago. Rural electricity was not high on patriots' lists during the wartime need for armaments. We rose at dawn and went to sleep at dark. I'll be quite at home. Don't worry. I'm looking forward to seeing where the logs jammed the devil's elbow."

Although darkness had fallen an hour before they drove up a rutted driveway, Ken continued on to the barn; he exited the car to raise the barn door to let Belinda park inside. Lights were on all over the house, and the warmth enveloped them both from his parents' arms and from the fireplaces.

"What is that bathtub for out in the yard?" Belinda asked Ken quietly.

"My mom grows herbs in it, dries them, and sells them at fairs for a pretty penny."

"Maybe she'll give me some mint, you think?"

"Sure. Mom," he said, "Belinda was wondering if you have any extra mint around."

"Of course, dear. I'll get it as soon as I dish up this goulash."

While Ken's mother set out a late supper for them, the new arrivals settled onto an old horsehide sofa, sagging at the end with a telephone on the end table. Interesting old party line hookup.

Ken noticed Belinda eying the cobwebs in the exposed maple beam ceiling. He watched her eyes settle on four items handing from the beam near them.

"On the first nail," Ken said, "is a gold-plated pocket watch that belonged to my grandpa. He sold sewing materials and clocks and watches from farm to farm. Was a peddler. The next nail has a metal spur dangling from it. My dad toured the rodeo circuit in the fall and won some cash. The third item is a Purple Heart that my brother won. Lew's eleven years older than I, worked in the Civilian Conservation Corps nearby in the Mark Twain Forest. Served in Europe. The fourth red item was not likely to make me money. Was my attempt to make a pincushion for my mother at Four-H camp. The reason she couldn't use it is that I filled it with clay, clay that made the needles greasy and soon became so hardened that she couldn't stick pins into it. I told her maybe she could bop a burglar with it."

"What great stories. We'll have to bring J. B. and Alberta here soon."

Belinda went to help in the kitchen while Ken brought in several logs that he stacked near the fireplace. The two couples visited long into the night after a great roast chicken supper with candied yams and also cranberries in a Jell-O mold. The meal wasn't *goulash* by any definition.

After supper, Ken took Belinda on a tour of the house. In his old bedroom, some animal skins were hanging on the wall. He told her how he had shot two raccoons, and his dad showed him how to skin them, as he now patted a stiff-haired pelt. But, he revealed, his mother had canned the meat and used it in mincemeat pie, which he hated. Knowing that the meat that was minced was coon meat was worthy of distaste.

At his brother's old room, Ken recounted some tricks he'd played on his brother, Lew, such as sticking a lump of clay in the bed pillow and replacing the Old Spice after-shave with his mother's Avon cologne. All he would reveal about retaliation was that both his brother and mother

173

were mad at him for the switcheroo of the liquids. And his brother did get back at him.

Ken remarked, "I'll know what symptoms of intrigue are brewing when J. B. is thinking of teasing Alberta. I'll subtly direct him to less dangerous things than we did."

"What you just told me, with those two tricks you played, doesn't sound dangerous." Belinda started down the dimly lit hallway. She glanced at him over her shoulder.

"I didn't tell you everything because some things we did were really dangerous. At the time, we thought they were funny, using fireworks and likewise ipecac. Don't ask, because I won't describe the stunts."

Belinda said solemnly, "My brother and I were perfect angels in contrast to you and yours. We would never contemplate jerking around the other one at any time, place, or merest opportunity."

"Uh huh, uh huh." Ken poked her back. "I would not bet a wooden nickel on that tale. Shall I interview Barnard Jones concerning this matter, investigate the truthfulness of the witness's statement? Or, perhaps the witness would care to revise her recall of events?"

"No. Quit poking my back. Barney and I will get together and reveal all. Some day." Maybe talk about the clever usages of persimmons.

After peeking into a small room with a treadle sewing machine, Ken said he was going to order his mother an electric Singer from Sears to be delivered for Christmas. He also wondered aloud if it were possible that a chain saw had been invented that was not too heavy for his father. His parents still used a lot of logs. He could tell Belinda was agreeable by her constant pressing of his arm, never interrupting his narrative, and looking at him with small, pleased grins twitching the corners of her mouth.

They returned downstairs to some hot hard cider in thick white ceramic cups and a plate of decorated sugar cookies. His mother caught Ken up on all his former classmates, and his father revealed the status of the neighbors' farms and their produce. His brother would be home for Christmas with his teen-age children. All the old toys had been packaged for the Masseys to take to J. B. and Alberta.

His parents could sleep late the next day and were reluctant to end the conversation, but the younger Masseys finally made their excuses about needing an early start toward Raumville. And collapsed into Ken's boyhood bed. Mattress filled with rustling corn shucks--confusing their ears, and pillows stuffed with chicken feathers needling through the muslin pillow covers--pricking their ears.

"This has been a wonderful experience, Ken," Belinda said, returning upstairs to the bedroom after brushing her teeth and washing her face. The one bathroom was by the kitchen, downstairs. "I think the varied skills you developed growing up are somehow eminently suited to your Air Force police and investigative career."

"Could be. With all the animal tracking, including being quiet and stealthy and sighting the slightest movement or animal dropping or broken twig or trampled grass, I did learn things. I never had put that together before. Thank you for your observation. It makes me proud of growing up here. We never felt poor although money was not falling out of the sky. My parents taught me so much about enjoying life, too, that I can never thank them enough." Ken threw himself on the bed and put his arms behind his head, scanning the animal skins hanging across the room on the far wall. "Our kids will enjoy the old toys as they grow older and use them in turn."

"And we'll enjoy the mint and canned goods. I'm going to put one sprig of mint in front of the car radiator to scent the interior."

CHAPTER SIXTEEN

"Come in, come in. I hoped it might be you." She had first cupped her hand against the window in the door but the frosted lines had obviously obscured their faces under the porch light. Mrs. Harver, *nee* Marlena Volks, opened the door carefully against the splatter of snow.

"I'm Belinda Massey, and this is my husband, Ken." Brushing snowflakes from her face, Belinda started stripping off her winter coat and boots in order to place them on the pegs in the foyer.

"I have hot coffee, tea, or cocoa for you. Even if you stopped by the motel first, I knew you'd get chilled."

"That's really thoughtful of you, Mrs. Harver."

"Call me Marlena," she said and ushered them into sit on the dark blue living room suite, a log fire burning away in the fireplace. She trotted to the kitchen to bring back three pots and three cups on a tray. "From your left to right, the liquids are coffee, cocoa, tea. Help yourself to the cookies, too."

The three chose their refreshments, sampling them in between bites of a gingerbread cookie, sinking into the warmth of the liquid and the soft cushions, taking time to glance around the room and observe each other.

Marlena said, "I'll bet you have a picture or two you

want to compare with my visage or for me to identify, given what Merrilee has told me."

Ken laughed. "Yes, ma'am, and she told us you wouldn't mind. But we don't have the pictures with us. We would appreciate having copies of pictures of you about age 30, maybe 40."

"I'll dig out scrapbooks. One of the things Merrilee didn't know was that Natalie Kilmer and her husband Richie, were on the way to see me. They had a new Lincoln convertible and were sailing along Highway 7 going from highway 71 to turn south on 13 at Clinton. Something happened when they went around a curve that made them keep sailing straight into the ditch alongside the road. They both died."

"We hadn't read the police report, so didn't know the exact circumstances of the wreck. Very little description was given in the newspaper article."

Marlena described the problem. "That highway sits high above a ditch, like the way a railroad track is built high above the surrounding ground. Tell me what's suspicious about these two things: a) new car, b) brakes fail suddenly? C'mon. I know Richie Kilmer was a crook on the shady side of the law. I think an enemy got to him, and Natalie was a casualty."

"I never saw that in the news story about the brakes," Belinda said, omitting that she'd heard about it from Ken yesterday, taking a sip that finished off her first cup of cocoa and helping herself to a second fill up.

"I did hear something alluding to that," Ken said softly. He hadn't told anyone that every time he went to the garage, even before he'd heard about the result of the wreckage examination, he had looked under his DeSoto for a brake fluid leak, that every time he pulled up, exited, and stopped the car, he had looked under it, while ostensibly tying a shoe lace, for a brake fluid leak. He had clearly heard the threat from his interview with the second pallbearer and Walt and gunshots and King's raging at them when they were tipsily inventing a news story.

Belinda and Mother Holly had not tumbled to his tactic of retrieving something from the car whenever they were going to take the car––he had managed to put the item on the garage floor and had bent down to check under the car. He was glad that he and Belinda had left town this week.

Ken glanced at Marlena. He nodded. "I understand what you're describing about the car sailing off the road."

"Something else Merrilee didn't know. She dreamed up the story about the twin girls owning jewels to play with because I said something like that to her and her sister when they were little and playing with my make-up."

"Dreamed up how?" Belinda asked sleepily.

"What you're doing is unnecessary; there's no twin girls' jewelry involved. Evidently I should have told them more. My uncle Henrik owned the jewelry hoard, not the girls. He worked for their father in Austria. The girls' father was a jeweler. Sometimes Henrik took his pay in some gems, but mostly he collected old antique items, artifacts, from people there in Vienna. Have you seen them?"

Ken responded, "I did see a strange list from the museum that I didn't much understand."

"Austria and Italy were destinations of people who traveled to the Far East and returned with bounty. That is what was termed jewelry in the appraisal that my cousin

Jacqueline had made. But the stuff isn't all gems, not pins, bracelets, necklaces."

Belinda was not sure what Marlena was saying. "I don't understand."

"Is a feathered cap a jewel? Come on; maybe to an antique dealer!!"

"They're parts of costumes?"

"Not costume jewelry as we know it, but accoutrements: things ladies wore to dress up their ball gowns. Faience beads, feather hair pieces, combs, shells."

Ken exclaimed, "The military calls our battle accessories 'accoutrements!' And, Walt had told me that part of the history.'"

"Well, I never. I needed to see that list, Ken. Where is it?" Belinda shook her head.

"I'm so sorry that I forgot to show you, Belinda. It's at home. We can even petition to go look at the stuff at the art museum, if you want."

"All right. All right." She closed her eyes briefly and then opened them.

Marlena said softly, glancing at Belinda's sleepy face, "My Merrilee knew only that Natalie Kilmer had given me a semiprecious pin. She blew everything up over that, as though we were even descendants from Henrik!! But this makes me feel elated to have you here concerning my ancestors. Before the Kilmers started over here before their wreck, my very own second cousin once removed Natalie sent me a box of family letters, pictures, certificates from Sunday School baptisms that I had never seen before. I hadn't bothered to open the box, after she never arrived, until you called. It was like opening a treasure chest."

"That's wonderful," Belinda said. "That sounds like an unexpected bonanza to add to the formal data that we have obtained so far."

"I put the stuff in stacks on the dining room table. It's not a library full of items, but different things that seem relevant to your pursuit." She finished her tea, placed the cup in the saucer, and stood to lead the way.

Ken and Belinda flanked Marlena on one side of the table. Ken picked up a Purple Heart and certificate of award for valor from the Great War. Belinda bent to sort a stack of pictures. Marlena had placed an embroidered stole aside on a chair, picked it up, and modeled it for them.

"If you're tracing descendants of the Volks to ascertain ownership of jewels that they brought from Europe, you should be aware that I'm keeping this brooch that Natalie sent me years ago. I've carried out the Homestead Act requirements, those that outlined squatters' rights to ownership, on it." Marlena laughed, touching the pin on her shoulder. It looked like ivory with some kind of yellow-orange beads imbedded, or pasted on, to form a flower. "You know that her mother and I played dress-up with the so-called jewelry and some old heavy brocade dresses in the attic of the big old house. The families of both brothers and their wives––who were twins––lived in the mansion."

Belinda yawned and hid her mouth with her hand. "Sorry. We've had a long weary day, winding on windy roads yesterday and then today all the way from Ken's folks. See how tired I am? I sound giddy. May we come back in the morning?" She glanced at the varied items of material.

"Of course, dear. Come for breakfast. I'll make pancakes with the strawberry preserves or maple syrup. I'll see if my daughter, Carole Maynard, can stop in. Her kids shouldn't be on Christmas break until the 19th."

"Thank you. Sorry to collapse. I can't seem to focus very well."

"No problem, dear. The warm cocoa was probably the best thing I could have made for you, tired as you must be. Good night. Come about eight a.m." Marlena hurried to open the door for them, and she waved goodbye after they exited.

Belinda mumbled from the passenger seat after Ken started the car, and it warmed up. "Ken. Ken? Ken, do you think we should take the box of toys into the motel where it's warm? Given that your brother's children are all teens, it was still thoughtful of your mother to pack all those elegant old classic toy engines, puzzles, kits, and games for our kids. Such sturdy materials things are made of. And I loved the carved cartoon characters your dad made."

"Yes, they are beautiful. Mom divided the carvings this fall, she said, between Lew and me. She packed our old teenage games and rifles for Lew's older kids. She said the attic space is becoming easier to sweep with that stuff disposed of to clutter up some other homes, with her permission gladly given."

"Umm."

Ken added, "I'm glad you pulled the plug on the evening. I'm really tired, too. And, no, I don't think the toys will get any colder, cold enough to be damaged, than they were in the attic for the past dozen or so years. Belinda, you awake? We're here at the motel. Belinda!"

"Huh? Did you and she mean that the stuff, that . . .

a cooter men's is ammunition--like pea shooters, or sling shots, or arrows made into jewelry?"

"Yes, honey, I mean, no, we'll talk tomorrow, honey. We're here at the motel."

"Umm."

CHAPTER SEVENTEEN

"Oh, ma'am, your house smells wonderful. I feel my strength immediately renewing, inch by inch," Ken Massey greeted Marlena Harver as the warm smells escaped into the frigid air outside. "Belinda's retrieving things that fell from her purse in the car. Here she comes."

A comely woman his age appeared behind Marlena. "This is my daughter, Carole Maynard."

Ken moved into the living room after following Marlena's gesture to hang his coat on a peg. The outside walk had been cleared so he had merely scraped his shoe soles on the entry mat. Carole remained by the front door to open it while Belinda came up on the concrete porch.

"We'll eat in the kitchen because I noticed you quickly sorted some items on the dining room table last night, but I didn't know your criteria for doing so. Ergo, I didn't touch anything after you left."

"I was doing a preliminary run through by dates. I was surprised that there are letters from before the turn of the century. Do you know what happened to your sister Irene?"

"One letter to Jacqueline mentioned that my baby sister had died soon after birth and was buried somewhere. I'll look again. I have barely heard of an Irene. My folks were rather distant and left me alone a lot. That's why I had five children. Merrilee is the oldest and Carole the second. Then there are their three brothers."

"I see."

"Letters were treasured because that was how families maintained connections. Giving a little history of one's family brought some reciprocal doings described in a return letter a few weeks later . . . when one could afford a stamp and the paper to write on."

Ken heard Carole and Belinda talking by the front door as Marlena led him to the kitchen and had him sit in the chair against the wall. A large iron skillet was on the gas flame with a huge red ceramic bowl nearby on a counter that was tiled in swirls of grey and white. The syrup, jam, sugar, cream, and butter were in the middle of the table in blue china containers. Four large white porcelain plates were posed between heavy silverware pieces. At one o'clock at each place was a glass of orange juice: fresh-squeezed, he'd bet a nickel.

Marlena had already turned the pancakes over and placed coffee into four cups when the young ladies walked in.

"My children are in kindergarten and second grade. I teach biology lab at the college Tuesdays and Thursdays," Carole was relating to Belinda. "I married a long time ago, right after the war. My wedding was just before summer term at college started. I graduated two years later."

Belinda said, "I've joined my husband and mother in an investigative agency. We trace data, people, and things."

"Sounds interesting," Carole said and took a bottle of milk from the refrigerator. "Milk anyone?"

The Masseys both nodded. Ken passed the syrup to Belinda after she had smeared her pancakes with butter that had softened in the warm room. Marlena already had flipped the second set of pancakes when Carole finished pouring milk and returned the bottle to the refrigerator.

"Do you have children?" she asked.

Ken replied because he noticed that Belinda had her mouth full, "One two-year-old boy and a seven-month-old daughter."

"My sister said you were hired to trace some jewels to us."

"Carole, let's just finish breakfast and then adjourn to the dining room where I've stacked artifacts from my cousin once removed, Natalie Kilmer. What you'll be discussing at that time is not really appropriate for table talk."

"Yes, mother. Sorry. It simply is interesting to be part of a trace."

"You need to know that the whole matter is based upon Merrilee's false memory of our family history."

Carole looked surprised, her fork halfway to her mouth, and then had it continue its journey.

The talk became desultory and intermittent as the young people enjoyed fluffy pancakes such as they had never eaten. "Oh, I put club soda in the batter," Marlena Harver revealed to their astonishment. "Read about it in *Good Housekeeping*. Didn't recommend any alcohol to accompany it."

They smiled at her joke and drank their coffee, juice, and milk in between bites. Belinda and Carole insisted on doing the dishes while Ken wiped the iron skillet carefully with salt and seasoned it with oil. Marlena put away the items requiring refrigeration.

As they repaired to the dining room, Ken pulled a small

notebook from his pocket while Belinda returned to the living room to pick up her Polaroid camera.

"The things are roughly sorted by chronology that I did last night, Carole," Ken said. "In Kansas City, we had newspaper articles and death certificates. What we've already found at Jeff City were birth certificates of Volks children . . . Frieda and Christian had one son, Jost: your mother's father. She married in 1920, you probably know. The other Volks couple had two sons, and one was Johann, the father of Jacqueline. Your mom played with his daughter, Jacqueline. With me so far?"

Carole nodded. "What about the other son?"

"He was named Josef, and we found no indication of marriage or heirs."

Marlena said, "I met Uncle Josef at Uncle Johann's house. He was round like a beach ball and wore a watch chain across his round tummy and a vest. I remember him being nice. He made me jump up in the air for a nickel he held in his left hand."

"Johann's daughter is obviously Natalie's mother, Jacqueline. We can't find out if there was another daughter who had no father listed, mother possibly was Jacqueline Volks. We'd been pointed to a lady that one of your sister's friends said was an orphan. Her name came up when her son broke some law."

Carole exclaimed, "Oh, you must mean what my sister Merrilee said. She was talking about the Clarmont mother. Meg called me one day about that. That lady died around the time my first child was born in early 1947. I'm sorry to say this, but the lady hadn't ever cleaned an inside toilet. The house they got over in east Missouri, by the vineyards, had a porcelain sink and toilet. She mixed incompatible chemicals trying to get rid of stains and stink, and she collapsed from the fumes. I could have taught her to avoid that! The son got out of prison a while back. My husband was busy tracking a Commie boy out at the rocket plant when that Clarmont son held up a family and was apprehended."

Ken nodded twice during the recital, acknowledging the background. "We've visited the Clarmonts. Drove over there Wednesday," he said. Picking up three letters, he handed them to Belinda. "I've made notes on these, but you should read them, too. And see if they photograph."

Belinda focused the Polaroid lens, snapped, and waited for a snapshot to emerge from the bottom of the camera. She peeled off the outer wrapping and squinted. "Not clear enough."

Taking the letters to a lamp table, she set the pages down and turned on the lamp. After another failure, she found the correct distance to obtain a print that was readable. "Ken, they're readable but in little letters. A magnifying glass will help."

Coming back to the table, she started through a book of snapshots that Carole had finished with. Ken was reading everything that was printed.

Carole asked her mother, "What are we searching for?"

"Anything related to the jewelry. Remember this brooch that Natalie Kilmer sent me ten years ago? It was from a mess of jewelry her mom and I used to play with when we were little. I keep telling this story so much I'm going to paint a sign-board and display it!"

"I don't really remember. I must have been in college."

"Yes, that's right, that's where you were when all this was

going on. What it is, is that an attorney in Kansas City and these Masseys––as Merrilee *told* us both––are trying to get clearance for the museum to have the jewelry permanently."

"Isn't that giving up a lot of money?"

"Look at this, Carole, and tell me it's worth a lot. It's simply an heirloom. Faience beads."

Belinda turned to Ken. "Fey aunts?"

He spelled it as Marlena kept describing the background to Carole.

Marlena fingered the brooch as she spoke. "Just because a man brought so-called jewelry with him to the United States of America does not mean that it was composed of precious gems set in designs that the twins' father had made. The jewelry was clunky and rough looking that we played with. Looked really old. Like part of clothes. Not regal. Not glittery. Play jewelry. Nothing someone would want to wear today. Natalie told me that her ring was made of moonstone, and, don't ask, because I don't know what that is."

"Mother, I get what you're describing. It's more likely to be something historically interesting but not worth breaking up––to be made into a diamond pin, for example."

"Right, Carole. I seriously doubt many gems that we value today are in the collection."

"Oh, look here at this picture. I never, ever, heard that you were a debutante, Mom."

"It was a long time ago. Jacqueline and I came out the same year. She brought back from France the most elegant dress worn at the ball. Such a tiny waist, upswept hairdo in a jeweled net, and with a sweeping train she gathered in one arm during each waltz. I was the most popular though, and had my card full before she did. My ball gown was made of lace with a puffed skirt. No, I'm wrong. She went to France two years before, in 1906, for the winter season and must have bought the dress then. We all envied her."

"What a different time that was," Ken Massey said, looking fondly around at the three girls in this day and age.

Marlena sat back. "I didn't like any of those beaux at the ball. No sense of humor. Just like that Gatsby guy, self-centered. Two weeks later I met your father at a party. He was funny, handsome. Just like your brothers, Carole. He had to finish college and then he went to war. When he returned, we married, were given a shivaree, and during the depression moved down here where he had a job offer. He was so successful at everything, commerce, politics. Died too soon."

"Don't you think my brothers might like something ancient from Europe? I want to talk about the jewelry," Carole said.

"There wasn't something to intrigue a boy from that collection, much less a man, Carole, except for my great-uncle Henrik Volks who liked to collect them or made them and brought them here to the States. He worked for his wife's father who was a jeweler. Let's try to find something in these pictures, and you'll see what I mean. Today I would characterize the things as more Oriental or middle Eastern than European. Maybe our twin grandmothers came from Austria, and the items were from all the trading going back and forth in the 1800s. They were like girls' costume accessories for play-acting. But, they were his, not great-auntie's."

Ken and Belinda had stopped looking at photos to listen to Marlena's expostulation. Ken knew she was correct, given the list of items that Walt had had him read and had had Marnie type for him. However, that the items were from a man's collection was new information.

"We had never heard that." Belinda sounded stunned.

"Well, yes, *I* did, Belinda, about the jewelry description," Ken said. "I told you that I saw a list of the items at Walt's office, and Marlena is correct. We haven't looked at the collection, though. *Mea culpa.* I had not the slightest hint that a man had owned them." Ken spoke at the same time as his wife and shook his head at her because he had forgotten to tell her about the strange collection. "That means the written information and pictures here all need to be examined for that interpretation. I'll go back to a couple of things that I put aside. Mayhap the items were merely intended so that the immigrants would have something familiar with them when they moved in with relatives in the States."

He turned to their hostess and said, "I have sorted out these pictures of the female children. Marlena, would you see if you recognize any pieces of jewelry on you girls? I know you were children, but often that's the time we remember things specifically that caught our fancy. Also, we need any photos you have of yourself or Jacqueline Schmidt when you were in your thirties. We have a lead on a potential relative that we need to compare with your visages."

Marlena took the three photos that Belinda handed her and sat down with Carole by a window on the south where sunrays were beaming through.

"None of these pictures, Ken, show what I was describing as the dress-up playtime with Jacqueline. Keep looking at the photos there. I'll go find another album of our family pictures for one of me in my thirties. My husband died in 1936; I started another scrapbook after that of my children and their activities. Honey, will you see if anything in that pile has a woman in her thirties who looks like me?" she added to her daughter.

Belinda left the room for a minute and brought back another role of Polaroid film that she'd carried in her purse. "Ken, I have eight more snapshots left on the film, and then I run out. Let's be choosy about our selection."

Carole had shuffled through the remaining items and found a picture that she showed to her mother as soon as she returned. Marlena was carrying three thick scrapbooks. "Mother, here's one of you in a flapper dress, so short, skinny, and fringy, along with some other girls. Is Jacqueline in this? She's wearing a flapper dress, too. I wonder why that fashion has never returned when so many other styles do."

"Yes, Carole, she's the one in the middle." The photograph had a lineup of five adults and one little girl. The women's hairdos were in close waves around the face in the black and white shot. Belinda made a copy with the Polaroid camera.

Marlena and Carole were flipping through the albums, exclaiming to each other about old antics and memorable outings to White River and Lake Taneycomo and Bennett Springs, to the local parks and zoo, and to shows at the Shrine Mosque, parks, and high school. It was nearly eleven o'clock when Marlena said, "I am about the same age as Jacqueline in the picture Carole found. Oh, dear, I pulled the corner off when I took it out. No problem. I have some more paste somewhere."

"Look at these shoes," Carole exclaimed. "I forgot I

loved my Mary Janes. And you have on some that look like old woman shoes with thick heels and laces up the top of the feet."

Marlena suggested, "You might want to make a copy of these, Belinda. I will try to find the negatives and make new copies. They'll be bigger than those Polaroids in case you need a better copy to compare our facial features with."

"That would be helpful. Thanks." Ken stood.

Carole carefully returned the items to the cardboard box as Marlena disappeared with the scrapbooks. Belinda wrapped the pictures, the ones she had dried in the air after taking them, placed them back to back in three envelopes, and carefully inserted them in her purse.

"Would you like a cup of coffee before you go?" Carole asked.

"No. Actually, yes, but I would like for you and your mom to be our guests at lunch. You pick the place." Ken looked at Carole with a grin.

"That would be fun. Mother?" Carole turned as Marlena returned to the dining room.

"Okay. Let's celebrate. We've helped the detective squad detect squat so far," replied Marlena. "Let's go over my recent history some more while we eat. For example, one tale from the 20s is about my husband's brother, Sonny, who stayed in Kansas City when Sam bought our farmstead down here. Sonny was invited by his barber to lay some carpet at a place over around 14th and Main. He went after hours, doing some freelance work. A curtain covered the entrance to the stairway, and an elderly woman sat there in a rocking chair. She gestured at the curtain, which he pulled back. He measured a staircase from bottom to top."

Ken was helping Belinda on with her coat by the front door as they listened. Marlena must be lonesome to be holding them up like this. And her daughter and three sons lived in the town. Not the kind of thing to mention off hand to Carole on such short acquaintance. Be better for Belinda to mention it to the other daughter, Merrilee in Kansas City, in passing, i.e., "Your mom is lonesome."

Marlena continued the story. "At the top, he noticed some huge vats and pipes and kegs. He returned the next night with the carpet on his back and, as he mounted the steps, tacking the carpet on the risers, found his feet sticking in some liquid. At the top he dropped the carpet and bolted, because all the vats had been wrecked: the smell of beer was heady. For a week, he went fearfully by vacant lots where bodies had been found and finally went back to his barber. 'I didn't tell anything about the place with the carpet you sent me to, Clip.' 'No matter, Sonny,' said the barber in a menacing tone. 'We know who did it.'"

"How frightening," said Belinda. "I'm glad Kansas City is no longer a fearful place."

"That may or may not be true, young lady. My uncle lived close to the Union Station where there was a massacre. You sleuths must be careful up there even nowadays." Marlena waved a finger at Belinda.

"Uh-huh," said Ken. He was going to have to emphasize the menace that connected to the Kilmer wreck. They themselves would indeed have to be a little more careful- -even if not fearlessly or fearfully so. *Have to be diplomatic about how I tell them what abyss we could fall into.*

"It's been gracious of you to have us over for breakfast, Marlena. We really appreciate it," said Belinda. "And your help in deducting the ownership of the jewelry leading to the younger Volks brother has given us the final clues. We'll send you a final report. You can share it with your children."

"Oh, oh. I forgot to explain what Walt had told me about the assignment." Ken threw up his hands with a feeling of chagrin marking his face, and advised, "It actually was simply to find out who owned the jewelry when after Natalie's mother died in the cemetery. So, let's meet for lunch to finish up. Our motel is over on the highway access, and there's a nice looking restaurant constructed of cedar logs close by."

Marlena said, "Carole, why don't we take your car, and then they can check out of the motel and take off for KC as soon as we've taken the last sip of coffee?"

The mother and daughter stood next to each other, and, although Carole was taller, Ken realized that they both showed their German ancestry in their plump bodies, dark hair, hazel eyes, and facial shapes.

In the car, he asked Belinda. "Does Merrilee look like her mother and sister?"

"Um, yes, except she's shorter and not as plump. She's the oldest of the five children."

"She doesn't seem interested in having the jewelry, just in helping the museum clear title, am I correct?"

"I'm not that sure, Ken. Merrilee may have designs on the designs," Belinda said. "Carole seems more interested in the value of the valuables."

"Not funny."

Belinda chuckled anyway. "Here we are at the motel. I already packed while you paid. I'll just run in and get the suitcases from the front desk manager, and you keep the car warm. I assume you meant that restaurant across the street?"

"Yes, I see the ladies pulling in now. I'll have to turn the motor off to unlock the trunk, and we'll have to make two trips with the suitcases. Don't fall in the parking lot."

"I'm wearing boots, sir, in case you haven't noticed. Although I'm not really wearing them to protect myself against ice and snow, but to kick your ass if you get out of line."

"Never happen. Just try."

PART THREE

TRAIL

CHAPTER EIGHTEEN

As the Masseys waved goodbye to the Marlena and her daughter and started for their car following lunch, Belinda said, "Let me drive. I like to drive. I get impatient if I don't get my turn to drive. The highways are straightforward from here on. And I don't need you from hereon to watch the map for the roads to turn onto. I know where I'm going. I just want to take the wheel and drive."

"Okay. How about you drive?"

"Okay back. Ahh, driving––the freedom of being behind the wheel. I studied the map and think we should go up 65 to Sedalia to Highway 50. That way, we go through Warsaw, which fortunately isn't as full of communists as its namesake is in Europe. I wish we could travel up 13 to Clinton and over highway 7. If we did, we could take a look-see at where the Kilmers met their fate."

Ken shook his head. "Out of the question."

Belinda said, "I know that it's not a good idea in this weather to take a little road like 7. After I master the trip up these hills in the snow, we'll be at Sedalia. I'll be tired and let you drive from there on home." She leaned forward and said, "I know what a mole feels like, carving his way underground. Our headlights are carving our tunnel through the snow."

He yawned and started rambling. "Sounds like a great way to move forward, my mole moll. Sedalia. Hmm. The

Missouri history that I learned in school described a fight between Sedalia and Jefferson City to become named the capitol city. Sedalia lost that conflict but won the State Fair. So, now both Jeff City and Sedalia get to contemplate the stubborn behavior of Missouri mules, if I may be so impolite in characterizing our legislature."

"It was more polite than behavior of the asses in the legislature that my dad fumed about. Don't look so surprised . . . you know I grew up on a farm and know the nomenclature. Look at that gas gauge. We'll need gas soon." Belinda turned on the radio station. "Wouldn't you know that snow and an empty tank would threaten my freedom; wouldn't you know?" She frowned as the KGBX weatherman finished his broadcast.

"Damn him!" she exclaimed as she pulled the car over to the right to avoid a head-on collision on the two lane highway. "That idiot was passing on a damn curve, swerving into our damn lane, and damn nearly wrecking us," she fumed. "And look——he also had to have been going around this curve on our side coming up the hill."

"You handled it well. Let your adrenaline subside," Ken said in an effort to soothe her.

"You needn't be so damned solicitous. Acting smarmy. I bet you were scared, too," Belinda hissed.

"I've been trained to face the danger first, and," he put a quaver in his voice, "wait to be scared afterwards. And you're acting snarky."

Belinda grunted and muttered that she certainly was no longer sleepy.

The leafless trees on either side of the highway were spilling snow from the wind, and the snow drifted over the car and highway like confetti at a New Year's Eve party. An occasional house off to the side had Christmas lights still plugged on in daylight, faintly blinking along the eaves or on outside evergreens similar to far off 4th-of-July sparklers. A beautiful rendition of *Oh, Holy Night* came on the radio after Ken found another station. They sang along softly and somewhat dramatically to that one as well as to every additional carol that played. The car had wonderfully soft cushioned seats, and Ken started to drift off while Belinda kept singing.

When the songfest ended, Ken, his head back against the seat top, started drowsily musing. "I wonder if your mother found out anything in her searches. I didn't want you to call collect again after your long talk with her Monday night. Walt Raleigh might think we're getting too deeply in his pockets."

"Wouldn't that be the museum's pockets? They're paying him, and he's just hiring us at the going rate." Belinda's voice was calm again as usually was her mien.

The car skidded as she drove up a hill on highway 65. "Oops." Belinda followed the skid expertly, turning into the forward momentum.

Ken sat up and said, "Good maneuver, wife." He grimaced inside, fearing that a compliment such as he had just made would insult her again. He flipped quickly to another thought and said, "Hey, I didn't tell you that Reverend Palmer's initials are O. O. P. He said his grandkids call him 'Oops' instead of 'Pops.'"

"That's funny. Hey, hubby, I've been driving cars since I was 14 and, before that, driving tractors. I know how to handle this nice vehicle. You may exclaim in fear. I won't become distracted."

"I forgot that you grew up on a farm, too. Being a farmhand was heavy work. Myself, I helped with all types of heavy work, lifting, dragging, sitting on the porch, and rocking."

"I've never asked you what you did for fun. Did you ever play baseball or any other sport at school? Football, basketball before you joined the Air Force?" Belinda asked.

"Lettered in basketball each year. I meant to ask if you've seen my letter jacket? I thought it was at the cleaners."

"No. I haven't even see you wear it this winter. So, what position did you play on the basketball team?"

"All of them, every year. It was a small high school. But, I was more interested in a foal than a foul, raising horses and mules with my folks. We had a couple of male donkeys and three mares that we bred with them. The mules were really amazingly strong, but willful, creatures. I'm sure you've heard of people being called 'Missouri mules.' Stubborn and contrary but capable of hard work. There was always a need for those animals when tamed. Even when the brutes would run under a tree to try to brush me off or scrape my legs against a fence, I'd hang on until I won them over. Usually." Ken remembered some episode with a chuckle. "Early on, I listened to *The Lone Ranger* and his side-kick Tonto on the radio. Then I watched the Roy Rogers and Gene Autry films at the Saturday matinee in town about every Saturday. I tried my best to copy them, even when I was too short to reach the stirrups."

"During our visit with your family, you didn't mention either horse training or Missouri mule sales."

"They're out of that business now, living on Social Security and renting out acreage."

"I see. Poor little a-lone ranger: no more gitti-ups for you."

"One airman who served in Germany told me that he heard a Lone Ranger radio program where Tonto said, '*Vas ist Das, kemo sabe*.'"

They laughed at the picture that rose in their minds. Belinda was silent for a few minutes and then added, "You also didn't tell me about the weird stuff loosely defined as jewelry brought over by some German, Prussian, Austrian whosoever immigrants." She paused and added casually, "Inherited from their fey aunts."

"Funny funny. That omission was an oversight. I hope Mother Holly has found the list. She might understand what the descriptions meant, but I certainly didn't, and neither did Walt. I'm glad we visited with Marlena in person. That was incredibly astonishing news about the younger Volks bringing the jewelry, gems, and thus whatever not being brought by the twins as we've been focused on. Merrilee sent Meg, Walt, and us on a wrong pilgrimage." Ken slapped his gloved hands on the dash.

"It's good we have the birth certificates now to straighten things out easily."

"Marlena's finding the old pictures and letters will help a great deal in identifying folks, Volks folks. Ha. I wonder how long it will take the Laura lady to mail us pictures of her mom."

"Marlena was adamant that no one and nothing indicated that the items were so valuable that they couldn't play dress-up with them. The items just looked like fun."

Belinda shook her head. The traffic was not too heavy. After driving for another hour, she started whistling a bit from *Rudolph the Red-nosed Reindeer*. Going downhill, the car started into another slide. "At the next gas station, I'm pulling in and ceding control to my wheel claim, hubby. You guide the sleigh tonight."

"There should be a Standard Oil station at the next intersection with highway 54. You're handling it fine."

"I know I am, but it's your turn to show me how well you handle sliding on the road. By the way, I didn't tell you 'cause you slipped out of the room to get another cup of coffee. Carole told me that the Laura once worked for Carole's husband, Dr. Maynard, at his clinic."

"Ah, that's how Carole heard about Mrs. Clarmont's death. I didn't think the Maynards, Harvers, and Clarmonts would exactly run in the same social circle," Ken said.

The radio station started to fade. Belinda said, "See if you can get a Kansas City station."

Ken soon found WDAF where the weatherman was issuing another heavy snowstorm warning: perhaps two inches of snow with light winds. "I noticed the snow is already deeper here than it was a few miles south. The area must have had snow all the time we were gone."

"I wonder why we didn't run into any of it."

"The storms tend to move from Kansas through KC to the northeast, and we stayed below the movement."

"We were below the jam being caused by the devil of a storm," said Belinda as she quipped, "over by Devil's Elbow."

"But now we're going into the middle of his armpit," Ken said as Belinda pulled into a gas station.

"You mean it's going to be hairy from now on to where we're heading?" Belinda joked.

He laughed. "That's one way of describing our two close shaves where you prevented our sliding into a snow bank. But you can cross your fingers in a hex, if you want, you little angel, to prevent a demonic storm."

Belinda punched his arm after she turned off the ignition, and then she turned to pull her purse from the back seat.

A gas station attendant ran out, pulling on a jacket, and started the pump for regular gasoline at Ken's direction. Belinda went inside to take the key to the ladies' room, and Ken followed her, doing the same for the men's room.

Coming back into the main room, Belinda put the key back on its hook, opened the top of a red metal soda pop chest, and plugged in a nickel for a bottle. She walked across the room and took a Three Musketeers from a box in the display behind the counter, and she put a nickel in its place.

Ken returned, replaced his restroom key, chose coffee, and put a cup under the spigot after inserting a nickel. He summarized their problem. "We're going to keep going until it's dark and/or dangerous. Going north, we have Warsaw or, then next up, Sedalia, as possible stops if the weather becomes too bad. Next, going west, we have Warrensburg as the biggest town. Warsaw, Sedalia, Warrensburg that we could stop in. The trip might take much longer than I thought. I'm going to call collect and alert your mom."

"Tell her to call Meg Raleigh to say that I won't make it to the gym tomorrow. I wrote Meg's number on the cover of the telephone book."

"And I just remembered that Walt told me days ago that

Meg knew someone who had had coins appraised: I need to alert your mother about her coins."

"Well, they may just be cooties-ments."

He shook his head in exaggerated resignation, went to a wall phone, made a quick connection through the long distance operator, and informed Mother Holly where they were. His part of the conversation consisted mostly of monosyllables, not furnishing Belinda with much information. Then he ended by saying to remind him to tell her about coin collecting.

After hanging up, he did report several bits of news, to wit: the weather has kept the family and servants inside all week; the neighbors had vandals damage their cars; no news had been received from the Clarmonts or Raleigh couple, by mail, phone, or visit; and, pans of gingerbread cookies were coming out of the oven as they spoke.

The attendant came back inside, stripping off his leather gloves that were grimy from gas and oil and lubricant. He dropped them on the floor and stomped his feet. His coveralls smelled faintly of gasoline but were fairly clean, unlike his stained Cardinal's ball cap that must have fallen onto the dirty pavement outside. "Oil's okay. Anything else I can do for you?"

"I put a nickel on the counter for the candy bar that I took from the box under the glass," Belinda said.

The guy rang up the costs of the gas and candy bar.

Belinda asked, "Have you heard from anyone driving down from Sedalia or over from Kansas City how the roads are faring?"

"The traffic has kept a lane pretty well open, going each direction on all major roads. That is going to change tonight as the snow combines with ice, and the temperature drops. Plus, going west, you're going to be closer to the river moisture blown around by the wind. The rivers haven't frozen over yet like the teeny cricks are."

"Thanks. We'll get moving."

Ken picked up the change and escorted Belinda back to the passenger side of the car. Outside of the warm station, they both took deep breaths. "Such cool, clean air, no odor, but plenty cold. So cold that I'm going to sit in the car while you do the windows, Ken."

He stretched and did a goose-step around the to the trunk of the car, first circling the hood. He could see Belinda laughing. She rolled down the window to ask, "Why are you pretending to be a German soldier?"

"It's a good way to stretch my lower back. I do think the passenger seat was a bit too comfortable. Watch how quickly you start to go to sleep. Roll the window back up so it doesn't get any colder in there."

Belinda pulled the lever on the seat to move it forward after she complied by twisting the window handle.

He went to work then, scraping snow from the edges of the windows, including where windshield wipers never worked. At those places, snow built up enough to obscure the few inches of peripheral vision, a blank spot that worried him. Someone might be sliding into them suddenly, and he would not see it.

"I'm glad we have a heavy DeSoto," he said as he climbed in, after putting the scraper on the back floor. "Better traction and wider tires than most cars."

A big Trailways bus paused at an intersection stop sign to their right. Then the bus crossed the junction, and it slowly accelerated away north. "I think I'll just trundle along behind the bus. Let it act as our snow plow," he muttered.

"As long as we don't have to breathe the smell from the tail pipe," Belinda cautioned.

He stopped at the entrance to the highway from the service station's driveway, signaling his "stop" first with his arm out straight and then, secondly, cocking it upright for the right turn onto the highway.

"And there you were, earlier talking about going into a devil's hairy armpit, and now you complain about smelly tailpipes? When when when will I ever figure you out, my darling princess?"

"Be serious. The emanation from a tailpipe is what people use to commit suicide," Belinda said. "I don't have the slightest compunction about repressing my opinion about dangers."

"I'll stay back ten yards, and the blowing wind will sweep the odor, or odorless, gas away." Once upon a time, he had been on a plane that was carrying his squad, composed of airmen who were lined up on the hard seats along the sides. After the plane landed, he remembered, too god-awful well, how he'd felt nauseous as if poisoned. Maybe it had been carbon monoxide he'd breathed. Would never know. Took hours to get rid of that feeling in the stomach.

Belinda commented, "Too many trees along side the highway for the wind to do much sweeping."

"Don't worry. I guarantee your safety You could go skiing instead of surfing? Win a couple of Olympic medals as Andrea Mead Lawrence did a couple of years ago."

The snow seemed to let up a bit, but Ken had to move farther back from the bus because the snow was light and swirling around in a vast eddy behind the big vehicle. After listening to a half hour of a soap opera on the radio, Belinda switched to a hillbilly music station.

"That'll keep you awake, all those wailings about love, horsies, home. If this snow doesn't turn to sleet, we're going to make it all the way home tonight."

"I think so," Ken agreed. "I want to see how much the kids have grown and how much your mom has found out."

"Do the first one tonight, but kindly don't wake them up. They'll never go back under. But let's put off catching up-to-date on our work until tomorrow morning."

"Deal. I can't wait for her reaction when we tell her what we've found out."

"You mean that Merrilee's interest in the jewels is off the page or out the window or off the clouds or high flown."

"Something like one of those. Hallelujah!" The bus turned west on Highway 50 at Sedalia, and Ken turned the steering wheel to follow in its tracks. "We'll be home in time to hear the Salvation Army band and chorus perform at the Country Club Plaza this evening. That is, if the precipitation is no worse than what we're into at this minute." He chortled at the possibility.

Two hours later they pulled up to the garage where Belinda jumped out and raised the door, permitting Ken to drive in. She clicked on the center light before he shut off the headlights, then she ran back and lowered the door, locking it. Ken unlocked the stair door, and they hauled their luggage up the stairs, plunking it down in the back porch. Ken automatically locked the stair door behind him before coming on into the kitchen.

Holly heard them arrive. "Welcome back," she called. "Good trip?"

"Tense," said Belinda.

"C'mon, it's 'past tense' now. Admit that 'it was' but now 'it is' over," Ken teased. "Mother Holly, our only peril was bad weather, and it didn't materialize. Belinda charmed it away, away, away up north from Dixie." He warbled the last part as he hugged her hard while grinning at Mother Holly. "We'll reveal all as soon as we've had something to eat. I smell a lingering odor of gingerbread. But just about the trip and adventures. The investigative data will wait until the morn."

"Mom, Marlena Harver told us a story about Kansas City in the old days. Seems her brother-in-law got caught up in a bad situation laying carpet over by between 12th and 18th streets somewhere where lots of cabarets were located. Some beer vats were there illegally as well, even during Prohibition in the 20s."

"That was the area with houses of prostitution, too, I think, around 14th Street."

"Whatever do you mean?" Belinda forgot the rest of Marlena's story, surprised because of her mother's statement.

Also, Holly had just pointed them toward the living room past the dining room. There they saw that there were three new, small tables by the seating area. "Go sit," Holly called. They walked in and sat on the sofa.

Holly came in carrying some low, rectangle boxes. "No. Sit in the armchairs. You're going to have your first TV dinners." She handed them each a fork and a knife. She left and brought back three mugs of coffee and paper napkins.

"No tea cart, Mom?" Belinda said in an impromptu, fussy tone of complaint.

"Of course not. The china is too delicate for these little tables that you clumsy oafs will probably knock over."

"Oh, Ken, Mommy excoriated me. Save me, save me."

"I'm busy preparing to eat right now, m'lady. Sorry. And I don't know what that word means, and I'd even bet that you don't know either."

"Well, it sounded good. This is a weird welcome home, Mom. At least we're promised gingerbread cookies for dessert."

The couple moved to the chairs, followed Holly's direction to arrange the tray tables in front of their knees, and pull the warm tops from the boxes.

"What is this?"

"Roast, potatoes and gravy, and green beans. Just what it looks like. If you need seconds, it takes only twenty minutes to cook a new one in the oven. Harriet laid in a supply of a dozen of these when we heard how bad the weather was going to get. You know where the drinks in the kitchen are, so help yourself."

"Are we required to watch TV while we eat?"

"Naturally." She moved her tray aside, and went over to the TV cabinet to turn on the station that she had selected for their listening pleasure, a comedy show from the offerings on the three channels.

Holly ambled back to her chair. She ate but soon paused, with her fork waving a green bean, while picking up the earlier topic of conversation during a commercial. "Certain areas of Kansas City thrived with prostitution houses and other areas built up with jazz clubs and beer joints, Prohibition or not. The city administration and police ignored all of the activity that is usually considered illegal. Wild and woolly town, famous for being so. Newsmen reported the town now and then to the American public."

"How did you find all that out?"

"Remember, I was talking history with Meg. Some about Europe, some about Missouri. Also, I was searching newspaper archives week before last. I was sidetracked a bit when I came to comments about Kansas City history. I wonder why we were never taught any of its raunchy reputation in our state history classes. 'Fascinating' doesn't capture the aura of the jazz clubs, the cabarets, the rousing nights in the downtown area." She ate the green bean, and remarked, with an apologetic tone in her voice, "Maybe that's why I found so little that was relevant to our investigation," she mused.

The Masseys laughed, ate, watched another TV show, and retired.

CHAPTER NINETEEN

"Ah, my bellissima, my belle, Ma Bell, etc.," sang Ken as he entered the room. "I hear her dulcet tones commenting on cuisine."

"Looks old and runny," she said. "Smells bad. I'm hungry. Not that hungry." Belinda had wandered into the dining room at mid-morning Saturday, opened a lid on a covered dish, peered into the covered dish, shuddered, and let the lid clatter back on top. She picked up a biscuit, poured milk into a crystal glass, letting it dribble slowly from the bottle after she shook the cream on the top into the bottle all the way, letting the milk foam a tiny bit.

"I wish you liked buttermilk. Today would be a good day for some, or some eggnog," her mom said from the table where she was finishing off a buttered biscuit.

"I shudder to think of how I spewed vomit after that time I took a big swallow of buttermilk, thinking it was real milk, and my stomach objected," Belinda answered. "Never could approach it again, even reacted strongly to the sour odor. Stomach always recoiled. But not to eggnog. The rum helps that stay down adequately."

"And, at least she isn't belladonna, Sir Kendrick. She would upchuck at the thought of being sorry rather than safe, just as she did to buttermilk," said Holly. "Miss Marple would find out, of course, if she were poison, and all would be solved, leaving us in the lurch. Or in church––in a coffin."

Ken grinned at Mother Holly with his eyes squinting. "You know what puzzles me? Those stories where the detective says, 'Aha, smells like bitter almonds. Victim died of cyanide poisoning.' Myself, I've never smelled sweet almonds. How would someone know what bitter almonds smell like?"

"A cook would, Ken. There's almond flavoring, but I haven't the faintest idea whether it would be characterized as a sweet or a bitter smell," Holly answered.

"Hey, Mom, what actually happened would have surprised Miss Marple. The Clarmont mother died of a cleaning combination that made poisonous fumes. Tell her, Ken. You know about such things. I'll have to look up the chemistry in the library. And note, in case Meg or Merrilee gets to either of you before one of them does to me, the missus' *cause* of death has nothing to do with our investigation."

Ken apologized because he was going to have breakfast before starting an oratory of events and information, choosing also to hear Mother Holly's findings first, and he would graciously let the cook bring him some warm sausages and a waffle.

Belinda walked to the kitchen with his order and added that a plate of the same would be welcome, too, for herself. Then, she refilled the percolator with coffee and water and waited while it perked.

The cook, who had been stuffing cloves in the top of a ham, stopped, washed her hands, and put the skillet and waffle iron to use. "What was wrong with the eggs on the sideboard?" she asked.

"The sterno lamp had gone out, and they were cold."

"I can use them to make egg salad sandwiches for your bedtime snack," she offered.

"Yes, thanks. I'll take the coffee pot in. I saw that there's already a trivet on the sideboard that I can put this hot pot on."

Ken told Mother Holly about the visit with his parents while Belinda was in the kitchen talking with the cook.

When Belinda returned, her mom said, "And, you need to call that Meg Raleigh. She already called twice this morning. When I told her yesterday that you wouldn't be back in time for the Y because you'd gone to Hermann to see the Clarmonts, she gave a great big sigh, and said, 'Ha, I was right.'"

"Right about what?"

"I thought you'd tell me," Holly said.

"We didn't find out anything that confirmed anything. Such an orphan descendant is still out in the ether somewhere, if it ever existed, and would have to be directly descended from Henrik Volks who was the original owner of the jewelry stuff, not the twins, as we'll explain in detail." Belinda said in singsong fashion. "If there even is one orphan descended from that Volks. Meg and Merrilee certainly were pumped up about that Clarmont mother being an orphan but, so far, we have no Clarmont connection to Volks folks so we think Merrilee wants title to the jewels and is in no way, no manner whatsoever, in line for them or any other female unless there's a strange will somewhere."

Mother Holly sat shocked. She sat up. "Did Marlena

say that the jewels belonged to a man? And, would you please use complete sentences instead of paragraphs in your elocution exercise?"

"Yes, her uncle, him alone. Yes, Teach, I'll add a period or exclamation point here and there. Just did! Satisfied?"

Her mother sighed. "Fine, Belinda, don't be so sensitive."

"Also, we're not charged with proving the provenance of the jewels; that is, where in the world they originally came from."

"No, Belinda, that was not our contract."

"Or what they're worth."

"Correct. Again, Belinda. Not in our contract."

"We were charged with finding who has title to them for the art museum's satisfaction. The museum can pay others to trace anything else, back through the ages, and also appraise anywhere else."

"Correct. Now you're finished telling me what I already knew, tell me what I don't know, please." Mother Holly raised her eyes to heaven.

"Uncle Henrik collected or made what was called jewelry in my school days but back then was called some strange word." Belinda looked at Ken who supplied "Accoutrements."

Holly stared at Belinda with a tiny frown on her usually smooth forehead. "Why didn't you ask Marlena that particular question about ownership when you called her weeks ago? Why have you traipsed all over the state looking for an answer that was a simple answer?"

"It didn't occur to me, Mother. We had not had a case like it. And, neither of you suggested that I ask only about ownership. I was getting a list of relatives."

Ken jumped in. "We thought, at the time, that we needed to know a complete list of Volks/Jufellear relatives, Mother Holly. Who could have guessed that one Harver lady had a simple answer?"

"Oh, very well. It's done. We have our case to present to Walt. We do have dates of births and some dates from tombstones and obituaries to give him, also."

Ken touched his wife's hand. "Belinda, well, that was a synopsis of what we found but rather breathlessly and beautifully delivered. I expected a long-drawn out story would have to describe what we found," Ken kidded her, giving Holly time to muse, conclude, and recover.

"Maybe at the swimming pool I shouldn't have repeated to those two girls what that Mrs. Shannon had hinted about to you, Ken." Belinda moaned and added, "So we've been tracking orphans on a sidetrack."

"Well, we've taken it in consideration now."

Belinda poured coffee for everyone, grabbed another piece of toast from the sideboard, slathered jelly on it, and patted her mom on the shoulder as she went by her on her return to the table. "Okay, Mom. We didn't want to run up the phone bill. What did you do this week?" She tasted the toast and sighed with delight. "Just smelling toast makes me hungry," she said, "and knowing your grape jelly is handy makes me hungrier."

"That grape jelly is almost gone. Finish it up, so the jar can be reused. I mentioned that I'd been snowed in most of the week, Belinda, when Ken called last night. I went through the 1915-1920 orphanage records earlier this month. I'd also decided, during my unexpected rest, that it would take all three of us to work through all those orphanage hand-written notes and printed forms for the dozen years to 1910. By myself, I wouldn't have gotten through them in a timely manner," her mother answered.

"But we don't have to. It's an idea that's been thrown at us, not relevant anymore. What is the weather supposed to be like next week?" Belinda asked. "Will we be able to drive around the city safely to finish searching relevant records--or go shopping?"

"Yes. It's supposed to be a great shopping week, just in time for Christmas merchants to be gleeful."

"Did you find out anything significant about orphans before the weather shut you in?"

Mother Holly turned her head toward the ceiling at Ken's question. "There is this. The printed forms seem to have had information that was verifiable about each of the orphan children's parents. Someone occasionally noted that the parents had died in a fire, or an epidemic, or the dad in an overturned farm wagon, or tossed from a run away horse. But not all data are on printed forms; some are handwritten."

Ken asked, "Another question. From your reading of history, is it possible that the twins and Volks brothers came from Austria in the mid 1800s? Have we any source at all for the name of their port of embarkation or where the family lived in Europe?"

Holly thought for a minute, her eyes downcast, then she looked up to the left as she thought about her answer. "It's possible. I'll tell you more about Austrian emigrants after I check some dates. Strangely, Austria just signed its WW Two accord with the Allies in May of this year, ten years, almost to the day, after we entered Berlin. Letting the Russians go first. Our big mistake. In fact, that country, Russia, is the one that held Austria down for the last decade."

Ken commented, "All that I remember in the news in Kansas City around last April was that ex-prexy Truman laughed as he threw out the first ball to our new, major league team, the Athletics. If, a month later, Austria was even mentioned around here in the news, I'd be surprised. The Athletics had the headlines."

Mother Holly ignored his side remark. "The jotted notes did make interesting reading. I preferred to concentrate on the printed items. Some of the children who were mentioned had occasionally undecipherable notes. I had no idea how we were going to find the two Clarmont orphans or their background information because if they are not in the printed info, we'd have had a mess to go through in the miscellaneous handwritten notes. And, now, we do not have to do that! Huzza!"

"Moreover, in our part of the investigation, we thought we were also stymied," Ken informed her, "until we found out about, and will receive, some pictures from a Clarmont daughter. They'll come in the mail, but I sincerely doubt they'll tell us anything, nothing that we would be able to discern about family traits. Moreover, in Raumville, Marlena, the first cousin of Natalie Kilmer, had been sent a box of family information. We went through that, and Belinda took some pictures of the letters and photos with her Polaroid. They'll be some help."

"You were gone all week, and that's all you found out? Pictures with information? No documents? More things resembling questions than answers?"

"Birth certificates, Mom. I'll make a table of descendants after breakfast." Belinda waved her fork.

The cook brought in four waffles already melting the butter on top, featuring a side of two pork sausages, and placed the plates on the table before the family members as well as her chair. She took the syrup bottle from the sideboard and set it on the table.

Belinda stuck her nose in the air and informed her mother, "We have six birth certificates with the Christian and Henrik Volks names on them and the six children's dates of birth. And, two of the pictures I took are of relevant letters from the ancestors down the Henrik Volks lineage. Thanks, Harriet," Belinda said to the cook. Cook then strolled to the butler's pantry, opened a drawer, selected heavy silver coffee spoons, and set them at the three places. Next, she refilled the coffee cups and then sat down. She finished her tasks before the family seemed to notice the food, so engaged in conversation were they.

Ken answered Holly holding up a "V" for victory gesture with his right fingers. "Mother Holly, the six birth certificates in Jeff City of the Volks' descendants solved the immediate descendant loop. It's the children from those loops that we're working on now. Marlena's hoard of memorabilia helped a lot. Only she and Jacqueline seemed to have survived and had children themselves. We could go report on this to Walt on Monday morning. What time can you search for the two obituaries?"

"Paper archives and library are closed on Monday. As well as Saturday, today. Courthouse just today."

Ken and Belinda groaned. "That puts us back days and days," complained Belinda. "You two finish your breakfast, or I'll finish it for you before it gets cold." She twirled a blond curl by her ear, frowned a tiny bit, and said, "We seem to be thwarted at every turn, don't we?"

Holly obeyed her daughter concerning the breakfast before her, taking a bite of her second waffle.

Ken wondered how Mother Holly could always eat so much more than he and not gain weight the way his mother had. He kept his face down in order not to betray his thoughts.

"Buck up, children. You can go do your Christmas shopping in the Plaza or at the Jones Store downtown. Ho ho ho. I think tomorrow you wanted to go to the Episcopal Church?"

"Yes. We need to find a church that has a Sunday School for the children plus a Vacation Bible School in the summer. It'll be the one where we feel the most comfortable."

The phone rang out in the office, the sound barely noticeable in the dining room.

"That'll be Meg for you, dear," Holly said to her daughter. "Go relieve her anxiety, feed her triumph, whatever she's after."

Belinda left the sliding door open across the living room from them.

Holly started to say, "One thing I . . ."

Ken put his fingers on his lips and pointed at the office, indicating that he wanted to hear Belinda's side of the conversation.

Belinda was speaking very little. "Yes, we did."
Silence.
"Yes, then we went to Hermann. And Raumville. And the landscape looked pretty desolate, cold as ever was. We

followed a bus home that helped clear the highway for us, or at least, it crushed down the snow."

Silence.

"No, Meg. We don't know. We'll report to Walt."

Silence.

"Meg, we don't know anything for sure. I simply do not know if you and Mrs. Shannon got it right about an orphan. Or if it was that Mrs. Clarmont you mentioned. An orphan, anyway, would have a tenuous relationship . . . yes, that's what I meant."

Silence.

"We'll tell your husband of our progress on Monday, Meg. Bye for now."

They watched as Belinda twirled the black handset in the air before returning it to the cradle. She leaned forward with her hands on the carved wood desk. "Quiet down, my old friend. I can't sing your triumph just yet, Meg," she muttered.

Holly noticed that her green corduroy skirt was losing its ribbed look on the backside before she blurted, "Belinda, don't wear that skirt anywhere except here in the house. It shows its age, dear. You can afford something better. Meg always is well-decked out."

Belinda pulled her full skirt part way around to her right to study the back. "I love the jacket to this outfit. I wonder if there's enough material in all these panels to allow a seamstress to make a straight skirt."

"Maybe."

Ken broke in, sounding impatient, which an unusual tone for him, Mother Holly thought. "Belinda, what did Meg say?"

"I know you were trying to hear my conversation." Belinda sat back down. "I was trying to be, I was trying hard to be, diplomatic, trying not to deflate her, trying to hint that her husband was the one who would be the recipient of what, if anything, we had unearthed. I think I worked it out correctly. We'll see."

Holly said, "I'm sure you handled it correctly from what we heard of the conversation. I was also careful to be discreet. I told her only of the cities you visited, not the people. Jefferson City, Hermann, near Devil's Elbow, and Raumville. Even if she had a phone book for every one of those cities, she'd have a hard time tracing your travels to the interviews, other than by guesswork."

"I do want Walt and Meg Raleigh to be friends but until we know how much Walt shares with her, we had better follow your example, Mother Holly," said Ken. He had been in law enforcement in the Air Force long enough to know that certain aspects of a case demanded confidentiality, within the law. However, Belinda, younger than he by three years, and only four years out of high school, was just becoming certified in higher degrees of discretion.

"Yes, I liked going to the Y with her and Merrilee. Yet I won't allow her to pump me."

"A school teacher, such as she, is pretty skillful at unraveling obfuscation on the part of tricksters in her class, I wager. It's good you're becoming equally skillful but yet maintaining a bland face, revealing nothing. I don't mean to imply you should lie, exactly, just divert attention by seeming disinterested, using a disinterested tone of voice, in whatever unfortunate direction her queries take," Holly said to her daughter.

"I thank you––if that's a compliment. If it's a criticism, I'll pretend it's a compliment, Mommy."

"What plans do you two have for today?" Holly asked. "Are we going to have enough to present a written report?"

"I have to get the laundry together for the washerwoman," Belinda said. "If you have any dry cleaning for her to drop off, put it on the bed. She'll be here about one, as usual on Saturday. You can pick the cleaning up on your home when it's ready, Ken. She'll do the ironing and bring the laundry back."

"I have to service the car." Ken pushed back his chair. "But, rest assured, a report is possible. We both have to sort through our notes so that Belinda can type them up, and you can file them. I'll write the intro and conclusions. Hope you didn't have anything else planned because we'll need to concentrate on our investigation for the rest of the day when we finish our chores. I'll be ready in about an hour, Mother Holly," Ken concluded his assessment of the duties to be done.

"I'll take the time to make a grocery list for the cook. She has the afternoon off so I'll be busy during your hour. I'll go with her to the store this morning. Or, maybe I'll just make a list, and you take her, Ken." Mother Holly glanced at him. "And, Ken, you might also find it as amusing as I did that the Athletics won no more ballgames after that first one. Zilch, nil, zero. Rest of the whole season, none. Ho ho ho."

"Mother Holly," Ken said, "I feared you would provide commentary on the Athletics' seasonal record. I noticed that, however they played, we did not surrender our tickets. We just laughed and yelled our 'rah rah sis boom bah' cheer, and we loved every minute of it at the ballpark. Now, admit it was fun, and winning isn't everything, unless it's in a life and death confrontation."

"Granted, sir, my son-in-law, Kendrick Massey, the Socrates of the family."

"I've bought a little Louisville slugger," Belinda said. "I stashed it away on the porch for when J. B. can run. I didn't know what size or type of ball to get him and forgot to ask you two experts."

"Baseballs are small but hard and rather dangerous with a little boy to play with. I like to play baseball, however, and will buy one for you and me, Belinda, to play catch with. For him, I'll find a tennis ball and the larger softball to start with." Ken felt a warm glow at the comradeship he had with his two girls. Their likes and dislikes were generally compatible with his.

Right now the girls resembled huge sunflowers. His wife was wearing a dark green crew neck sweater that complemented her blonde hair and fair coloring. She had a white collar folded over the neckline. Her skirt didn't look old and tatty to him, and the sweater was perfectly all right, for sure. His mother-in-law had on a yellow cardigan and green skirt while her hair was silvery like a spider web on top of the sunflower.

"I guess Harriet's going to be gone this afternoon after she gets the groceries." Belinda was spreading a blanket on the floor. Ken would bring J. B. down with some of his toys while Lillian brought the baby downstairs. The family always took care of the children during the two maids' afternoon off.

"Yes. The weather was too bad for Harriet's regular time

off, so I gave them both extra time off today." Holly helped even up the edge of the blanket by her chair, and she then started on the grocery list out in the office.

Lillian brought Alberta down singing a quiet repetitive song in a rich contralto. Belinda followed, leading J. B. by the hand into the living room and carrying a sack of blocks and little cars and trucks. Holly put a folding cardboard protective shield over the coffee table and started helping J.B. unload his vehicles.

She said, "J. B., let's draw a highway."

"Yes, G'annie."

Holly brought out some pieces of crayon. She wrinkled her nose at the waxy smell when she opened the pack. Seated on the floor, she leaned over and drew a snaking highway on the cardboard.

After climbing onto the table and racing a car over the cardboard, bending it under his knees, J.B. put in an order. "Tram, too, tram, too. Whee! Nana!" Holly drew straight tracks in front of her and a bridge over the indentation his knees had made. He switched a Lionel train engine carefully around the track she then outlined on the cardboard.

"I'm going to break out the Lionel train tracks, Mother Holly. He's old enough." Ken left for the storeroom.

The baby's diaper had to be changed, and the task fell to Belinda. She knelt on the floor and cleaned and replaced the cloth, using the big safety pins to secure the front folds.

After rinsing the diaper in the toilet and putting it in its laundry sack, Belinda brought the swing chair into the living room from the storeroom and then had Lillian place Alberta in it. Lillian waved goodbye. J. B. waved goodbye to her and then started bawling with his arms raised beseechingly after her. She kept going toward the front steps anyway.

Ken amused the kids by making noises with the toys, incidentally quieting J. B. as his interest was captured. J. B. climbed down into Ken's arms and then wiggled out to run around the room. That peaceful interlude allowed the others to complete their chores.

Belinda collected the laundry and dry cleaning, setting two baskets full by the back porch door. After going down the stairs and unlocking the back entry door, she returned and kept her hearing alert for the sound of the rapping at the stairway door.

Holly finished the grocery list and settled down with a book. Ken took Harriet with him, to drop her off at the store while he continued to the service station. He would pick her up on the way back home. She would be free for the afternoon after they brought the groceries upstairs. He had not found his letter jacket in his closet. When he picked up the cleaning next week, he'd inquire if he'd forgotten it last week when he had picked up the rest.

CHAPTER TWENTY

"Mother, I need you to clarify one item that you mentioned on the phone to Ken. What did you mean about vandalism to neighbors' cars?" Belinda began the professional session just after the noon hour. She was moving back and forth between the living room and their office, arranging her supplies while attending to the children. She put the extra release forms into one divided drawer in her desk.

"Two neighborhood cars had oil pans pierced. None from our garage, but then we always have the last person in at night lock the door. The police came by, said they'd keep an eye out, but that they had little to go on. The damaged cars were both Chrysler models. That is why I jumped when the police knocked and told me what had happened. I thought we should be extra careful. The police said it might just have been some kids."

Ken sighed. "I mentioned earlier that the second man that I interviewed on the Tuesday before last is a car lot manager, Walt told me. The man seemed to believe I was investigating Richard Kilmer's death-by-accident, not our search for Natalie's relatives. The bully warned me off. He would have noticed that I drove a DeSoto because it was sitting out at the curb in front of his face. A lad was down the hall with a big, ugly grin on his face. Walt said calmly that it would be hard to prove something, or someone, damaged the Kilmer's new car after the wreck."

"You think that car guy cared enough to send kids to damage our neighbors' cars?" Belinda said, disbelief in her voice. "Why, Kendrick Massey, do you keep adding tidbits of threats instead of telling us the whole story to start with? Do you think we're sissies?"

"No, hon," he said hurriedly. "I wasn't sure enough of what I sensed, I guess."

"Ha. Some excuse."

Holly asked, "What was the salesman's name––battymobile?"

"Some generic name, such as, maybe, Jones," he kidded in return, "or Ford, Chrysler. Just minute, I'll find it."

Holly said, in a put-on huffy tone, "Jones is *not* a generic name, John Doe, Jane Doe, type of name. I will guess: aha––his name is Lincoln of Lincoln's Lincoln Cars."

"Yes. That sounds right. How did you know that?"

"There's a picture of him in the newspaper; he's bleeding all over his office chair; his body's slumped backwards; his head hanging toward the floor. Pretty gruesome. No guts in view, thankfully. Glad it wasn't a color picture. Somebody took him out while you were gone." Mother Holly bent to the magazine rack beside her overstuffed rocker to pull out a stack of newspapers. "I haven't thrown the papers away because I know you like to read them."

Ken reached over and took the newspaper. He read the article but something made him keep looking back at the newspaper's picture as he read. Great Christ! His letter jacket was beside the man's chair, the MASSE and PULAS (raised embroidered letters showed clearly, as did a stain, probably blood.) So, he had lettered years ago at Pulaski High School. So, the jacket *had* been taken when he brought back the cleaning days ago. So, was someone trying to implicate him? Obviously, you dolt; couldn't be any other explanation. So why was his breath now coming in gulps as though he were afraid? Because he was.

"It amazes me how low class people who are always in trouble with the police also call on the police for help. Then go ahead anyway and take care of eliminating their troubles violently," Belinda said apropos of nothing, arranging some typing paper on the office desk, "Maybe if the shooter is another Chrysler auto dealer who sells DeSotos, if Lincoln is the one behind the vandalism, and our DeSoto dealer found out, why, he'd come to our rescue. Marshal DeSoto aimed a shot in the dark Chrysler Earp. Powie! It worked. Bloody shame." Belinda twirled her pen, aimed it, and pretended to press a trigger.

Ken asked Mother Holly, "Did you enjoy that story?"

She grinned and nodded at Belinda.

"Did the police ask you any questions when they told you about the cars?" he asked.

Holly answered with a quizzical look on her face. "No. Why? I wouldn't have had any answers to any questions, would I?" Pause. "Do you have some?"

Ken persisted in his questioning without answering. "Did you mention the shot-out window in the storeroom?"

"No. It's just a hole in the glass. Could be a bird expelled a gallstone. Except for the hole in the wall opposite the window where the shot landed. A bird would've had to dive bomb sideways to do that."

Ken shook his head. "All right, ladies, you're passing

these events off lightly but we shouldn't. We are being drawn into an old quarrel that I'll try to explain to you. It covers a number of years, and I have only a vague outline. If you look at the newspaper picture, you'll see that that it is *my* high school letter jacket on the floor. It was stolen from our car when I had two loads of dry cleaning to bring up that first week in December. Furthermore, we do have a bullet hole in our storeroom window and the opposite wall. Walt and I were shot at downtown when I visited his Kansas City Club. Heard about vandalized cars in the alley, anyone?"

"When were you shot at?" Now Mother Holly sounded indignant.

"The day Belinda typed and mailed the releases the university kids signed."

"I smelled whisky on you, not gunpowder." Belinda aimed her pen at him.

"Oh, we weren't hit."

"But now you're trying to scare us? I agree with Belinda about these constant bits being added to your tales of fire and fury."

"Warn you. We should all remain alert and go about with our pistols at hand until we can think of some way to get out of this jam. The other side refuses to understand that we are investigating only the ownership of the jewelry. We are burdened with *their* belief that we're trying to find out who killed the Kilmers."

"Good god, Ken. What can we do to allay their fears, to rebuff their mistaken assumptions?" Belinda shot up on her feet and stared at him.

"When I interviewed those two pallbearers early on, I recognized a menacing aspect in who the dead Lincoln fellow described in that article was. He was the second one I've told you about, the one who thought it was the wreck involved, not Natalie. Did you notice that he is now murdered? Dead as a dodo? However, Walt told me the bigger menace was the first fellow I interviewed: Clyde Shannon. He was Lincoln's boss, and, if Lincoln is dead, that's one threat that is laid to rest. The police will not find out a single thing about who-dun-it, I would bet. But I don't know about that Shannon."

"Nor can we find out anything." Belinda returned to the living room couch and gave her daughter a push in the swing with her foot. The baby played with a mobile hanging against the front of the swing. "Let's quit talking about any of our connections to nearby DeSoto vandalism, generic names, or Lincoln's Lincoln. We'd end up making something out of nothing, and I'd never sleep at night. We have children to protect calmly."

J. B. was asleep below a corner of the couch.

"Walt's old partner, Clifford King, is what Walt called 'connected.' The lawyer made a great fuss last week when Walt and I were considering ways to stop any threats against our families. Also, Walt said that his house was shot at by a kid. Eh, also, I'm glad to say that Walt's police friend is my old sarge, Phil Tyler. He was at Walt's house and took off after a kid, probably the Lincoln boy. Didn't catch him."

"A kid is doing the shooting? Did he murder Mr. Lincoln, too? His own dad?"

Holly said, "You never said a thing about that before. I am a bit worried about that, Ken. We need to know what is facing us. Personally, I demand that you tell us all about this type of background and events as soon as you find out something. Or experience it."

"Will do. I asked Walt to look into why the man Lincoln was so jumpy about being Richard Kilmer's pallbearer that he threatened me. Walt finally pushed for a thorough investigation of the car from the wreck. He found out from a subsequent police search that Kilmer's brakes had been tampered with as we discussed. The oil pan had a tiny hole, too. Probably the vandalism and the threat to us are both pretty much over."

Both ladies clapped. "I certainly hope so," "It better be," they chimed in.

He went on, "It's not part of our aegis to investigate murder. Mr. King, that former boss of Walt's, promised to correct the misconceptions the pallbearers had of our assignment. He was flinging lightning bolts at us that day, he was so angry. I mean when he confronted Walt and me the day we were shot at, and he caught us making silly plans. We'll proceed cautiously about ancillary matters, and the implied connections will hopefully disappear," Ken said, reassuring his girls. "Just because cars like ours were vandalized by kids next to our building, why should we suspect that there was a connection?"

"I would, now," Belinda said, with a sober look on her usually cheerful face. "After having this conversation. I'm glad King chastised you, calmed you down, and said he'd intervene."

Distracted by her serious tone, Ken quietly studied her. "We're safe, Belinda," he said to allay her fears. Ken liked her choosing to wear only a touch of lipstick. That way, she didn't look strange to him in the nighttime from having to remove layers of mascara, rouge, powder, and anything else he didn't even know about. She even looked pretty without the touch of lipstick. Even when she was as pale as that white fabric she is wearing under her cardigan sweater.

Holly commented, "At least my building has doors on our garage under the first floor porch, and twelve inch square beams framing floors, walls, and ceilings. We can't be poisoned by carbon monoxide or easily shot or bombed, except by pigeons. I do admit windows are a vulnerability. See, those tenants in adjacent buildings, if they're lucky, get to park under a roof in an open sided shelter. Otherwise, they park in the snow and rain and sleet and dark of night. Their building may not be as sturdy as ours, either."

Belinda said, "You were smart in having the leases for the two second floor apartments and for the three third floor apartments contain the clause about opening, closing, and locking the garage doors each time a car was moved, Mom. Neither being able to see inside nor to get inside has probably saved all of us multiple problems generated by hoodlums."

"The mailboxes in the foyer that have combination locks are a fine idea, too." Ken added his remark to expand their growing sense of safety.

Holly replied, "The reason I thought of all those things to examine before I bought this building is that I had always lived in a rural area where we never locked our doors. Neighbors did pop in and holler, 'Anybody home,' but we didn't have any people threatening us––after the tramps disappeared when the Depression era was over, and everybody worked on the war effort."

"Time for me to finish gathering up the dry-cleaning

for the washerwoman to take by the shop on her way home with the rest of the dirty clothes," Belinda said.

"I'm off to the kitchen for a few minutes," Holly remarked, "because I hear Harriet coming up the back steps with the groceries. I had to send her back because I forgot the meat for next week. Remember that your brother, Barney, and my brother and his family are coming up on the afternoon of the 23rd. We'll have a turkey dinner Saturday and ham early on Friday night, Belinda, so we can walk over to the Plaza festivities. They'll return home Saturday. The Saturday dinner will be at 11 a. m., a little early for our usual dining, but they want their three kids to be at home Christmas Eve. A week later, their oldest boy will have to return to Ft. Hood."

"Mother. Please do not make those meringue shells for dessert. I hope you did notice that 'desserts' spelled backward is 'stressed.' Yes, they're pretty. No, it is not easy to eat one without it shooting off the plate when I try to cut a piece. Stresses me out just looking at them."

Holly looked amused. "I remember how you shot it like a hockey puck every time. All right. I'll do mincemeat pie, okay?"

"That is a great idea, Mother." Belinda nodded her head.

Ken with a tentative note in his voice, queried Holly. "Uh, Mother Holly, isn't that pie made of animal guts?"

"Not any more. It does sometimes still have meat in it but I don't use it in mine. It's raisins, suet, and other things, spices the way I make it."

"That's a relief. Not that I'm squeamish, but it always sounded like a weird dessert when I read about it."

Holly summed up the anticipated holiday activities.

"We'll have a fun family celebration Friday into Saturday, twenty-four hours' worth, yet the timing frees our family for Christmas Eve and Christmas Day activities."

Alberta began wailing, and J. B. joined the chorus. He burbled, "I wanna cookie." Belinda said, "Break time, snack and nap for the kids."

Belinda directed people with her hands, Holly through the butler's pantry and Ken to a chair by the round desk to open the mail. Belinda said, "I already paid the bills and Mother opened the Christmas cards. The rest looks like advertisements but you better check."

She picked up Alberta and started walking to their bathroom to change the baby's diaper. A she walked past the others, Ken called from the office, "We need to get back to discussing our investigation as soon as you return, mothers."

CHAPTER TWENTY-ONE

Mother Holly supervising, Ken and Belinda Massey compared their findings, working at the round desk, arranging categories of related items, and crosschecking relevant subjects. Belinda took certificates, began typing up everything in duplicate, inserting two pages, with carbon paper between them, in behind the roller. She handed a sheet to Holly.

SLEUTH WORKS REPORT FROM DEPARTMENT
OF VITAL STATISTICS DEC. 15, 1955,
GRAVEYARD, AND NEWSPAPER DATA
H. JONES, K. MASSEY AND B. MASSEY

1. Christian VOLKS (1843-1893) and Frieda JUFELLEAR (1846-1897) (tombstones)
   2. Jost Christian VOLK September 13, 1873-September 11, 1914 (Jeff City, obit) m. Clara FINLEY (1871-1909) Kansas City, Missouri
      3. Marlena None VOLKS dob April 3, 1892 Kansas City, Missouri m. Samuel Harver June 7, 1919
      4. Merrilee, dob. Aug., 24,1920, Raumville, Mo
      4. Carole, dob March 31,1926, Raumville, Mo
      4. three sons, unk dobs

> 3. Irene Schlenk VOLKS (May 6, 1894-1894) Kansas City, Missouri

1. Henrik Mann VOLKS (1845-1903) and Helga JUFELLEAR (1846-1898) (tombstones)

> 2. Johann Scheid VOLKS September 1, 1874-January 4, 1921 (Jeff City, obit) m. Frances DALE (1872-1924) Kansas City, Missouri

>> 3. Jacqueline Jayne VOLKS April 10, 1892- May, 16 1946 (Jeff city, obit) m. Dean Schmidt

>> 4. Natalie Schmidt Kilmer (unk dob?, -9/2/1955)

> 2. Josef Zimmerscheid VOLKS August 17, 1895- April 17, 1918 Kansas City, Missouri(never married)

Belinda said, "Yes, we know Irene died young and that Jacqueline died in 1946 here in KC. I am finish making the chart and will put copies on the table for you to read at leisure."

"Indeed. Thanks for reminding me. These other two, then, demand research. AH, how quickly we move," Holly said. "Excellent." She looked down the list. "I searched the newspaper archives for other Volks descendants. I found those obits of Jost and his wife and Johann and Frances. It seems definite that Marlena is the only one still alive. Plus she's a descendant of Christian. I can't do any more."

Ken waved a hand to halt her departure as he tried to read through her notes from the orphanage. He wasn't able to comprehend her abbreviations. She walked over to as he frowned in concentration, trying to suss out her meanings from the conglomeration of notations.

"Oh, I should have given you a translation to start

with. Abbreviations consist of symbols for male and female, estimated age in months, such as 23 for a year and eleven months. A question mark when the date was estimated for the birth. I'll write the items out completely for you to read. Here is the first page to show you what I mean. Make notes alongside the margins if any problem interpreting catches your eye. As I said, I had assumed we were looking both for a girl and a boy who ran away in 1920 and became the Clarmonts. They may have made up that name."

"I'll keep that in mind that as I read your notes," said Ken. "I'm afraid we're spending too much time on an insoluble, insignificant problem."

Holly explained further, "I was concentrating on identifying kids who were no longer in the files, as far as I could ascertain their absence. That should shorten the search. I mentioned that we're all three going to have to go look through the earlier decade of handwritten notes for information about when orphans arrived. The orphanage probably couldn't afford printed forms for a while, and no one ever bothered to go back and update the material."

Holly penciled in notes on several sheets from her notebook, ripped them out as she finished each one, handing them across the round desk to Ken who, also still seated at the round desk, swiftly read them, and made a few notes in the margins, chart in hand.

The two Massey children had scattered toys all over the room and fallen asleep on the carpet, covered with small blankets over their legs. They had eaten everything Belinda and Ken offered them for lunch and were sated.

Finally, Belinda stood and marched over, moving her stiff legs out straight in front, in imitation of Ken being a

Nazi storm trooper at the gas station. Holly had finished with her own notes so Belinda handed her more sheets of paper that she scanned and approved. Ken gave Belinda the items he'd finished and back she went to the typing duties. The same triangle moved information around during the next hour.

The trio paused for a tea and ham sandwich break in the kitchen with the kids before returning to their big main the office to discuss impressions of the data that were on hand and decide what data were still needed. Holly made notes of the discussion for a written summary to take to their visit to Walter Raleigh Monday morning.

Next, Ken outlined plans for his tracing of the military service of brothers of the two young college students. Finally, Belinda listed their hours for the statement they'd submit with the report.

Their work completed as far as possible, the trio sat back on soft, luxurious sofas in the living room and relaxed. The huge old oil paintings of Missouri towns in the early days of the state provided a feeling of space even beyond the dimensions of the elegant room. After another hour and a half, J. B. would demand the bubble bath and toys to play with in it. His mama frequently mentioned that she preferred his having the bath before supper in order that a warm bath and warm food developed into warm sleep.

Belinda left to wash her hands in the lavatory down the hall, off the living room. The hallway led to the master bedroom/bath and the Masseys' bedroom and bath. Belinda had told Ken how much she enjoyed letting J. B. have a bubble bath in their tub. It was a huge, boxed-in porcelain tub that was two feet deep and six feet long. Their bathroom had actually been a maid's room in the early days when people went down and out through the rear door to the outhouses. A section adjoining their bathroom but opening off the hall was the guest lavatory.

She returned to the living room singing, "Sorrowing, sighing, bleeding dy-i-in-g, sealed in a stone-cold tomb."

"I guess that myrrh is yours, that bitter perfume?" her mother asked from the floor where she was again drawing the landscape around the tracks and highway.

"No, actually it's Chanel #5. I put a dab behind my ear even though we're not going anywhere tonight."

"Did you know Chanel designed suit jackets with a unique sleeve that allowed a lady to raise her arms without raising the hem of the jacket?"

"No. You'll have to draw me a diagram because I can't imagine how that works."

The baby was sitting up focusing on a nursery rhyme book that Holly began reading to her, both seated on the blanket. J. B. was obviously listening to the rhymes because he would recite them along with her. His doing both maneuvering the toys and reciting the words fascinated Ken. The kid would make an alert soldier.

Belinda sat down by her husband and slipped her shoulder next to him. "I'll have my husband raise his arm, and I don't care if the hem of his shirt comes *up* because his arm is going *around* me."

"Mother Holly, I remember that Barney was in the JROTC in Granstadt High School. Why has he never been drafted?" Ken asked, kicking off his slippers, wriggling his toes, and sliding the soles of his feet over the tufts in the dark blue rug.

Holly gave the book to Alberta because it was made of oilcloth and virtually indestructible. She ignored her daughter's comment and answered Ken as he obeyed Belinda's 'call to arm.' "Barnard has the same irregular heartbeat that my husband had, that eventually killed him. Barnard was depressed when he couldn't join the service, after practicing to be a military man for two years in high school. I offered to pay for half his college, if he put together the other half of the monies. My brother popped over one day and asked Barney to help with the books and sales from the farm. Barney has saved his money for two years and will start college next semester."

The adults took turns playing with the little boy and baby girl while resting occasionally with a cup of coffee. Eventually the kids started cranking up their displeasures with this and that. Belinda swooped J. B. off to the bathtub with his two rubber cars that would float. Holly and Ken took Alberta to the kitchen for her supper.

Eventually, both kids were put back down on the blanket to wait for the nanny to return. With relief, the adults put themselves back on the cushioned furniture. Working with the children was alternately exhilarating and exhausting.

Belinda slipped out of the warm arm for a minute to go to the television console where she clicked on the Arthur Godfrey show and came back to sit next to Ken. "My brother is more interested in college than I was. My one accounting class satisfied me perfectly. And, I could date you while I was taking it. One of my friends was studying nursing. The girls had to march to the hospital for practice and were sequestered in a dorm every night. I thought that was a dreadful way to learn a career."

"It sounds like detention," said Holly. "I hadn't heard that. Wonder why any girl would want to be a nurse that badly."

"Well, it beats military boot camp, but only because the girls get to sleep inside," Ken said.

Holly lifted a finger. "Hey, I just heard Lillian go upstairs. Take J. B. up, Ken. Harriet won't be back until later this evening. I'm off to the archives. I now have only two obits to check because we know what happened to Marlena, Irene, and Jacqueline. Shouldn't take long."

Ken picked up the sleepy boy while Belinda took the baby in her arms, and up they went to relinquish their bundles to the nanny.

CHAPTER TWENTY-TWO

Walt Raleigh received them at 2:30 p.m. Monday. The evidence in their reports consisted of the snapshots that Belinda had taken from Marlena's photographs and letters; and, six legal birth certificates plus three short newspaper obituaries constituted the remainder. These Holly had found for Jost Volks, as well as Johann Volks and his son Josef. Ken had added a section and clearly labeled any conjectures in the written reports about an orphaned descendant as separate from their proofs.

The attorney motioned for them to be seated in the conversation arrangement of furniture. He seated himself and started leafing through the report.

The attached summary of expenses didn't raise an eyebrow on the attorney's face when he scanned it. Calling for Marnie, Walt indicated the expense sheet he had separated from the report. She smiled at both men and ignored both ladies. "Certainly, Mr. Raleigh. I'll be happy to draw a check for Mr. Massey's agency and his employees," she said. She took tiny steps; her personality appeared as tightly wound as the pencil thin skirt and jacket around her. Her body was as straight up and down as a straw.

Holly laughed out loud––deliberately. She spoke leisurely as Marnie made for the door. "We have written that report on the proofs we have ferreted out, Walt. Ken added a short report on a rumor. Your Meg contributed a direction to that rumor, the one other lead, a vague one that we're following up this week. Do you want to know more about something that may not prove viable?"

"I prefer not to be surprised."

"Behind the cover letter is a table summarizing the birth certificates Ken and Belinda found. The Volks' sons and their daughters are identified by the six certificates." Holly had separated the Vital Statistics copies from their report and pointed out the overview as she saw him look at it. "My colleagues found six birth certificates in Jefferson City. Then I found the obituaries of the three Volks. Descendants Marlena, Irene, and Jacqueline we already knew about."

She reiterated, "Marlena on that list is the only one still alive, and she has five children. I also found one obituary for Henrik Volks in 1903. In addition, Belinda obtained copies of the marriage certificates of the two Volks sons. Those are in that next envelope there. We have not yet unearthed the older marriage certificates for the twin sisters to the Volks brothers. They may have married in St. Louis and moved here to Kansas City. May be in some church archives in a dusty basement."

Walt opened the envelopes that were with the typed report. He stopped and went through the usual ceremony of lighting his cigar. That was one way to buy time to think, Ken figured.

Holly said, "Belinda took those pictures you have in the envelope. She'll explain them."

Belinda stood, walked behind Walt's chair, and looked over his shoulder. "We stopped to see a third cousin of that Natalie Kilmer, the one who would have had sole title to the jewelry. The cousin is Marlena Harver. Natalie had sent some mementos from her family hoard of pictures and letters to Marlena. I had a Polaroid and made copies of those letters and pictures. That first picture is of Marlena in her 30s. That next one is Mrs. Schmidt, Natalie's mother, in her thirties, with her husband and young Natalie. Hold those next Polaroids under the lamp to read them. They are letters reminiscing about family lore. Because the film is small, the letters are barely discernible, but with a magnifying glass, they can be read."

Holly concluded, "And Marlena says she wants nothing to do with the so-called jewels and was never in line to inherit them! It was a shock to me to have Ken and Belinda tell me that it was the younger Volks, Henrik, who had collected or made the jewels while he was working for the twins' father, a jeweler in Vienna. She so informed her daughter, Carole, in the Masseys' hearing and admitted that Merrilee was probably ignorant of the true history of the stuff. Marlena Harver is the first and only remaining direct descendant of the Volks brothers, but a descendant of the brother who owned a boarding house in KC. I repeat, she stated firmly that she had no legitimate claim, and that what Merrilee was purporting to know was blatantly erroneous."

She undid the buttons of her brown angora sweater in the too warm room. Walt stood and helped her off with it. He placed it on a coat rack beside the door.

"You mentioned that there's another thread, or snag. That must be this addendum."

Ken said in an undertone, hoping Marnie wouldn't hear, "Here we go about the rumor. One wife of a pallbearer, Mrs. Shannon, I earlier mentioned I had interviewed."

Ken gave Walt an inquiring look. Walt gave a small nod of understanding in return. He then squinted an eye in recognition of shared danger.

Ken related, once again, "The Shannon name I found from the obituary about the Kilmer pallbearers. The missus told me a rumor. She indicated that a Volks daughter was a real scamp, a round heels. The girl supposedly went to France with her mother the winter before the debutante ball. The implications were that she was *enceinte*, out of view, and delivered of an out-of-wedlock child. And, not only your wife, but also Marlena's daughter, Merrilee, made suggestions regarding the rumor that we tried to follow. The two girls had lived in Raumville and knew of a married couple who were orphans--knew that because the couples' son had gotten in trouble, trouble involving Natalie Kilmer's mother in a graveyard here in KC. Sorry, for the convoluted explanation."

Holly added, "Note that *nothing* in the pictures or commentaries mentions anything at all about a missing, illegitimate child. Then check the pictures from Paris-- those two," Walt had separated out two more Polaroids, "and look then at the picture of the Jacqueline Schmidt girl, the Volks debutante, I mean, from the newspaper photograph."

Walt pulled out a picture Holly had taken of a 1908 society section from a local newspaper.

Holly insisted on her viewpoint, stating, "She couldn't have been recently pregnant. Girls didn't run around the world in plain view back then. Such a period as that, of four or five months before a baby was due, was called 'confinement.' That's my opinion."

"I am not as sure as Mother is about that," Belinda said.

"We're trying to be thorough. What we have been tracing, as you'll notice from our mileage, is Meg and Merrilee's wish for us to follow up on that orphan lady they knew about. Of course, that all was the result of my mentioning to them the rumor Ken heard from the Shannons, slap my wrist. Yakety yak, yakety yak. Mother may be correct that our investigation of an orphan is going up a stovepipe belching smoke. But about this orphan lady: she and her husband had fled a Kansas City orphanage some forty-fifty years ago and ended up in the Raumville vicinity and later moved over to the wine country. That is the reason we took the trip to Hermann, Missouri, last Wednesday."

"The male orphan is a widower and still lives there. He and his daughter talked with us. The daughter is going to find pictures of her late mother, make copies, and mail them to us. We talked with them; his name is Clarmont, and his daughter, Laura Helsinger. My parents live between Hermann and Raumville where we stopped overnight to save money on not having to get a hotel." Ken's voice indicated that he was half-joking.

Holly Jones regained the stage to conclude, "I've already found names of children in the Catholic orphanage who were mentioned one year and not mentioned the next year during the span 1907 to 1920. The three of us could go back through earlier records tomorrow when the orphanage records are available, if you wish. We'd need to find out when the names first appeared, in case any ancestral information accompanies the entries, and note when they entered the orphanage, perhaps with an age written down," Holly Jones said. "Then this off-the-road juncture will be ended."

"I appreciate your progress so far. Do you think we'll

have this wrapped up by Christmas? The museum is extremely busy over the holidays and will not be expecting anything until January." Walter leaned back and took a cigar from a box, waving it at Ken, who shook his head. Walt twisted the cigar in his mouth after he clipped the end, before he lighted it.

The smoke drifted warmly and pungently around his head and into their faces. The walls in his office had a brown overcoat from smoke dusting the white paint. The colors matched his mustache––brown more than white. The sun's rays coming in the south window danced through the smoke. Ken would bet that all Walt's clothes identified him with the smell. It had been noticeable when Walt welcomed Ken at the to his club.

The Masseys nodded, and Holly noted, "Maybe. Depends on when the Clarmont girl gets the photos to us. We need to compare them with the Harver and Schmidt ladies at the same stage of life. Mrs. Clarmont was near forty years of age when she died from combining some cleaning fluids that created lethal fumes. That was about ten years ago. Mr. Clarmont, however, Walt, was adamant that he wanted nothing to do with any claims on jewelry that would engender publicity. The problem is that he wouldn't be a claimant anyway because his wife left no will. Ergo, the lady's children would inherit. But, these are all slim possibilities." Holly emphasized her remarks with a raised hand, finger pointing up.

"But didn't you say that he was also an orphan?" Walt aimed his cigar at Ken before placing it in a ceramic ashtray.

"Yes. Both Merrilee and Meg described him as such. Those two pointed Belinda at Mrs. Clarmont. We'll have to ask them why they mentioned the lady and not the man," admitted Ken. He began to see why Mother Holly suspected that this trail led nowhere. Too nebulous.

Marnie gave a tap on the door, entered with a large ledger and a checkbook, and gave them both to Walter Raleigh. He signed a check. "That takes care of us to date. Along with the allowing for the legal forms I gave you to take to the printer."

He placed the check in an envelope that he put over on the desk by Ken. Holly picked it up and put it in her purse, which she closed with a secure sounding snap.

"Do you anticipate having to travel out of town again?"

"No, sir. But, we'll know whenever we've closed all possibilities from the orphanage records," Holly Jones said. "We're going over the old, handwritten notes from the defunct, closed orphanage tomorrow morning, as I indicated. When the copies of photographs arrive from the girl in Hermann, we'll come over and compare the picture with the two Volks' descendants in those Polaroids we're leaving with you."

Walt said, "All right. Do close out that orphanage angle. I'll be going out of town in a few days. We're going to Meg's folks for the week from December 25th through New Year's Day. I doubt anything pressing will come up, but you'll find us at the phone number that I wrote on the envelope."

All stood and shook hands, with the **Sleuth Works** contingent leaving past a tiny, stiff-necked Marnie who nodded brightly through her round glasses at Ken. "Hurry back, Mr. Massey, sir," she chirped.

She shut the door behind them, and they headed down the stairs to the street.

"This interest of the museum in jewelry surprises me. What art comprises, as I think of it, is paintings or sculptures. Furthermore, I don't spend my hard-earned money on jewels," Belinda commented in a thoughtful tone. "I cannot see why anyone would do that." She pulled a new blue wool knit cap onto her head and matching mittens onto her hands.

"It's a way to indicate that one has enough money beyond water, food, housing, etc." Ken was thankful that she wasn't a wastrel, buying useless things merely for show.

"Like gilding a lily? Meaning wealth and waste are synonymous? But everyone needs food, water, shelter. I guess it's just what a person chooses––or is able––to spend, such as dining on a pork chop or on a pheasant stuffed with a partridge stuffed with cheese."

Holly laughed. "And we ourselves are much better fed than many. I'm sure that not only females, but also males, throughout history adorned themselves. I don't mean the poor people, but royals and nobles. Remember why the *Magna Carta* was signed?"

"Because the King needed his princes to give him money, and he signed citizenship concessions that they demanded in exchange," Belinda said. "I wish that Marlena had had pictures of the odd things called jewelry. Wonder if a king bought some of them. I couldn't get my mind to envision them from what Ken showed me of the list."

Holly said, "I'll try to set up an appointment through Walter Raleigh with the museum. It would be a good idea to know what we're concerned with, wouldn't it?"

"Right you are, Mother Holly. I'd like that."

"Speaking of princes, I did look at what was happening

with the inhabitants in 1840s Prussia, Germany, and the Austro-Hungarian Empire. Some Germans were enthralled by movements in France during that time, such as revolts against royalty and so on by the proletariat. The revolting Krauts demanded a Constitution, and elected people to Frankfort plus offered the head of state to Hohenzollern Frederick, who was not happy about the offer. When troops came to his palace grounds to give a cheer for him, he set his troops against them––believe it or not, as Ripley would say. Moreover, the little Princelings in Germany and Prussia didn't like the idea of giving up their fiefdoms. Meanwhile . . ."

"This would make a *very* complicated motion picture, Mother." Belinda inserted her comment in the monologue, twirling her finger around her ear.

"Yes, indeed. Meanwhile, the Hapsburgs in Vienna had domain over neighboring countries where various and assorted languages were spoken. To put down any uprising, the Hapsburgs merely shooed the army of one country against the rioters from another of their countries. A smart Royal Austrian noble had the Emperor abdicate in favor of an 18-year-old Prince, whom he could control. Also, the Hapsburgs did not like the Hohenzollern, Frederick. Turmoil was everywhere. That is probably when our female twins probably sailed out of Bremen or some other Harbor and, days later, made it to the east coast. Their husbands-to-be had prudently left the European area earlier; I would hazard a guess that they came over during the 1830s."

Ken and Belinda watched a veritable pageant as Holly illustrated her history. Holly chose to act out a pantomime to become a king, placing a crown on her head in an almost believable fashion. Next she was a member of the proletariat toiling with a bundle on her back slogging her way around the room. As a deposed Emperor of Austria-Hungary, she looked despondent while arranging make-believe royal robes around herself.

Portraying these different characters with a haughty look and sneer or a sneaky look and an imaginary weapon illustrated her history lesson. Her Hapsburg consulting Prince orders out the army of one country with the wave of her hand and a finger pointing toward the next country. Shells are flying over her head in that country, and she reels pretty well for someone her age.

"And, then as they left the boat, the twins were wrapped in midcentury dress and carrying a single bag each. I can envision them, frightened and excited at the same time, weary from the voyage yet eager to see everything in their new country. They didn't have to wait long for an introduction to the vast country. That's because I can also see an aunt from St. Louis waiting to take them to her home and heart. And arrange the marriages with the Volks folks." Holly sat down with a grin. She had pretended to open her arms wide and hug them and then to usher the girls ahead of her through a doorway into America.

"I never consider our Revolution, with 13 states finally banding together against the British, difficult to follow," Ken vowed. "You've just taken me on a trip in European territory smaller than the US of A borders, and, frankly, left me a little confused."

"Amen," Belinda said. "But also, thanks, Mom. You know how to encapsulate a lot of information into a short lesson. I wondered what could drive so many people across the ocean to here, merely from hearing a promise of life, liberty, and the pursuit of happiness. Apparently, the driving forces were *threats* to their life, liberty, and pursuit of happiness!"

Ken coughed and said, "Mother Holly. That reminds me that the clerk in Jefferson City said that the word 'Volks' translate as 'folks.' 'F-o-l-k-s.' He said someone at Ellis Island had probably made a mistake in entering the boys' surname. That means we would have a very difficult time trying to trace anything back to either the German or Austrian branches of their real names, if those are the countries of origin."

"No one has given us the faintest indication that we were to do that kind of tracing. The myth of the so-called possible-maybe-heiress who was an so-called orphan has sidetracked us. Both are moot points. We're after the lineage of the so-called jewelry in the United States of America after the brother arrived. Period, over, and out."

"I'm indebted to you," Ken grinned, "for the summary, mother-in-law and heart and soul."

CHAPTER TWENTY-THREE

After they left the attorney's office, the purchasing of many Christmas presents was on the agenda for Ken and Belinda before the stores closed at seven p. m.

Mother Holly went back to her apartment. She had already finished her shopping in November and chosen antimacassars and had had leather wallets inscribed with their initials for her daughter and sister-in-law. For Ken, her son Barney, and her brother, she purchased brown leather belts and wallets. All the young nephews would receive a dollar in a Christmas card. Consequently, she spent the remainder of the day in a comfortable chair reading while taking an occasional sip of eggnog. In the background she could hear the splendid symphonic records she had selected for the record player.

The Christmas tree would be erected in the living room Friday evening away from the fireplace's live embers. All the youngsters would enjoy decorating it. The tinsel had been carefully repackaged last year, what of it could be retrieved from the fir's branches.

Belinda's brother, Barnard, had graduated high school two years before. He now worked for his uncle, Chuck Osborne, on his farm. Barney would be coming in with that family. Because, come spring he'd be going off to college, Belinda also bought him two handkerchiefs and ties.

Belinda told Ken as they parked and headed for the Jones store, "My aunt, Deedee Osborne, is pretentious, although she is quite familiar with what naturally goes on, living as she does on a farm. But she pretends that she's strait-laced while I know that no expression, no vulgarity can faze her because she understand how life begins, how it lives while growing up, and how it ends in the slaughter house or graveyard. I'll drop a couple of off-color remarks, and you watch her. She won't appear shocked out of her shoes. She'll understand exactly what I'm saying . . . and ignore my humor. Not my favorite person."

Ken and Belinda spent all Monday afternoon in a toy section at the department store. They ended up with a Monopoly set, chemistry set, and Dopp kit for her three young cousins, who were 13, 16, and 19 years old. The oldest, Gene, had been drafted into the army.

She chose a leather scrapbook for her aunt and uncle Osborne in the camera department, Holly's brother and his wife. Ken liked it so much he said he was going to buy one for their family after the holidays . . . when things went on sale.

"You keep telling me that I have good taste––other than that needed for cooking well––and am diplomatic. I remember my first taste of diplomacy was when I was 10 years old, and Aunt Deedee showed me a baby boy of theirs. I thought he was ugly, but I straightened my face and cooed, 'He's cute as a bug's ear.' At the time I was waging war on cockroaches in the hayloft."

Ken laughed. "You also have a very quick mind. We make a good team with your intelligence and mine working so differently."

"You're such a compassionate man, Ken., and work well with Mom. Does it bother you to have a lady boss?"

He was surprised and a bit shocked. "No. She's experienced and easy to understand. I've had bosses all my life. My parents, my older brother, teachers, coaches, master sergeant. I've developed the ability to grasp what is needed. Doesn't bother me to be directed when I'm let to do it my way. I've simply moved from physical labor through to brain work."

"But you don't react when she's terse or sarcastic."

"No. I just listen. I don't have to react. You do react to her tone of voice because you two ladies are so much alike. Pretty and fervent."

"I'll have to think about that a while. I'm not sure what you mean."

"Don't worry your pretty head about it. We're fine as a family."

Belinda studied him a minute with her head to one side, then shrugged her shoulders and gestured him toward the bookstore section.

For their children, she bought a Jack-in-the box and a xylophone set for the two-year-old and a teddy bear and cloth doll for the baby. For her mother, she and Ken bought an encyclopedia set because the woman loved to read about everything. The Massey couple then separated for the selection of gifts for each other, promising to meet back at the car in an hour or so. Each could wait for the other in a nearby coffee shop Mother Holly had recommended for its succulent French silk pie.

For Ken, Belinda had had a bespoke tweed jacket made by his tailor that would match the trousers on either his brown or his black suit. Belinda also found a coonskin cap and cap gun ala Davey Crockett for a dollar and a half. She would salt those away for J. B.'s third birthday.

Ken bought Belinda an aluminum suitcase and a cosmetic case and inserted an invitation, in a card inserted to the luggage tag, to travel to St. Louis for her birthday. The brooches he had hid until he could put them in the stockings Christmas morning. Belinda and Mother Holly's stockings would be draped from the fireplace mantel in the living room by then. Those would replace the stockings for the nephews on Sunday morning, he guessed, not be hung on Saturday morning with the boys'.

He and Belinda met up in good time for the pie and drove a ways back southeast to the Christmas tree farm to ask that his chosen one be cut down on Friday instead of Saturday because of the Osborne's plans. When they returned to the apartment, he pulled boxes of ornaments from the storeroom that was next to the kitchen.

The out-of-towners would be introduced to the apartment house for the first time as well as to Kansas City. Each person in the Kansas City apartment knew where the others hid packages but politely ignored the evidence under their eyes and noses.

Ken and Belinda had one large bedroom on the first floor, and Holly had another. Each was furnished with a double bed comprised of a soft mattress over bedsprings, knit bedspread in fall colors, and headboard and footboard of ash wood. A matching chiffonier, next to a dressing table with a bench, was against one wall. Before another wall, under an oil painting of an old European family, were two overstuffed chairs covered in warm colors of washable chintz cloth. Lined drapes were hung in winter with the colors matching the autumn hues. In summer, sheer curtains were hung with a window shade behind them.

The bedside tables of ash wood had brass lamps on top. Holly insisted on placing doilies under the lamps although Belinda didn't particularly like the crocheted frills. The window seat became a bed for J. B. when needed. A playpen could be quickly erected for the baby. Sometimes one or the other was sick or needed to lie down when the nanny, Lillian, was absent.

The servants' rooms and the guest room on the second floor were furnished with items moved from the Jones' farmhouse, in particular from Belinda and Barnard's rooms.

Consequently, some of the sycamore wood pieces were slightly marred and darkened with age but still well polished, and the fabrics were clean.

Friday night, the family would erect the tree, go to church, sing carols, and see the crèche pageant. The group would then walk over to the Country Club Plaza to look at the lights and listen to the singing. And finally tumble into bed, drained by the excitement.

On Saturday morning, they would open presents. The adults hid presents until early morning before the kids awoke to find them under the tree. Breakfast would be available all morning in the form of boxed cereal and juice. Hot coffee was always ready.

"What do we give the servants?" Belinda asked her mother Monday evening.

"I guess you were busy having a baby last year and didn't know what I decided," Holly said. "I give them a new apron, your good used clothes to alter, clean used bed sheets, and a bonus of a week's salary plus the weekend off this year on both Christmas Eve and day and New Year's Eve and day. They receive room and board all year and two dollars a fortnight. They're satisfied and would tell me if they were not. I know how to prepare the holiday food and will be glad to have the kitchen to myself. You'll have a child for both you and Ken to tend to. Works out nicely. And, Belinda, I've been trying to teach you how to cook well by winging it, although you try to ignore the lessons."

"Cooking bores me," Belinda said. "It's creating something that doesn't endure."

"Then think about something interesting while you're using half your mind on tasting the concoctions. We'll make noodles in the butler's pantry Friday morning before the guests arrive."

"I've had a few disastrous results thinking of something else while cooking," Belinda said. "Ken said the brownies resembled hockey pucks. Hard on the teeth."

Ken laughed at the memory, sitting with the newspaper folded at the crossword puzzle and pencil in hand.

"Never mind. Your family will get used to your disasters. But experiment . . . a sense of flavors develop with a pinch of this and a dusting of that," Holly suggested while Belinda groaned.

Ken grunted in disbelief with a twist of his mouth that exaggerated and underscored his reaction.

"I mainly seemed to do all right the first time I prepared something. One time I made an ice cream cake that was terrifically good. I had bought a container of egg whites for the icing. The problem is that I didn't see that one brand had sugar added to the eggs but the next brand I bought did not. The second one was terribly bad. I never made it again."

"But you did learn. Pay attention to exactly what is written. That ability is why you turned out to be such an excellent librarian and accountant. Details do not often escape you, Belinda."

"No, you're correct. I have learned a lot. I enjoy our agency. You mentioned the other day that my green corduroy skirt was showing wear. I think I'll take the streetcar down to the department stores after the holidays and buy some new winter clothes. There are usually sales then."

"Yes, there are, if you can stand the rush and crush. Good idea, though."

"First, I'll wait to see if anyone has bought me any new outfits for Christmas, hint hint."

Holly laughed. "Star light, star bright, wish I may, wish I might, grant my wish I make tonight."

"And Pinocchio said, 'When you wish upon a planet, makes no difference if you want it.'" Belinda sang the revised version of the lyrics while giving a bow with a regal flounce of her red plaid pleated skirt.

Her mother retorted, "If wishes were horses, all beggars would ride."

"You just know all those sayings because you've been reading the Mother Goose book to the kids."

"One chooses one's literature where one can find it." Holly opened her latest library acquisition, *The Strange Career of Jim Crow* by C. Vann Woodward. "You taught me to find mine at the library's recent acquisition section and thus not have to buy it."

"And, I'd like to read that about a strange career when

you're through. I'd like to know how not to pay for other things than just books or without having to ask you for money. Maybe I'll find a strange career to enable me to go it alone." Belinda's voice was a bit choked and strained, as though she were about to cry in frustration.

Ken came into the discussion. "Did I hear a heated discussion going on here? The apartment is plenty warm enough without our needing high blood pressure. The coal bin is full. You could don sweaters."

"It was nothing. Just us quoting loving quotes at each other, Ken," Belinda snapped her comment.

Holly reminded Belinda, "Remember what happened to Pinocchio's nose?"

"Pshaw, Ma, Ah'll go check on supper and powder mah nose. Keep mah nose outta yore way."

"You're fine just where you are and the way your nose looks," replied her mother. "Simmer down. The hired help does not receive more than you, if that's what you're worried about."

Belinda looked at her mom, surprised. "Oh. I guess I did sound like that."

"Look, Mother Holly and Belinda. I hadn't thought about this before. Why don't we each set up a separate bank account that we can use anyway that we choose?" Ken sat back with a serious look on his face. "We've been putting our company money into one account and the rental monies into another. That means money piles up in those causing us to ask permission any time we need clothes or something. We can keep the expenses for the separate enterprises clearly delineated for income tax purposes."

Holly was thoughtful but kept silent.

Belinda said, "And which account would be used for the children's expenses?"

"Well, perhaps you and I also need a joint account."

Holly said, "That makes six accounts for Belinda to keep track of."

"Oh, Mother, that would be no problem for me. It's just six separate sets of books. The accounts will be pretty straightforward. No problem at all."

"All right. Bring in the Housing income and expenses ledger and the **Sleuth Works** costs and income ledger. Let's see what can be sliced out of each. I certainly don't mind divvying up the rental income somewhat. I think we should set up **Sleuth Works'** incomes with a specific salary for each of us."

"Yes."

"Yes."

Belinda went to the office, unlocked the file cabinets, and extracted some ledgers. She found a tablet and three pencils. She labeled columns in each ledger. The three went to work seated alongside each other at the round desk with two ledgers spread in front of the middle person, Holly Jones.

"My goodness, Mother, you've really done well. When you've already paid the real estate taxes and insurance this month, look at what's left? And you haven't collected this month's rent yet, Ken!" Belinda said. "And our office is in the black. I really don't pay attention to the columns I'm dealing with; it's simply routine for me."

"We *do* do well." Holly grinned at Belinda and then Ken.

CHAPTER TWENTY-FOUR

On Tuesday morning, the three investigators spent two hours hunched over bits of fragile notepaper, lots of dim writing, and scattered information. Each had a copy of some of the orphan names that Holly had found days before. Any item that held potential relevance was noted out loud in order that all three kept up. Bit confusing, too. Ken, suddenly attuned to their voices, wrestled with deciphering a comment from Belinda that was superimposed on one from Mother Holly.

Belinda said, "Horatio Bridge!!" And Mother Holly followed that exclamation as she snapped, "Horatio at the bridge.

They looked at each other.

Ken raised a finger and said, "There's more things in the heaven and earth, Horatio than are . . apparent to me! What were you talking about?"

Holly said, "It's a poem by Thomas Babington, Lord Macauley, about a brave Roman named Horatio who stopped invaders at a bridge to Rome. A couple of his friends were alongside."

Belinda said, "Oh. My reference was the name of a kid. I was recalling that Slim Anderson's given name is Horatio. Didn't mean to speak aloud. We don't need our bridge defended." She bent her head back over her collection of papers. "Well, if we ever do need a Horatio, that's Slim Anderson."

Ken started to reveal that Walt and Meg had suggested such a defense back when, back before old man King threw a fit, or was it a caber? Naw, he let it go.

They ended up with 37 names. Now, the archives of deaths, wills, and obits would get another, but shorter, scrutiny. Ken threw up his arms and said, "Enough work. Let's secrete ourselves and wrap presents. After lunch, we can hide them and play Monopoly. P. S., I intend to win again. After supper, let's watch television. I think the Ozzie and Harriet program is on ABC tonight."

And so it went until bedtime. Nothing remembered after bedtime.

Wednesday the sleuths continued to mine slips of paper that bore, perhaps, significant details. It was a wearisome effort, Ken decided, as he rose and paced the room. "I can find nothing in our notes that indicates anything other than a) there were five girls named Barbara, and b) two boy children named Ted. I'm speaking of ones that appeared no longer in the information by1920. Mother Holly took that data down two weeks ago as being from the five previous years. That's too many to follow up on. Shall we hang it up and tell Walt to close off the investigation with the Harver lady being the only close--and deniable--claimant?"

Holly demurred. "No, no, Ken. I wonder why Marlena was married so many years after the Schmidts? Did she say her husband was in the first world war?"

"Yes. He was a sergeant in the AES, American

Expeditionary Service. They didn't marry until after he returned."

"That explains the difference in why third cousins Natalie and Merrilee were ten years apart in age. We've found no descendants of the Schmidts other than Natalie. We do still need the pictures from Laura, Clarmont's daughter."

"That one last clue, that about an orphan, will be rejected as a possibility, if I may predict the outcome," Holly argued. "All right. We'll let it rest until we hear from her. And it better be soon. Or I'll insist the case is finished. Ken, you need to put some time on the case set out by the two students about tracing relatives who served in the military."

Belinda went from the main office to the small front reception foyer. She opened the door to the stairwell and walked down. She left the bottom stairwell door open at the building's entrance hall. The afternoon mail was usually delivered by now, and she eyed the mailbox front. The outside door opened. Belinda looked over her shoulder at the intruder and said, "Hi, Meg Lowe Raleigh. You're heavy laden."

"Hello. You must be clairvoyant to know I'd be arriving on your doorstep this very minute," said Meg, pulling off a scarf from her blond hair. She'd had it cut in a pixie, and Belinda complimented her about her haircut.

There was a sound of metal and wood as Meg must have tried to open a doorway to the upstairs rental apartments. She said, "The pale green Christmas lights around the foyer are beautiful. The floor is covered with a beautiful carpet. How do you keep it clean in this weather?"

"Don't try that other stairway door. It goes to our

tenant's apartments. Let me carry the sack. We go in this way. It's going to get chilly in our apartment if we don't move." Belinda had opened the heavy door with a large key when she came down. She turned behind Meg to lock up. The door allowing ingress to their accommodations was on the wall adjoining the brass-plated mailboxes.

"Mother does the seasonal decorating. Has always had a knack I lack. I preferred sports like archery."

"Archery is better than debauchery," Meg said, kidding her.

"I'll agree with that. Although a quiver might be involved with either . . . This is the way up these few steps to our entryway, remember," Belinda said.

"Let me help you with your coat," Belinda said. "Just put Lynn down on the rug and let him hold the package."

"I've brought you some divinity and fudge that my mom made. She's been making tons of candy for my twin brothers' college years. Their fraternity has a big Christmas party after classes close. The exams are after they return in the New Year. We're leaving for our annual visit with them after this weekend, stay for the holiday week. This is Lynn; say 'hi', buddy."

The boy did so, best he could, and it lisped out, "Hi, buthy."

"We're having relatives up this weekend. The candy will be welcome."

Meg said, "I told Mom about meeting you. She said you were a tall, strong, accurate archer and rifleman––rifler?–– well, person who shoots rifles. She adored having you girls come to the farm to practice. She said Dad met you once, but was usually at work, and my brothers were at college.

Your visits helped fill in days that were too quiet for her liking. She loved meeting you and your husband, too, last week. She wrote me all about it."

"Hey, look who's here. You haven't met my latest friend, Mrs. Meg Raleigh, and her baby. She's the one got us into this latest case. There's my mother, Mrs. Jones, and my husband, Mr. Ken Massey."

"Oh, we've met. Hi, Ken." Ken nodded at her and returned to his work on the desk.

Meg greeted Mrs. Jones warmly while she unbuttoned and removed her coat after putting the child on a davenport. "My son, Lynn, was walking before he was a year old. He could say eight words, in his own language, too, and the pediatrician was very impressed." Lynn hopped down from the couch and went to the pile of toys.

"I'll get the coffee," Holly said. "Let me signal the nanny, and you take Lynn up to play with J. B. He's just turned two. He's gentle with his younger sister and entertains her. Lynn will entertain them well in turn, I'm sure."

Upstairs in the nursery, J. B. was leaning over the playpen with a washcloth, dabbling at his sister's face. "You're a s'obber bots, baby," he said.

Belinda laughed. "I called the teething one a 'slobber box,' and J. B. loves the word."

As they descended the stairs to the landing, a landing that offered five stairs going down to the kitchen on one side and five stairs down to the dining room on the other, Meg commented on their beautiful and roomy apartment.

"And, Belinda, let's let our boys play with each other frequently when a nanny is off for the afternoon. I mean play at the other boy's house where the nanny *is* present. I'm going back to teaching next semester, and I want to start Lynn on being around other people before then." Meg gave the suggestion with enthusiasm.

"Great idea." They walked back into the living room.

Ken rose, went to the coffee table, and opened the two containers of candy and sampled each one, looking up at the ceiling as if he were a gourmet taster. "Those are excellent. My compliments to the chef," he said. He offered everyone a choice of divinity or fudge.

Meg refused. "Don't look at me. My mother made them. I'll pass along your remark. Walt and I are making an early December visit with my folks. His parents are visiting us over the next few days. They flew in from North Carolina. They have the most delightful soft, Southern accents, 'y'all?' Then we go back to my folks in mid-Missouri after Christmas. I'm so bored at not being in charge of anything. I'll be glad when school starts."

Meg accepted the mug of coffee and a shortbread cookie. The cook had wheeled in the tray with cookies, cups, and coffee pot. Belinda and Ken helped themselves.

Holly Jones also brought in a tin of her decorated sugar cookies for Meg to take home. They turned on the record player so that Meg could hear *White Christmas* from Bing Crosby's album that the Masseys loved.

At the end of the music, Ken asked, "What was it you did in Japan, Meg?"

"I taught history to the dependant children of the Occupation Forces from 1949 to 1952. And, I also taught English to the Nagoya Mayor's daughter and two of her friends. That was interesting. Then, too, I toured the Japanese historical places such as Kyoto, Miyajima, Tokyo,

Hiroshima. I met a lot of Americans and Japanese, but the Korean War, sorry, *engagement*, was regrettably vicious. Guys I knew with great personalities and futures were killed, maimed. No reason for it––the country was already divided. Politics and history are things I'm supposed to understand!"

Holly held up her hand toward Meg. "No, I know exactly what you mean, Meg. I've lived long enough to know that the wars are the result of some megalomaniac sending young men to be killed. And, it seldom achieves for the perpetrators the riches and territory that they wanted."

"Or conversion to their religious beliefs," Ken said.

"But Walt said you were invited to meet with Japanese diplomats who came to Kansas City," Belinda persisted.

"Yes. It has happened once. Actually, the Japanese diplomats are not impressed with a female, even if she can say some polite, obsequious things in the Japanese language and bow her head slightly. I'm not sure I'll answer that request ever again," Meg said, thoughtfully. "I have more years of education than those diplomats . . . but the only prestige goes to the male species in Japan. They think more of tortoiseshell cats than human females."

The Masseys looked at her in surprise.

The nanny, Lillian, rang the bell from the nursery, calling for attention to some matter, causing Belinda to hurry back up stairs with Meg at her heels. The summons turned out to be because Lynn was half asleep, sprawled on a rug with his head half under a giant stuffed elephant. The alarm had been because J.B. kept trying to wake him up by poking him.

"What does J. B. stand for?" Meg whispered to Belinda as they returned to the living room. She had the sleepy Lynn over her shoulder. And put him down carefully while she replaced their outer winter garments.

"Jeremiah Bartholomew, after both his grandfathers," Belinda whispered back.

Meg gave her an amused look. "He'll learn to write quickly, just to sign his name." Holly chuckled at her remark and nodded.

The adults quietly made some more promises to meet after the holidays, both at the gym for exercise, or socially, with or without their family members depending upon the event.

Meg added, "You'll receive an invitation after the holidays to our annual 'Break a Resolution' party. We hold it the second Saturday night after the first Monday in January. Our friends and colleagues from my school and from Walt's practice all come. You three fit in both categories. Friends and colleagues. We have a bridge group, too, if you feel like filling in when another couple can't make it."

"That would be fun. We'll be there at your Resolutionless party. Maybe we can substitute nannies with our children every second and fourth weeks. I know how to play bridge, but I don't know if Ken does."

"I know how to play but it's been a while," he interjected. "Do we bring anything like wine to the gala?"

"No; we take pertinent expenses off our income tax as business entertainment." Meg started down the stairs after she put wraps on herself and the boy, following Belinda with the big key, and stepped out the front door. "Cold out here," she called back, pulling the outside door shut.

The frigid air sent a sharp temperature contrast through the office into the living room. "Dear me, I didn't realize how stuffy this apartment was becoming, all shut up. Both times that outside door opened with the door to the stairs also open, we had some fresh air. Maybe we ought to open a window now and then." Holly went over to the oriel window. "This window and its twin in the office don't open but the ones in the dining room and kitchen slide up. If the temperature is around 40 degrees, I'll have Harriet open a couple for a cross breeze, maybe for half an hour."

"That won't cause us to use much more coal. I agree that some fresh air is better," Ken said. "It's odd how great fresh air is, and yet it doesn't smell. If we have damp air, like from the river, we'll get musty smells. Mothballs do help keep out moths when packed away with winter coats. Not a pleasant task when unpacking them in the fall for our professional team of sleuths."

"I certainly think putting mothballs around winter coats would make us smell worse than a farm smells. I can think of nothing better to freshen up our rooms except outdoor air," Belinda said. "Ken, the next time you talk with the tenants, ask how they handle odors. Maybe it's something easy and less offensive than cold air or certainly better than mothballs or musty odors that we've been talking about."

"Ken, I didn't notice anything like a musty odor in here last summer." Holly objected to his prediction.

"I did, for sure. I'll do it, that is, ask the tenants a discreet question. I doubt that cologne or after-shave would conceal that smell that's similar to forest mushrooms. I used to put lime on toadstools and mushrooms when they invaded Mom's garden. We can't make use of that on our rugs or furniture: it'd dry our skin like Egyptian mummies." Ken sounded serious.

"Don't want an asp to get me!" Belinda said. "Don't wanna be a toadstool to be limed. I wonder if any limes are around this time of year. Ask cook to check for limes when she's at the IGA, Mom. Ask the neighbors how to rid musty odor, Ken, when you collect rent."

"I bet gin would taste good in limeade. Be something for our punch bowl when we entertain." Holly went to the office to make a note on the weekly grocery list.

CHAPTER TWENTY-FIVE

The Osbornes arrived in good time from their farm. Holly had written to her brother to tell him to park in the alley, lift the garage door, turn on the stairway lights, drive in, shut the garage door, mount the stairs, and knock on the first door he came to. And so he did. Followed by his family and Belinda's brother, Barney.

Holly bustled into the kitchen when she heard the knock on the porch door. "Come right in and park your carcass," she said cheerfully. "The boys will sleep here on the porch so have them dump their gear here. Hello, Deedee, dearie, come right on in."

Chuck hugged his sister and told her that they'd brought a 100-pound sack of potatoes and a smaller one of turnips. She directed him to the storeroom before she stood by the stairway door to open it as he and his son, Gene, returned from the car, lugging the sacks.

Ken told Chuck how to lock the garage door back down the stairs and showed the boys to their cots while Belinda took the aunt up to the bedroom. The newcomers followed directions and shed outerwear and suitcases in the rooms where they'd be bedding down. The three nephews and Barney wandered around the downstairs apartment rooms like a recon troop but settled into the nursery upstairs to play games.

Holly exclaimed over how much Gene (named for his grandfather Osborne), Michael, and Perry had grown. Her son, Barnard, she gave an extra squeeze, but not obviously enough to embarrass him, yet hard enough to let him know that she had missed him.

The four boys continued exploring the house. Up in the nursery they started in by dropping toys into the crib to make Alberta laugh her glorious laugh, and by trying out every plaything J. B. owned. The two older lads, Barney and Gene, settled into a game of Chinese checkers with the board and marbles Ken found for them on a shelf. J. B. soon tired of watching the match, mainly because they ignored him and prevented his grabbing a marble here and there. Michael began reading a Hardy Boys book to him, with enough expression in his voice to keep even a two-year-old entranced. Perry observed all the activity without joining in and then stepped down to the main level.

Belinda had placed Alberta into a stand-alone swing next to the couch in the living room. The baby couldn't seem to stop staring at the activity around her, Ken noticed.

"Any chores you need another man to help with?" Chuck asked Ken after they'd shared a glass of wine over by the oriel window in the living room and nibbled on some cheese and crackers, looking out at the lights coming on in the late afternoon. "Gene's home on furlough and can lend a hand, too."

"We need to bring in the Christmas tree and set it up after supper. Hmmm. Come to think of it, your sister asked me to secure the dumbwaiter in the butler's pantry. It lifts into a narrow hall upstairs that has an ancient lock on the door. I've found no way to lock the lift nor have I found a key to the upstairs lock."

"I have a padlock and hasp in my tool box, but you'll need a bolt or new door lock for the hallway down here. I might even have two padlocks, one for each end of the dumbwaiter. I'll go see. I'll bring in my screw driver and drill," Chuck said.

Ken nodded, walked to the storeroom, looked over the pegboard, selected a hand drill from its place on the wall hook, and returned to the butler's pantry. Chuck emerged from the downstairs door into the porch and came into the area.

Opening the dumbwaiter, peering inside with a flashlight, Ken's nose noticed that a mouse seemed to have made its home there. And died there. The fetid air was shockingly bad. He towed out his handkerchief, coughed into it, and said, "Maybe we better put some moth balls inside there before we start, something to counter the smell, air it out a bit."

"But that'd take ages. Let's stick Vick's or Vaseline in our noses and forge ahead, man," Chuck responded. "Belly-roo, can you bring us a jar of Vick's or Vaseline?"

"Certainly, Uncle Chuckie-pooh."

His youngest son, Perry, wandered into the pantry and peered under Chuck's arm into the dumbwaiter. "Smells, Dad. Something died in there."

"I noticed."

"Looks like there's a secret treasure chest in the wall," Perry said.

"What?"

The short boy put his head into the dumbwaiter. In

a muffled voice––he was holding his nose as he held his head against the wall and peered inside––he said, "There's something I can see glittering inside on the floor on this side."

"What can you see?" Ken asked.

"Uncle Ken," the boy replied, "somebody hid something." Reaching in with his free hand, pushing against a low board that was extremely dry and splintering, tugging harder, jerking back as a bunch of metal dropped to the floor of the dumbwaiter, he then backed out, no longer holding his nose but holding round silver and black coins in both of his hands. Others littered the floor of the lift.

Perry hollered, "Look at all this money I found! Lots of silver, lots of money! Hey, Auntie! Look at my treasure!"

Chuck and his son then moved back to let Ken gather the remaining items in his handkerchief. He handed the packet to Perry.

"And, there's something else." Perry stuck his head and one arm in. A splintered sound and a thud followed. He stood up holding a brocade bag. "Something heavy inside. Maybe a huge gold piece," His voice trembled with excitement as he danced around, cradling the bag in both hands.

Ken said, "Or a pin cushion filled with clay like I made my mother."

Chuck took the bag from Perry's hands and set it on the sideboard counter. From inside, he carefully pulled a long necklace of dirty, dark grey beads. "Some costume jewelry, I bet."

"Oh, man," Ken moaned. "Some little girl is missing her precious jewels. Now we have another jeweled mystery. I hope her name is in that bag."

Chuck upended the bag, but nothing fell out. He said, "It may not be dime store stuff, Ken. Manufactured beads, play beads, would be perfectly round. These are misshapen." He rubbed one on his front tooth. "May it's some kind of pearl. It's rough when I rub it on my canine."

"Let's find out who sold this building to my old sister," said Chuck, and the three turned back toward the living room after sliding down the door of the dumbwaiter. "Maybe there's other loot hidden in the walls."

"We've not discussed the sale except about the real estate people who were involved. The realtor and his family who lived here then moved out to her farmhouse on that acreage. She settled in comfortably as we helped," Ken noted. "I was getting out of the Air Force, and Belinda was having our second baby. I asked Mother Holly a few days ago who had conducted the transaction, just in case it was part of a local mob. She remembered the name of the fellow and the out-of-state company he worked for."

"I heard the negotiations were intense."

"So did I. I wanted to steer clear of any involvement with the vestiges of the gangs still around and was happy to hear the company was not from here. They're developing a suburb called The Meadows on her old land. Maybe gangs are waiting underground to spring into action, like a Class B movie plot. But, she assured me the people who sold it to her were from an out-of-town corporation."

The ladies looked up as the men hurried into the living room. "All fastened up safely?" Belinda asked. "I was just bringing you the salve."

"Um. Not quite. We found something in it," Perry

blurted, opening his hands. He added on a hopeful note, "Your sign says 'finders, keepers.'"

"Not quite: it says 'we finders, you keepers.' That means whoever finds something turns it over to the keepers," Aunt Holly teased. "The finder gets to keep ten percent of the worth of the items, if the finding has a price."

Perry sneezed. "It smelled dead in that little elevator. But it held a treasure of coins and a nasty necklace in a bag."

Aunt Holly said, "*Gesundheit*. You sneeze that hard very often, you'll sneeze your schnozzle off, Perry. And, stay away from Alberta. We have survived the winter so far without anyone having a cold."

Deedee scolded him. "Perry, put those metal things away from you. They're making you sick. Who thought you'd find something like that in a clean house?"

Belinda looked from Perry's hands to Ken with a lifted eyebrow. "And what, may I inquire, are those? More ancient jewelry?"

Perry answered her. "Money, looks like. It's jewels, too." He showed her the coin collection. Chuck displayed the necklace.

Ken looked at Belinda and Mother Holly with a beseeching look. "Another jewelry mystery, my dears, but the coins are yours, Mother Holly."

"This is the first time we've seen this fine building, Holly," Chuck butted into the conversation. "Who sold it to you? Ken is vague about the company you dealt with. And why put coins in that dumbwaiter? And did you put this necklace in there?"

"No one actually sold it to me, Chuck. If you must know, I traded the farm for it."

Chuck laughed. "Don't be teasing me. We're not in elementary school. It's important. Who sold it to you?"

"Chuck, I am not teasing. The corporation that wanted our farm wanted to get rid of this building, rid of the upkeep, and rid of taxes. They felt bogged down, wanted to expand, capitalize on the growing population in the area."

"But, Holly, they'll be liable for more taxes with the farm acreage."

"Chuck, I guess you don't know that my farm is going to be turned into a housing development called The Meadows. They'll sell off housing plots to other people. Kansas City is expanding like crazy all around the edges."

Chuck, Deedee, and Barney looked at her, now speechless. Perry was on his knees, sorting through the coins and arranging them by size on the desk at the far side of the room from the family. He had ignored his mother's directive to leave them alone. He unwrapped the ones in the handkerchief and began scrubbing at a coin with the cloth.

"If those are antique coins, honey, you must not rub them. I read that rubbing them could remove some fine etching on the coins. Dealers have a special way of doing that type of repair work," Holly said. "I put them in the dumbwaiter to protect them. I feared the guns in the safe would get oil on them. But, this odd-looking old grey necklace isn't mine. Junk." She looked down at it on the table.

Chuck looked at her with a frown closing his eyebrows toward each other. "I think it is real pearls. Black pearls. Look at the knot or silver bead between each bobble. Look how uneven the grey pearls are. I think that they are definitely black pearls. Rubbed against a tooth, they rasp. Do you know who lived here before?"

"It'll be in the documents. Just a second." She looked up to the left. "Ah: a Jerry Winslow, who represented the company locally, lived here with his family. He and I had a few toe-to-toe negotiations. I think we both were satisfied. I'll give him a call and see if it belongs to his young daughter or his wife."

Perry, proud that he'd found the stash, called to her, "Did robbers live here, Auntie? Someone stashed these old coins and that thing in the dumbwaiter."

It was Holly's turn to be secretive. Silence hung in the air. She turned an innocent look on her brother and the others and shrugged. "Later, Perry, later. I said I put the coins in there, but I'll tell you more later."

Ken, ever sensitive to the nuances in conversations, said, "Let's all sit down and have a drink. Sherry okay with everyone? We've finished the wine. We need to sort through several bits of information––obviously, bits that the family haven't thought to share. I'll pour. Belinda, is there another crystal glass? Only four are out here in this cabinet."

"Yes. It'll be in the butler's pantry." She left and returned immediately. "Sorry, Barney, you'll have to share mine," Belinda said to her brother. "The others were broken or, as I just found out, cracked when we unpacked."

Holly began her story, after taking a sip, and wrinkling her nose at the taste. "The people who rent the five apartments upstairs had been here for years and intended to stay, I was told. I therefore would have a steady income without running a tractor or doing a rain dance to overcome a drought."

"But how could such a transfer of properties be made?" Chuck asked.

"Paid the register of deeds and signed some papers and paid the tax guy and the title search company and paid the lawyer and whatever other fees. You probably know that Jeremiah and I had adequate life insurance, and I had some money left after his funeral." Holly sounded as though she was proud of the transaction.

"I swear, I've never heard of swapping property. Did you have the farm and this building appraised?"

"Well, of course, little brother. I wasn't born with a silver spoon in my mouth. I know quite a bit about business matters. Both sides were very careful to have neutral real estate appraisers, from people not normally used by either side. I have this big apartment, a covered garage under the porch; and, Ken and Belinda and I have an investigative agency that uses my skills. The skills that helped our family, even when you and I were children, Chuck. And, with Jeremiah gone, I needed to quit dealing with tenants and sharecroppers on the farm. Furthermore, I know how to unclog a tenant's drain if Ken isn't here. And I'm teaching the skill to Belinda."

"Do you have a copy of the deed here?"

"No. Why?"

"I'd like to see who owned it."

"It was The Meadows Corporation, as if you need to know, my tiny brother," she said, looking up at him, a head taller than she. "I left some of my furniture at the farmhouse so that they could use it as the sales office and have a manager live there. The rest of the furniture I brought here to supplement the few pieces left by the previous tenants. I bought new appliances for the kitchen. It was a furnished apartment. Some things I had hauled away. That local rep, Jerry Winslow, moved from here out there with his family."

"Holly, fatty one, I didn't need to know that. We need to know the names of people who owned this building––or, at least the tenants who lived in this apartment since the Civil War, even before Wrenslows. I'm assuming the building's that old because of the dates on the coins I looked at. If they are a collection, were put somewhere for safe-keeping, and were not stolen, you've been given another source of income."

Holly laughed, Ken noticed, but said nothing.

"Uncle Chuck, I do know that the building was erected in 1879 because that is etched in the stone over the front entranceway. The numbers are probably full of snow or ice but, come, I'll show you," Belinda said getting to her feet. She disappeared and returned with a broom.

"The first families that lived on this property did not *own* it, Chuck, and you should be aware of that," Holly told her brother as they and Perry followed Belinda. "An acquaintance, Meg Raleigh, and I discussed this a couple of weeks ago. The Missourian tribe here didn't believe in, or understand the concept of, owning land. The Indian tribes in the 1800s were all moved out of Missouri––into Kansas and Oklahoma, mainly––with a sincere promise from The Great White Father that they'd be safe and secure."

Holly shook her head at what had actually transpired. She said that the tribes were tossed into reservations and ignored generation after generation. Even when benevolent Presidents were in power.

"I never knew that you were maudlin, Holly, a pitying

Patty," her brother said as they traipsed down the stairs and through the front door, shivering.

Ken concealed a laugh by coughing into his fist.

"No, realistic is more like it, chubby Chuckie. Now, how we trace subsequent pioneers' ownership through the years since the government's dispersal of tribes––with little disbursal of wherewithal––I'd vote for it being the Register's Office for deeds. We can do that next week during the hours it is open."

"See there," Belinda pointed at the stone lintel outside, shivering harder as snow and ice fell on her uplifted face.

They trooped up the stairs and back inside to the warm living room through the foyer and office. Chuck and Deedee looked at the desk and padlocked file cabinets with interest. "This is where **Sleuth Works** works out, to coin a phrase?"

"Yes, Uncle. We have plenty of room and can close off the living quarters like this." Ken prevented the people from walking into the living room by holding out his arm in front of them, and then he slid the door in place that made the section appear to be a seamless piece of the wall.

Chuck said, "That's a pretty good piece of engineering. Keep sticky-fingered strangers out of your private lives. Although previous owners knew that, too, with those pearls hidden in the dumbwaiter. The door looks pretty sturdy even though it seemed to slide shut easily."

Perry still on the hunt for involvement in a pirate's tale, with excitement gleaming from his Saxon grey eyes, said, "Maybe some robbers took the loot in a train robbery, came to visit their grandmother, and hid it from the U. S. Marshalls chasing them by sliding shut that secret door. And it was destined that I, Perry Osborne, should come to visit my aunt and find the loot. And, I didn't even have to confront the pirates the way Master Jim Hawkins did in *Treasure Island*. Especially the one with the hook."

"And maybe those are play money pieces, such as from a gambling game like poker or from a filthy organ grinder wandering the streets with a monkey," Deedee said. "You need to wash your hands, in case there are infectious microbes on those metal pieces, Perry. Dead things, like a mouse, can leave bad germs. And, when you're vomiting your guts out, remember that I've warned you more than once. Wash your hands with soap and hot water."

PART FOUR
THRUST

CHAPTER TWENTY-SIX

"I hear your brothers having an argument upstairs. I'll go get them and J. B. and treat them to a little snack," Aunt Holly said. "I showed them how to twitch the bell if J. B. bothered them but haven't heard it go off. I'll take Alberta up and change her because my nose says she needs it."

Chuck said, "Ken, we better finish putting on the locks on that door upstairs and down here in the pantry before the rest of the boys hear about the dumbwaiter. They'll want to ride the lift up and down, if I'm not mistaken, and they're too big. It'd break. Perry, let's put the coins and necklace back on the floor of the dumbwaiter and lock them in."

"Oh, Dad, can't I keep them?"

"I glanced at a few of the coins, and I think they're from maybe the late 1800s, but we don't have time this evening to do any research on them. Aunt Holly will let us know what she finds out about this building, who lived here, and who could possibly have put them there."

Belinda said, "Uncle Chuck, those coins are hers—I don't know why she's being secretive about them. But I've never seen that necklace before so we'll do that if you really think it's pearls, ugly pearls at that. We're pretty skilled at tracing ownership of things—that's how we make a living."

Perry added, "It could have been to hide everything

from marauders . . . or from a nosy little brother or even from the tax man."

"Just put the stuff back, Perry. Your aunt said she'd discuss the coins with you later, in case you didn't get the cue. After we fix the dumbwaiter, I'll get the tree up from the garage." Ken dismissed the whole set of speculations in favor of moving on. "We can decorate it after supper," Ken said, moving back toward the butler's pantry after he put down his glass. "The sherry bottle's empty, too, Belinda. Do we have any more?"

"Sure. I'll replenish this cabinet while you finish the locks." The wine bottles were kept in the storeroom, lying on their sides in the wine cabinet. They liked the white wines cold but the red wines at room temperature.

The drill screeched and the hammer tapped as the gentlemen made the dumbwaiter secure. While Ken went after the tree in the garage, Chuck put a bolt high across the hall door to the dumbwaiter upstairs, preventing children's hands from accessing the dumbwaiter.

Holly came downstairs holding the baby girl in a frilly dress, and two nephews, son, and grandson followed her, although J. B. bumped down the stairs on his rear end rather than walked. "They were merely arguing over a game of Chinese checkers," she said. "J. B. wasn't helping by asking 'why?' 'Why did you move that one?'"

She mentioned something about peanut butter cookies and milk over her shoulder to the boys following her down the five stairs leading into the warm, brightly lit kitchen. A Formica table, with eight folding chairs surrounding it, sat plunk in the middle of the wide floor. Barney helped his mother fill the glasses and two baskets with various cookies, including Oreos. Perry showed J. B. how to separate one in order to lick the icing from the center. Next up was dunking the chocolate halves in milk. Messy, but delicious.

Belinda and Deedee carried in boxes of lights and ornaments from the storage closet behind the kitchen. Ken and Chuck steadied the tree in a heavy wooden bucket of sand, lined with foil so that they could add some water. The men handed the lights around the back of the tree to each other and to Belinda standing in front. The metal clips on the cords were stiff, and Belinda nipped a finger, but it didn't bleed so she didn't complain.

Holly cleverly arranged a crèche set in the corner beyond the tree. The Magi, parents, and shepherds were made of wood, delicately painted. The wood manger had tiny slats and a pair of rockers on the bottom, making it resemble a cradle rather than a hay bin. Baby Jesus was smaller than J. B.'s index finger. Next, Holly placed a wooden picket fence set in lumps of clay in front of the manger set, as well as having similar slats encircle the tree, in order to protect the lowest branches. She finished the display by stooping over and hanging a silvery star on a branch above the crèche.

"I hope we can make it clear to the children that these items are not toys," she said to Deedee.

"Well, certainly my boys are certainly old enough to understand that." Deedee sniffed as she replied.

The warm room took on the odor and ambience of an evergreen forest represented by the high tree and reflected in the huge framed paintings of Missouri scenery on the walls. Ken and Chuck, Gene and Barney, Deedee and Belinda sampled the wine.

Because the cook, Harriet, had set the dining room

table before she left on her vacation, two leaves that had been added in the middle that extended the table. Ten chairs were arrange with one on each end and four down each side. A long lace tablecloth was on top of a linen one, underlying crystal glasses, silverware, china plates, and salad dishes. Trivets at each end were ready for the platters and bowls of food being kept warm in the kitchen.

Smack in the middle of the table was a long oval decoration made of evergreen fronds, pinecones, and small ornaments of wooden animals. These carved animals nestled in wool in little barns made by Chuck during indoor times forced by wintertime weather. The barns would be handed to the children, after the streusel dessert was downed. Or at least, before they left for the church pageant.

Holly dusted off her hands and walked through the butler's pantry, glancing at the security on the dumbwaiter. "Okay, Belinda, we need you to help carry the food. Perry, why don't you come lend your muscles?"

The nephew and daughter trotted back and forth up and down over the stairs from the kitchen to set out the food that Deedee dished up, including a bowl of sauerkraut, and the platter of hasenpfeffer. They toted in a basket of rye bread and a dish of butter, bowls of gooseberry and blackberry jelly, a large bowl of warm German potato salad, and another with pickled pigs feet. The salad dishes were for heaps of canned strawberries and loganberries with a dash of cream on top.

Ken poured all the drinks of water or milk, plus another round in the goblets of wine from the bottles that Belinda had unearthed and uncorked.

A couple of Ma Bell telephone books boosted up the chair for J. B., and the baby was plunked into a high chair.

Ken Massey, at one end of the table, opposite Mother Holly Jones, said grace as everyone, except the two youngest nephews and J. B., sat with bowed heads. The youngsters spent the time eyeing the food. They all chirped in at "amen."

"What is that meat, Mother?" asked Perry.

"You know it's the rab––"

"*Chicken*," Chuck interrupted Deedee to inform his son, "that I killed and prepared the other day. It was already cooked at home. We just warmed it up here. Your mother spent all week preparing the food, put it into pans or into baskets. Remember, you helped put them in the trunk to stay cold on the way here. Then, she started warming food up two hours ago while you weren't paying attention, kiddo."

The hasenpfeffer platter was too heavy to pass around thus Ken had people simply pass him their plates and "say when" he'd added enough meat.

"Tomorrow we'll have the traditional Christmas dinner at noon before you leave for home. After we finish dining tonight, we'll go to the Christmas Eve service at the church near here and then stop back at the Country Club Plaza to hear the singers and look at the decorations," he promised.

Chuck said, "I'd really like to drive by the Liberty Memorial for the WWI soldiers, the Great War, it used to be called before the Second World War came along. Our dad, Gene, was in the same division as Truman. You may have heard that Truman was an excellent officer. Boys, the flame is always lit on the top of the Memorial. I think the Union Station is by it. It's supposed to be another beautiful building. Busy, too, with all the goods flowing across country."

Spates of conversation about Kansas City attractions and commercial strengths were all that occurred the family for the next twenty minutes. As well as making significant inroads into the food.

The sound of either a fire engine or a police car siren wafted into the room. Ken looked at Belinda's brother and cousins. "Do you guys know why fire engines are red?"

The boys looked at him with puzzled faces. "No." The vote was universal. They put down their forks.

"See, it's because two times two is four; three times four is twelve; twelve inches is a ruler. Queen Elizabeth is a ruler. Queen Elizabeth is also a ship; the ship sails the ocean. There are fish in the ocean; the fish have fins. The Finns fought the Russians. The Russians are called 'Reds.' Fire engines are always rushin', so fire engines are red."

The boys clapped or laughed. The adults shook their heads; they had continued eating during his tale. The lads picked up their forks and took another bite.

"Now," Ken said. "Do you know why firemen wear red suspenders?"

The family stopped eating again. "No. Why?" They all looked at him, eating suspended again, waiting for another dissertation.

He glanced around solemnly. "To keep their pants up!"

The family members hooted at him.

"What a bunch of gobble-de-gook." Belinda shook a finger at him as she laughed. There were no takers for "seconds, anyone?" The plates had been heaped high on the first go-round.

"Let's wait for dessert until we come back," Belinda suggested. "We need to hustle to make the church service."

Every single person carefully carried a plate and silverware to the kitchen. Then ladies returned to the table and followed the path with the salad dishes, and remaining pieces of silverware. The men carried in the glasses and heavy platters and bowls.

Belinda started a big sink of hot water and put the glasses into the soapy water and immediately under the faucet, wiped them and set them into a drainer. The plates she left to soak. Holly and Deedee arranged the leftover food in the refrigerator. Belinda carefully washed the huge platter and large bowls of heavy china. Deedee placed one dishtowel under the large blue platter and handed Ken another to wipe the top carefully. He dried them carefully and put them back on the shelves in the butler's pantry.

"Aunt Deedee, how did you meet Uncle Chuck? I mean, like I first met Ken at a church social," Belinda asked.

"Oh, I grew up with a German couple from when I was a baby and raised to work on a farm. I met him when he was running a Four-H Club in our area."

"*Grew up* is an odd expression? What do you mean?"

"Well, I felt like an orphan. The way they treated me. Little Orphan Deidre. Unloved. Worked to the bone. Actually, another girl in third grade told me I dressed like poor Shirley Temple in *The Little Princess*. And, that's bothered me ever since, especially after I saw the movie. I can't shake the label from my sense of self."

Belinda stopped and gazed at Deedee. "Who would your parents be otherwise?"

"Don't know. Never asked if they were. They were

probably my parents, really. But I would hate them anyway, if I knew, you know," Deedee showed her straight white teeth with a feral smile, then laughed derisively. "I didn't think to ask. We spoke German all the time––until the war started, then it was guttural English. I acquired all the experience I could ever desire cooking German recipes. Chuck rescued me after they died within three months of each other, and my background was of no importance to him. My parents' farm was repossessed by the bank. I'm about six years younger than he is, and our oldest boy, Gene, named for your and Barney's grandfather, is about Barney's age. Those two formed a great team until Gene was drafted last spring."

Belinda said, "Yes, brother Barney finally chose to use his strength and intelligence rather than his mischievous side. Well, let's not hold the group up any longer. The rest of the dishes can wait. I'll just leave the them to soak." She dried her hands on the cotton dishtowel that Deedee handed her.

Deedee looked for a place to hang the dishtowel. Belinda took it and placed it over the handle on the stove.

"The pilot light's always on. That means that there's a faint wisp of steam in the air along with the heat from the radiator," Belinda said.

Deedee replied, "We still use a wood stove in the kitchen. Soon we'll have a gas line coming through the area. We already have had electricity for years. Makes our work days longer in summer but makes us more productive in the winter with longer hours of light."

"Yes, that's about the way it was when I was growing up on our farm Mom and Dad were working all year round.

They certainly didn't go south to Galveston for the winter as our neighbors did."

"Our animals need us during the winter as much as in the summer. We really loaded up the hay bins before we left just to get away for two days. And, I'm so glad we did. It's wonderful meeting you again as a housewife and mother, instead of a single babe, one that I envied," Deedee said, and turned around to give Belinda a long, warm hug.

CHAPTER TWENTY-SEVEN

"Now, let's take both cars," Ken called over the hubbub in the living room. "I'll take Aunt Deedee and the four boys and you, Chuck, take my family. Holly or Belinda can carry our kids and show you the way and where to park at the church and leave them the cars there when we go on to the Plaza."

"Good idea. I don't know my way around, and it's hard to read street signs in the dark." Chuck helped Deedee on with her fur coat that he had brought down from the guest bedroom.

"We drive out the far end of the garage. I'll lift the door when we go down. When we return, you parallel park in the garage again, and have your crew follow me up the stairs. We've room for four cars to park down there. One of Mother Holly's tenants doesn't drive, but we all use those stairs at the end of the porch and garage to deposit trash as well as we all use the front stairs for the mailboxes and front door. And, watch your heads. The doorway is short, low, if that's a proper description. I conk my forehead all the time."

Belinda carried the baby bundled into a one-piece zip-up outfit while Holly had garbed two-year-old J. B. in a snowsuit;, he who was almost hyper with excitement. His mother and grandmother agreed that he was darling. Even

Deedee smiled at him. He wriggled every which way trying to see what everybody else was doing.

The church service, on this evening before the Christmas Eve service, featured a pageant of the nativity scene. The kids sat, entranced, on the front edge of the pews where their parents sat, and watched wide-eyed. J. B. stood in front of Ken, having slid off his lap to stand on the floor. Alberta sat up straight on Belinda's lap.

One nephew whispered, rather loudly, "There's the Three Wise Guys," as the Magi entered the crèche scene in the stable.

The choir performed a selection of yuletide songs. After the recital of Bible verses by youngsters from the Sunday School, the caroling congregation completed the service by singing *Silent Night.*

The family members moved down the aisle and emerged into a shining night of moon and stars and frosty air. Brilliant Christmas lights on the Country Club Plaza drew them toward the exciting area. The roofs, domes, and cupolas were beautifully outlined with the strings of colored bulbs. The families jostled jollily in the crowds there.

Ken carried J. B. on his shoulders to start with, but that was becoming awkward, J. B. hanging onto his ears and hair, knocking his hat askew in doing so. Ken moved him into his arms and set his hat on straight.

He heard someone repeating behind his back, "Make way, make way" in a loud voice.

He turned toward the person speaking just in time to be shoved by a man's hand, shoving strongly against his rib cage, causing him to hit his back hard against a brick store wall. Luckily he had turned toward the voice or J. B. might have hit the wall.

"What the . . . " He caught a glimpse of a faintly familiar figure leading an elderly couple through the crowds down the middle of the crowded street.

His brain, his nerves, fed his body with an aurora borealis of emotions, reacted with flickers of red rage, white ferocity, emitted green resentment, yellow fright–– intertwining, changing, shifting behind his eyes.

J. B. might have been injured if he hadn't turned at that second, at that voice! His brain struggled to register the scene around him.

What? Who? Why that's the Shannon's tall, burly chauffeur, Chaz, smiling like the Cheshire cat, smug, moving out of sight. Plus the Shannons are being chauffeured, as usual--guided along the way--by walking, on their feet, not in a car.

The short elderly couple seemed to be deliberately delighted at the lights on the building across the street, pointedly avoiding him, heads turned away, big grins on their faces.

And, brother, that does it! My family will now lay down the defense against your gauntlet: think you're powerful, do you, you Shannons and your Chaz?

"Ow, Daddy," said J. B.

Ken then realized he was squeezing him too hard. "Here, I'll kiss it and make it well." He kissed the top of the boy's head. He let his emotions settle back down. Never in his life had he felt that angry before. Nor had he had such a swirl of mixed reactions surging through his system.

Next, Ken shrugged and pointed over to a huge lighted

wreath to distract J. B. who was looking up at him with curiosity. "I bumped into the wall myself, owie owie," he explained to his son. "You kiss me and make it better."

J.B. shifted around and planted a kiss on Ken's chin, bumping his forehead hard against Ken's nose.

The sharp pain, worse than his nose hurting from eating ice cream too fast, not as sharp as when his nose had been batted by a mule's head, about the same feeling as when he'd been k.o.'ed in boot camp, brought him completely back into control.

Ken was tall enough to overlook most of the crowd, to spot Belinda, her tam-covered hair nearby, her brother Barnard some distance away. Mother Holly was surrounded by the crowd but tall enough to be looking back at him in concern and following his eyes on the chauffeur although she couldn't see the short Shannon couple. He could not see Chuck's family but assumed that they were somewhere in the immediate area.

Time to go home. Time to walk back to the church and find their cars because they'd decided that leaving them there was easier than trying to find parking on the Country Club Plaza streets.

Patience was supposed to be its own reward. He'd been patient, waiting for Mr. King's promise to control events, insure that the threatening occurrences had dissolved and/ or would be concluded. Mr. Almighty Powerful (obviously not an Air Force **AP**) King had not fulfilled the promise. Maybe King'd bid a suit in trumps when no-trump won the bid. Or been out-bid. Or someone had reneged.

In that holiday crowd of good cheer, Ken began coldly

calculating. Enough. Tomorrow p. m. he'd revive-ruffle-rustle the retaliation plan.

The Raleighs had said they were attending a Christmas Eve party with American Bar Association colleagues. He hadn't forgotten one of Meg's sidebars. She'd suggested that she could mention, during a break at a dance, seated before the long mirror in the ladies restroom, re-doing make-up with the other ladies, that she'd heard a rumor that Mr. Shannon was being investigated by some senator: Symington? Senator McCarthy? Without making eye contact, ask quietly, "Had so-and-so next to her heard anything like that?"

Meg said all the ears in the room would hear, would repeat, would expand on the news, and would swear by the accuracy of the information. She would guarantee that it would spread back to her a week later, greatly embellished. Sounded like a sneaky defense, well suited to the situation at hand. Will she, won't she, will she join the dance?

CHAPTER TWENTY-EIGHT

The carolers on every corner sang harmoniously, either popular or classical noels. A repertoire of one included titles ranging from *White Christmas* and *Jingle Bells* to *Away in a Manger* and *Adeste Fideles.*

Santa's elves distributed candy canes, and helped children find a place in line to talk with a Santa on this corner, or with another one on a side street in front of those stores. No cars could dare to enter the crowded streets.

Over on one street corner, a sign acknowledge thanks to the Catholic college that had erected a crèche with live actors posing. One extra goatherd stood to the side with a goat that children petted.

The Jones/Osborne/Massey family spread out in twos and threes and moved up in turn through the lines of people to observe displays in store windows. In one display, a beautiful scene of little old-fashioned homes and snow-covered streets reminded onlookers of the Kris Kringle legends. There were tiny female dolls that had wreaths around their hair and wore long white dresses. Wooden sabots in front of a tin stove held cards that read **Naughty** or **Nice**. One pair with **Naughty** was in front of a wooden boy puppet who had a wicked look on his face, lips pulled down in a sneer, one eye winking. That resembled what Chaz had most likely been like as an unlikable kid.

The window that captured the nephews' attention featured intricate train tracks running through pine forests where lumberjacks in various poses hewed the trees. The engines tooted warnings before crossing a bridge or entering a tunnel. Other tiny men loaded cut trees on horse-drawn wagons that were aimed down a snow-covered road. The road went up over, or down under, three railroad tracks.

A number of dolls were arrayed at a party in another window display. They held cups as they stood by a fireplace or sat on couches or the floor.

Next door, a number of baby dolls appeared asleep in cribs. Santa had already crept down a chimney, left presents, and was leaving the way he had come, because he had his back to the room, his head turned with a finger beside his nose. Tiny bows decorated miniature gifts around the hearth.

Slowly collecting the family members, Ken shepherded them back toward the church parking lot. They moved in shifting pairs, discussing what they had seen, their favorite displays. Perry gave a long recitation of the Christmas poem he had learned for his school holiday presentation.

Mother Holly came up next to Ken, and she tucked her arm into the crook of his elbow, and said, "That tall guy who shoved you and J. B. was in the newspaper archives, arriving after I did one day."

"Did he accost you?"

"No: who is he?"

"The Shannon's chauffeur."

"Someday, Kendrick Massey you will spill your guts to me, won't you?"

He nodded and, she moved off.

Returning home, climbing wearily up the back stairs from the garage, all family members pitched in to help with drying dishes and putting them away. Then, while completing those chores, they had the odor of Deedee's warmed-up *Kakao* and *Kuchen* that settled people further into relaxed sleepy states. All family members hugged each other good night, awaiting Kris Kringle. Or Santa Claus. Or St. Nick. Whoever it was that brought all those presents during the night in spite of the fact that the chimney continued to send smoke into the ether from lighted logs in the fireplace.

Belinda used the window seat in their bedroom as a bed that J. B. loved. She had covered the wood seat with a long, thick cushion, put on a protective plastic cloth under the sheet and blanket, arranged two chair backs as a rail, and left enough room for J. B. to slip out in the morning and pounce on his parents in their own big bed. Ken put down his son on the cushion and started singing *Silent Night*. The boy's eyes finally closed.

By another wall, they had the playpen that served as a crib for Alberta. She had fallen asleep on the Country Club Plaza tour and been passed around to all the adults and the three oldest boys. She was still sound asleep when placed in the playpen, slept through the removal of her snowsuit and change of diaper.

Ken and Belinda moved quietly readying themselves for sleep. "I'll get up early and put out the presents and fill the stockings," she whispered. "I should have thought to get them out of the bedroom closets before everyone went to bed. If I could stay awake long enough, I might be able to tiptoe in tonight yet. But then I'd have to hide them from our kids, especially J. B. who'll probably get us out of bed."

She started brushing her hair 100 times at the dressing table. She would follow that with a bit of cold cream for protection against the frosty time they'd spent outside tonight.

"I'll permit you to do that, whatever you're talking about, for sure. I'm exhausted." Ken yawned and fell into bed, the odor of toothpaste emanating from his mouth as he pretended to snore. She kissed him, leaning over his prone body, and pulling the cover up to his chin. He was still tense enough to feel a charley-horse trying to form in his left thigh. He had to get his mind off the Shannons and their Chaz. And that newspaper picture of Lincoln slopped over his chair. With his own letter jacket peeking out of the picture.

He concentrated on the surroundings, trying not to keep looking up at the ceiling but to keep his eyes closed. He needed to relax. The linens smelled as though they'd been hung outside to dry, a virtual impossibility this time of year or in this place where they lived. Dried up old Shannons. Dead old Lincoln. Stop, think about how to dry sheets in the winter. Ken, his eyes firmly, determinedly closed, sniffed, melted out clues, and pondered the problem. He'd have to remember to ask Harriet how she did it. Getting old dried up, those Shannons. Using the chauffeur. Maybe it was Chaz who shot at Walt. And him. No, the washerwoman took the sheets with her. Maybe she did have a way to hang them outside. But, how would they even begin to dry in this cold weather. Belinda would have to inquire of her. But, why bother? He couldn't get ahold of the problem.

He had himself to ask Belinda and Mother Holly their opinions to help knead that plan he'd begun to mix. Now, come to think of it, both his stint as an Air Policeman and recent events held yeasty possibilities.

Sleep, go to sleep, ex-Sergeant Massey. Reveille will be soon in the form of a small body jumping on him eliciting a grunt from his stomach. Quit rehearsing what you're going to tell Mother Holly and Belinda tomorrow afternoon. Need their approval to do. This minute, the plan sounded stupid. Walt needs to know it's Chaz that's the shooter. Agate marble shooter. Mother Holly must hear it, mothballs for must. Why does my brain make these connections?

Ken barely heard Belinda go into the bathroom, shut the door, and start filling the tub with the really hot water she liked, probably scented by lilac bath salts. He faintly pictured her stretching out with a sigh into the warmth, closing her eyes for a few minutes. Sure enough, she must have returned sometime later, and he hadn't noticed, but when he woke once, he smelled the lilac as well as Palmolive soap and peppermint toothpaste. Oh, spring will return sometime, and nothing is so fine as a day in spring, unless that something is my Belinda.

The fright and retaliation flipped into his mind. A surge of anger followed. Idea for a plan set in Meg's rumormongering taking on a sturdy foundation.

Tomorrow, he'd give her a couple of presents, but he had not figured out how to deliver the birthday present. He must have been able to keep his poker face on, because Belinda could usually read his mood. He drowsily considered putting her present into a wood stocking, because it was a trip to St. Louis next week that she could bop an intruder with.

That didn't sound right, must be getting drowsy again. Her birthday came between Christmas and New Year's. Maybe he'd hold off giving it, not on Christmas Eve or . . . No, better to . . .

CHAPTER TWENTY-NINE

Saturday morning, Mother Holly awakened early, and Ken heard her tiptoe down the hall. She had quietly placed a beautifully wrapped package for each member of the clan in front of the picket fence surrounding the tree and crèche. "Oh, I forgot about filling Christmas stockings for the kids," she whispered as Ken and Belinda tiptoed into the living room.

"I know what to do. There're some little red sacks in the box of wrapping paper. We can put an orange and some candy in five of those for the boys. I'll go get them," Belinda whispered, turning toward the storeroom behind the kitchen. "They may range from age two to 21, but they'll all expect a personal gift from Santa like those the other kids have." She hurried out of the room.

"I'll get the oranges and ribbon candy now. Then I'll go collect the rent upstairs," Ken offered. "The tree looks wonderful, even when the lights aren't on, especially with the presents in front of it. Too, I'll set out the candy from Meg on the coffee table with us adults having first choice of that fudge and divinity."

Holly touched some straw decorations on the tree. "Look at these straw angels that Belinda made when she was in first grade. I was thirty-two when she was born and thirty-six when Barney came along. She made the angels for her baby brother's first Christmas."

"Took nimble fingers as well as delicate handling all these years." Ken gave Mother Holly's shoulders a hug as he went by. He gave Belinda bear hug, and said, "My talented wife."

Ken walked to the office door, preparatory to leaving for the stairway in the foyer to the upper apartments. "I'll be back shortly. I need to take these jars of walnuts up to the tenants and pick up the rental checks. I know they love having these nuts from that place near Stockton."

"Coupled with the fact that we don't have to shell them and cut our hands," Belinda said, returning with shiny red crinkled paper bags. "The walnuts may be expensive, but they're worth the price. Tell the people Happy New Year, too, when you give them the Christmas Cards."

Four boys charged into the room from the porch, clothes askew, and Christmas presents took precedent over solving mysteries or eating breakfast.

Deedee and Chuck came downstairs just behind the boys. Immediately Belinda heard Alberta prattling in her own language to J. B.––and he answered her! Belinda hurried to her bedroom and dressed him, sending him back to the living room. She dressed Alberta in a red velvet gown, white hair ribbon around her skull, and white anklets with lace around the top.

"What-ho, I'm going to set out boxes of cereal on the kitchen table with bowls and spoons and glasses of juice. I decided not to make Cream of Wheat because I didn't know when the others would get up. The coffee is already perking," Holly said as she left the room through the dining room into the kitchen. "Breakfast," she called back. "Whenever you want a bite to eat."

The kids, except the oldest one, Gene, were too excited to eat more than a spoonful of cereal——and that only because their mother insisted. They ran back to the living room, sat down at Aunt Holly's order, er, suggestion, and by age, oldest to youngest, walked to the tree and found his name tagged on a present. Each person opened a present, starting with the youngest, as the others watched and exclaimed.

Grandmother Holly watched J. B. working over his present; finally she became impatient and slipped the ribbon off. He ripped the paper but couldn't open the box. Until lifting off the top was demonstrated for him. As well as replacing the top and lifting it up again, as a hint for being neat.

"My train. See. My train," he said, walking it around to the others to be admired. He next opened a package from the Osbornes. Uncle Chuck showed him how to turn a handle on a box. Upon doing so, the child jumped when a Jack-in-the-box popped out at him. Uncle Chuck shut the lid on the puppet, and, this time, J. B. laughed when the puppet bounced up.

Then the lads spied the pile of red Christmas bags and opened them. Deedee had put a packet of pfefferneusse cookies in the red sacks after she came downstairs. Crumbs littered the floor, as the hard cookies became breakfast for the boys.

"Sorry, Holly. I didn't make them early enough in the month, else they'd have become softer," Deedee said stiffly.

"No matter, I have a vacuum cleaner. They're good cookies, crunchy or soft. Crunchy food adds a sensation to the tastes. Did you have any frog legs this fall? I've always loved the taste and crunchy skin of those. I want to fry some when J. B. is a year older so that he can watch them jump as I cook them in lard," Holly said to Deedee.

"No, but Perry did catch some crawdads that we roasted. They weren't as filling as the frog legs but he had found them in the same creek area," Deedee replied. "Oh, look, J. B. just crushed more cookies in the blue carpet. I'm so sorry, Holly."

"It's no problem. We also have a cleaning service come twice a week. He doesn't have enough teeth yet to chew very well. We're used to crumbs. Indeed, we'll continue with crummy behaviors until Alberta has finished teething."

Deedee shrugged helplessly with a timid smile on her face.

Holly read her accurately and changed the subject by saying, "We'll have our Christmas turkey dinner at noon. Gooseberry or mincemeat pie for dessert. And also sliced ham, with brown sugar and syrup on top. On the buffet will be candied yams, mashed potatoes and gravy, cranberry sauce, biscuits, rolls, butter, jams. I'll have a bowl of cabbage slaw with vinegar and mayonnaise dressing there also, along with bowls of canned carrots and canned beets (from the stash you brought, Dear). You've spent a busy year canning wonderful food."

Her sister-in-law looked at her with surprise all over her face. "Why, Holly, that's the nicest thing I've ever heard from you."

"My dear. I've stood in a hot kitchen sterilizing Mason jar after Mason jar, followed by the pressure cooker emitting bits of steam while I hope it doesn't explode. I've peeled and cooked––and I think beets really smell bad cooking. I realize how many hours and how much energy you put into the cooking and canning you brought. Our men folk seem to think it drops from heaven."

"Well, Chuck does mention what he likes to eat after he comes in from working on the farm and growing the vegetables. The farm crews who move up the country through the farms helping with the harvests eat anything and everything in sight. They drink lots of well water and pour a bucket of water over their heads before they come inside for some meals."

"I remember how hot those days of harvest time can get."

"I cook huge pots of potatoes and beef shoulders. And, your Barney is complimentary, too, about the regular meals I make. Nice kid. Helped my sons at their work a lot this past few months," Deedee said, with a swipe at her auburn hair. "At least, I refuse to let the men folk treat me like a servant, the way some of my friends let happen in their marriages. The kids and farm hands say 'please, ma'am' and 'thank you, ma'am.'" She added under her breath, "And not like the way I was treated growing up. I was treated like an absent-minded afterthought, pet dog."

Holly heard the soft remark but didn't react. If Deedee wanted to explain further, she would, sometime, some place. That is, if the sister-in-law meant the remark to be heard and wondered at. Most likely, she did want it to be heard as a dramatic clue to more about her childhood, imagined or real.

Ken returned from collecting the rent checks and delivering the walnuts. His arms were loaded with gifts from the tenants: fruitcake, fudge, coffee table book, Edam cheese, and three pairs of knitted gloves. He placed the items on the coffee table in front of the couch where Holly and Deedee sat. "They loved the walnuts," he said.

"Put the checks and cash in the safe, please." Mother Holly looked over the presents.

He added with excitement, "Look here, Mother Holly. I asked each of your tenants about getting rid of the dead mouse smell. One man said to boil vinegar and put the pan in the affected room. Another said to just throw everything out. But, look what the third man said, 'Gilda, bring that scented candle from the bedroom. We need to show this youngster how to deal with odor.' He gave me this big candle and said to keep it going until the smell dissipates."

"Oh, my goodness. That's a great solution. Put it near the dumbwaiter on the shelf in the butler's pantry. I'll get some more scented candles at the drugstore when I go to the bakery for sourdough bread next week."

Deedee said, "I didn't know that you liked that sourdough bread. Next time I'll bring you some yeast that you keep in the refrigerator. You just use a bit of yeast every time you want to make the bread. It keeps growing forever, replacing itself. It doesn't smell great but works well."

Ken laughed. "At least that red wrapped Edam there isn't smelly like Swiss cheese. The holes in Swiss are made by introducing a kind of bacteria that makes gas, and the holes form when the cheese is sliced. For a while, a scarcity of rennet used in cheese processing meant that bacteria from calves' stomachs were used. I know because we and our neighbors provided some from our fall slaughter to the local dairy that served four counties," Ken said.

"I didn't need to know all that, people. Please think,

censor, and process such enzymes before they leave your mouth," Belinda said. "My stomach recoils at your background information on how things are created in what I eat."

"I'll cheese it for my sweetheart," he answered. "Speaking of gas, Apartment Three-A said the drain is clogged again. I promised her I'd look at it this afternoon. I bet she put tealeaves down it again because they swell up when she lets hot water drain. I usually get by with using a plunger. After I do that, Belinda, I'll polish our shoes that have picked up spots from the snow. We have to be more careful in removing our galoshes."

"Yes, I'll remember. Shoe polish. It smells funny. You know how to do so many things so well. You're a marvel. Better than ole St. Nick who simply said people were either naughty or nice." Belinda gave him a quick squeeze.

Belinda took a deep breath, beckoned to her mother and husband, and began to whisper in a conspiratorial manner. "Listen. Deedee told me that she felt like an orphan brought up by a German couple on a farm near your childhood home, where they still live. She said she's about six years younger than he is and knows next to nothing about her parents."

"Oh, for the love of heaven. She said something like that to me, too. I don't suppose . . . " Holly exclaimed.

Ken snorted. "Such malarkey."

Belinda rounded on him with eyes flashing. "For someone who prides himself on his interviewing skills, I'm occasionally surprised that you still cannot distinguish between when I'm teasing and when I'm contributing to an investigation."

Ken said not a word, just looked at Belinda, as he seemed to calculate the possibilities in the information. "No, no," he said. "That history of hers is really too far-fetched, Belinda. This time you're teasing? I . . ."

"I know I am. If I'd been allowed to finish telling her story, you'd have heard that she was joking, that she simply liked the idea of a being a poor little rich kid like some Shirley Temple story that she knew."

Mother Holly contributed a morsel of information. "Shirley Temple in *The Little Princess* was banished to the attic at her boarding school when her dad was lost during The Great War. She was NOT an orphan."

"Sorry, ole soul, merry ole soul," Ken said, putting his hands together and bowing with contrition.

She scolded him. "And I noticed that there's still an unrepaired hole and crack in the storeroom's window, you tarried, ole soul, and didn't repair it." Her tone was no longer teasing. "It seems to have become damaged some more, in fact, Ken. The cold or something else is causing a widening crack." She gave his ear a tug.

"Why don't we bundle up and go for a stroll, and let the kids have a snowball fight out in the alley?" Ken said, walking up to the parents. The boys were examining each other's gifts and had quieted down.

Chuck said, "I find that a perfect project before we have four pent up energies, young whirlwind males, in the car for three hours after lunch. Then maybe we can entice some sleep from them." He gestured to the boys to follow him to the sleeping porch to collect the coats and rubber boots they'd discarded last night.

"Let's do go outside for a while," Holly agreed with Ken

and spoke loudly enough for everyone to hear. She would have to tell Belinda to lay off the snuggle bug stuff when other people were around.

"That porch is a fine idea," said Chuck when he came back bearing his heavy sheepskin coat. "You can toss confetti and roses on the people below if you open a window.

Holly grinned at her brother as she said, "The porch was cantilevered when I moved in.

Chuck said, "I read that the Country Club Plaza by here is patterned on buildings in Seville, Spain. If I remember my American history, Seville is from whence dear ole Christopher Columbus came. The Plaza was also the first shopping mall built to accommodate cars. The cars are parked either in underground levels or on tops of buildings. I'd like to see how that was accomplished! In contrast, now, your parking is on the *ground* but completely boxed in——a third way of having parking spaces."

"I loved the cantilevered porch when I checked out this apartment. Ken suggested adding the wall along the alley to allow our cars more secure parking inside," said Holly.

"It has worked well. Some recent vandalism hit the cars that were in the alley outside the garage," Ken said. He shook his head slightly at Holly because he immediately regretted making that remark about vandalism.

"First," Belinda suggested, "let me take some Polaroid pictures of people around the tree. Line up, you Osborne boys, by size, like stair steps. That's it. Now, I'll take one of you holding up your gifts. Now, one of you sitting around your folks, you on the floor and Uncle Chuck you and Aunt Deedee on the couch." She had first plugged the lights on, but the lights appeared with weird haloes when lighted, as it were, so she left them unplugged. She waited for the film to process between each order for posing.

"Hey," Chuck said after she had ejected the film to show them each picture. "Show me how to take your family's picture."

Belinda complied with her uncle's request. She and Ken picked up their kids and sat beside Holly in front of the decorated Christmas tree. Chuck took two pictures for them.

"Now, outside for some fresh air and flung snow." Chuck acknowledged the earlier suggestions with a wave of his hand at the adults.

Ken carried J. B. to the bedroom to collect the woolen winter wear from last night. The rest of the family trailed off through the kitchen.

CHAPTER THIRTY

The group walked down the rear steps, out of the garage, shutting the doors behind them each time, last person out responsible for doing so, and out into the gravel alley. An early morning snowstorm had left the right texture of wet snow for snowballs. However, teenage Perry gently put his hand on Holly's arm, wanting to talk rather than play, restraining her from keeping up with the others, and said, "Auntie, what can I do about the coins I found?"

She shifted Alberta to fit more comfortably on her arm and shoulder. "Perry, my child, they are from my coin collection. I didn't want to disillusion you guys who were inventing a cops and robbers story."

"Oh? What do you mean?" His voice trembled with shock.

"When we were moving in, we had so many strangers putting in hours hauling and arranging that I didn't want to leave money in sight, and, yet, I didn't want to keep toting those coins back and forth to the farm. I also didn't know much about my tenants, and I needed a safe place. That butler's pantry is dark, and the dumbwaiter isn't noticeable until one is looking for it. I thought it was a perfect hiding place. I put the coins against the wall and shoved that scrap of old plywood against them."

"Oh. I see. They're not a treasure trove from some bandits."

"Don't be disappointed. I just let you play with the fancy idea for a bit until I could speak with you privately."

"And are the pearls yours?"

"No, I don't have the faintest idea where they came from and how they got in there behind my board—unless they're from the lady who lived here before me. I'll call long distance this afternoon and check."

"Can I give them to mom if they don't belong to her?"

"Whoa, there!! Let me check them out first. Your dad said they might be worth lots and lots of money. I'll want to go slow about disposing of those, but we'll see."

"Okay." He put his head down to conceal his disappointment.

Holly tapped his shoulder, shifting Alberta to the other shoulder beforehand. "But, back to the coins. They actually gain in value every year because I started with coins I found where a Civil War battle had taken place just a bit southeast of here in Westport. Those are the black, dirty looking ones. I'd read somewhere not to rub them clean. None of the coins were from the rebs . . . their southern states issued paper money. I add coins all the time that are shiny, almost unused. You know what I mean? Coins that I receive as change from a purchase, ones that that look new. Haven't been circulated much."

"I don't buy things, Auntie, so I don't handle money except to take three cents for milk at school lunch. Mother and Dad do any buying so I don't know what you mean. I can imagine it, though. A coin gleams at you. There are some in your bunch I was looking at."

"You want to join me in coin collecting?"

"Oh, Auntie, can I? I'll be real careful."

"You must cross your heart and hope to die if you ever let your brothers or any of your friends know about any coins that you have. Some kid will swipe a penny from you to buy penny candy that is gone in one bite––and that penny could be worth $69! See, the valuable coins just look like any ole money to most people, not something to be treasured. Not something that would actually grow in value by becoming older. Just like you will, kiddo."

"I swear, Auntie, I swear."

"I swear, too. Shake my hand as we make this promise . . . we tell no one."

They shook hands, and Perry's brothers eyed him. "Hi, fellows, I just congratulated Auntie on her apartment," he called to them. They turned back to the manufacture of snowballs.

Alberta reached out a hand to him. He kissed her fat knuckles.

Holly saw Belinda run back inside, and finally come back down with her 8-millimeter movie camera in hand. "Everyone. I want to take our pictures. The whole reel of film lasts only three minutes. What I do is count for three seconds for each scene. It's in color. First, Chuck and Deedee, line up in front of the brick wall. After I have counted to one thousand and three, Gene, you walk in beside them; after the next three, you Michael; and, then same for you, Perry."

The Osborne couple obeyed, as did their sons. Belinda handed the camera to Gene and showed him how to focus and film.

She said, "Next up, Mom and Uncle Chuck together.

Finally, Gene, take Mom and me and Barney and, lastly, have Ken walk into the frame holding the two kids, if they'll stop squirming long enough. Be sure to count to three aloud, as I told you, before Ken comes in."

The filming completed, Belinda promised to show it to them the next time they met. She had bought a projector and screen but had to send the film out to be processed.

Holly casually walked over and returned to her nephew's side to discuss their interest in coins. "Perry, I will also let you have my blue folders that have slots for coins. I put them in a bookcase when I hid the coins in the dumbwaiter because they made the plank bulge too much. I can buy more at a bookstore for my set. I will give you duplicates that I collected."

"That'd be great, Auntie."

"Oh, dear. We have to retrieve the coins before you leave and sort them. The most precious coin I'm proud of is the 1921-quarter that the United States Mint issued for Missouri's centennial celebration in Sedalia. Of the Sedalia Fair."

"Our Sedalia?"

She nodded.

"You mean that the Federal mint made a coin for our fair at Sedalia, the State Fair where I'll sell my lamb, whose name is Minty?"

She nodded again. "I kept trading and bartering with my friends until I had two of them. I'll let you have one. That's what we'll do to start with. Coin collectors are called 'numismatists.'"

"That's a weird word. Say it again."

"Numismatists."

"I like that. Numismatists. Sounds like a scientist. And when I do get something, and it's a duplicate of a coin I have, I'll save it for you. I'm going to have money when I sell my lamb at the fair next fall in Sedalia." He danced up from his feet and hugged her arm holding Alberta. "That's when you'll hear from me for sure."

"*Minty*, Perry, is a well-chosen name for your beginning enterprise in coin collecting. You can *mine* more coins at an antique store from the U. S. Mint with the proceeds from her sale."

"Yes, yes."

"Ouch!" A snowball hit Holly in the back of her neck. She handed Alberta to a surprised Perry, stooped, formed a snowball, and hurled it straight as an arrow at Ken who was looking mortified. She made a bull's eye on his chest.

"I meant it for Chuck, but he dodged behind you, Mother Holly," Ken apologized, "but you obviously can defend yourself."

"Ken! You noticed my little brother, Chuck hiding behind me there? He and his friends always liked to set traps, and my friends and I would outfox them––when we could. We're pretty even-stephen on victories, eh, Chuck?"

"Right you are, Sis. You were so tall for a broad that the blond hair was a dead give away, but I never told you how we'd found you, as I remember. Actually, we won nearly 100 per cent of the hide 'n seek wars."

"Naturally you'd skew the results," scoffed Holly.

"That forest that was our outpost along the creek is a place that Barney likes to hunt in now. It's still full of animals and fowl as you can imagine," Chuck said with a grin.

"Do you mean f-o-w-l- or f-o-u-l?"

"Take your pick. The stream is still running clear where we collect the frogs and crawdads."

"I'm glad you took over our folk's other farm, Chuck. That house and grounds were wonderful places to grow up in, especially during the rationing during the war. We never suffered from lack of food, for sure," Holly said. She patted Perry on the shoulder. "Perry, let's leave all these relatives so that they can take a walk or run around to the front of my building for the mail while we'll take care of some numismatist business."

"Are you sure that's wholly legal, holy Holly?" Chuck teased.

"We're forming a partnership, and I need the key to the padlock on the dumbwaiter that you put in yesterday. I didn't see where you put it. This weekend, you've found out that I know a lot about business, particularly the legal issues that may arise, where the solutions are, and how to finalize contracts, you duffer. Note that we advertise, too, that we can find items, people, and historical facts. Anytime you need to consult us, we'll give you a really good price, one that'll satisfy your penny pinching ways, completely chunky Chuckie."

"I'll take you up on that when I decide to retire, if ever. I don't intend to wither away like an old sister might. The key to the dumbwaiter padlock is on the peg-board in the storeroom," Chuck said. "I repeat: did you notice the window has been damaged in there and is leaking cold air?"

Ken nodded, busy brushing snow from the back of Mother Holly's coat. She had Alberta held in front in her arms again.

"Let's go around to the front door and then upstairs, Perry," she called to him where he was helping with the snowman construction gang.

Mother Holly, Belinda, and Ken all noticed the yellow snow where an animal had visited the alley. There were also three brown-gold glistening spots where two cars had had lost a lot of oil. Ruts in the snow down to the tar and gravel were evidence of cars being towed away. Their eyes signaled to each other but no word needed to be said. Damage to oil pans.

Chuck must have seen them glancing at each other because he said to the youngsters, "You kids have snow on your hair and coats and animal pee on your boots. Let's brush stuff off as we go around to the front door and climb through the foyer where the hemp mats are for your boots. The coats can finish dripping in that room." His command indicated that he interpreted the looks among the Sleuths as being worried about the mess the kids would create going back into their apartment. However, he watched his sister's face carefully as he spoke.

Ken and Holly stopped Chuck from moving away. She lowered her voice while Ken just kept nodding as if a pleasant tale were being told. "Chuck, seriously, I noticed that you guessed that we have been targeted by a scoundrel. Be assured that we'll take care of the problem. But, I need to know Deedee's background. Today, if possible. Take me aside and tell me what you know about her origins, I mean forebears, and the place where she grew up, I mean with the German couple. She isn't an orphan, is she? I don't remember a German couple farming by us, is the problem. Act as though we're consulting about business, okay?"

"Why? I saw you guys peering at the snow on the side of the alley. Those are oil stains, not animal pee, I'd bet. She couldn't have done those."

"Correct. I'm sorry I stated things awkwardly. When I wish upon a star, I always think of you going off to war," Holly said in her normal voice, catching sight of Deedee edging toward them. "I wished you home safe. No matter how I tease you, you're my darling brother." She reached up and pecked Chuck on the cheek.

Chuck came up behind the Kansas City family and made his way to Holly as they left the foyer and entered the living room through the office. He said in a normal tone, "Deidre is a farm girl who had parents older than ours, much older. They were austere and hard working and expected the same approach to life from her. She loves to be held and cherished, and I and our sons make sure to treat her like an angel. She probably mentioned she felt like a waif, but that was simply her imagination, I'm quite sure. I would have heard something if she hadn't been their daughter. Neighbors love to gossip on the telephone party line, you know."

"For sure I know that. Thanks, Chuck. I was trying to make sense of something she had mumbled and you defined it for me––an orphan remark."

The Osborne offspring had clattered upstairs and walked back into the porch to change out of wet clothes before they returned to their gifts and candy by the Christmas tree. The ladies moved to the kitchen after conversing with the men for a while in the living room and enjoying an aperitif. They had spent time looking through the bookcase and discussing the reading matter. The shelves held Holly's high school textbooks in physics, English, Latin, and speech. Besides those textbooks were some Spode figurines from Belinda and Ken's wedding presents. Ken's Air Force manuals and Hardy Boy books were on a lower shelf above a complete set of Belinda's Nancy Drew books and two Rex Stout detective books. A new set of shelves would be needed for the encyclopedia set.

"Are your ancestors British?" Deedee asked Holly while busy basting the turkey, a hot pad in each hand, while she maneuvered the roaster around in the oven.

"Yes, as far as we know. I inherited the painting in the hall wall of an English family. I think Chuck has one also. Don't you know where it is?" Holly was carefully adding and stirring cornstarch into the large gravy skillet of juices.

"You must mean the one in the living room at the farmhouse," Deedee said. "Yes, they look English. My folks had one of a girl in a Dutch hat and apron. I don't think it was from Germany, but I could be wrong. Maybe Holland. I'll see if I can decipher the artists' names when I go home and write to you about them so we can do some research."

"That's a good idea. We have fine libraries here. I'll look for the artist on our painting, too, and do some research. Maybe we have a hundred dollar painting and don't know it."

"Mine's rather dim with age."

"A museum art division knows how to clean those things. You're surely making enough money now to indulge in a few whimsies."

Deedee looked at her, smiled, and winked. She spoke, tongue in cheek, "Holly, plus we could have it appraised. We'd probably find out we have a Rembrandt where we can watch it at night."

"Sure you would. You made me laugh at your quip. I've seen pictures of *The Night Watch,* and the dimensions would cover the whole wall in that hall."

Deedee lifted the roaster from the oven rack and transferred the turkey to a platter. She scooped dressing from its insides. "Turkey's ready, let's call the troops. The guys can haul this stuff in and pretend they've had something to do with feeding the clan," Deedee said and called for the male aides. "We've got male aides here, but we girls can be ale maids."

"Deedee, you're going to make me laugh out loud and have to try to explain why to those fellas, without insulting their delicate feelings. Unfortunately, we have no ale, but we do have hard cider. Sorry it's not moonshine." Holly snorted in laughter. She poured hot cider into a pitcher from a warm pan. "There. That smells enticing. The spices add more flavor to savor." She picked up the pitcher with hot pads and carried it into the table.

"Men! Bring in the food, please. The platters and bowls are too heavy for us weak females." Deedee laughed at Holly's entreaty.

Chuck and Ken obliged by toting in the food while the boys all went to wash their hands. Belinda placed Alberta into a high chair by her place and J. B. on two thick Ma Bell phone books on the chair between his two oldest cousins.

Gene and Michael flanked J. B., seated across the table from Barney. The three boys could keep the toddler well supplied with laughs, making funny faces, gesturing how to hold a tiny spoon properly, giving him his small cup to drink from. The two boys beside him cut up his meat and replenished his plate.

Holly left the table to bring in a bottle of wine. She chose to go up the five steps to the landing and down the same number in the kitchen rather than going through the butler's pantry. She turned, started because she was startled, when she heard a sound at the kitchen door. She opened it, surprising a young fellow who had a pistol in his hand.

The kid gasped, "I didn't hear no one home. I just need the loot." He clattered back down the stairs, intent upon running through the garage door that Ken had forgotten to lock.

"Hey, you!" Holly picked up a big can of V-8 juice and hurled it at the boy. It hit him in the back of the head, and he tumbled down the stairs. The noise caused Chuck and Ken to shove back their heavy chairs and run into the kitchen.

Chuck and Ken ran down, jerked the kid up, and twisted his arms behind his back, causing him to howl with pain.

They eased their grips. Ken yelled back upstairs, "Call Sergeant Tyler, Belinda, or corporal, whatever his rank is now. The number's in my address book." She had appeared at the top of the stairs and then, at his request, she ran back to the office to call for help.

Family members crept down the stairs. "There's a pistol on the garage floor!"

"What happened?"

"Whom're you yelling at?"

"Why did you holler?"

Chuck held the boy up on his toes.

Holly stood and answered the questions from family up on the stairs as she walked over to the pistol. "There was a noise at the door; that young, dumb looking kid was trying to open the knob. Thank god I had locked the kitchen door.

But, Ken forgot to lock the garage door downstairs when we came back inside earlier. The kid had this weapon, not a cap gun, believe me, said he wanted the 'loot,' turned to clamber back down the stairs when I threw that heavy can and hit him. He fell for it." Holly laughed shakily. She could've killed the boy.

"Who is he?"

"Darned if I know," Holly shook her head up at the entourage. "Some neighborhood kid or a bum or someone with a wrong address. Who knows what Sherlock Holmes could have told Dr. Watson from merely one glance that enabled him discern the answers to any and all of your questions?" She gave a significant look of complicity to Kendrick who nodded back.

The kid had a bloody scratch on his cheek., and held one wrist awkwardly. He said, "Mr. Shannon tole me to git you all outta town. I heerd you discussin' the loot inside the wall upstairs. He said I could have it. I got my ole man outta town with one bang. I wus gonna wait for you inside and pick you off after I found the loot. I saw you all wus traipsing off toward the church outta the alley a while ago."

Chuck said, "Unfortunately for you, boy, we were 'traipsing' around to the front door while we cooled off. What's your name?"

"Abe Lincoln."

Chuck shook the kid. "Don't get smart with me, boy."

"That's my name. You asked me. It's Abe Lincoln."

"Are you the son of the owner of Lincoln's motors?" Holly asked, events clicking into order in her mind.

"Yeah. He's dead. I hated my dad, but Mr. Shannon

pertected me. I forgit mah jacket when my dad hit me, and I slugged him a good 'un."

"Have you been in this alley before?"

"Found me mah jacket hereabouts. I had me a knife but hardly not sharp and could not go plumb through them tires but poked through the oil cans in the engine right smartly. I rised up the hoods. Garage man showed me how when I were a young'un. I'm strong. 'Twas easy to climb them stairs when I git in thet there garage."

Deedee came down the stairs holding coats for everyone and passed them out. "Belinda is feeding the children and will put them down for their naps soon. When she reached Phil Tyler he said he doesn't have jurisdiction in this neighborhood, but he is sending a colleague he trusts named Donald Specter. That must be him now."

A police car came down the alley. Holly urged every "young'un" back upstairs to allow some peace and quiet while the adults related what had happened. Saying "Dinner's getting cold" certainly helped urge the youngsters inside.

After the explanations that Ken and Holly related to the young sergeant, the sniffling kid held out his limp wrists to be handcuffed. Holly handed the pistol by the barrel to the officer who received it in his handkerchief.

She had repeated what the kid muttered about his father and Mr. Shannon. The officer shook his head. "I doubt anyone will believe that Mr. Shannon put Lincoln's own son up to killing him. We'll see what eventually the charges are that stick. He did try to break into your house. Armed with a weapon. The kid ain't too bright." He drove off in the police car, boy in the back seat, siren wailing on top.

Holly and Chuck climbed the steps as Ken revealed

more background to what explanation had been given the policeman. Chuck shook his head and said, "I was beginning to envy your easy life here. I guess we all have unexpected threats. I'd carry my shotgun with me if I were you."

Holly remarked, "What an anticlimax. A *kid* shooting a gun at us. At least it's not us against a local gangster." Holly had a bland expression as she looked at her brother and briefly included Ken. She telegraphed *downplay this incident*. Ken nodded.

Upstairs again, Ken picked up the wines and handed a milk bottle to Gene, standing alertly by the kitchen door when they entered, and asked him to pour more cold milk for those who wanted it while he brought a bottle of cold white wine for the adults. Returning to the dining room over the steps and landing, he shook his head slightly as he smiled at Belinda and Mother Holly. He had brought back two types of white wine, dry and semi sweet, and gave each oenophile the preferred choice.

Holly raised her replenished wine glass and gave a toast to the holidays and family ways. "May we be ever as joyous and secure as we are here together this second, minute, hour, day, month, and year."

"Hear! Hear!" the family responded, sipping wine or milk. Alberta and J. B. sat enthralled and gurgled and giggled, respectively, in appreciation of the clan's warm spirit. And some of the clan appreciated the cold spirits. The boys raised their glasses of milk in response.

CHAPTER THIRTY-ONE

The Osbornes took off in the long Ford with the boys sprawled in the back seat, except for Perry who sat between his mom and dad. They were laughing and remembering the visit. Deedee exhorted Belinda to make copies of the pictures she'd taken. Plus send them picture postcards showing the lights on the Plaza.

Ken furnished Chuck with a hand-drawn map of directions to the Liberty Memorial by the Union Station and then to the highway down to their farm.

The Sleuths returned upstairs and finished cleaning up the kitchen and dining room, the porch, and the spare bedroom and bath. The children played by their toys in the living room. Alberta kept crawling off the blanket and was finally encased in her swinging chair with an animal cracker and a new rattle.

Belinda brought in the teacart with ample supplies for their rest period.

"That visit went well," Mother Holly said to her two young compatriots. They responded with remarks about the German dinner, the streusel that waited to be sampled, coins, red suspenders, crèches, and then, the stroll to Country Club Plaza. That was the opening Ken had been waiting for. "Mystery solved at end, even."

"But something else serious happened last night," Ken

said, putting out a hand on each girl's arm. "We need to talk, decide, get moving. We need to take *more* steps. Come into the office, and let the kids play in the living room. We can keep an eye on them through the door. They look like they're falling asleep on the blanket."

Alberta was already sleeping, thumb in mouth. Holly lifted her carefully out of the swing and put her on the blanket. She curled up with her legs tucked up under her stomach. J. B. was sleepy-eyed, his mouth dribbling saliva as he lay on his side, pulling a model truck around.

"You sound as though we're going to have to circle our wagons," Mother Holly said.

"What is the matter, Ken?" Belinda touched his arm and looked up at him with concern all over her face and her body tense with alarm.

He walked over, slid open the door to the outer office, and looked at the amateurish paintings on the wall, keeping his back to them, as he steadied his voice. "A few days ago, Mr. Walter Raleigh invited me to his men's club one morning for a talk. He had warned me that his receptionist, Marnie King, eavesdropped. What's worse, she reported on his doings to her father. King is an attorney with connections on both sides of the civil line."

Puzzled, Holly asked, "You mean State Line Road between Missouri and Kansas?" She and Belinda were still arranging items away from the children.

"No, the shady and the sunny sides. Criminal versus principled behavior."

Belinda said, "I'm not following you."

Ken turned back. "Let me finish telling you about our meeting." He managed to keep his voice even by taking shallow breaths, barely expanding his chest, and speaking slowly. He removed his turtleneck sweater, buying more time to arrange his revelations in his mind. Following that arming of his report, he walked back to the living room, after sliding shut the door.

"The meeting at Walt's club," Belinda prompted him.

"I've mentioned a lot of this. He told me that the two pallbearers at the Kilmer funeral were actually there so as to make a point. That is, carrying his casket was a warning to others who might defy Shannon's clan. Richie Kilmer had not only jilted . . . Well, the two men were Lincoln and Shannon whom we've discussed before, Lincoln being Clyde Shannon's underling. Richie, as a laddie, had jilted Shannon's daughter but survived that mistake, through several decades, because he was a good enforcer. He goofed up by skimming too much money from Shannon's betting rackets."

"Why should that cause something serious to happen? What happened next, I mean, was it like what happened last night or this morning?" Mother Holly prompted him as though he were reciting from a script. "Why did that boy say he killed his own father?"

"Yes, why? Nothing makes sense," Belinda said. "We went to the Plaza together, and you two saw something I didn't. I saw you whispering by that store."

"Wait, I'm building to it. You need to know—or remember--the background of what happened the day I met Walt at his club." Ken turned, began pacing slowly, speaking slowly. He reiterated the comments Walt had made about the Kilmers' "accident," Marnie King, Clifford King,

Mr. Lincoln, Clyde Shannon, plus by certain emphases, he included Walt's tone of voice——a tense tone of voice.

His partners listened with eyes fastened on him, not wanting to interrupt a coherent account. Even when he spoke of being target practice upon leaving the Club, or dropping to the pavement when a car backfired, they did not make a sound, waited him out. He also admitted, with a small chuckle, that part of his dropping flat on the sidewalk might have been the second glass of bourbon he drank before lunch.

A recital of the ensuing events, such as the lunch that Meg Raleigh prepared, the introduction of the police sergeant Tyler, and their practicing a news segment for Slim (Horatio) Anderson, left his colleagues frowning.

"'Red and white and pink all over?' Maybe you and Walt were still a bit tipsy . . . think so, Ken?" asked Mother Holly gently.

"It was a perfectly rational idea at the time. Your point, however, is well taken."

"You never told us to watch the news for that report on Slim's broadcast," Belinda said.

"No. It never went that far. I haven't finished the story." Ken continued telling the them the consequential confrontation: Clifford King came storming into the Raleigh's library, after slamming the front door open, and roughly pushing past the maid. "He hollered that we were obtuse and obstructive, that he'd be taking care of the game and that we were not to up the ante. Marnie had informed him on our meeting there. Walt looked guilty; he hadn't meant for her to know about us being at his home."

"Oh, wow, that's great," Mother Holly said, sitting back and relaxing. "So we're home free."

"I thought so, too. I thought if he'd been the one to put the kibosh on us verbally like that, he'd do it to any people threatening us." Ken stood up from the chair and shook his body, head drooped as if brooding but with his shoulders and back as tense as a wire guyed to a radio tower.

"Something else happened. What was serious about last night? We were together all the time," Belinda asked softly.

After a minute Ken turned, shoulders still at attention, and now his head was up erect and commanding. "Yes. First, it was my stolen jacket next to the dead man in the newspaper picture. That boy who ran up here probably stole it from my car, Lincoln's son. It implicated me, if anyone thought to check whose it was."

"And?"

"In just a minute, I want to go back to the ideas Meg had at the luncheon that King terminated with his warning. The second thing happened yesterday evening, as we moved through the crowds at the Plaza. I kept my billfold protected in an inner pocket. J. B. and I enjoyed the noise and festivities. We all were feeling so serene. And, here is why I've changed my idea about our peaceful, nonconfrontational tactics: last night I heard a voice say 'make way.' As I turned toward the voice, Chaz, the Shannon's chauffeur, deliberately shoved me--remember that I was carrying J. B. in my arms--into a brick wall. I hit my spine and head hard. Knocked my hat forward."

"It would have been J. B. who hit the wall if you hadn't turned!" Mother Holly exclaimed, her voice exploding quickly into anger as she pictured the deed.

"Yes. And, I hit so hard that the hurt lingered until after we were home. I became so mad when I saw who it was that I couldn't move for a sec. J. B. said I was hurting him. I was holding him so closely that I squeezed him."

"Did you go after them?" Mother Holly asked.

"Why did it make you mad, other than that you were holding J. B., and it hurt you?" Belinda added her question as though confused by his description of events.

"Because the Shannons were following him, were grinning at what he had done to me. I could see Mr. and Mrs. Shannon pretending to grin at something across the street, but they didn't shift their eyes quickly enough. They were sniggering at my being shoved back into the wall."

"Wh-what can we do? I'll have to think," Mother Holly said, obviously trying to catch an idea from those swirling in her mind. "This episode today with the boy coupled with what happened last night is almost unbelievable. If you, Ken, hadn't been describing it, I would have thought it was a figment of someone's imagination."

"Shall we go to Mr. King and tell him?" Belinda suggested. "Or go to the police? Why haven't you mentioned it to him?"

"Today's intruder is so dumb he thinks shooting people is a great idea. No to both ideas, Belinda. The police have the kid and, if a single charge against Shannon comes out of the kid's mumbling, I'll yell up and down the street in gratitude. I am quite sure that I will not be doing that. Moreover, King has obviously not been able to intercede on our behalf, to convince people we're not trying to solve Kilmers' accident. We don't know how these people are twisted together. Here's the plan that I want you to critique.

Let's pick up on Meg's idea but do it more subtly than within a newscast."

"I don't see how you can make it work," Mother Holly said, leaning her head to one side and brushing a hand over her hair, leaving it mussed up. "King was correct in stopping that dumb drunken idea."

"Walt told me some time ago, or maybe it was Meg when she was here once, that there's an attorneys' banquet and soiree after work this evening, Christmas Eve, something running from five to midnight at a downtown hotel ballroom."

"Yes, I remember her mentioning that." Belinda continued to study him, trying to fathom what he was suggesting.

"I do, too." Mother Holly stood, walked over to him, and put her hands on his shoulders. "I didn't mean to sound so critical, Ken. Tell us what you suggest."

"How about this? I'll ask Meg to lay a hint, while refreshing her make-up at the long counter in the ladies' room. The hint will go something like, 'Have you heard anything about Senator Symington investigating Clyde Shannon, or was it Senator McCarthy, the Wisconsin one?' Or perhaps she'll say, 'Have you heard that the two *H*'s, J. Edgar Hoover and HUAC, are interested in the Shannons?' She could say something along those lines that feels natural. Picture it? Her speaking to the woman in a quiet undertone? To the lady next to her?"

"Yes, indeed. That'll spread like wildfire. It will grow and grow. I'd love to hear what it finally grows into. It will be the pinko thing you and the Raleighs were trying to wrap your strategy around. Before King stomped in and prevented your gleeful idea to try to get Slim Anderson to broadcast a weird bit of news. He wouldn't have done that, so you were lucky King stopped you." Belinda clapped.

Mother Holly looked at him fondly. "Ken Massey. From acting like a relative of a mule, you're using assets that no one can trace to this origin. More subtle than locked doors and mailboxes or our p. o. box address in our ads."

Ken asked, "You two agree?"

Holly hadn't finished her assessment. "You're the scamp even if you don't have round heels. It's a grand idea and cannot be traced to us. Or back to Meg."

Ken phoned the Raleighs and asked if he could drop in for a few minutes. He put down the phone with a sigh. "They are busy but said I sounded like I had an emergency, and I should rush right over. I'll drive to their house and ask for their help. Your remarks about the rumor being untraceable should convince them. I'll come from that angle."

And, thus the Sleuths worked a new protective scheme. Using a little help from their friends. Plus they would tell Walter Raleigh, Esq., that, when he returned to town, they would have finished a report for him, releasing the jewelry to the museum in perpetuity.

CHAPTER THIRTY-TWO

On the Monday after the Christmas weekend, the investigators woke up rested and eager to discuss their investigations. The past few days of excitement, visitors, and threat had slapped them into somnolence–indeed, almost cataplexy––on Sunday afternoon. Both of the servants had returned in time to take over the chores and free the adults to sprawl among newspapers and toys in the living room. Or work.

Mother Holly had taken the dirty necklace to a jeweler downtown last Saturday afternoon and left it to be cleaned and appraised. She also wrote to Jerry Wrenslow at her old address and asked if his wife or little daughter had lost any jewelry. If the necklace was a treasure, she didn't want to give away what piece of jewelry it was to a fast-talking negotiator.

Consequently, the next order of business had the trio studying the two students' tracing of their brothers in more detail. Retired sergeant Kendrick Massey had made no progress on the two signed contracts from Nettie and John. He had had no response from entities in D.C. that he had written to, Arlington Cemetery and Department of the Army at the Pentagon. He liked the useful form Walter Raleigh had drawn up for the Sleuths to use in just such an endeavor. All efforts have not been tried yet.

Ken has access to the files kept by the national registry in St. Louis as well as at the Veterans' Administration in the same city. Good thing he's made reservations so that he and Belinda could take a vacation to eastern Missouri for her birthday. That way, he does not need to charge the youngsters for mileage. He knows that the college kids are not exactly as wealthy as an attorney like Walt is. If Belinda wouldn't mind, maybe he could use some vacation time to do some work.

"Belinda, I felt as though I maybe cheated you by giving you your birthday present at Christmas." He gave an apologetic shrug.

"Not to worry. This has happened all my life. 'Merry Christmas' and 'Happy Birthday' on a single gift. Meanwhile Barney had separate presents because his birthday is in May. Not that I was *ever* jealous. Ken, this is a second gift, solely for my birthday. Besides, the brooch is so beautiful. I've neither seen any gems like those on it before nor had any such. The diamond wedding ring you gave me is the only other expensive jewel that I have." She kissed him.

"I thought you'd like it," he muttered as he returned the kiss. "Well, we'll take off tomorrow for your birthday trip, be gone from the 27th through New Year's in St. Louis. Sorry I couldn't rustle up a World's Fair for you."

"It will be fun."

"I'm also sorry that I have to ask if I can do some sleuthing for the college kids while we are there?"

"No problem, Ken. Wish I could help. But I don't have your military credentials."

Holly came into the room. "Say, you two, I just remembered that Meg told me quite some time ago that

Walt had arranged for us to see what the so-called jewelry consists of. We have to go before the museum opens and be there at 8 a. m. tomorrow morning. She and Walt saw it last Friday when the Osbornes were here with us."

"Mother, why do we need to see the stuff?"

"Meg and I think it would help a lot to trace the history—just to satisfy my curiosity! After we examine the brief description that the museum antiquarian attaches to each piece, we can look at portraits in history books and biographies from century to century. It's probably something the museum already knows, but I wanted the historical context revealed in our extra, and I know, unnecessary, search through generations. Meg will help me if you're not interested. That'll make a great history lesson, you know. I'd write a short addendum on the historical context for Walt. and Mrs. Marlena Harver, and her daughters. OF course, it might all be speculation about the historical background. He can submit it with his report if he chooses to, if he doesn't have to hand it over immediately but can wait a bit."

Ken said slowly, "That's a grand idea. You have fun, Mother Holly. Belinda, we have plenty of time to make it to St. Louis to help close the college kids' cases if we leave later in the morning. We should first view the set of jewelry in order to understand what your mom can trace historically.

Belinda agreed. "We certainly know the cities most of the way there in case we do run into foul weather. We can stay over in any or each of them, if necessary. Hard to predict with this winter weather. Let's go see the display, see something from history.

"We'll perhaps wrap up both cases, then, during this week. Particularly if we get those pictures from the Laura girl." Belinda winked at the other two with Ken's (and Churchill's) "V" for victory sign on her right hand.

Holly said, "When we have time, we'll start tracing our own ancestry. Deedee and I talked about having those old paintings appraised that could be part of our history. But, first I have to assist Ken with tracing those soldiers. The students Nettie and John thought that their brothers might have been born in Jackson County and gone to Lincoln High School. I could take a cab over to check those places out while you're gone. At least we have their parents' names as well as the soldiers'."

Ken said, "Thanks, but wait until I see what I can garner from the sites in St. Louis, Mother Holly."

Belinda was silent. She looked a bit stricken; is she heartbroken, Ken worried, is something taking attention away from her birthday again? Her lips turned down in a moue, and she looked up at the ceiling.

"Eet eez a mah-velous idée, *ma mere* and *mon mari*," she drawled like Marlene Dietrich, then switched to Greta Garbo. "To mix my multi-language lesson further, 'I do not vish to be alone while you see hees-tory, meesterious, heestory. I vill ride mit vous/toi/you."

"Belinda!" Both her mother and Ken laughed as they reacted.

"Also, Mother Holly, we must jot down what you found out about Deedee and see if her tale, at least what Chuck told you, coincides with any of our documentation. Moreover, I can't think of anything that connects from her background with the orphan investigation, unless her German mother was a maid of the Volks and became a foster mother to an unwanted child," said Ken.

"Far-fetched idea, just like those of Meg and Merrilee and your Shannon dame. You're correct, she is not an orphan, and you two must quit worrying about a Volks orphan. Chuck knew about her parents and where they lived. He was quite sure of the information he knew about her. They met during the awful Dust Bowl and Depression days. The farm where she worked was closer to a river than his, and Chuck was trading produce to her folks for barrels of water. He helped with a Four-H fair where she had some sewing exhibited. Both of her stern old folks died, leaving the farm without an owner. It was foreclosed. Chuck said that all it took was for both of them to pitch into saving his farm during those bad years in the 30s, and their future was sealed."

"But we need to know if a birth certificate exists." Belinda held up a file. "If it exists, like the Volks ones we found in Jeff City."

"No, we don't. One does not necessarily exist. Some children who were born on farms or in back alleys had no legal notice taken of their origins." Holly blew on her coffee. "Chuck's sure she was their daughter, the only daughter of a dour couple."

"At least we have the picture that you took of her by the Christmas tree to compare with the photos from Marlena's albums. Compare Deedee's picture, I mean. Maybe Laura's pictures will come this week, too," Ken said stubbornly. "Likewise, you brought in that newspaper copy of the debutantes in 1908, and Belinda took a Polaroid of the Schmidt girl's snapshot when she was in France––the skinny Volks girl, same skinny as in your ballroom picture a year later. The pictures of Marlena and Jackie from their 30s look nothing like Deedee does now."

Holly mused, "Chuck did say he feared that the farm she was raised on was in the county where the courthouse burned. No one knew what caused it, but the records were all lost. He'll look at the church they went to in case records of a baptism are there, if she agrees. Moreover, she seldom had anything positive to say about growing up because the parents were old when they had her and simply used her as a worker from the time she could walk."

"She has red hair," Belinda pointed out. "Germans are supposed to be dark or blond, blue-eyed."

"You mean tall, blond, and blue-eyed like Hitler thought Germans should be––and he wasn't?" laughed Ken as he spoke.

"*Touché*. You won that round," Belinda said, poking her chin at him.

Ken said, "There's no way that Deedee could be a missing heiress, partners, so let's quit playing around with the idea. She merely made a remark about growing up unloved. Well, she has Chuck and the boys now. Our investigation awaits only the pictures from Laura. To be concluded, that is. Agreed?"

His partners agreed after thinking over their documented information.

The jewelry collection that they viewed at the museum left the three investigators befuddled. "Why this is called jewelry, I do not understand," Belinda complained. "Those beads on that pectoral look like something I made in grade school. And a baby would mess up a bib like that Thing."

Their guide looked affronted. "It is, madam, jewelry, and not for a baby."

"True. Faience is merely earthenware that is decorated and strung," Ken said. "I looked up the definition after Walt gave me the list."

"Who'd wear a feather cap? We always say that we put feathers in our cap when we win," Belinda said. "Or call it macaroni," she finished, singing the line from the *Yankee Doodle* tune.

The guide looked toward the ceiling in dismay, perhaps jotting her down as a peasant. Certainly uncouth.

Ken hastily said, "Seems that royal ladies in the Orient do wear them. Marco Polo and his father and uncle are supposed to have brought back a wide group of items around 1300, only 600 years ago, you realize. Those items would probably be mirror images of these. Henrik Volks may have worked for a jeweler and collected antique things that he brought ashore to the US even if they weren't of much value in this country, except to a museum years later."

"Those different colored stones are cut in intriguing ways," commented Holly. "I could see wearing them for decoration, but I wouldn't put it past a neighbor to ask if I were wearing costume jewelry. The worth of these items simply has to be because they are ancient and from far distant lands."

The weather staying cloudy, with no snow predicted, permitted the Massey couple to drive at a steady pace toward and into St. Louis. Holly had informed them that Highway 40 looked a bit shorter than Highway 50 to St. Louis, and they took that advice and that highway.

The trip lasted about seven hours with a stop here there, now and then, food or gas, restroom or water. A bakery in a grocery store in Columbia offered some luscious looking rye bread, and Belinda tried a bite, then made a note to stop back at the store on the way home.

"We've timed our trip well. We're able to slide into the metropolitan traffic after dark. I don't like driving on unfamiliar roads after dark, but streets with street lights and headlights from other cars help in a city."

Belinda asked, "Do you think that's what happened to the Kilmers?"

"What?"

"Driving in unfamiliar territory?"

"Or the man encroached on enemy territory," Ken replied. "Walt virtually ordered me very clearly to stay away from inquiring about the accident. Still sounds to me like an accident on purpose. When the Lincoln man was found shot in his office last week, the police also closed the case on the Kilmers' deaths, Walt said. He and Meg did agree with the rumormonger approach when I spoke with them last Saturday. We'll see if it works."

"Wouldn't it work better if Shannon knew that we started it and could just as easily threaten him if he threatens us?"

"No. Walt, as well as Meg, agreed with me about our staying behind the scenes. No need to beef up any of his reasons to go after us. Shannon will soon be busy worrying about an investigation from the Washington, D.C., direction."

"Is that good for us and the Raleighs?"

"Yes, very good and also Walt told me more. I haven't mentioned or had time to mention that the Lincoln son confessed to vandalizing the cars in our alley, firing at our window, and shooting at Walt 's house and us at the Club. Lincoln, his father, had told him to harass Walt and me before he killed his old man. The boy told the police about that, bragging, about everything he'd done."

"How very odd. I'm glad we were busy with Christmas," Belinda replied with a shudder of relief. "And the kid shows up here, kills his dad in an argument over money or something, hides in our alley, tries to sneak in until Mother hears him and hurls the can at him, comes slithering in as if he is going to rob us or wipe us out!"

"Not a smart young man," Ken agreed, turning on the headlights as the evening dimmed.

"I'll just stay aloof from crime, behind or beside you. Mayhap any other threat is gone," she replied, giving a little shudder. "How did these guys find where we live? We simply advertise a post office box number."

"Well, a car dealer would have pretty good connections at the Department of Motor Vehicles, wouldn't he? Mother Holly told me the Chaz chauffeur showed up when she was at the newspaper archives. She didn't know if it were by chance."

"Ken! That would explain our vulnerability. I thought we had a safety barrier. Oh, my. We'll have to be careful from now on."

"We will."

"I don't even like movies with a dark theater and huge screen unless they're musicals. I haven't been to many. I'm not scared of drive-in theaters, however."

"And just whom did you go with to drive-in theaters, my sweet?"

"I have had a date or two before you, my sweet," she replied with a wink of a blue eye and her jaw a bit sideways. She gestured at a sign on the corner, and Ken turned into the next street.

The small hotel had a discrete sign advertising an entrance to a circular driveway. They drove in, stopping in front of a door from which a valet came, accompanied by a doorman. The valet took the car keys, promising to leave them at the desk. The doorman took their suitcases, ushered them inside, and placed the valises beside them on the floor at the desk. Arriving a little late at the hotel, they were pleased to find that their room had not been canceled.

The desk clerk knew that Holly and Jeremiah Jones had been regular visitors to the small hotel over the years and that Belinda Massey was their daughter. He bowed slightly as he greeted her. Holly had suggested the hotel to Ken.

Ken suggested to Belinda, "Why don't you get a copy of the *Post-Dispatch* over there while I check us in? There might be a good revue on tomorrow night."

Belinda joined him at the desk with the newspaper under her arm. The bellboy picked up both suitcases and, over at the elevator, told them he was the son of the hotel owner.

Their room was large with big pieces of furniture, including those in a seating area next to the windows. Everything was brown, tan, or ochre: wallpaper, cushions, rug, bedspread, and drapery. Furniture, too, of course. The brown tones swirled before his tired eyes like muddy creek waters.

"It's not too late––if you're not too tired––let's drive downtown and look at the lights, maybe park and listen to some buskers, and go for a walk, maybe do some window shopping on Euclid Avenue." Ken rubbed his eyes, took a deep breath, and looked out of the second story window toward the street. He turned away and watched her a minute. "What are you looking at?"

"In the desk I found this Gideon Bible, probably been here since I was little, a city map, and a brochure from the Chamber of Commerce. There're a lot of really old, spectacular churches. One has a magnificent dome. And some buildings in the botanical gardens are left over from the 1904 World's Fair. I wonder if the garden paths are cleared of snow. Tonight, I think we should drive over near the river and landings, and I'll show you where we boarded a boat one day. I don't feel like going for a walk tonight. Tomorrow we can do the churches and stuff."

He flipped through the newspaper. "Sounds like a plan. Maybe we'll run into Laura Helsinger's brother who caused the family to disown him by some criminal action. Dress warmly. You need to put on your wool skirt, leggings, and fur-lined boots. Too bad but I can't see anything here in the entertainment section that I want to go to, but you look and check out the offerings."

"Do you think we should try to trace records on the Jufellear twins from when they first emigrated here?"

"What for? We know when they died and thus ceased to have an interest in that so-called jewelry," Belinda said bluntly. "But you will do the college kids' brothers."

After a light breakfast the next morning, the bad weather still holding off, they first circled around the construction of a memorial arch commemorating the Louisiana Purchase (and its purchasers: Thomas Jefferson and the U. S. government) as well as saluting the pioneers who traveled west from here. The grand arch, when finished, would allow visitors to see far vistas.

They viewed a neighborhood of magnificent homes built decades ago, built to last, behind gates and elegant lawns. The area seemed aloof to the changes that occurred nearby over the years. Belinda noted that the stores here now were not here when she'd looked at these mansions when she was much younger . . . if she remembered correctly.

"Oh, I've been by here. Years ago," Belinda exclaimed as they pulled into a parking lot outside an elegant building. "We went to the zoo and botanical gardens. Lovely vacation. Took a riverboat down and back one day on the Mississippi River. My brother almost fell over the side, but Dad grabbed his britches in time."

"Sounds like a tourist boat the Clarmont boy works on," Ken said.

"It does at that. I'll go look inside the botanical greenhouse while you look up the veterans' information. There's always a magnificent display of poinsettias here in December. The Linnean House is interesting but takes a while to tour."

"My search may take a while. There's been a gap of ten years since the war ended. Both of the kids who asked me to trace soldiers would have been young enough to have been in elementary school during WWTwo. Maybe that's why the GIs didn't list them as next of kin, I'm thinking. Both sets of parents died a few years back and left the kids with relatives, shifting around from one family to the next."

"That really could be why contact was lost. Go, do your

part," Belinda said, exiting the DeSoto and walking up the path to the indoor garden, noticing through the glass walls that the interior was flush with greenery and flowers. Maybe it would smell like spring in there, iris and lilies.

Ken quickly found addresses of both GIs at the archives. He silently thanked Walter Raleigh, Esq., who had drawn up the permission slips that John Johnson and Nettie Rugger had signed to ease his quest to find each one's missing brother. Walt had told him that he could find a notary republic at any courthouse or bank when he had time to take the youngsters for that purpose: the kids located one at their university. That meant it had been easy to accomplish obtaining their signatures before Christmas.

Before they left home, he had read over the notes Belinda had typed of the two youngsters' interviews three weeks ago. The Washington. D. C., offices had not even yet responded to his letters. He had packed the notarized statements into his suitcase and now he carried them into the Administration building, feeling that he had enough data to separate out, from a from a hundred Johnsons, a particular one with the same first name of 'Bill.' Big brother Ralphie Rugger's identity would be easier to trace for Nettie.

It took only an hour and a half. Bill Johnson now lived in Marysville, Missouri, where he received disability payments, his Purple Heart awarded seven years before. Ralph Rugger was in Chicago. Ken would call both men from the hotel, inform them of their New Year's surprises, that is, a sibling looking for each of them.

Belinda had been ready to return to the hotel when he picked her up from the greenhouse. She'd bought a small poinsettia that she knew she had to keep warm all the way home, however awkward that would be.

When they were in their room, Ken made the long-distance calls to each of the ex-servicemen and told them of the inquiries. Both were taken aback and somewhat stunned, somewhat suspicious at first, then responding with degrees of delight and wariness evident in their voices. And, both asked for the addresses of their young kinfolk, and agreed, first of all, though, for the kids to be notified by Mr. Massey about his findings. He immediately dialed the dormitories where each student lived and delivered news of a fantastic New Year's gift, a long-lost brother.

The late afternoon was spent touring two elegant churches followed with a late supper downtown at a German restaurant, followed by a stroll they took to look in window displays and listen to buskers. During the next two days, they woke late, had brunch, and spent the time in the history and art museums, with final stops at an elegant ladies' clothing emporium and at a gentleman's store.

New Year's Eve, they dressed up, went to a nightclub, blew whistles at midnight, and kissed in the New Year. "Next year," Ken said, "I'd like us to go to Vienna and ride the Ferris wheel that we saw in *The Third Man*. I've seen and heard so much about Salzburg and Vienna."

"I'd be happy to accompany you, my dear, as long was we do not run into any intrigue such as portrayed in that film. That's one that scared me in the dark theater. I'd be looking for the shadowy guy to show up even if you promised he wouldn't."

"Maybe we could find some more ancient jewelry there."

"Nor do I want to buy anything that is so-called jewelry

like that museum stuff. However, I've been intrigued by the way emigrants from there also clap to part of *Colonel Radetsky's March* when it goes by in a parade. Duh de duh, duh de duh, duh de duh de duh," she hummed. "I hear bystanders at parades do that every time, but I don't know why and when that clapping started to be a fashion. I think Mom said Radetsky was a hero in those mid-century wars, didn't she?"

"Don't remember. You're heroine enough for me."

The rest of the evening became a vague memory of dance, song, and champagne.

The Masseys left for home on Sunday, after a brunch of English muffins, steak, and strawberry pie. Belinda was wearing her new brooch and a new brown wool coat. With a sable fur collar and cuffs. To match a new fur hat. Ken had on his new tweed sport coat under a belted beige raincoat. It fit his fit body to perfection. They sang and kidded all the way on the homeward trail.

CHAPTER THIRTY-THREE

Meg Raleigh brought Lynn over for a visit with J. B. while she visited with Belinda. Holly and Ken were in the living room as Belinda asked Meg and the boy in. through the foyer and office. Belinda took the boy upstairs, and returned to find her mom had already served the newcomer with a glass of sherry.

Ken appreciated that Mother Holly had let the Masseys sleep off and on through the day Monday after their late return the evening before. They had awakened Tuesday feeling great and had been busy telling her about the St. Louis attractions.

Through the window, snowflakes were falling like a soft white lace mantilla onto the land below. The windowsills had a brief dusting of snow, with pigeon tracks making a pattern.

"It's really not very cold outside. Wish we knew where we could take the kids for a sleigh ride. I'd like to learn how to ice-skate, too," said Belinda walking to the windows. "I'm very pleased that you found out the total history of the deeds to this place, Mom. Now I know how many people have looked out on this very view, watching it grow up, and spread out over time, being tamed, and tossed into world history. Immigrants were really brave, to come across the oceans, facing an unknown."

"And freedom from tyrants. History is the very thing that has interested Meg and me all our adult lives, Belinda. I'm pleased that you've been caught up in exploring it."

Meg said, "And brave even when a tin tyrant in the local vicinity turns out to be rumored to be under investigation by a Congressional committee." Meg laughed.

Mother Holly said, "You mean the rumor you started has blown up satisfactorily?"

"Oh, yes. It went out over the grapevine quickly and sprouted twisted offshoots and fruit. The concatenation is virtually impossible to trace back to me."

"I'll go get the mail," Belinda said, rising swiftly, and leaving the room without bothering to don a coat. "There should be a delivery this morning or, maybe, this afternoon. Perhaps something historically important occurred. Or, an op-ed column in tonight's newspaper mentions a rumor of Federal inspectors sniffing around."

"The history of this area can also be traced somewhat by looking at newspaper archives," Meg said. "I have my students do that. Then the class works on pulling the conglomeration together in a coherent, chronological review of a certain stretch of time. One topic is the Kansas City Massacre which is macabre, and the kids like to shiver studying it."

"Already been studying some of the history here during our Volks' descendants search," Holly replied.

"Ken! Mom! Look the photos have come from that Laura! There are two of them." Belinda hurried into the living room, hurriedly shutting the sliding door behind her. She took a sharp-edged letter opener from a desk drawer first. After that she opened the envelope, and dumped the snapshots out on the coffee table. "And there's a letter." She read it aloud.

Dear Masseys,

Here are pictures of our family taken ten years ago. My mother is the older lady. My husband took the picture and my brother is absent.

I remembered after you left that she told us that she was born when the World's Fair was in St. Louis, and her folks were mad because they couldn't go because of her arrival. She said they died when the whole neighborhood died, and she was riding in a farm wagon to a big building. That is all she told us about her childhood.

My father was orphaned when his parents were killed in a tornado when he was four and huddled in an underground storm cellar. His folks had gone to try to hold onto the cow and horse when the winds started.

Neither one had any brothers or sisters.

Sincerely,

Laura Helsinger

Belinda had put a lot of drama into her voice.

One picture was of a couple and six girls of various heights in shapeless housedresses. The other photograph included three men wearing overalls standing behind three of the same girls, their wives, Ken assumed.

"My goodness. The World's Fair in St. Louis was in 1904." Holly sounded intrigued. "She is too old to be of interest."

Meg peered at the photos that Belinda put on the coffee

table and said, "How do you know the Otoes in those pictures? The older lady looks familiar to me."

"The what lady?"

"The Oto Indian female. Used to be lot of them until they and the other tribes were moved out a hundred or some years ago to Kansas and Oklahoma. Of course, some Indian braves were off hunting buffalo that were bouncing around the prairie, although the herds were pretty well depleted by 1900. But those Indian hunters stayed on in this area. Just as there are still Cherokee Indians in the southeastern states to this very day. Not all Cherokees were on the Trail of Tears. Then, along with settlers and pioneers, Indians occasionally moved off to the happy hunting ground in the sky––dead of smallpox, flu, measles, typhoid, and so on."

"I still don't get you. These are pictures of the Clarmont family. The name 'Oto' hasn't been mentioned anywhere, Meg."

Meg overrode the objection. "Don't you recognize the features of the Oto tribe? See the nose, big eyes, skin color in the mother and most daughters? It is fortuitous that you asked for these pictures. My fears of a side heir are allayed. I think I saw the mother some years ago in Raumville."

Ken studied the picture after Belinda handed it to him, grinned, and then he put it back on the table. He studied it, turned it to face his colleagues, and shrugged.

He said, "I'll be. You mean the Clarmont wife named Barbara is from the group of five orphaned girl babies Mother Holly found out about? We found out that they had been brought in from the enclave of Indians just over the border? Around 1904? We have that list somewhere in our stack of names. The adults perished in a typhoid epidemic."

Holly tapped one picture and sang, "One little, two little, three/four little Indians; five/ six, seven little Frenchies."

"Where do you get Frenchies from, Mom?" Belinda asked.

"The French trappers were the first white men through these parts, a long time before the settlers came. Hitched up with Indian girls. The French were here before other anyone else, except the Indians, guys. The Louisiana Purchase was made in 1803 by Jefferson and occurred around the time Lewis and Clark were planning a long hike to the west coast and back. The European settlers by then were already rapidly coming into the territory Prexy Thomas Jefferson bought. Plus 'Clarmont' sounds French to me."

"But Louisiana kept changing hands, Spanish to French and back again during all those wars in Europe. Maybe the father wasn't French. Or even Spanish. Lots of immigrants from different countries." Meg helped educate the group.

Holly said, "I know, but Jefferson had his envoys buy the area from France, and there were more French settlers hereabouts than Spanish to start with. Spanish were mostly in the southwest and west. The President needed a clear use of the Mississippi River for exporting goods, and the threat of embargo hung over another country's having title to the mouth of the river."

"Okay. Point taken. I noticed, too, that you alluded to a name being 'Clarmont.' I concur that it could be French," Meg exclaimed. "Clear mountain . . . maybe."

Belinda said, "It isn't a French word, I don't think. It sounds like wine, Italian."

Holly noted, "Maybe it's anglicized French. But, the name doesn't matter anyway. We're not looking at the father, although he was an orphan, now that I think of it. We concentrated on the females because of our notes about an orphan who was a mother."

"Meg, you and Merrilee had never mentioned that the father was an orphan, too," Belinda remarked. "I don't know why you, too, ever picked on the Clarmont mother."

"My conjecture is that it could be because you were investigating jewelry, and neither of us associated men with jewelry," Meg said defensively.

Ken left the room and then could be seen began unlocking a file cabinet out in the office and flipping through their notes. He called, "And now we're no longer looking at the mother. False chase."

Meg called to him, "Shucks. That means that you and I didn't conjointly connect a relevant Volks unwed orphan clue after all, mentioned by the Shannons, with a local female orphan. Compounded and problematic. Well, at least, I recognized the Indian origins of the mother in the Clarmonts' photograph. Are you going to tell Walt or should I?"

"Oh, we must do it, by all rights. Let's see if we can all convene in his office right now. We'll make one check of the features of the mother against those pictures of Marlena Harver and Jacqueline Schmidt when they were of the same age, approximately. Those two women are clearly of German origin with the noticeable features of forehead, chin, nose, and eyes."

Meg admitted, "Yes, it is your place to finalize it. I'll call him and see when we can traipse over." Belinda went to bring Lynn down with his winter coat.

After a hurried gathering of wraps, and a single

additional sip of coffee, undiluted, the four started slowly across the wide avenue, paced by Lynn's ability to keep up, because he "didn't want to be carried like a little kid", and the two blocks over to Walt's office.

Marnie looked quite surprised, even a bit put out, when they burst in. She looked as though she wanted to demand if Walt Raleigh's wife had an appointment, Ken surmised. Without deferring to the others, Ken knocked on Walt's door, and the group poured in without waiting for an invitation, all explaining at the same time the reason for the impromptu visit.

Walt finally asked Holly to be the person describing why they were here. "We have the picture of the lady who was an orphan and is of the age to perhaps be related to a Volks' daughter. We are agreed that we first must compare her features with the Polaroids we left with you of the verified daughters, Marlena and Jacqueline."

He frowned with those bushy eyebrows and deciphered her remarks. "Marnie, bring me the art museum's file, please." Ken saw that she has kept her head low, peevish expression somewhat hidden, but not hidden all the way, has choked back a protest when they didn't allow her to announce them, and is being overall quite subdued from the way she had acted during their earlier visits.

Ken would bet a nickel that she'd been scolded by the same policeman who had had a meeting with her father, Mr. King, attorney to the various sides of the law. Her interference in Mr. Raleigh's cases was unethical and deplorable, to say the least. Ken would also bet that she'd keep right on reporting to her father. If Walt couldn't find a way to dispose of her.

She appeared promptly with the file, however, having been smart enough and so eager to be of indispensable use that she had already discerned its need. She also liked to know what was recorded in its pages, another type of reporting on the fortunes of the Raleighs. She hovered a second until Walt waved her out.

"Here we go." He pulled the snapshots out of the envelope.

"There was no doubt in the common ancestry of these two. But, this new picture is doubtless, undeniably, a stranger to the German clan," Walt said, and Ken agreed.

The three ladies searched carefully for any resemblance and also found none.

Holly said, "I wish the new photos were in color so that we could see if the other three daughters have hair with red glints in it like the father's."

"They seem to have the same coloring as his, anyway, Ken. Lighter colored eyes like his. It's clear enough that their mother is not a descendant of the Volks," Holly said.

Walter Raleigh, Esq., smiled as he said, ""The museum has its claimants identified: Jacqueline Schmidt and daughter, all deceased. The heirs are not Marlena Harver and children, namely Merrilee Anderson; the heirs are only descendants of Henrik Volks, of whom Natalie Kilmer was the last. The art museum will be able to finalize ownership."

"All hunky-dory, Walt," said Meg. "Although I rue that all I contributed to the pursuit was stultification."

Walt commented, "No matter, dear; it wasn't your chore."

"At least it's in the Sleuths' favor that it's completed before we leave."

"Yes." Walt turned toward Mother Holly. "I remember you reported that Mrs. Harver said she was not the least bit interested in those weird items titled 'jewelry.' She thought they were useful only for historic display or for dress up for Hallowe'en parties. I'll follow up now for her to sign with a legal disclaimer for the museum. And mention her comment as being an accurate analysis!"

"That historical display scenario was our conclusion, also, after viewing them," Ken said.

"Send me your final bill. I trust we'll be seeing more of each other, at church and at the gym and parties," Walter said. "You've conducted a fine-tooth-comb investigation, and I'm much impressed. Good work."

"Thank you."

"You're welcome."

Holly opened her purse and removed a fountain pen. "I have the statement with me. It will just be the $77.20 for wrapping it up today. We're grateful that you made us the legal notary documents, and we have allowed for the cost of doing so. I can make the final cover letter out to you if you hand me some plain paper, that is, without your logo and address on the top."

"Marnie. please bring in two sheets of plain stationery. Here she is already with them." He gestured for the secretary to give them to Mrs. Jones.

Holly made two copies, signed them, and had Walt sign them. She handed over the statement that Belinda had typed in detail.

He called Marnie to bring in the checkbook ledger. She did so, and he signed the check with a flourish and stood to shake hands. "Fine. We're finished with this small endeavor, with its odd ancillary issues. And now, I and my family wish you and yours an interesting New Year. We hope to see you at our party next week."

The sleuthhounds responded in a cordial manner, walked happy and relaxed, proudly, to the door, and waved goodbye to the Raleighs. Walt waved back, and they heard him speaking softly to his wife.

Walt murmured, "You stay, Meg. You must get something else going before you go back to teaching to take your mind off the results of the investigation. You seemed caught off guard and disappointed. You didn't hit a grounder this time, sorry to say."

Meg shook her head and replied, "At least I didn't *start* the wrong rumor about an out-of-wedlock baby. I just suggested an orphan's name, a solution, Walt. And it wasn't the first time I've been caught being somewhat inaccurate in my game of chances, and when I didn't swing things in the correct direction."

"You got me long ago, Meg, and what more could you ask?" He stood and took her in his arms, with Lynn clinging to both their bodies.

"Not a single thing, Walt." She rested her head against his chest, her blond hair appearing to be added to his bushy mustache.

The three investigators swiveled their heads back to look through the door and laughed gently. Holly Jones said, "We'll leave you to get on with things. And, Meg, you did remember the Otoe mom."

Ken shut the door behind them carefully. "We need to drum up some more business. Let's see how much putting ads in the other major papers in towns around here would work. We will ask the art museum to be on our list of references when people inquire," Ken suggested. They nodded goodbye to Marnie King.

Holly noted, "We can also use Jerry Wrenslow. When I asked if his wife or daughter had misplaced any jewelry, he described the pearl necklace. His daughter, Bennie Lou, when she was six, had taken it from his wife's jewelry box some time back. Three years ago, when her mother yelled at her for getting into her jewels, the girl was frightened and hid it. She only now admitted that it was in the dumbwaiter when his wife asked her calmly where it was. The jewelry storeowner had told me it's worth maybe a hundred dollars. Jerry is sending me $10 to reimburse my 'search'."

The Masseys laughed. Belinda commented, "That sawbuck won't pay the bills but does enhance our reputation. But you should give it to Perry because he found the chamois sack with the pearls."

"Perry?! I paid $12 to have it re-strung and appraised!"

Belinda bowed her head in mock apology. "Oh, right. The ads in the phone book and the *Kansas City Star* have already worked well and don't cost all that much. Ken, check out how much those other ads would cost. Pay me attention about the coming weeks' of financial matters: we'll have to file taxes and pay our quarterly reports in a few weeks, and I have kept the books current.

"Plus, I suggest we write to Laura, not only to thank her for the photos, but also to tell her what you found about her mother's tribal relationship. That will help pay for her cooperation."

Holly shared additional tasks and information. "We can put the jewelry, necklace, coins, and college kids' investigative reports in the inactive files. While you were gone, I was told by your old sarge, Phil Tyler, that the pistol that idiot boy dropped in our alley matched the bullets that killed the kid's father. Luckily, we had Tyler over for coffee earlier and then called him at the time the kid tried to rob us. Nasty lad is done for, done for. Phil told me about that when he brought your jacket back, Ken. The kid had stolen it from your car while you were taking the other cleaning bags upstairs, but it wasn't evidence needed for the trial."

Ken had each of his girls by an elbow and guided them toward the fancy restaurant. "We did find the kid but not because of our sleuthing; the police can keep him, thank you very much. We'll get some lunch and get going on getting to be finders for more of the fascinating keepers."

REFERENCES

Hall, Walter Phelps and Davis, William Stearns. ((3rd ed.). *The Course of Europe since Waterloo.* New York: Appleton-Century-Crofts, Inc. 1941, 1947, 1951.

Meyer, Duane. *The Heritage of Missouri: A History.* (Rev. Ed.) St. Louis, Mo: State Publishing Co. 1965.

Montgomery, Rick, and Kasper, Shirl. (Edited by Monroe Dodd). *Kansas City: An American Story.* Kansas City, MO: Kansas City Star Books. 2007.

The WPA Guide to 1930s Missouri. Lawrence, KS: University of Kansas Press. 1941, 1986.

TIME, Inc. Archives for quotes from *Miscellany*, October and November, December 26, 1955.

Lyrics © Bourne Co. Washington, Ned, and Harline, Leigh. (1940?). *When I wish upon a star.*

AND

Thanks to editor extraordinaire: Lacey Brummer

Printed in the United States
By Bookmasters